GHOSTS OF
ASCALON

GUILDWARS®

GHOSTS OF
ASCALON

MATT FORBECK
AND
JEFF GRUBB

Based on the Acclaimed Video Game Series
from ArenaNet

POCKET STAR BOOKS

NEW YORK   LONDON   TORONTO   SYDNEY

The sale of this book without its cover is unauthorized. If you purchased this book without a cover, you should be aware that it was reported to the publisher as "unsold and destroyed." Neither the author nor the publisher has received payment for the sale of this "stripped book."

Pocket Star Books
A Division of Simon & Schuster, Inc.
1230 Avenue of the Americas
New York, NY 10020

This book is a work of fiction. Names, characters, places, and incidents either are products of the authors' imagination or are used fictitiously. Any resemblance to actual events or locales or persons, living or dead, is entirely coincidental.

Copyright © 2010 by ArenaNet, Inc. All rights reserved.

NCsoft, the interlocking NC logo, ArenaNet, Guild Wars, Guild Wars 2, Ghosts of Ascalon, and all associated logos and designs are trademarks or registered trademarks of NCsoft Corporation.

All rights reserved, including the right to reproduce this book or portions thereof in any form whatsoever. For information, address Pocket Books Subsidiary Rights Department, 1230 Avenue of the Americas, New York, NY 10020.

First Pocket Star Books paperback edition August 2010

POCKET STAR BOOKS and colophon are registered trademarks of Simon & Schuster, Inc.

For information about special discounts for bulk purchases, please contact Simon & Schuster Special Sales at 1-866-506-1949 or business@simonandschuster.com.

The Simon & Schuster Speakers Bureau can bring authors to your live event. For more information or to book an event, contact the Simon & Schuster Speakers Bureau at 1-866-248-3049 or visit our website at www.simonspeakers.com.

Text design by Jacquelynne Hudson
Cover art by Richard Anderson; cover design by AJ Thompson; map design by Robert Lazzaretti.

Manufactured in the United States of America

10 9 8 7

ISBN 978-1-4165-8947-1
ISBN 978-1-4391-5603-2 (ebook)

Dedicated to the millions of gamers everywhere who breathe life into the worlds the designers create.

Thanks to everyone at ArenaNet, especially Will McDermott, Ree Soesbee, Randy Price, Stephen Hwang, Colin Johanson, Bobby Stein, and James Phinney. Also, many thanks to our editor, Ed Schlesinger.

From Matt:
As always, the greatest thanks go to my wife, Ann, and my kids, Marty, Pat, Nick, Ken, and Helen. Without their love, support, and understanding, I can do nothing.

From Jeff:
A special thanks to Jeff Strain, Patrick Wyatt, and Mike O'Brien, the original founders of ArenaNet and Guild Wars. Hope you like what we've done with the world.

Timeline

10,000 BE: Last of the Giganticus Lupicus, the Great Giants, disappear from the Tyrian continent.

205 BE: Humans appear on the Tyrian continent.

100 BE: Humans drive the charr out of Ascalon.

1 BE: The Human Gods give magic to the races of Tyria.

0 AE: The Exodus of the Human Gods.

2 AE: Orr becomes an independent nation.

300 AE: Kryta established as a colony of Elona.

358 AE: Kryta becomes an independent nation.

898 AE: The Great Northern Wall is erected.

1070 AE: The Charr Invasion of Ascalon. The Searing.

1071 AE: The Sinking of Orr.

1072 AE: Ascalonian refugees flee to Kryta.

1075 AE: Kormir ascends into godhood.

1078 AE: Primordus, the Elder Fire Dragon, stirs but does not awaken. The asura appear on the surface. The Transformation of the Dwarves.

1080 AE: King Adelbern of Ascalon recalls the Ebon Vanguard; Ebonhawke is established.

1088 AE: Kryta unifies behind Queen Salma.

1090 AE: The charr legions take Ascalon City. The Foefire.

1105 AE: Durmand Priory is established in the Shiverpeaks.

1112 AE: The charr erect the Black Citadel over the ruins of the city of Rin in Ascalon.

1116 AE: Kalla Scorchrazor leads the rebellion against the Flame Legion's shaman caste.

1120 AE: Primordus awakens.

1165 AE: Jormag, the Elder Ice Dragon, awakens. The norn flee south into the Shiverpeaks.

1180 AE: The centaur prophet Ventari dies by the Pale Tree, leaving behind the Ventari Tablet.

1219 AE: Zhaitan, the Elder Undead Dragon, awakens. Orr rises from the sea. Lion's Arch floods.

1220 AE: Divinity's Reach is founded in the Krytan province of Shaemoor.

1230 AE: Corsairs and other pirates occupy the slowly drying ruins of Lion's Arch.

1302 AE: The sylvari first appear along the Tarnished Coast, sprouting from the Pale Tree.

1320 AE: Kralkatorrik, the Elder Crystal Dragon, awakens. Creation of the Dragonbrand. Breaking of Destiny's Edge. Founding of the Vigil.

1324 AE: Dougal Keane enters the crypts beneath Divinity's Reach.

GHOSTS OF
ASCALON

Over the years, Dougal Keane developed a personal rule: Never adventure with people you like. If pressed, he might modify it to: Don't adventure with people you'd hate to see die. Now, in the depths of the crypts beneath Divinity's Reach, he was getting his wish. Dougal disliked his comrades intensely. He also hated his task. Most of all, at the moment, he hated the stifling heat of the crypts themselves.

The sweltering summer heat that enveloped Divinity's Reach above had stolen deep into the bowels of these hidden burial grounds, where it festered like a hidden wound. The prevailing winds that caressed the burial ground's cliffside entrances might carry the stench of the warm, dry rot away from the city, but inside the crypt's twisting passages, Dougal had no means of escaping it. People had been bringing their dead here since before the founding of Kryta's new capital, and Dougal swore he could smell the dust of every last one of them.

Their explorations had taken them into parts of the

crypts that even Dougal was unaware existed. At each branching of the path, Clagg had consulted his glowing map, then indicated they take the less-traveled option. The smooth, polished flagstones of the Skull Gate in Divinity's Reach gave way to less-used paths, and finally to rooms and corridors that had been untouched since the dead were left here to desiccate centuries before the founding of the city above.

Still, as he stalked forward, brittle skull fragments of all shapes and sizes crunching beneath his feet, Dougal reminded himself that these crypts weren't as bad as some places he had been. The ruined temples of the Caledon Forest, or the Bloodtide Coast, its beaches awash with twitching, malevolent corpses.

Or Ascalon. Never as bad as Ascalon.

Dougal stopped and rubbed the stubble on his chin as he scanned the bone-covered passage before him. It opened into a wide chamber that stretched far beyond the reach of his torch's light. It was clear of bones.

He didn't like that.

He signaled for a stop, and his companions—the sylvari, the norn, and the asura riding his golem, the one who'd hired the rest of them for this expedition— pulled up short behind him.

"What is it?" snarled Clagg. The asura was irritable when they first met, and the closed, stuffy air of the tomb had done nothing to improve his disposition.

Clagg's people had bubbled up from the depths of the world over two centuries ago, harbingers of the fact that the nature of Tyria was about to change. They were a small people with oversized, flat-faced, ellipsoid heads, the width of which were made more pronounced by long ears, drooping in Clagg's case. Their skin came in varying shades of gray, their large eyes a product of lives spent in magic-lit caves. The asura arrived on the surface world not so much as refugees as settlers confident in their intellectual and magical superiority over every race they encountered.

And, Dougal had to admit to himself, they were often right in that assumption.

Clagg was seated comfortably in a harness fixed to the front of his golem, the creature a masterpiece of polished and painted stone and fitted bands of bronze. Its articulated limbs hinged on glowing blue magical jewels that held the independent parts of the angular, headless creature together without actually touching them. Magical force, magic beyond that which Dougal was comfortable with, held the creature together. A single large crystal housed between its carved shoulders served as both its eyes and ears. The sharp-faceted gem constantly swiveled around in its socket, scouring its environment for more input.

Clagg called it Breaker, and seemed more concerned about its well-being than that of the other members of the party.

"I said, 'What is it?' " snarled the asura, its shark-like teeth flashing with irritation. Dougal rarely saw an asura smile, and was never reassured when he did.

"Something's wrong," Dougal said, keeping his voice low.

"Humans," Gyda Oddsdottir muttered, shaking her head. The silver sleigh bells woven into her long, yellow warrior's braid jangling loudly. "Always taking stock instead of taking action." She set her huge hammer before her with a resounding thud, crushing a dry skull to dust.

Dougal winced, not at the norn's words, but at the racket she made. At nine feet tall and bristling with weapons, she thundered down the halls, making more noise than the asura's golem. This daughter of the distant snowcapped Shiverpeaks didn't care who heard her coming: she wanted to warn them of her approach. In the heat of the depths of the crypt, her heavily tattooed flesh dripped with a sheen of sweat.

Gyda's grandsires were refugees as well, fleeing from the power of one of the great Elder Dragons to the north. The norn were a healthy, hearty, proud people, quick to anger and equally quick to forgive. In his time since leaving Ebonhawke, Dougal had met good norn and bad norn. The good ones treated every day as an adventure, every problem as a challenge, and every foe as a chance for personal glory. Most people didn't understand how dangerous the dark places of the world could be; the norn actually relished exploring them.

Gyda, though, was definitely in the latter category of norn: boastful, judgmental, and unpleasant to those around her. She was both bullying and insulting, as if any achievement by others diminished her own. Dougal didn't like it when she smiled, either.

"The floor. It's too clear," said Dougal, talking to Clagg but meaning it for Gyda. "No bones. No one was buried here."

"And that means a trap," said Killeen, the last member

of the party, the sylvari, in her soft, melodious voice.

Dougal nodded. The sylvari necromancer was probably the most pleasant individual of their motley krewe, himself included. Shorter than a human but not as diminutive as the asura, her skin was a verdant green, her hair more similar to the leaves of a succulent plant than that of a human woman. When she moved, golden pollen drifted off her.

The humanoid appearance, Dougal knew, was a lie. Killeen and the others of her race were born fully formed from the fruit of a great white-barked tree far to the south. There was no animal warmth to her flesh. The sylvari were a recent addition to the world, their entire race only a little older than Dougal himself, but they had already spread far and wide, like an invading weed. Killeen had all the traits attributed to her race: she was honest, direct, and focused. In many ways she was better than most humans he knew.

That may have been what made Dougal most uncomfortable of all.

Killeen took Dougal's statement at face value, but Gyda instead snorted, "I think you are just trying to delay us from our goal."

The sylvari ignored Gyda but said, "What do you think would set it off?"

Dougal looked at the norn. "Not noise. Maybe vibration, or maybe weight."

"The human's probably right," Clagg said, sitting in the relative safety of his armored harness. "I guess even a blind dredge finds a diamond some days."

The asura fiddled with a row of crystals set into his

harness's front rim, then nodded to himself. "Ah, yes. There it is. Crude, but effective."

"What is it?" Dougal hated asking the question. He knew the asura was fishing for yet another reason to explain how brilliant he was. To an asura, the other races of the world existed primarily for heavy lifting, taking risks, and asking stupid questions.

"If one of us were foolish enough to walk into that room," Clagg said, enunciating every syllable, "it would trigger a lethal blast that could kill those present."

Gyda harrumphed as if no explosives could slow her down, magical or otherwise. Still, Dougal noticed, the norn's feet stayed rooted where they were.

"If it is a trap, can't Dougal disable it?" Killeen asked. "Isn't that what you hired him for?"

From any of the others, such a statement would have come laden with sarcasm and bile. The sylvari, though, meant every word in earnest. It was, indeed, why he was part of this expedition: his knowledge. Of traps. Of history. Of the way the world used to be.

"He hired me for my experience in recovering powerful artifacts," said Dougal.

Gyda let out a deep chuckle. "Robbing tombs, you mean."

Dougal ignored her. "Does anyone have something helpful to add?" Dougal asked.

"The petal-head's comment stands," said Clagg, prim as a schoolmaster, "That *is* why we brought you along, human. We know the trap is there. Now take care of it."

Dougal reached down and picked up a skull, trying not to think about if this was an ancestor. He aimed for a spot about in the middle of the room and touched the locket beneath his shirt for luck. Then he pitched the skull underhand into the room.

Nothing. He pitched another skull to a different area. Nothing again. He pitched a third.

Gyda rolled her eyes at his uselessness and folded her thick arms with impatience. Clagg shook his head at him as if Dougal were an addled child.

"Not set off by noise," said Dougal. "Not vibration or motion, either. That leaves weight. We should send in something heavy." He looked at Gyda.

"I will not be an experiment for you," said the norn quietly, her face clouded.

"Well, then, the golem," said Dougal.

"Strike that suggestion," snapped Clagg, "I did not craft Breaker from scratch just to see it blown to smithereens. This is your problem, human."

"You care more for that walking statue than you do for the rest of us," said Gyda.

"Untrue," said the asura. "I just have less invested in you than in it."

Killeen brightened, her eyes glowing a faint green. "Perhaps I can help."

The sylvari set her chin and concentrated on a patch of the bones lining the left side of the passage. She swung her arms and fingers in a complex pattern and spoke words that made Dougal's head ache slightly. A greenish glow formed in the wall of bones and coalesced around a human-sized set of remains.

As Dougal watched, the bones detached from the surrounding patch and assembled themselves into a coherent skeleton. The deep-green glow, rather than sinew and tendons, held it together. The right side of its skull had been bashed in, and its jaw was missing, as was the lower part of its right arm, which terminated in a pair of jagged breaks. It stood before them like a servant presenting itself to its betters.

Dougal shuddered as Killeen gave the creature a satisfied smile. She gestured again, and the skeleton tottered around and stumbled off down the passage toward the room beyond.

Dougal glanced up at the bone-covered ceiling and reminded himself there had to be some stone and earth up there somewhere behind the remains—that they weren't just moving through a tunnel carved out of a mountain of bones. "Hold on," he said, reaching toward Killeen as she smiled at the way her creation shambled away. "We should back up and take—"

The explosion cut him off. The animated skeleton disappeared in a cloud of flame and smoke.

Dougal ducked down and wrapped his arms over his head as a cascade of bone fragments rained down on him, bouncing and clattering on the floor. One flying shard of their animated helper shot into Dougal's heavy leather shirt and stuck there like a revenant's fang.

Dougal stood up and saw Clagg gazing into the cavern, pursing his lips. "Crude," the asura said. "But effective."

Gyda shouldered past Dougal and laughed. As she strode into the chamber beyond, she grinned at the scorch mark where the skeleton once stood. "Well done, sapling," she said to Killeen. "At least *you* are earning your pay."

Dougal winced at the implicit insult. To the group at

large he said, "We need to press on. It may take minutes or days for this trap to reset. It may just be a single use, but we have no way of knowing."

Now Gyda laughed. "He means to say, 'Thank you, sylvari, for doing my job.'"

Killeen's cheeks blushed a deeper green. "My apologies," she said to Dougal. "I did not mean to upstage you. I did remove the trap without hurting anyone."

Dougal grimaced. He didn't doubt that her apology was heartfelt, but that made it feel even worse. He said, perhaps not as kindly as he could, "You could have given us more fair warning, or time to back out of the explosion. As it was, you could have brought the ceiling down on top of us."

"I see," Killeen said, thoughtful for a moment. "I did not intend to endanger our quest."

"Of course not," Dougal said, feeling bad for upbraiding her. Despite himself, he couldn't help but enjoy her sincerity.

"Perhaps it's the wonder of this place," the sylvari said, raising her chin once again. "It's fascinating. To my people, death is an integral part of life. We revere it wholly, even the darkest parts of it. But we don't quite understand it—yet." She gazed around the chamber, her eyes wide with wonder. "And even so, we would never build a monument like this to it."

"It is not a monument to the dead but rather a testament to those who lived," Dougal said gently. He felt his irritation ebbing away—toward her, at least. "Let's go." Then, raising his voice to the others: "Let's be careful moving forward. We should see more traps like this."

"You are such an old woman, human," Gyda snorted. "My great-granddame Ulrica would not hesitate as much as you do, and she's been dead for seven years." She kicked aside a pile of bones and held aloft a torch. "You worry too much. What's life without danger?"

"Longer," Dougal said.

He followed the norn as she strode through the exploded room and into the chambers beyond. He'd worked with other norn before. They were larger than life in many ways, but norn bullies were just like everyone else's. Gyda's bluster was meant to cover some other deficiency. Dougal didn't mention the norn's own reluctance to enter the trapped room, despite her bragging.

"Bah. Such a life only seems longer, like a tasteless meal," concluded Gyda. As Dougal followed her, he noticed that the air had grown slightly cooler. Once they were all inside the next chamber, both he and the norn held their torches aloft. The light found something thick and gray hanging among the bones at the apex of the room's high-arched ceiling.

Dougal held up a hand to shade his eyes against the torch and peered at the substance. At first he thought it hanging moss, but suddenly it was clear what it was.

Webbing.

Dougal cursed. He shouted out a warning, but Killeen's high-pitched scream behind him cut him off. He spun about just in time to see the sylvari disappear into a hole in the ground.

2

In an instant Dougal knew what had happened. Killeen's assailant had waited as the larger forms of Dougal and the norn had passed over its concealed hiding place, and sprung its trap on the lighter footfalls of the sylvari. And in that moment Killeen was gone, pulled into a hollowed-out space beneath the ancient flagstones, a trapdoor made of webs and bones slamming down after her, blending once more into the bone-littered floor.

Gyda spun around, too, and scanned the room for any sign of Killeen behind her. "The necromancer! Where is she?"

"Down there!" Clagg shouted, pointing at the trapdoor. "Spider!"

Dougal raced toward the trapdoor, dropping his torch and drawing his sword as he went. He smashed at the disguised covering with his blade, and the trapdoor shattered as if he'd struck a dinner plate.

Killeen screamed again as she popped back up out of the hole, like a swimmer breaching the surface. She flung out her hands and scrabbled for a handhold among the bones before her, but they pulled away loose in her hands.

A black-haired spider the size of a small wolf appeared on the sylvari's shoulders and reared back to strike her on the neck. Dougal made a desperate stab at it. His blade sliced through one of the creature's legs and lodged itself in its side. The beast hissed in pain, its twitching mandibles dripping with viscous venom.

Before Dougal could pull back his blade for another strike, though, he heard Clagg shout at him. "Stand back, you fool!"

Dougal turned in time to see Breaker's boulder of a fist coming down at him. He threw himself to the side, leaving his sword buried in the spider's abdomen. The golem's stone fist narrowly missed both the thrashing spider and the sylvari but smashed Dougal's blade to pieces.

Gyda stormed up then. She grabbed Killeen by her arms and hauled her out of the hole. The sylvari wailed in pain as the spider sank its fur-covered fangs into her back.

Swordless, Dougal snatched a knife from his belt. He wondered how much good it would do him. The spider's fangs were longer than his blade.

Gyda dropped Killeen to the ground, then snatched the spider from the sylvari's back with one hand. The black thing struggled in the norn's grasp, its legs twitching helplessly in the air. Ichor flowed around the shard of Dougal's broken blade, still stuck in the creature's side, and hot blue fluid trickled down Gyda's heavily tattooed arm.

With a flick of her wrist, the norn flung the beast

toward Breaker and Clagg. A moment later, the golem's heavy foot had smashed it into paste.

Clagg, from the safety of his harness, snapped, "Watch it! It has a brood in here!"

"Watch over the plant-girl," Gyda ordered Dougal. "I will take care of this beast's spawn." And the norn turned back to the web-filled room, not caring if Dougal followed her orders or not.

Dougal scrambled over to Killeen to examine her wounds. Her back was covered in a warm bluish blood, most of which he hoped had come from the spider. He'd never seen a sylvari hurt before, and had no idea what might leak out of one that had been injured.

Dougal wiped the liquid off of Killeen's shoulder with his sleeve, uncovering a pair of puncture wounds from which spilled a golden fluid that sparkled with life. Most of the mess had come from the spider, then. The holes in Killeen's shoulder hadn't bled much, but the skin around them had already started to swell a bright yellow. Her skin was firm, like the shell of a horse chestnut. She was cold but not clammy. Was that good or bad? Dougal didn't even know if she could sweat.

"It hurts a bit," Killeen said as she craned her neck around, the glow in her large eyes dimming. Then she noticed the grim look on Dougal's face, and she blinked and rallied herself enough to ask questions.

"Do you think I'm dying? How can you tell? Is there some special way to know?" She tried to ask more, but a coughing fit stopped her. Her skin was lightening to a pale yellow around the wound and spreading to the rest of her body.

While Dougal turned her over and held her, the norn and the golem began smashing a pack of spider-shaped shadows into a blue-black paste. Dougal hunkered down over the weakened sylvari to protect her from the flying bits of dried bone and arachnid with his body. He looked down at her face, golden and pale.

Dougal realized he had violated his first rule. He was going to feel horrible if she died.

He glanced back to see Gyda breathing hard and holding her hammer in a two-handed grip. Splats of spider corpses formed a ring around her. Clagg's golem had ground out a mushy blue mixture beneath its stone feet.

Once the slaughter ended, Dougal saw that the sylvari had passed out, and he beckoned the others to her side.

"Raven's wings," Gyda said, barely breathing hard from all the exertion. "She's getting paler than you, little man."

"It's the poison," Dougal said. "It's working fast."

Clagg climbed down from the harness on Breaker's front to get a better look at the sylvari. "I estimate she has only a few minutes remaining before the venom takes her. Do either of you have a potion, poultice, or spell that could aid her?"

Gyda shrugged. Dougal grimaced and said, "Do I look like an alchemist to you?"

"Given your background," Clagg said, "I thought you might have stolen one somewhere. No matter: I have something that should do the trick right here."

Clagg rummaged around in a pack he wore strapped diagonally over one shoulder and across his chest, producing a clear vial filled with a viscous blue liquid. He dribbled the contents of the vial into Killeen's pale mouth, past lips that had gone dry as autumn leaves.

Clagg stood back up and recorked the vial. "That should be sufficient to prevent her expiration," he said, "at least in the short term." He bent over the sylvari and said loudly, "This will be coming out of your share." Clagg smacked the norn on her kneecap and added, "Strap her body to the back of my golem."

Gyda scooped up Killeen as if the sylvari were a limp doll.

"If we take her straight back up to Divinity's Reach, she should be fine," Dougal said.

"All too true," Clagg said, "but we've not made it this far to turn back now."

"Forget it," Dougal said. "We're down a member. This expedition is over." He reached to take Killeen from Gyda. The norn was a statue and wouldn't let go. Brushing Dougal aside, Gyda moved around the back of the golem and began to laboriously craft a suitable lashing from rope and the back of the harness.

Dougal glared at Gyda but spoke to Clagg. "We get back to the city and we get her taken care of. Then we come back later, when we're all healthy."

"We don't have time for that," Clagg said as he scrambled back up into the armored seat hanging from his golem's chest.

"This is a boneyard," said Dougal, exasperated, turning to glare at the asura. "They're all dead. I'm sure any other spiders will wait. What's the rush?"

Clagg, now looking down at Dougal, raised his

eyebrows and clicked his tongue. "If I figured out who is buried here, then others may have as well. Knowledge propagates. We press on. The Golem's Eye awaits."

Dougal had seen the greed that danced in Clagg's eyes before in others. It was a herald for disaster. Greed made people careless, and in tombs like this, being careless made you dead.

"That's insane. I'm heading back to the Skull Gate and Divinity's Reach. I know the way. I'll take Killeen with me." He moved toward the back of the golem, but Gyda's immense form loomed up before him.

Clagg cleared his throat. "I'm afraid we can't let you abandon us quite yet," the asura said. "Your presence raises our chances of success, even if only by a few percent. That's why I hired you in the first place. You stay with us."

Dougal snarled, more at himself than Clagg. "I don't have a sword."

Clagg gave Dougal a cold smile. "I didn't hire you for your sword. I hired you for your mind, such as it is."

Gyda let out a cruel chuckle.

Dougal looked at the other two tomb robbers. Without a blade, it wouldn't be a fair fight against either one, and even properly armed it would be a chancy encounter. Heading back alone would mean that Killeen would be left with them, and she would perish when their stupidity brought about their own demise.

For a long moment Dougal glared at them, then turned, picked up his guttering torch, and pressed deeper into the crypts beneath the city. Gyda marched along behind him, kicking up bone fragments that bounced off Dougal's heels. Clagg guided Breaker after them from the rear, the golem showing no sign of noticing the unconscious Killeen's weight on its back. At each intersection, Clagg would check his glowing map and choose the most inconvenient route.

Dougal spotted several more traps as they grew closer to the tomb, and he made quick work of them, rendering them useless. Similarly, the few locks he encountered were easily sprung by the fistful of steel tools he kept in a moleskin pouch. They moved forward in silence now, except for the regular orders from Clagg and Killeen's occasional moan. And through it Dougal thought about the asura whose tomb they were going to rob.

Blimm.

When Clagg first hired him, Dougal rooted through ancient texts and tomes in the city's archives but learned damned little about Blimm. He had to hope it would be enough. Blimm, a genius even by asuran standards, had lived a couple centuries back. He served his apprenticeship as a golemancer, a maker of golems, with Oola, another legendary member of that diminutive race. After leaving her service, Blimm made his home in what would become Divinity's Reach, where he made (supposedly) some amazing advances in golem construction that were now lost to time.

Blimm's greatest triumph, according to Clagg, was the creation of a large mystic gemstone, infused with arcane energy. The stone was called the Golem's Eye, and apparently was lost along with Blimm's knowledge and the location of the asura's tomb.

Until now. Clagg had uncovered that knowledge,

and rounded up a krewe in the asura fashion: talents gathered together with a specific goal. For this goal, that meant spellcaster, muscle, trapspringer, and leadership, the leadership supposedly provided by Clagg and unquestioned by the rest, entered the crypts in search of the Golem's Eye.

"Why have we stopped?" Clagg shouted from the back of the marching order.

"We're stuck," said Dougal, trying to keep the relief out of his voice.

He was faced with a simple thing, a door bound in bands of iron. Clagg piloted his golem forward and shook his head at the human's reluctance.

"Open it," said Clagg.

"Can't," said Dougal. "It's not locked, it's stuck. Swollen in the frame. The lock doesn't matter. It might as well be a wall."

"I know how to handle walls," said Clagg. "Gyda?"

The norn stepped up and motioned for the human and asura to step aside. Dougal pulled back, half hoping for some trap he hadn't seen to suddenly reveal itself.

Gyda stood in front of the door, staring at it, and for a moment Dougal thought the norn was trying to wither the door with her glare. Then she growled a deep, feline growl. White fur began to sprout from her exposed flesh, and for a moment it was as if her armored form were overlaid with another, ghostly image of a great beast. Then the image solidified, and Gyda was transformed into a hulking two-legged feline, her pelt snow white with black spots, her armor and weapons subsumed into the new creation.

Gyda had summoned her totem, the snow leopard. She sprang forward, her heavy paws slamming into the door.

The door held, but the hinges did not, and the entire door flew off its frame and back into the room. Even Dougal was impressed with the norn's strength and prowess, and he started to say, "That was very . . ."

His praise died in his throat as Gyda snorted and said, "*That* is why your people are dying out and better races are taking your place."

Dougal reddened with anger but just pressed past Gyda, holding his torch high, into another passage with more bones lining the wall. Dougal was convinced that Divinity's Reach, the shining human city, was built on a mountain of bones.

"One thing I never understood about Blimm . . ." Dougal called back over his shoulder to Clagg.

Clagg cackled. "I would guess a bookah like you could fill Blimm's tomb with the things you don't understand," he said.

Dougal ignored the crack. "Bookah" was an asuran term for humans, and not a very complimentary one. "I always heard that asura traditionally burn their dead. But not Blimm. Why did he build a tomb in the first place?"

"At the end of his life, he didn't believe in the Eternal Alchemy: that we are all part of a greater equation," said Clagg. "Blimm considered himself a function apart. That's likely why he made so much progress with necromantic constructs, using bone and dead flesh in his golemtric creations. He was willing to test ideas no lesser asura would consider."

"And since he didn't fit in with other asura, he didn't want any of them to enjoy the results of his research," said Dougal.

"Close, but that's not quite all of it," said Clagg. "He kept strange company in his later years. Humans. Necromancers. No offense, sapling," he added over his shoulder. Killeen responded with a grunted moan.

"Sounds full of himself," said Gyda. The norn's interjection surprised Dougal, who had guessed she wouldn't bother listening to Clagg and him blather on. "But then, what asura isn't?"

Clagg barked a cold laugh at that. "Many of my fellows have outsized egos, I agree, but Blimm was a raving paranoiac on top of that. They say that some of the best minds were the most disturbed. And Blimm was definitely disturbed."

The passage beyond opened into a wide hall lit by unnatural light. At the far end, a staircase made of polished green stone banded in bronze led up to a great brazen door flanked by great bowls of blue-green flame that flickered from unnatural sources. The gilded frame of the door was carved with the swooping rays and tangents of the asuran alphabet, which danced in the unearthly radiance. Dougal, despite himself, was speechless.

"Gentlefolk," said Clagg smugly, tucking away his glowing map, "we have arrived. Welcome to Blimm's tomb."

3

They climbed the steps three abreast, Dougal flanked and overshadowed by the larger norn and asura-piloted golem. The stairs themselves were wide and flat, almost a ramp up to great double doors.

Dougal shot a glance at Killeen, slung to the golem's back like a child in a cradleboard. She managed a weak smile and tried to raise an arm. Perhaps Clagg's potion was having some effect, or the sylvari's own recuperative powers were kicking in.

They reached the top. Dougal feeling like a supplicant in the great temple. A large steel bas-relief image, as tall as Dougal himself, hung to one side, as if emerging from the wall itself. It portrayed the image of a golem of the ancient style staring back at all who approached. A bright red gem sat affixed in the carving's stubby head. Gyda gasped at the sight of it.

The norn reached out and pried the gem from the door. She considered it for a moment, then squeezed it in her bare hand as if it were an overripe nut. It crunched between her fingers, and a moment later she opened her fist to let a handful of pink dust cascade from it.

"A fake," she said with a dismissive sigh. "To have found such a grand treasure so easily would have shown a real lack of imagination on the part of your Blimm."

Clagg scoffed. "You really think that an asura like Blimm would be foolish enough to leave the Golem's Eye mounted on the outside of the door?"

Dougal barely stifled a laugh at the scorn dripping from Clagg's lips. It was good to see someone else at the end of Clagg's verbal lash.

"I have seen things far more foolish in my own lands," Gyda said.

"Or in any mirror you passed," Dougal muttered as he stepped forward to examine the writing scrawled over the door and frame.

"Hold! What did you—"

Dougal cut the norn off with a wave of his hand. "Shush. Reading."

"You can read this?" said Clagg, with mild surprise.

"You did bring me here for my mind," said Dougal, a little sharper than he had intended.

He stared for a moment at the words carved into the surface of the door. They were written in asuran script but used an archaic dialect popular before the subterranean asura had been forced to the surface more than 250 years earlier. It was a half-mathematical, half-structured sentence, and the syntax would make a human scribe take to the bottle. Many asura could no longer even read it. According to Dougal's research, Blimm's paranoia had driven him to write his notes in this script for that exact reason.

Dougal ran his fingers along the text as if he could peel the meaning from it with his fingernails. "It's very old, but I think I can make it out." He cleared his throat and began to read aloud: " 'Here lies Blimm, the greatest of the golemancers, favored counselor of Livia, apprentice to Oola, whose brilliance he has surpassed, the finest mind to grace Tyria in his or any other generation—' "

"Yes, yes, yes," Clagg said impatiently. "Blah, blah, blah. Get on to the promises of curses on any who would disturb his rest. There may be something useful there."

Dougal shrugged and skipped over the next several words. "Here we go: 'Let those who would dare to disturb his rest be cursed for eternity by the bones that line these tombs. Let the earth rise up against them and their remains serve as a testament of his greatness. Let their remains join those that surround him.' It goes on like that for a while."

"How absolutely human of Blimm. He must have spent far too much time in the sun," said Clagg. "Sounds like standard-issue warnings, though. All those tomb-door epitaphs read the same. 'Look on me and know fear,' 'Leave me be lest I haunt your nights,' and so on and so on. Toothless. "

"That doesn't mean they're not true." Dougal scowled.

"Please," said Clagg. "If these people had the power to do what they claimed, they'd still be wandering the world in one form or another. Those are just words."

Gyda laughed at this, a low rumbling under which lay

a note of malice. "If this Blimm of yours is beneath your notice, then why are we bothering to rob his grave?"

"Blimm was one of the most impressive golemancers ever," said Clagg. He patted Breaker's stone chest. "Most of the time, you need several arcanic motivators to move a golem's exo-frame about at a reasonable speed: at least one for each joint, plus another for the senses. And you need to arrange them in a very particular way or it all falls apart.

"Blimm, though, figured out a way to imbue a fist-sized ruby with the same amount of power as you see in Breaker here. His secret died with him, but legend has it that it was buried with him too. Once I get my hands on the Golem's Eye, I should be able to reverse engineer the process and establish myself as the greatest golemancer of *this* age."

Gyda held up a large hand, her brow furrowed in what Dougal thought was confusion. "For someone so small, you talk a great deal. Let's find this ruby of yours and be gone. I would like to quit this place." She stared hard at the double doors, and Dougal knew what she was considering.

"Hold on," he said, holding up his bag of tools. "Let's try this the easy way first."

Dougal stepped up to the hole left in the golem's forehead. The bas-relief was hollow, and beyond it was a maze of thin wires and interlocking gears, some of them glowing softly of their own light. Dougal opened his moleskin pouch, selected a thin flat tool with an end that looked like an asuran summation sign, and slipped it into the gap. He twisted it, and the great double doors rumbled outward. Gyda and Clagg had to step back down the broad steps.

The room within was circular, its walls and domed ceiling jutting with the bones that adorned the rest of the crypt. The granite floor was set with a pattern like slices of a pie, forming a series of concentric circles centered on the bier in the middle of the room.

The bier at the center of the pattern was a pile of skulls, although from the doorway Dougal was hard-pressed to say if they were real skulls or just carved stonework. Probably the former, he decided, to instill fear into would-be robbers. Atop the bier squatted a large marble box, its sides etched with the swirling script of the asura. Dominating the lid of the sarcophagus was a larger-than-life effigy of the deceased, dressed in ornate stone robes gilded with precious metals, its arms crossed over its chest.

And hovering over the forehead of the reclining stone form floated a red gem the size of Clagg's fist. It turned and glimmered in the light from the door.

Clagg had Breaker nudge Dougal forward. "Do your job," said Clagg.

Dougal pushed back. "My job is to spring locks and locate traps."

Clagg sniffed. "You are guaranteeing that there are no further traps and that that gem floating there is free for the taking?"

Dougal did not respond, but Gyda clapped him on the back. "Get in there," she growled. "Get the ruby for us—or I'll toss you on top of the coffin from here."

She reached for him, intent on carrying out her

threat, and Dougal stepped into the room. Safe from his companions for the moment, he pulled a length of thin rope from his pack, uncoiled it, and tossed an end to Clagg. The asura made the rope fast around his golem's waist. Dougal held the rope with one hand, wrapping it over his wrist and letting it play out behind him as he advanced. The stonework felt spongy beneath his feet, like a road after a soaking spring rain. It looked solid enough, but Dougal chose his steps carefully as he moved toward the center of the room.

On nearing the coffin, Dougal could clearly make out the asuran script that he'd seen on the door. From what he could read, it repeated many of the same warnings found on the doorplate, only in more strident and emphatic tones.

Dougal dropped the remaining few loops of rope at his feet and stood on his toes, leaning over the sarcophagus perched atop its bier of bones. Above Blimm's forehead, the gem danced in the doorway's light, its facets catching and reflecting the glow. This was no paste-work fake.

"It's the real one," Dougal said.

"Bring it to me. Now." Clagg's voice betrayed a clear eagerness.

Dougal considered the gem for a moment. A faint glow swirled deep inside it, something that had lain dormant for untold years, hidden in this buried room.

"It's sure to be trapped," Dougal said.

"Do you *see* a trap?" Clagg asked.

Dougal scanned the gem from every angle. There were no wires, no gears, no hidden plates or moving panels in the coffin. It was magic. Asuran magic. He really hated asuran magic.

"No," he said finally, "but that doesn't mean it's not there."

"Bear's blood!" Gyda said. "You are the most worthless burglar I've ever met. I could have *not* spotted a trap myself!"

Dougal ignored the norn and spoke to Clagg. "Do you detect anything?"

The asura checked the row of glowing gems in his harness, then shook his head. "It appears safe."

Dougal snorted at that. He'd heard those exact words at such moments before. They never turned out to be true.

He gritted his teeth and reached for the gem. The glow inside it gained strength and swirled faster as if something within it meant to meet his touch. As he brought his fingers closer to its sharp-cut facets, the floor beneath his feet seemed to vibrate softly, although he wondered if that was just his nerves betraying him.

He drew his hand back.

"Get Killeen out of here," Dougal said. "This isn't going to go well."

"You spineless coward," Gyda said. "It's just a rock! Take it and be done with it."

"This requires care and precision," said Dougal sharply, "not brute force!"

"You know nothing of force! Cowardice holds your hand!" thundered Gyda. "I should come in there and show you!"

"You'd just make a mess of it," said Dougal

automatically. "When I need a lumbering ox, I'll call for you!"

Dougal regretted his words the moment he said them. Sputtering in rage, the norn slung her hammer over her shoulder and stomped into the chamber, the floor shaking beneath her massive boots.

As she lumbered forward, Gyda snarled, "I came down to this filthy land of civilized cowards to make a name for myself, and despite working in the shadow of my legendary cousin Gullik, I have done a damned fine job of it. This is only the start of my saga, tales of which will be sung around norn campfires for centuries to come! And you, human, will be no more than an aside in it!"

Dougal dropped the rope and put the coffin between himself and the now-furious Gyda. She lunged at him. Dougal ducked around the bier, keeping the mound of bones between them. From the doorway, he could hear Clagg laughing at his predicament.

Calming the bullying norn was not an option, Dougal realized. He would have to make the best of his situation.

The norn, her eyes burning with fury, lunged at him again, but he danced around the end of the sarcophagus. He did this to her twice more, eluding Gyda's grip. On her final lunge, she launched herself at him over the top of the stone effigy, hoping to snare him between her massive hands, but she missed and wound up sprawled across the lid of the sarcophagus instead.

That's when Dougal snatched up the free end of the rope he'd dropped, reached out, and plucked the

Golem's Eye from its place at the head of Blimm's stone form.

Gyda's bright blue eyes flew so wide that Dougal could see the whites all the way around them. Dougal grinned at her as he took three quick steps back. If something bad was going to happen, he was going to face it along-side a crazed norn. The gem glowed in Dougal's fist like caged fire.

The first warning of "something bad" was when the floor buckled and warped like the deck of a ship that had just run aground. Dougal was knocked from his feet. Gyda clutched the top of the sarcophagus with all four of her mighty limbs. Dougal looked about, and the floor appeared to ripple around him.

Clagg yowled, "Don't drop it, you fumble-fingered bookah! Toss it to me!"

Scrambling back from the bier, Dougal hefted the gem in his fist. If he threw it to the asura, he was sure that Clagg would cut the rope and leave them both to their fates. Instead, Dougal dramatically dropped the gem into a shirt pocket and buttoned it shut. Then he grabbed the rope with both hands and started to pull himself back across the undulating floor.

Before Dougal could start for the door, the walls shuddered as much as the floor. Dougal glanced all around the room and saw that the bier was coming apart.

The bones peeled away from the sarcophagus's stand one by one, hovered in midair for a moment, then came together in a cluster collecting at the head of the coffin like a swarm of skeletal bees. Within moments the sarcophagus slipped to the floor, crushing the remaining bits of the bier beneath it. Still clutching Blimm's gilded form atop the coffin's lid, Gyda roared in a mixture of terror and enthusiasm as the flying bones thrummed about her.

Dougal struggled to his feet and made for the exit in a running crouch, working his way along the rope that still hung from Breaker's waist. He saw Killeen prop her head up over the golem's shoulder and goggle at him with her bright green eyes, her arms flailing as she tried to untie herself from the back of the golem.

Now the bones had begun to tear themselves from the walls as well. They raced from all angles toward the thing forming at the head of the sarcophagus.

Dougal shouldered his way through the tornado of skeletal hail toward the door. After a few more steps, he lost his footing on a spinning skull and hit the floor hard, knocking the wind from him. Taking a moment to catch his breath, he realized he'd fallen below the worst part of the sideways rain of bones. Glancing back at the sarcophagus, he saw Gyda standing there before the coalescing creature, roaring and swinging her massive hammer at it with double-handed force.

The creature was roughly human in shape, but far more than that: It stood three times the height of a man, and each of its body parts formed from fragments and clusters of similar bones. Where its legs should have been, it had a serpentine bundle of femurs and tibias encrusted with random shards of bone and bound together with magic. Its skull was formed from at least a dozen broken heads smashed into pieces and plaited back together to form a human shape. It towered over the norn.

Gyda raged with determination and delight as she brought the battle to the newly formed bone beast. "At last!" she said. "A fight worthy of me! I will show you how a norn handles this!"

Gyda's hammer smashed the bones to bits over and over again, churning them from fragments to pieces to dust. It seemed as if the norn might gain the upper hand over Blimm's construct, and for a moment hope rose in Dougal's heart. Still keeping beneath the buzzing bits of bone, he wrapped the rope tight around his wrist to keep it secure.

"Tomb guardian!" he heard Clagg say, excited now. "It's forming a massive tomb guardian from the bones! A self-replicating, ambient thaumaturgic construct! I never realized that Blimm had solved that problem!"

As fast as the norn shattered the bones, though, they came right back together again. The flying shards had sliced through her skin, and she bled freely from at least a dozen small cuts. Her eyes went wild for a moment, and for the slightest instant, Dougal swore she looked afraid. Then she pressed on with her relentless attack, determined to bring the creature down. Her efforts seemed as effective as attacking a sand dune.

"Yes! Keep fighting!" Gyda shouted at the creature, her bloodied face split into a wide grin, even as her breathing grew more labored and the swings of her hammer became less vicious. "Keep growing! Bear's jaws, give me a fight to sing legends about!"

Clagg was giddy. "If we defeat the guardian, we can

raid Blimm's bones as well. There may be greater wonders within the sarcophagus. Breaker! Help the norn destroy it!"

The stonework golem lumbered into the room, the asura still in its front harness, a struggling Killeen lashed to its back. With a sickening feeling, Dougal realized what was about to happen. He shouted at Clagg to stop.

It was too late. Breaker stepped out onto the wobbling floor, which immediately crumbled beneath its weight.

Clagg screamed as he, Killeen, and his golem tumbled through the floor and into the blackness below.

4

In his shock, Dougal forgot about the rope wrapped around his wrist until it went taut and nearly yanked his shoulder from its socket. The weight of the golem on the other end of the rope dragged Dougal along the undulating floor, right toward the Breaker-sized hole. As Dougal sped across the granite tiles, he swung his feet forward and tried to set his heels against any sort of edge he could find.

Dougal heard a massive, earthshaking crash from somewhere below, just as the heels of his boots caught on the edge of one of the wedge-shaped tiles. The impact caused the tile beneath Dougal to give way, and a brand-new abyss yawned under him. He tottered for a moment on its edge and then toppled backward into the darkness below.

Dougal fell only a half-dozen feet before the rope snapped taut. Pain radiated from his extended arm. He swung wildly, suspended from the edge of the hole above him. The rope stretched straight up to the edge, across a few bony tiles that had yet to give way, and then back down through the first hole to where Breaker anchored it on the floor below.

Spinning about like a pendulum, Dougal looked down. Through a thick haze he spotted the blue glow of Breaker's arcanic motivator gems moving around as it struggled to climb back to its feet. He could see the asura beat his fists against the rim of his harness.

"I should never have opted for strength over speed!" Clagg shouted. "Up, Breaker! Now!"

As the rope's crazy swinging slowed, Dougal began climbing for the floor above and realized he was covered in thick, ancient webs, thankfully abandoned. They filled the lower chamber from one end to the other. These were what had made his vision down here so hazy. They must have been spun over decades by spiders that lived beneath the crypt's floor, the ancestors of the trap-door spider that poisoned Killeen.

Dougal understood then what had happened. Blimm had designed the floor of his crypt to give way under any significant force—like the pounding feet of some-one racing away from a gigantic tomb guardian—but the staggering quantity of spiderwebs woven under the floor had lent the fragile floor strength. That had helped it hold far greater weights than Blimm must have intended—right up until Gyda weakened it and Breaker provided the last straw.

The analytical part of Dougal's mind admired the nature of the trap. Originally, Blimm had probably meant for the victims of his trap to fall into the lower chamber, where the tomb guardian could have an easy time with them. Dougal suspected that a pillar supported the sarcophagus at the center of the room, keeping it from sharing the victims' fate, but it was impossible to tell in the darkness.

The rest of Dougal's mind concentrated on survival, and carefully he began to pull himself up the rope to the remnants of the chamber above.

Something overhead thundered and the room shook, the false floor above him twisting against the mortar of the abandoned spiderwebs.

Dougal had time to curse, but only just. Gyda and the tomb guardian broke through the false floor nearer the bier. More light spilled into the lower room, revealing the central pillar, safe and stable and completely out of reach. Gyda roared in triumph as she fell into the lower chamber, her last blow with her hammer having smashed the tomb guardian straight through the floor beneath them both. She landed hard but on top of the tomb guardian, which once more scattered into pieces before starting to re-form.

"This," Gyda bellowed as she staggered to her feet, ready to do battle again, "is a battle worthy of a norn!" She sounded winded but no less enthusiastic.

Dougal didn't stop to watch what happened next. Instead, he clambered up the rope as fast as he could. He reached the floor of the upper chamber in an instant and hauled himself onto it. From there he scrambled back toward the room's entrance, hoping that staying on all fours would distribute his weight enough that he would not break through the floor once more.

Skirting the hole Breaker had created, Dougal reached the threshold of the doorway, which seemed stable. Only then did he loosen the rope, which had bitten painfully into his wrist.

Dougal's brain, the analytical part that admired the workmanship of a trap that had almost killed him, told him it was time to leave. He already had what they had come for, and he was safe. He could just find another asura willing to buy the Golem's Eye and keep all the profit himself. Sticking around here any longer only meant risking death.

The norn was a bully anyway, and the asura was insulting, and the sylvari . . .

The sylvari. Dougal thought about it for only a second, the sound of Gyda's hammer blows getting fainter and more infrequent. He cursed and muttered about never adventuring with people you would hate to see die.

Peering down over the edge of the hole, Dougal shouted, "I'm up here at the entrance! Let's go!"

Suddenly the rope jerked out of Dougal's hand as Breaker fell over on his side again. Dougal managed to grab the line again before it got away from him, but rather than allow himself to be dragged back into the lower chamber, he let the line play out through his grasp.

"Hold it, Clagg!" Dougal shouted, hoping the asura was somehow still alive at the other end of the rope. "I can pull you up. I've got the rope!"

"They're shattered!" Clagg sobbed. "My Breaker's beautiful legs. I carved them myself. They're destroyed!"

"Forget about the golem!" Dougal said. "Cut your end of the rope free, and I'll haul you and Killeen up!"

"Right, right," Clagg said, blithering as if to remind himself of the details of this most basic plan. "Cut the rope and you haul me up. To safety."

"And Killeen too!"

"She's dead," Clagg said. "She *must* be dead."

"No, I am *not!*" said Killeen weakly. "I just can't find a way out of these straps!"

"Cut her free!" Dougal said.

"No!" Clagg said, his voice rising hysterically. "No time!"

A crash came from the other side of the lower chamber, and Gyda screamed, this time in pain. Then Dougal heard her hammer start pounding again, even faster than before.

"Cut Killeen free and I'll haul you both up!" Dougal shook his fist with the rope in it at Clagg and snarled. "Do it now or I'll toss the rope down and let you die with Gyda!"

Clagg squeaked something inaudible, then set to work with a knife.

"Thank you," Dougal heard Killeen say to the asura.

Gyda bellowed from the other side of the room. "By the Bear! How many times must I slay this damned thing?"

Dougal peered deeper into the gloomy hole. The norn stood near the pillar, stooped with exhaustion, her body heaving to catch a breath, her warrior's braid shredded, sweat and blood from a hundred small wounds pouring over her tattoos and fur. The fragmented tomb guardian continued to re-form, pulling replacement parts from the walls and floor. Gyda's eyes met Dougal's, and for the first time Dougal saw real fear in her face: the fear of someone who had realized she had picked an unwinnable fight.

Gyda raised her hammer and pointed beyond Dougal and toward the tomb's entrance. "Go," she said, and turned back to the re-forming guardian, her hammer raised.

"Ready!" Clagg tugged on the line. "Haul us up now! Please?"

Dougal backed up into the chamber leading into the crypt and set his feet against the top step. He began hauling on the rope as hard as he could, reeling it in an arm's length at a time. Individually, the asura and the sylvari weren't heavy, but together they added up to the weight of a good-sized man. Dougal let his fear of the beast below—and the knowledge that it would soon finish the wounded, exhausted norn—spur him on.

Then Dougal heard something that sank his heart. The hammering had stopped.

"Hurry!" Clagg screeched. "It's coming!"

Now Dougal heard the rough clacking of dozens of bones smacking rhythmically on the stone floor in the chamber below, coming closer with each beat. Dougal tried to brace himself when he heard Killeen scream, and the rope yanked him up the top step and back into the chamber, toward the gaping hole. He strained against it, knocking several bones over the threshold before him. He watched them skitter into the hole as he came closer and closer to following them down.

As his feet reached the edge of the hole, Dougal held on to the rope with one hand and snagged the door frame with the other. The strain threatened to rip his arms from their sockets, but he somehow managed to hold on, and planting his feet against the bottom of the frame, gripped the rope with both hands. Staring down the length of the rope, he spied Clagg and Killeen hanging from its far end. Clagg had knotted a loop under Killeen's arms, and now he clung to her shoulders with a grip so desperate, his gray fingers had turned white.

Just below them, the blood-spattered, mostly shattered tomb guardian had snagged the sylvari's leg with a composite arm fashioned from dozens of people's limbs. Still reassembling itself, the creature swung a wild punch at Killeen and Clagg with its other arm, but the partially formed limb fell to pieces even as it swung. A wave of bone dust buffeted the two trapped adventurers.

"Help!" Clagg wailed. "Damn you, Dougal! Save us!"

The tomb guardian brought its already re-forming arm back again, stronger this time. Dougal looked around for an option, a tool, anything within reach, that could be used to distract, dissuade, or defeat the creature. Dougal closed his eyes and knew that it was over. He could do no more than hold on until his arm gave out or Blimm's beast killed the asura and sylvari and hauled him in after them.

He couldn't help them. He could only die with them. One hand went to his chest; beneath his shirt, he could feel the cold metal of his locket, a reminder of the last time he had failed this badly, when he had stumbled out of a haunted city alone. When he had left friends behind.

He knew what had to be done. His hand kept moving

now, almost of its own volition, and fumbled to unbutton his shirt pocket.

A deafening crack sounded in the chamber below, echoing like thunder and accompanied by the sound of hailstones clattering on the stone floor. Dougal wrenched open his eyes to see that the half-shattered Breaker had stumped forward on what was left of its legs to smash its fractured arms into the tomb guardian's chest. Blimm's creature let go of Killeen's leg and turned to face this new threat, leaving the sylvari and asura to dangle over its head. The guardian turned to the task of reducing Breaker to gravel.

"Haul us up!" Clagg said.

Dougal tried, but his aching arms would not comply. He'd already put every ounce of his strength into trying to save the others, and he didn't have anything left. It was all he could do simply to keep himself from letting go. "It's no good. I can't!"

"You humans!" Clagg barked. "What good are you?"

Dougal closed his eyes again and strained with all his might. Try as he might, though, he couldn't bring the end of the rope up an inch. He bellowed in frustration with the effort, but nothing he did made any difference. He felt the end of the rope begin to wobble like mad and realized that if he didn't release it soon, he'd only wind up dead with the others.

The instant before he could finally allow himself to let go of the line, though, delicate fingers grasped his wrist. Then a sweet, desperate voice said in a ghostly whisper, "Dougal, help me up!"

Dougal almost dropped the rope in surprise. While

what was left of Breaker had kept the tomb guardian busy, Killeen had climbed all the way up the rope, with Clagg's arms clamped around her neck.

Dougal moved his numbed fingers from the rope to Killeen's arm and then fell backward, letting his weight haul Killeen and Clagg up over the lip of the hole to land upon him.

Blushing just a little, Dougal and Killeen disentangled themselves from each other and stood up. As one, the three of them leaned over and peered into the pit.

The tomb guardian gave Breaker one last stomp, and the blue glow in its central arcane motivator crystal faded and died.

Clagg howled in despair. "Do you know how much of my life that represents?"

As if to answer, the composite tomb guardian turned and stretched its arms up at them. Clagg leaped back, but Dougal stood his ground, confident that they were well beyond the creature's reach.

"I hate magic," Dougal said. "I mean, sure, we *knew* that grabbing the Eye was going to make something happen—an asura like Blimm wouldn't just leave it there unguarded—but with magic, you can't ever know what it's going to be."

Killeen leaned up against a wall of the bone-lined corridor, trying to restore the circulation to her legs. She looked like a newborn colt struggling to its feet for the first time. "Blimm must have been very determined to protect his crypt. Guarding a tomb with a beast like that strikes me as overkill."

Clagg snorted at them both. "You idiots. The Golem's

Eye isn't just a pretty rock. It is an ambient thaumaturgic construct. It contains the construct's mind. That tomb guardian didn't even exist until we showed up to disturb it." He glared at Dougal. "When you touched the ruby, you *activated* the Eye. The Eye in turn *created* the guardian."

The tomb guardian slammed its limbs into the side of the chamber directly below. Dougal watched as pieces of the construct crumbled away. It hit the wall again and again, knocking loose more pieces every time until little of it was left but a few twitching skulls that seemed to stare up at Dougal and accuse him of thievery with their empty eye sockets.

"So passes Blimm's great creation," Clagg cackled. "And now the Golem's Eye is mine!"

Dougal started to grin, but his sense of triumph faded when the bones lining the corridor began to thrum.

Dougal looked about them. "You say the ruby is that thing's mind?"

The asura nodded, still delighted in his anticipated prize. "In a sense. Blimm designed the central cereoimpulse unit so that the guardian could assemble itself out of appropriate materials in the surrounding environment. I'd think even a human could grasp that."

"So, assuming the ruby is still intact, the creature could reassemble itself anywhere?"

Clagg's face darkened. "Isn't that what I just said, bookah? It could re-form anywhere it could find enough appropriate . . ." The asura's voice faded to silence as the rattling of the bones surrounding the three of them grew louder. Clagg's eyes opened wide as he realized what he had just said.

". . . material." He finished softly, looking at the bone-lined chamber around them.

"We should run, now," suggested Killeen.

As the bones began to peel themselves from the corridor's walls, Dougal grabbed his torch in one hand, Killeen's hand in the other, and ran. He didn't look back to see if Clagg was keeping up.

Through the chambers and passages they fled, the dry clattering of bone against bone behind them. They slowed only for a moment where the spider had ambushed Killeen, and again where the explosive trap had detonated. Only after they reached the far side of both chambers without incident did Dougal call for a halt. Clagg bent in half, desperate to regain his breath. Killeen was practically yellow from exhaustion as well.

Over their deep gasps for breath, Dougal listened for the sounds of pursuit. Nothing.

"We've outrun it," he said at last, wiping the sweat away from his forehead.

"Not possible," panted the asura. "We are still surrounded by bones. Show me the Eye."

Dougal fished out the gemstone and held it out to the asura, but did not let go of it. The fire in the jewel's heart was gone, and the stone felt dead and lifeless.

"As I thought," said the asura. "It is deactivated. Exhausted the stored malagetic field. It could recharge naturally over time, or someone with sufficient skill"—Clagg paused just long enough to indicate he meant himself—"could reactivate it. Give it to me."

Dougal closed his fist. "Not yet."

Clagg snarled, "I hired you to retrieve the Eye."

Dougal said, "You hired *us* to accompany you into these crypts to recover the gem. We are still in the crypts. Once we are safely out and, may I add, paid, I will give you the gem." With that, Dougal made a show of placing the gem in his breast pocket once more.

Only, this time he palmed the gem and kept it in his hand.

Clagg opened his mouth to abuse Dougal further, but looked at the human's smiling face, said "Bah," and stomped away in the general direction of the Skull Gate and daylight.

Killeen said, "You think he is going to cheat you." It was a statement, not a question.

Dougal nodded. "Definitely. Well, likely. Best to be sure." He looked at the sylvari, and she returned his gaze with a quizzical look. He coughed and followed the asura.

The Skull Gate, a main entrance to the crypts beneath Divinity's Reach, was named for the long tunnel lined with the lacquered skulls of the deceased. Nameless souls whose bodies had washed up when Orr sank, and when that lost kingdom rose from the depths once more at a dragon's command. Dougal thought of the power of the Golem's Eye unleashed here and shuddered.

Up ahead, around a corner, was daylight. They had been underground for most of the day, but even in the deep shadows of the elevated main thoroughfares of the city, the natural light was welcome.

Clagg disappeared around the corner, then returned at once in a sudden rush—so sudden that he barreled into Dougal, knocking the human over.

Dougal felt small fingers snatch at his shirt. Instead of the gem, however, the asura came up with a closed gold locket hanging from a chain around Dougal's neck.

Dougal reached up with his empty hand and pulled the locket loose from the confused asura. "I'll take that, thank you," he said. "What's wrong?"

"City guards," said Clagg, recovering. "Seraph. We have to wait."

"Show me," said Dougal.

They crept forward. Going into the crypts was not illegal, but needed proper paperwork and passes. Paperwork and passes they, of course, lacked. Meeting the Seraph would be a bad thing at this point.

Clagg stopped at the corner and leaned out. Dougal leaned out over him, placing the hand holding the gem against one of the skulls.

The asura was not lying about the guards. Decked in heavy white armor trimmed in gold, the Seraph were the city guard of Divinity's Reach and the army of Kryta. They should not be gathered in such large numbers in the plaza outside the Skull Gate, thought Dougal. They did not appear to be on alert, and were not apparently waiting for the krewe, but a battered human, asura, and sylvari coated with bone dust and stumbling into the plaza would no doubt be brought in for questioning. Questioning that would turn rather pointed when they found the Golem's Eye.

Dougal slipped the Eye deep into the eye socket of the nearest lacquered skull. It was an unsuitable hiding place, but it was the best he could do for the moment.

"So, do you have a plan, human?" said Clagg.

"Let me see," said Killeen. "Is there a problem?" The sylvari climbed up on Dougal's back to see past him, putting her slim, booted foot on the back of his belt to boost herself up.

Despite himself, Dougal shook her off and wheeled on her. "What are you doing?" he said sharply. "Aren't things bad enough?"

The sylvari shrank back from the reproach, and Dougal swallowed any further words. He turned back to the asura, towering over him.

"Here's the plan: we wait."

Clagg, visibly frustrated and tired, shook his head. "What if they are checking the crypts?"

"Fine, then one of us goes out and draws their attention. Then we regroup later for the split."

"Dougal . . ." said Killeen.

"By 'one of us,' you mean me or the sylvari, don't you?" spat Clagg.

"If you want, I will go first," said Dougal, looking down on the asura, his own anger rising. They had been through too much to end it with a stupid argument.

"Dougal . . ." repeated Killeen.

"So you can fast-talk your way past your human friends and leave us here to be caught?" snarled Clagg.

"We can't go out together!" said Dougal hotly. "They will get all of us!"

"Dougal Keane!" said Killeen firmly.

"What?" snapped Dougal, turning toward her again. This time she didn't shrink back.

"We have company," said Killeen.

Dougal turned back and looked down the drawn

blade of a Seraph lieutenant. Two other Seraph stood behind her, their blades drawn as well.

"Dougal Keane—I believe she called you that," said the lieutenant. "You and your friends are under arrest, Dougal Keane. Come along now."

5

The manacles, Dougal felt, were an unnecessary insult. His cell was carved out of living rock, without mortar or purchase. The bars that bisected the room were old and stout and as thick as his thumb. The only light was from a thin chimney far overhead, also barred. The door to his partitioned cell was secured by a heavy padlock, which Dougal could pick with the proper tools, but those tools were now denied him. Beyond the barred partition was a small hall leading to an ironbound door to the rest of the jail. If Dougal had a norn, he could get past that as well, but that luxury was also denied him.

Given the security, the heavy iron leggings and wrist cuffs—all held together by a single loop of chain and set into a ring in the center of the room—were simply overkill.

It had been four days since his arrest, and except for a bored, grunting servant who brought porridge in the morning and stew in the evening, he had not had any visitors. That changed on the afternoon of the fourth day.

The outer door opened and a heavyset, mustached Seraph guard entered, followed by a young clerk carrying a writing desk. The heavyset guard stared at Dougal through the bars while the clerk positioned the small desk, then left the room. The clerk returned with a stool, set it before the writing desk, uncorked a small vial of ink, set it in the appropriate hole in the desk, opened the desk, selected a quill, sharpened it, removed a small sheaf of paper, peeled off the topmost sheet, sat down on the stool, dipped the quill in the vial, and waited for the guard to speak.

"Dougal Keane—" began the officer.

"Present," said Dougal, interrupting him.

The officer scowled, then started again. "Dougal Keane, you are accused of grave-robbing in the crypts beneath Divinity's Reach. How do you plead?"

"Did you find any grave goods on myself or my companions?" asked Dougal.

"No," said the officer, who seemed unbothered by the admission.

"And did you find much in the way of weapons on the three of us?"

"No," repeated the officer.

"Then," said Dougal, "If we are tomb robbers, we are extremely ineffective ones."

"Your effectiveness is not the issue," said the officer. "Your intent is."

"Then I will go with 'Innocent' as a response," said Dougal to the clerk, who dutifully noted it.

"You were found at the Skull Gate, injured and coated with bone dust. You lack the proper exploration permissions. Your answers have been less than satisfactory." Here the guard smiled. "And one of your compatriots has already confessed that you were seeking the Tomb of Blimm and the Golem's Eye."

Clagg, thought Dougal, and all the air went out of him for the moment. "So, why are we having this discussion?" he said.

"Formality," said the officer, his teeth showing white beneath his mustache. He walked over to the writing desk and motioned to the clerk, who opened it and produced another sheaf of paper. The Seraph guard read the form.

"Dougal Keane," he said.

"Still present," said Dougal, his heart sinking.

"Born in Divinity's Reach, but emigrated to Ebonhawke as a child. Served in the Ebon Vanguard. You are listed as missing, presumed dead. Deserter?" His teeth flashed.

"We were caught behind charr lines on an extended patrol," said Dougal, choosing his words carefully.

"You disappeared five years ago," said the officer.

"It was an extremely extended patrol," said Dougal, hoping he sounded more authoritative than he felt. He felt compelled to add, "There were a lot of charr between us and Ebonhawke at the time."

"You never went back," said the officer, smacking his lips in disdain. Then he added, "The queen strongly supports Ebonhawke. We could send you back to rejoin your unit."

"I'm sure those who are still alive would welcome me back," bluffed Dougal.

The officer shrugged and returned to his list. "Wanted in regards to numerous petty crimes in Lion's Arch."

"Does the queen strongly support Lion's Arch as well?" said Dougal, raising his eyebrows in mock disbelief.

"A crime is a crime," said the officer. "Even in Lion's Arch."

"Lion's Arch was founded by pirates, corsairs, and wreckers," said Dougal, and for the first time the Seraph nodded in agreement. Even the clerk smiled.

The officer returned to his paper. "You worked for the Durmand Priory, apparently."

"Briefly. We parted company after a disagreement about their book-lending policy," said Dougal.

"I was unaware that the Durmand Priory lent out its precious books," said the Seraph.

"My point exactly," said Dougal. This time the clerk smiled and nodded, but the Seraph only shrugged.

"Your name turned up in an incident involving the sunken Temple of the Ages."

"Never been there," Dougal lied.

"Several landlords are looking for you about rent owed," continued the Seraph officer.

"A series of simple misunderstandings," said Dougal.

"You've been to Ascalon City," said the officer. "And came out alive."

The accusation was sudden and unexpected, and left him breathless. It hung in the air a moment, and even the clerk looked up. Dougal just nodded.

"Yes," he said at last. "That part is true."

The Seraph shook his head. "With all your . . .

apparent abilities, I am surprised you have not made more of yourself."

Dougal struggled for a moment, then said, "Such is the nature of our lives in these dragon-haunted times. Perhaps I have a problem with my work ethic."

"Very well," said the heavyset man. "I think we can provide you with a little work ethic. You'll be joining a work crew on Lake Doric."

"Don't I get a trial?" asked Dougal.

"You get a hearing," said the officer. "This was it. In the name of Queen Jennah, the city of Divinity's Reach, the nation of Kryta, you are found guilty. Tomorrow morning you'll be escorted to a work gang north of the city."

Dougal started to protest, when the door opened and another Seraph entered the room.

If his original interrogator was ill-made to wear the uniform, this one seemed to have been born in the armor. Tall, with dark brown hair parted in the center, the long locks framing a stern face with noble, chiseled features.

Dougal inhaled sharply: this was Logan Thackeray, captain of the Seraph in Divinity's Reach, champion of Her Majesty Queen Jennah, protector of Kryta. The man had been legendary even before he had joined the Seraph: he was a member of one of the most famous guilds in recent history, Destiny's Edge. Although that guild was no more, Logan Thackeray's legend had continued to grow.

The interrogating officer immediately stiffened and saluted, while the clerk laid down his pen and bowed in respect. Even Dougal felt his spine stiffen and stood up straight in the captain's presence.

"Lieutenant Groban," said Logan sharply.

"Sir," said Groban, dropping his salute with a snap. "I was about to assign the prisoner to a work gang."

"Dougal Keane?" said Logan.

"Yes, sir!" said Groban, pleased that the captain was following his caseload. For his part, Dougal felt a little sick: when someone in power knew your name, it never boded well.

"He is to be released," said Logan.

A confused look spread over Groban's face, as if Logan had suddenly manifested a godly aura and levitated before him. "Released?" the lieutenant repeated.

"On orders of Her Majesty, he is to be released into the custody of the Vigil," said Logan, and Dougal's stomach felt like an abyssal hole. The queen? Why would the queen have anything to say in this?

Lieutenant Groban fumbled with his heavy set of keys and unlocked the cell door. Then, selecting a smaller key, he began working on Dougal's manacles.

Dougal's thoughts raced. Why was this Vigil interested in him? They were a group of would-be knights and heroes engaged in fighting the Elder Dragons and their minions. A fool's errand if there ever was one.

Why did they want him? He checked his ongoing list of people he had offended, stole from, or owed money to. He came up empty.

"You are a lucky man," said Logan, speaking to Dougal now. "You were specifically asked for by someone with enough influence to get you out of here." From the tone of his voice, it was clear that Logan would prefer to see Dougal rebuilding a dock somewhere on Lake Doric under armed supervision. "Were I you, I would strongly recommend that you not disappoint her. I don't want to see you back here again." He failed to elucidate whether he was referring to this cell, Divinity's Reach, or Kryta in general.

Dougal's mind was spinning now. " 'Her'?" he managed.

Logan walked to the doorway. "Ma'am?" he said.

A slim woman in chain armor entered the room, and for a half-second Dougal's heart stopped. She had tightly wound auburn curls that stopped just short of her shoulders, and her icy blue eyes had the cold look of a military professional.

"Riona," said Dougal softly.

"Riona Grady of the Vigil," she said, holding up a document sealed with purple wax to the captain. "Here to take charge and responsibility for the prisoner on behalf of my order."

Dougal held up his bare wrists to Groban. "If it's all the same to you, Lieutenant," he said, "I think it'd be safer for me if you put the manacles back on and closed the cell door on your way out."

6

Riona did not say more than three words as Dougal regained his few confiscated belongings and followed her out of the jail.

The city of Divinity's Reach was laid out like a great six-spoked wheel, with each spoke being a great high road that arched from the outer walls of white stone to the uppermost reaches of the city. The upper city, with its palace and senate and domed gardens, was at the hub, and the lower reaches between the arched high roads were where most people lived. Over the years, the divided sectors took on a regional flavor. The original Krytans predominated in one sector of the city, while the descendants of the Ascalonians, their homelands blasted by the charr centuries earlier, gathered in another. Other spaces between the bridges were dominated by Elonian and Canthan immigrants, their distant homelands now unreachable, thanks to the rise of the Elder Dragons.

The southernmost of the two sectors were given over to an assemblage of inns, alehouses, general services for travelers and merchants, and the carnival. The last was a collection of ornate rides and vendors scattered through the area, funded by a powerful minister in the Krytan bureaucracy. It gave the area a surprisingly festive appearance and a false feeling that everything was safe and secure in the last human kingdom.

Riona and Dougal wound their way among the hawkers, merchants, and revelers. Confetti drifted down from the sky, and in the distance the deep brass tones of a clockwork band drifted over the proceedings.

Riona stopped at a shadow show, and Dougal stopped with her. The shadow show was an opaque white sheet set up at the base of one of the High Road's supports, lit from behind. About a dozen townspeople and a similar number of children gathered in the shade. Silhouetted puppets danced across the screen.

"Riona, I . . ." Dougal started to say.

"Hush," said Riona, her eyes locked on the screen.

The shadow show told the tale of the kingdoms of Tyria. First was Ascalon, defended by its Great Northern Wall. The charr attacked the wall, their heavy-shouldered feline troops striding across the screen from the left. Human soldiers appeared on the wall, led by their heroic king, and drove them back in a cascade of arrows. The charr returned with great cauldrons, and out of the cauldrons sprung huge crystalline missiles that struck the walls and breached them. This was the Searing, when the charr broke through the wall and overran Ascalon.

The screen darkened and brightened again. Another city, this one with more ornate, delicate structures, twisted towers and great arches. This was Arah, the greatest city of Orr. Again the charr, with their mystic cauldrons, arrived from the left, and a man in robes appeared in the tallest tower and summoned a great spell. The screen flashed and the charr were blown back, but the city itself was shattered. A wavy line representing the ocean rose up, and the pieces of the city settled to the bottom of the Sea of Sorrows. This was the Sinking of Orr.

The screen darkened again, and the scene shifted back to Ascalon, where the charr were besieging its greatest metropolis, Ascalon City. The feline assailants broke through the gates and were soon on the walls, fighting the human soldiers. On the tallest tower the human king, Adelbern, fought with a powerful charr. The two locked their blades and there was a great explosion. The charr were all blown away as if by a wind, and the humans all went pale: they had become ghosts. This was the Foefire.

After another flash, a large black blot ran from one edge of the screen to the other under the waves. Then the blot opened a great draconic eye. Now the ruined city of Arah rose from the waves, and at its tallest point a great winged form spread its wings and roared at the sky. This was the Rising of Orr, and with it the waking of the undead Elder Dragon known as Zhaitan.

The dragon roared again and flashed its wings, kicking up a great wave as it did so. The wave traveled to the right, the risen city retreating to the left, and now a new city appeared at the right hand side of the screen. This was Lion's Arch. The wave struck it, and pieces of the city flew in all directions. When the dragon rose, the original Lion's Arch was flooded and swept away into the sea.

The screen darkened one more time, and now the scene was of refugees entering from the left. They were dressed like Krytans and Ascalonians and Canthans and Elonians, and brought wagons with their belongings and great packs. Rising up before them came the walls of Divinity's Reach, and with them the upper city, and atop the upper city the Queen's Palace. Atop the tower the queen appeared, clearly modeled after Queen Jennah, welcoming the refugees to the city, and confetti drifted down from the sky as the happy travelers reached safety. The last of the refugees traveled into the city, the gates closed, and the banner of Divinity's Reach was raised from the queen's tallest tower.

The crowd politely applauded, and the puppeteer, a small, smiling Canthan woman, stepped from behind the screen to take her bows, her puppets mounted on slender sticks. Riona did not applaud but simply moved on, and Dougal followed. She passed the ale tent and took a pint of lager. Dougal took one as well, careful to let her pay. She sat down at one of the nearby tables. Dougal sat across from her, and they were silent for a moment. Riona looked at the rough, knife-carved tabletop.

"Riona, I . . ." Dougal started again.

"I want you to know . . ." she said, bitterness in her voice, then stopped. Dougal held his tongue, and in the distance the band shifted to a different tune, more of a waltz converted into steam and strained through brass fittings.

She continued. "I want you to know that, were it up to me, I would have left you there to rot. Like you left me."

"I didn't mean to—" Dougal said.

"Like *you* left *me*," repeated Riona, piercing him with her blue steel eyes.

"It was . . ." Dougal started, then realized that the words "not my idea" would not be well received, nor would they be true. ". . . a mistake. I'm sorry. We shouldn't have left you."

"You didn't just *leave* me," Riona snapped. "You knocked me out and left me for the Ebon Vanguard to find. You left me to pay the price for your crimes."

Now it was Dougal's turn to look at the table. Five years ago, he and Riona and the others had all been in Ebonhawke, members of the Ebon Vanguard. They weren't very good at soldiering, and all of them talked about various schemes to get them to Lion's Arch, to Divinity's Reach, to anywhere but within a city besieged by the hated charr.

Then Dak found the map—the map to the original Ascalon City. A map that showed the towers and streets of that ancient human city from the times before the Searing and the Foefire, before the devastation of the charr. A map that showed the royal castle of King Adelbern.

And, most of all, showed the royal treasure vault and inventoried its contents.

Dak had found a treasure map and Jervis suggested they go after it. Marga asked why they should wait, and Vala and Dougal agreed. Riona, alone among them, said it was a bad idea, that they would be put to hard labor if they were caught, or slain by the charr if not, because Ascalon City was in the heart of the charr territories.

So Marga hit her over the back of the head one night when they were scheduled to go on patrol beyond the battlements. Marga and Dougal then loaded her into her bunk and told the commander she was ill and left her there. And they left Ebonhawke and never came back.

"When your patrol didn't return, the Ebon Vanguard came for me," Riona said, filling in the blanks on the table. "I didn't tell them what was going on, and they didn't believe me. I took the blame. They put me at hard labor in the quarries for two years before even considering reinstating my position. And they never let me patrol beyond the walls."

"And you're with the Vigil now," said Dougal, looking away as the carnival swirled around them.

"I served my tour. I left. I looked for a purpose. I found one with the Vigil and I came here, to Divinity's Reach. I've been here a year, and in all that time I never tried to hunt you"—she almost said "down" but brought herself up short—"out . . ." she finished.

"And the Vigil wants me. Why?" Dougal returned her glare. Her accusing eyes still hurt to look at, but it was clear he was going to have to learn to live with it.

"You survived Ascalon City. The others?"

"Dead. Dak, Jervis, Marga . . ." The locket felt heavy around his neck, like a stone. "And Vala. Dead in Ascalon City."

"And yet, you survived," said Riona, smiling. It was not a friendly smile. "Why am I not surprised?"

Dougal stared back into the angry eyes and said, "We were wrong. I apologize on behalf of the dead. Now you need me. Why?"

Riona bit her lip. "I need you to promise you won't run when I tell you," said Riona, and her expression softened just a bit.

"Would you believe me if I did?"asked Dougal.

"No," said Riona, "but I need you to promise anyway."

Dougal thought a moment, then said, "You need something in Ascalon. The Vigil needs something in Ascalon. You need someone to go there."

"Are you going to promise?"

"I don't understand how you ended up with the Vigil," said Dougal. "Their leader is—"

"I know what their leader is," said Riona. "I was looking for a purpose. For a chance to change myself, to change the world. I found it there."

"Riona," said Dougal, leaning forward, dropping his voice as if sharing a confidence. "They think they can defeat the Elder Dragons."

"Don't worry, they aren't asking you to fight a dragon, Elder or otherwise."

"Then what are they asking me to do?" Dougal took a pull on his ale.

"Go to Ascalon City," she said.

Dougal looked over the rim of the glass. "And do what?"

"That we'll talk about once we get to Lion's Arch."

Dougal thought for a moment and said, "I'll need a sword."

"You always were a horrible swordsman," said Riona.

"I've gotten better," said Dougal.

The two sat there for a moment, each daring the other to break the silence.

"Fine. Finish your drink," said Riona. "I'll get you a damned sword."

They returned their glasses to the vendor and weaved their way through the crowds. Riona kept shooting Dougal looks as if she anticipated him to melt away into the masses of carnival-goers.

Dougal had to admit that he considered escaping, ditching her in the bustle of the festival, recovering the Golem's Eye from its precarious hiding place, and quietly heading for some small village far from Divinity's Reach. Although Riona's offer was intriguing, the idea of returning to Ascalon City was insane. He had barely escaped with his life before. But the chance to make good on previous failed promises . . .

"A new shipment came in from Claypool," said the merchant, a squat man who, despite being surrounded by sharp blades, was in severe need of a shave. "Finest kind, fresh from the forge."

Riona's brows bunched up. "You must be kidding. Look at that pocking. The grip wobbles. And the edge isn't even true."

The merchant gave an irritated shrug. "You're not expecting Seraph quality, are you? And the really good stuff all gets shipped out to those Ebonhawke soreheads."

"What do you mean by that?" said Riona, her eyes narrowing.

"Ascalon is dead and buried," said the merchant. "Let the charr have it: it's blasted and filled with ghosts, anyway, from what I hear. Sending men and supplies to Ebonhawke—supplies we can use here at home to fight centaurs and bandits, mind you—is a waste of money. Good gold chasing after bad."

As the merchant spoke, Dougal noticed Riona's visage grow darker and her hand drifting to the grip of her own sword. "This will do nicely," he said quickly. "Pay the man, Riona."

"I'd rather—" started Riona, her jaw clenched.

"Pay the man," said Dougal. "Let's move on."

The two walked away from the merchant, Riona muttering, "That traitorous moron! And this is what people think of us in Divinity's Reach."

"Ebonhawke is far away, like Orr and the dragons," said Dougal. "You can understand if they worry more about centaurs raiding their caravans and bandits robbing their fields. You're right about one thing, though." He flicked the blade back and forth a few times. The other pedestrians watched him cautiously as he executed some textbook moves. "This blade is miserable."

"Told you," said Riona.

"Most modern blades are. Modern human blades, anyway." He sheathed the sword. "Such is life in our dragon-haunted times."

Someone called out Dougal's name from behind him.

"Now what?" said Riona, but Dougal saw a green face flickering among the crowds, a verdant arm raised overhead.

He smiled and shot a glance at Riona, who scowled at the approaching newcomer. The fact that the sylvari's appearance frustrated Riona made him feel even better.

And Killeen looked fully recovered from her sojourn in the crypts beneath Divinity's Reach.

"Riona Grady, member of the Vigil, may I present—" he began.

"Killeen, born of the Cycle of Night," she said, holding out a hand in the human fashion.

Riona scowled and nodded, leaving the hand unclasped. "It is good to meet you, Killeen of the Night, but I am afraid Dougal and I have business to discuss—"

"Would you like an ale?" Dougal broke in. "There is a tent not more than twenty feet from here that does a passable brown lager."

The look Riona shot him would have slain a devourer at ten paces, and Dougal allowed himself a smile. New sins for her to be angry about might help heal the old.

"It's very nice," said Killeen a little later, sipping the ale. "Is that butternut squash in the mix?"

Dougal shrugged amiably while Riona, leaning back in her bench, kept her arms crossed. She said, "I don't know many sylvari." From her tone it was clear that she would prefer to know one fewer.

"And I don't know much about the Vigil," said Killeen, "other than they are a group made up of members from many races, nations, and guilds. They are dedicated to resisting the depredations of the Elder Dragons by force of arms. Are you hiring Dougal to fight dragons?"

"I'm glad you're not still in jail," said Dougal, realizing that this was the first time he'd thought about Killeen since they had been arrested.

"I spent the night there, and then a pleasant human with a mustache asked me questions, and I answered them, and they let me go." She sipped the ale again.

Dougal thought about what Lieutenant Groban had said about one of their group confessing. "*You?*" he managed. "*You* told him?"

"Of course. I told him about Clagg and Breaker and you and Gyda and where Blimm's tomb was and where you hid the gem by the entrance," she said. "They had forgotten about Blimm's tomb and were happy I told them where to find it. That's something that is strange to me: I hadn't thought about it before, that knowledge can die. It makes sense, when you think about it: someone who knows something dies without telling anyone else, then the knowledge is lost. But, to a sylvari, it is odd."

Killeen did not notice that Dougal was now cradling his face in his hands and that Riona was chuckling. "So," began Dougal, "you told them where I hid the gem . . ."

"Yes," said Killeen, smiling. "Honesty works out best, I find." At this, Riona actually laughed. "And that reminds me," the sylvari said, reaching for her pouch. "I wanted to give you this."

She produced a small object wrapped in a lace handkerchief, about the size of an asura's fist. It thunked heavily on the table. Dougal picked it up, and a flash of red crystal flared in the late-afternoon sun.

"Nice," said Riona, catching a glimpse as well. "Looks just like the type of thing you would risk your life for. Not magical, is it?"

Dougal pushed the entire gem in his pocket,

handkerchief and all. "I'm confused," he said, shaking his head. "You just told me—"

"That I told our jailers where you hid the gem," said Killeen. "I didn't say anything about where I hid it afterwards . . ."

"Where you . . ." The pieces of the puzzle fit together in his mind. "I see. When you climbed up my back . . . ."

"I pulled the gem from where you put it and moved it further up, and quickly sealed it up inside a skull for good measure. When I saw you leaving the jail, I went and retrieved it."

Now it was Dougal's turn to laugh. Killeen leaned across the table and, in a conspiratorial tone, said, "So, what is the new job? Is it dragons?"

Riona shook her head. "I'm sorry, Killeen of the Night, but this is a private matter between me and—"

"Ascalon City," interrupted Dougal, ignoring Riona's glare. "She wants me to go to Ascalon City for the Vigil. She won't tell me why yet."

Killeen leaned back and put her palms together. "Ascalon City is in the center of charr territory, and filled with ghosts."

"I know," said Dougal, "I've been there."

Killeen blinked in surprise. "I didn't know," she said, and was silent for a moment.

Dougal felt compelled to add, "It did not work out well," and looked at Riona. For the first time Riona nodded in agreement, her mouth a tight line.

Killeen looked up and said, "All right. Count me in."

Riona looked up in shock and stammered, "I'm sorry, that's impossible."

"Why?" said Killeen. "You're taking *him*." She motioned at Dougal with the glass and Dougal felt vaguely insulted.

"Ascalon City is filled with ghosts . . ." Riona began, repeating Killeen's words as if explaining something to a child.

"She's a necromancer," said Dougal. "That argument doesn't have a lot of traction."

"Indeed, Riona Grady of the Vigil," said Killeen. "My people are less than twenty-five years old. None of us have died, save by violence, poison, and disease. We don't know much about what it is like to die. I find the dead, and the undead—and ghosts and everything similar—to be fascinating. If you are going to Ascalon City, I am in."

Riona looked at Dougal, who smiled. "You should have heard her in the crypts," said Dougal. "She was practically poetic."

"I'm sorry," said Riona, spreading her fingers out toward Killeen, "that's just impossible."

"She's in," said Dougal.

Riona goggled at him, an angry color returning to her cheeks. "*You* don't get to decide."

"Of course I get to decide," said Dougal. "If she doesn't go, I don't come to Lion's Arch. You march me back to Captain Logan Thackeray and his Lieutenant Groban and I spend the next few years repairing docks on Lake Doric. Which, you might think, is poetic justice. And you get to go back to the Vigil and explain how you let the one man who's been to Ascalon City and lived to tell the tale get away, and your entire plan, whatever it is, falls apart." Dougal leaned back on his bench. "Your choice."

Riona was flush with rage now, and for a moment Dougal feared that he had pushed her too far. The new sins were quickly overwhelming the old. She choked out a few words and, glaring at Dougal, finished her ale in a single pull.

"Fine," she said. "Killeen, born of the Cycle of Night, would you care to join us, at least as far as Lion's Arch?"

"I'd be honored," said Killeen.

"Good," said Dougal. "And, in return, the answer is yes."

"Yes?" said Riona.

"I promise not to run when I find out what you really want," said Dougal. "At least until we get to Lion's Arch."

The next morning Dougal surveyed the contents of his life, spread out across his bed. The moleskin pouch containing his tools: picks, wrenches, flats, hooks, and skeleton keys. His knife. The few crumpled and tattered notes he had made about Blimm's tomb. A change of clothes, including a warm cloak, suitable for sleeping in. A new sword, human-made and rough, inside a fine old scabbard, looted from some ruined temple in the Caledon Forest. And the Golem's Eye, still bound in Killeen's handkerchief.

Dougal packed light, as always. Everything he owned fit into the worn leather backpack that he'd had with him since his youth in Ebonhawke. After his mother had died here in Divinity's Reach, he'd gone to live with his father in the last human outpost in Ascalon, and his aunt Brinna had given him the pack to carry his belongings in. The backpack had long outlived everyone else in his family and proved trustier than any friend.

The night before had been restless and his dreams were plagued with the faces of the dead. Even while he packed, Dougal still considered the merits of bolting. All he would have to do was not meet Riona in front of Uzolan's Mechanical Orchestra, as they had agreed. All he had to do was slip out the front gates, or even hide elsewhere in the city, perhaps go to ground in the Canthan district, where she didn't know anyone. If he ran, he knew that Riona would never find him—at least, not in time. Turn left instead of right when he left his quarters, and he would be gone.

He had buried Ascalon City deep, intent on never returning. Indeed, who would want to go there? The city was wrecked, first by the Searing, then by the Foefire, its inhabitants reduced to ghosts, its walls surrounded by extremely possessive charr.

And yet, he could feel the tug. Of failure. Of the price paid. Of things left undone.

Dougal reached into his shirt, fished out the locket, and looked at it for a long time. He carefully undid the clasp that opened it to reveal a cameo, ivory set against jet, of Vala in profile. Its twin, the one with his portrait, jet on ivory, was lost in Ascalon, along with everything else.

Dougal replaced the locket and carefully packed his gear in the battered backpack, and when he left the building, he turned right, toward the meeting with Riona. A low, thin mist still clung to the streets where the sun had not yet arrived to burn it off.

Both Riona and Killeen were waiting for him at the feet of Uzolan's Mechanical Orchestra, a frozen explosion of giant hornbells at one end of the festival grounds. It was early, and the orchestra had yet to be activated;

its silence left the permanent carnival with an empty, lonely feeling. Bits of excelsior and other debris littered the pavement, and a few workers, fitted with the heavy leather collars of criminals, swept the remains of the previous celebration into larger piles.

The two women were waiting but not talking. Killeen seemed interested in the construction of the clockwork in the orchestra, while Riona paced, her arms folded. The official representative of the Vigil had regained that hard professional look that she had had the day before. Dougal wondered how well she had slept the previous night, now that she knew for sure that the others were well and truly dead.

"It's time," Riona said. "Let's go." She was just as sour as she'd been yesterday, a thundercloud on an otherwise clear morning. Killeen, of course, was the sun.

"This should be exciting," Killeen said. "The idea of a city filled with ghosts is just too intriguing. To my knowledge, no sylvari has ever ventured into Ascalon City. I will be the first of my people to see inside the city's walls."

"It's not that exciting," said Dougal. "More like terrifying."

Riona grunted at him.

"Surprised to find me here still?" Dougal asked Riona.

She shook her head. "Thackeray's people have had an eye on your place all night."

"And you don't think I could slip past them if I wanted to?"

She shrugged as if it didn't make a difference. "You didn't."

Dougal arched an eyebrow at her. "And you could have told Thackeray and his people that we had recovered something from the crypts after all."

"Captain Logan Thackeray only tolerates me at best," Riona said. "Telling him you had this gem would only have forced him to toss you in prison again. I need you in Ascalon City."

Dougal slung his pack over his shoulder. "Then let's move."

Dougal turned southward, to the main gates, but Riona instead moved north toward the Ascalonian district. Killeen was left in the middle, unsure which way to go.

Dougal pointed. "Main gate to the city is this way."

"We aren't using the main gate," said Riona. "Time is of the essence. We're going to use an asura gate."

Dougal walked back to Riona now, Killeen following and trying not to look like she was listening. "You didn't say anything about using an asura gate," he said, trying to keep the worry out of his voice.

"Don't tell me you're afraid of them," said Riona, smiling slightly.

"Of course not," said Dougal. "It's magic. I don't particularly trust magic. Worse yet, it's asuran magic. They operate at such a level that even human spellcasters are still lagging in their wake."

"You *are* afraid," said Riona, with a tight smile. "You've faced a city full of ghosts and gods know what else, and you're afraid of a magical gate."

"An *asuran* magical gate," said Dougal. "There's a difference. Half the time they are taking it apart and putting it back together. And have you ever had one of them explain how it works?"

"It is a simple immobile-location dimensional transporter," said Killeen, "that shortcuts normal reality by bringing together two fixed points with suitable equipment tuned to the same metavibrational aetheric frequency." Dougal stared at her, and she added, "We have them in the Grove. The asura were one of the first peoples we met when we appeared."

"You have my sympathy," said Riona, and led the way into the Ascalonian district.

Divinity's Reach was waking up. The people who worked for an honest living were shuffling off to their jobs, but laughing children still raced through the streets, darting from doorway to doorway in their carefree games. The Seraph patrolled the streets, alone and in pairs, always on the hunt for innocents to protect and lawbreakers to bring to justice. Merchants' voices started to sound, hawking everything from apples to armor. Elders stood ready to train students in various specialties. Criers called out announcements from the queen and news from both inside the city and beyond its limits.

They passed through another set of walls, built within the city itself to separate it from the asura gate. Dougal noticed the walls were patrolled by white-armored members of the Seraph, armed with the newer, smooth-bored muskets. The Golem's Eye in his pocket felt suddenly heavy. They passed within the picket line without being challenged, and Dougal assumed that Riona's Vigil authority extended to these watchmen as well.

And that Captain Logan Thackeray was delighted to get them out of his queen's city.

The gate itself was up on a low earth platform against the city's outer wall, a great stone loop filled with bronze pulsing energy. Even looking at the shifting surface of the gate's opening made Dougal a little queasy. The area around the gate was filled with wagons and bearers, golem carriers, and a small group of soldiers in dark armor: Ebon Vanguard. Dougal remembered that the Ascalonian district had a hospital for the more badly wounded soldiers from the fortress city of Ebonhawke.

Riona walked past the collected wagons to a smaller group, mostly human, but with a couple asura and their golems mixed in. The asura seemed unfazed by the crackling energy before them, but the humans apparently shared Dougal's nervousness.

"Aren't we cutting ahead of people?" said Killeen.

"Those are here to go to Ebonhawke," said Riona, pointing a chin at the larger group. "They have to tune the gate for the jump around noon. Requires a lot of energy. We're going to Lion's Arch." She looked at two asura arguing in front of a rune-inscribed pillar bristling with crystals and levers.

Dougal knew that the asura gates were used by the diminutive race, and they would never risk their own lives for something that had not been (mostly) tested and safe. The gates were leagues upon leagues apart, yet simply by stepping through the oval archways, they would be at a similar gate in Lion's Arch. Still, the asura's continual tendency to modify and meddle with their own work gave him pause.

The two asura in front of the plinth of crystals concluded their heated argument and the older of the two walked over to them. The younger stayed behind, shooting sullen looks at his elder.

"Sorry," said the older asura, a female. "Training day. My apprentice has his own ideas about the process of tuning two gates into alignment, and I have to beat some sense into him." She turned toward her sullen apprentice, who immediately brightened, then returned to his black cloud of resentment as soon as the elder's back was turned. Dougal watched the younger asura eye the arcane runes on the plinth and was concerned that the upstart apprentice would suddenly try to prove his point by changing the settings.

"Papers?" said the asura, and Riona presented a folded letter with a purple seal similar to the one she had presented Logan Thackeray in the jail. The asura reviewed it, grunted, and said, "Are you carrying anything from Orr, the Dragonbrand, or any other territory that has been dominated or altered by the presence of the Elder Dragons?" She recited the question with the complete lack of inflection born of repetition.

"No," said Riona.

"Are you carrying any items that are illegal in Lion's Arch or Divinity's Reach? Are you entering Lion's Arch with intent to commit any illegal actions or to flee Divinity's Reach authorities?"

Killeen started to say something, but Dougal quickly said, "No, we are not," and shot the sylvari a look to indicate that the asura really didn't want or need to hear about the Golem's Eye and their recent incarceration.

"Very well," said the asura, returning the document to Riona, "we should be ready to go in a few moments, if *somebody*"—she turned toward her assistant—"will stop sulking and tune the gate to its correct aetheric frequency."

The apprentice began to touch the various runes and jutting crystals in order, and the bronze light within the archway turned a deep golden shade. One by one, the various travelers approached the golden glow and disappeared.

Killeen stepped through without pausing. Dougal hesitated and looked at Riona. She made an "After you" motion, and it was clear that she wasn't going to leave him alone on this side of the gate. Mentally noting the lack of trust in these dragon-haunted days, Dougal stepped through.

It was no more difficult than stepping through the surface of a soap bubble. One moment he was in Divinity's Reach, the rising sun just cresting the walls ahead of him, the city around him in deep shadow. The next moment he and the others were in bright sunshine, leaving him blinking and raising a hand to protect his eyes. The air itself was different, changing suddenly from the cool, damp morning air to something warmer, fresher, and smelling of salt. The quiet energy of a city awakening was immediately stilled and replaced with the clamor of merchants and townspeople at work.

One moment he was in Divinity's Reach, and the next moment he was here. Dougal did not want to think about where he was in the space in between.

They stood on another low set of earthworks overlooking the merchant district of Lion's Arch. Around them, in a slight arch, were other gates, some with golden energies in their arches, some bronze, and some with a purplish hue. Next to them, three more asura were squabbling about performance issues.

Riona ignored them, passing Killeen and leading them down the steps into the Great Bazaar, following the other travelers.

The Lion's Arch of long ago was gone, its only remaining memory consisting of the battlements that survived the great waves from the Rising of Orr. When Zhaitan, the undead Elder Dragon, brought long-sunken Orr back to the surface, all lands surrounding the Sea of Sorrows were awash in great waves. Lion's Arch was almost utterly destroyed, and in its place was left a swamp of broken ships, snapped trees, and dead creatures.

Out of that morass, the new Lion's Arch arose over the past hundred years. The town was re-established by pirates and corsairs looking for a safe haven, and salvage crews reclaiming the flotsam and jetsam that had washed ashore. It soon blossomed into a cosmopolitan trading center.

The city showed its recent origin. Some of the newer buildings were stone, but most of the city was of wood. The original structures were built from the remains of wrecked ships tossed up on the beach, and that architecture so defined the city that even new construction was built along the lines of hulls and keels as opposed to walls and roofs. It was a scratch-built city, a lash-up made permanent, a temporary site that might yet outshine

Divinity's Reach or the Black Citadel or even the asuran city of Rata Sum.

The people of Lion's Arch were as motley as its buildings. Before the Rising of Orr, it was a human city, a Krytan city. After the floods uprooted the houses and replaced them with shipwrecks, a transient population took hold, a brotherhood of the coast seeking nothing more than survival in an overturned world. The crews of the surviving pirate ships colonized the wreckage that was Lion's Arch, and their captains became the first leaders. As a result, Lion's Arch was ruled by a council of captains, and its morals and legality were always more flexible than in other great cities.

The new population was also more diverse than anything else seen in Tyria. Here you found humans but also equal or greater numbers of norn, asura, and sylvari. The occasional bloated, amphibian hylek or hunched, bucktoothed dredge stalked through the streets. The castoffs of a half-dozen nations and a plethora of societies all gathered here.

And charr. That was the part that concerned Dougal the most. The humans and charr were still at war in Ebonhawke, yet in Lion's Arch charr and humans lived, if not in harmony, at least within sight of each other without open hostilities. That was something Dougal, who had spent much of his youth hating and fighting the charr, had a hard time understanding.

The term most people used when describing charr was "feline," but beyond a few basic attributes, they were no kin to any cat Dougal had ever seen. They were huge, half again as tall as a man, not as massive as a norn but still towering opponents against a single human. Their faces were elongated muzzles, and their jaws were those of carnivores, filled with long teeth. Both males and females had four horns jutting from the sides of their skulls, the males boasting an impressive set and the females a smaller pair on each side, just behind the jaw-line. Beneath the horns hung two pairs of sensitive ears. The males had huge hunchbacked and maned shoulders, and while the females were more lithe and swift, they were no less deadly.

When Dougal first came to Lion's Arch, he was stunned by the presence of the charr, including charr dealing with humans and other races. He had a hard time looking at them without thinking of the implacable foes who drove the humans from most of Ascalon and besieged them in Ebonhawke—the creatures responsible for the Searing and the Foefire.

He never dealt with them, preferring a norn or human merchant to a charr one when he could. Even when forced to talk to one, he could feel his skin crawl and the small hairs on the back of his neck stand up. The charr were legendary for their tempers and their violence, and he was unsure what would set one of them off. And while he was fairly certain they could not smell his fear and unease, the charr were excellent observers, and his reticence to deal with them was obvious. He would never go into the crypts with a charr, or want to be left alone with one.

Now, walking down the stairs into the Lion's Arch merchant district, he saw charr for the first time in over a year: none would come to Divinity's Reach, any more

than he would go to their main base, the Black Citadel. Already he felt uncomfortable by their very presence, even though the leonine creatures seemed more
at home here than he was.

The Great Bazaar occupied a low spot surrounded by
hills near the center of town. Great posts were driven
into the hills, and from those posts were strung rope
riggings and lines, the entire web covered by sheets of
sailcloth dyed blue. From above, the patchwork of sails
looked like a choppy ocean, and from below the cooler,
sheltered market felt like it was cradled at the bottom of
a shallow azure sea.

Around them brewed and bubbled the population
of Lion's Arch, engaged in the trade that was the life-
blood of the city. There were farmers from the estates
to the north and salvagers from the southern bays and
estuaries. Asura and sylvari squabbled over the prices
of glowing floating platforms and weapons made of
twisted wood and butterfly wings. Norn roiled through
the crowds like bears fording a stream. And the charr
moved around, living their lives and ignoring the three
new arrivals just like everyone else.

"Killeen!" came a shout behind him. The sylvari
turned, and Dougal along with her. Riona hesitated for
a moment, then kept walking.

Wading through the crowd was a heavyset golem, a
crude creation of lumber and stone, as temporary as the
rest of the city, a flat pane on its headless chest emitting
a blue-green glow. One arm was much larger than the
other, and both upper limbs ended in claws, making it
look like a crude combination of man and fiddler crab.

More important was the small asura directly in front of the golem, who became visible only as the crowds parted for the larger golem.

Clagg. In all his self-involved fury.

Dougal blinked and wondered if Logan Thackeray kept *anybody* in his jails anymore.

"Betrayer!" said Clagg. "You sold us out! You told the Seraph everything! For this you are going to pay!"

That definitely sounded like a challenge, and an opening appeared in the crowd with Killeen and the two humans at one end, the asura and the golem at the other. Dougal looked around and saw two Lionguard in the crowd. They were curious, but neither was stepping in to take matters in hand. As long as the disagreement didn't threaten any trade or merchants, Dougal doubted they would.

Lion's Arch was a good distance away from Divinity's Reach and its vigilant Seraph.

Dougal stepped forward, hand on his sword, to stand beside Killeen, but Riona put a hand on his shoulder. "He is talking to her, not you," she said, clearly enough for the sylvari to hear. "This is her problem."

"I don't see it as much of a problem," said Killeen. "I suppose you don't want to chat about this first?" she asked Clagg.

The asura responded with a curse and pointed at the sylvari. Emotionless and obedient, the golem lumbered forward. Killeen dropped into a crouch, and bright green motes bunched and flamed from her palms, gathering into swarms of necrotic energy.

She was too slow. The golem crossed the distance

between them and smacked her hard with a limb the thickness of a ship's yardarm. She stumbled to one side and a second arm punched her hard back the other way. Killeen lost her footing and fell to the paving stones. Golden blood appeared at the corner of her mouth.

Clagg had apparently chosen to invest in speed over raw strength this time.

Dougal let out a shout and, shaking off Riona's hand on his arm, ran forward, drawing his sword. The blade came out roughly, catching the sides of the scabbard and threatening to pull it along with it, but he got the sword out and closed on the hulking golem.

Clagg shouted a command and the golem changed targets, wheeling quickly from the fallen sylvari and bearing down now on Dougal. The human reversed himself and danced backward a few steps, the heavy arm swinging through the space where Dougal had been seconds before.

The golem overextended itself and Dougal lunged forward, driving his blade into the joint where the huge claw-arm met the rest of the body. The blade dug deep into the juncture, and Dougal heard a very satisfying crack as he loosened the armatures holding the golem together.

The golem flexed its shoulder back, trapping Dougal's blade, and with a sharp snap crushed it in its joints. Dougal pulled back the shattered stump of his sword, stared at it a moment, and cursed.

The golem had regained its footing now. The smaller arm lashed out, its claw-shaped hand closing on Dougal's sword arm, and pulled him off the ground. Dougal let out a yelp as he dangled there, the golem drawing back its arm to deliver a blow that would knock the human into the Sea of Sorrows.

Riona leaped in at that moment, her own weapon jabbing quickly into the gap in the construct's shoulder held open by the shards of Dougal's blade. She was quicker than he had been, so that she pulled the blade out in a cascade of arcane sparks, and the lethal arm hung there, its internal runes and spells grinding to regain control.

Having gained the advantage, Riona did not hesitate but instead struck against the golem's now-exposed chest. The fragile pane at the golem's heart shattered at the blow, and elemental lightning spilled out in a shower of sparks. Dougal twisted in the creature's grasp as the energies played over its body.

The Vigil warrior was not done, and dropped to one knee and lashed out again, this time striking at the joints of the golem's knees. Another cascade of elemental energy spilled out as the crystals within were smashed open with the skill of a chirurgeon with a scalpel.

The golem froze up and let go of Dougal, who dropped the few feet to the ground. Then it pitched backward, leaving a surprised Clagg exposed beyond it.

"Stupid second-rate sword," said Dougal, looking over at Killeen, who was moving now, though not very fast.

Dougal pulled himself off the ground, but Riona was still quicker than he was, and flung herself on top of Clagg like an owl on a rabbit. Grabbing the asura by the throat, she hefted him up and pulled her sword back to skewer him. Clagg made a rattling noise, and his eyes were wide with fear.

Now it was Dougal's arm on Riona's shoulder. "Let him go," he said.

She paused, and Clagg managed to gurgle, "She informed on us! I lost the Golem's Eye because she told the Seraph! You said . . ." The rest of his words were lost as Riona tightened her grip around his slender windpipe.

Gods, thought Dougal. *He doesn't know about the Eye.*

"Not so smart now, are you, you little monster?" said Riona. "You and the rest of your deformed race should be stomped out. We should skewer him right here!"

Dougal looked at Riona. Her eyes were angry, her jaw set, her words hissing through her teeth. She had changed since she was the voice of reason in their platoon.

"No, we have a mission," said Dougal, looking over to where Killeen was pulling herself upright. "Don't let the little stuff get in the way. He's little stuff."

Riona looked at Dougal, then took a deep breath and let her hand open. Clagg dropped to the ground, gasping and clawing at his throat.

"Scat," said Dougal. "We're done here. I don't want to see you again."

Clagg pulled himself up and shot a poisonous glance at Riona. He started to say something, and Riona dropped into a battle crouch and growled at him like a charr. That was enough: Clagg spun on his heels and fled back into the crowd, catcalls from the observers at his back.

Killeen stumbled up, rubbing her side where the golem had connected.

"Are you all right?" asked Dougal. Riona was still intently watching the space where Clagg had disappeared.

"In a moment." She staggered over to where the fallen golem was still sparking elemental essence. She knelt down next to it and for a moment seemed to be swathed in a greenish shroud. She placed her hands on the golem and the last of its energy drained out of it and into the sylvari.

She stood up and nodded at the others. "Better now," she said. She pointed to the golem and said to the crowd, "Scrap." The golem's body disappeared under a tide of opportunists.

Dougal looked at Riona. "What about you?"

Riona took some deep breaths and said in a low voice, "It just seems that every time we turn around, there is some lesser race that is making trouble for us. I'm just getting tired of it."

Dougal opened his mouth to argue but looked at Riona's face. There was pain there—and something else. Hatred. Instead he said, "We were going somewhere, right?"

Riona nodded and headed off across the marketplace without a word, Dougal and Killeen in tow.

They emerged on the far side of the blue-tinted sails and found their way to a more permanent part of the city, where there was more stonework among the wood, although it continued with the nautical theme. Finally she stopped at an innocuous-looking doorway. Riona knocked.

A hylek, taller than Killeen, opened the door and

Riona backed off a moment, surprised by the wide, monstrous face. It was a frog-like being, in the same fashion as the charr were cat-like: bipedal, a great-mouthed head topping a round, neckless body. Its eyes were wide and accusing.

She gathered herself together and said, "Crusader Riona Grady of the Vigil in Divinity's Reach. I have brought Dougal Keane for the general."

The hylek responded in a deep, rasping voice. "Crusader Naugatl of the Bloodtide Coast, also of the Vigil. Come in. I will announce your presence."

They followed the hylek into the hallway, and Dougal got the definite feeling that they were being let in through a side door. Whoever Riona was working for in the Vigil, he or she apparently didn't want to make a lot of noise about their arrival. Dougal wondered how the Vigil would react to Clagg's attack or Riona's sudden burst of temper.

The hylek led them into a small waiting room. They sat there, Killeen composed as if a half hour earlier she had not been assailed by a golem. Riona twitched and rubbed the back of her neck, trying to work out the tension. Dougal left them to their thoughts, for he had his own broodings.

After about fifteen minutes the hylek returned and with a booming "Follow me!" led them back out into the twisting hallways. Dougal figured that the Vigil chapter house must occupy most of the block, with numerous exits and probably access to the sewers as well.

Finally they were led into a large chamber dominated by a great table. Maps of Tyria hung from the walls, and the walls were lined with heavy cabinets. At the end of the room a large figure stood before the fire in full armor, her hands clenched behind her back. When they entered, she turned and regarded them with sharp feline eyes.

She was a charr, and for a brief moment Dougal felt she could sense the hairs rise on the back of his neck, an instinctive reaction he could not suppress.

"Dougal Keane, Killeen born of the Cycle of Night," said Riona smoothly. "May I present General Almorra Soulkeeper, founder of the Vigil."

The amazing Dougal Keane. Your reputation precedes you." General Almorra Soulkeeper thumped a fist over her heart, charr-style, and then extended a paw. Dougal could feel a cold trickle of sweat drip down his back as he gripped the charr's firm, strong hand, which wrapped around his own, the nubs of her sheathed claws grazing the back of it. The general gestured to the chairs opposite the broad table. The two humans and the sylvari took their seats and the charr lifted a ewer. "Wine? This is a good vintage from the Almuten estate."

Killeen said, "Thank you." Dougal said, "I may need the drink." Riona said nothing but nodded respectfully. Dougal was amazed by her sudden change in attitude from the violent warrior of an hour before.

Almorra poured the wine into four goblets and offered one to each guest. Then she raised her glass and said, "Death and despair to the dragons and their minions!"

"Death and despair!" repeated Riona. Dougal and

Killeen looked at each other, said nothing, but raised their glasses in response. Dougal sipped his wine. The charr was right: it was a good vintage.

"A pity we could not meet in Vigil Keep, north of the city," said Almorra, seating herself on a wide bench of the type preferred by the charr. "It is a proper and more secure place for such discussions, but when Crusader Riona's message arrived that she had located you, I thought it best to meet here. Still, the Vigil appreciates your efforts on our behalf."

"I have made no real effort so far," said Dougal, shrugging. "And I will make none until I understand what exactly you want. I have agreed to come here and talk, nothing more."

Almorra looked sharply at Riona, her four ears flattening slightly. "You did not tell him?"

Riona looked almost abashed. "I thought it best if he were briefed once we arrived. It was difficult enough getting him here."

Almorra let out a noise halfway between a purr and grunt and said, "What do you know of our organization?"

Killeen said abruptly, "The Vigil is a group made up of members from many races, nations, and guilds. They are dedicated to resisting the depredations of the Elder Dragons by force of arms." Riona scowled at her interruption, but Killeen ignored her.

General Soulkeeper nodded. "We have a number of your people in our organization, including my second-in-command. Your knowledge is always appreciated."

"You want to fight dragons," said Dougal.

Almorra nodded.

"But you don't want *me* to fight dragons. So I've been told." He motioned to Riona, and Almorra nodded again.

"You've been to Ascalon City," said the general.

"So people keep reminding me," said Dougal. "What do you want that's in Ascalon City?"

"We seek the Claw of the Khan-Ur," said Almorra simply. She took a long sip of her wine and let the silence in the room draw out.

Finally Dougal said, "You're completely mad, you know."

"Others have suggested that," said Almorra. "*Most* of them have been charr." There was a mild sense of menace in her words that Dougal always heard from the charr, intended or not.

"Why would you want the Claw?" he asked.

"I'm sorry," said Killeen. "This one I don't know. What is the Claw of the Khan-Ur?"

Riona looked into her goblet. "A legendary weapon, highly valued by the charr legions. It is an ungue, a four-bladed weapon with a central grip. Two blades jut forward, two blades backwards."

"More importantly," said Almorra, "the Khan-Ur was, in ancient times, the ruler of all the charr legions: Iron, Ash, Blood, and Flame. The Claw was a symbol of unity among the charr, the last time the legions were fully united. It was lost in Ascalon City."

"In the Foefire," said Dougal.

"We have reason to believe that it is still there," said the general.

Dougal looked at Riona, who from her uncertain expression fully expected Dougal to leap to his feet and try to find the nearest exit. Instead he remained seated and said, "Why do the Vigil want a charr artifact?"

"We don't," said Almorra. "Your human queen wants it."

"Very well," said Dougal, feeling as though he were being lectured by an asura, "why does Queen Jennah want it?"

"She wants to give it back to the charr," said Almorra, and Dougal shot a glance at Riona. She said nothing but was scowling.

Dougal shook his head and said, "Obviously I missed a step here."

General Soulkeeper leaned forward and put her paws on the table. "Your people and mine, we have been fighting for how long?"

"Since the Searing," said Dougal.

"Longer," said Almorra. "When man first came to Tyria, the charr were here. All its lands were our hunting grounds, all its creatures our prey. Your people drove us northward to found their kingdoms, and resisted us when we rightfully sought to regain our lands." Riona stiffened at Almorra's words but said nothing. Again, the sense of challenge was in the charr general's voice.

"Since then there have been victories and reverses for both sides," she continued. "The human nations are now gone from east of the Shiverpeaks, with the exception of the fortress city of Ebonhawke, which has been besieged for generations."

"A siege that has so far failed, I should note," said Dougal, feeling he had to speak up for his original home.

"And the conflicts between charr and man have

blown hot and cold for generations. But now there stands a chance for peace," said Almorra.

"I find that hard to believe," said Dougal.

"Both sides are tired," said Almorra. "And both sides have other worries in their lives. The humans have been driven back on numerous fronts, almost to the gates of Divinity's Reach itself. You are plagued by marauding centaurs and human brigands.

"Similarly," the general went on, "three of the charr legions stand united: Blood, Iron, and Ash. The fourth, the Flame Legion, which once commanded the other three, stands against us. And the ogres have come down from the Blazeridge Mountains, seeking land for their herds."

"And Ascalon is haunted," added Dougal.

"And Ascalon is haunted," agreed Almorra. "The legacy of the Foefire."

"So, how does the Claw fit in?" said Dougal.

"A peace faction has grown among the charr," said Almorra, then stopped. "Perhaps I give my people too much credit. Call it a truce faction. They seek to end the hostilities with Ebonhawke, so that they may better deal with the Flame Legion and other matters."

"And the humans, as you've noticed," said Riona flatly, "have other foes as well."

"The Vigil has been acting as go-betweens," said Almorra. "We have human agents in Divinity's Reach and charr crusaders in the Black Citadel. The discussions have been extremely secretive to date. There are humans—and charr—who would reject out of hand any attempt at peace and ban our order for promoting it."

The charr general leaned forward again. "The discussions have gotten to the point that the charr legions have agreed to open formal negotiations, combined with a cessation of hostilities. But they want a sign of good faith from the humans."

"The Claw," said Dougal.

"The Claw," said General Soulkeeper.

"What is in all this for you?" asked Dougal.

"The Elder Dragons," said Killeen, and Dougal looked at her. She had been listening intently throughout the discussion. "If the humans and charr can stop fighting, you hope they can turn their armies against Zhaitan, Kralkatorrik, and the others."

Riona nodded curtly, and Almorra said, "The sylvari have a talent for cutting to the heart of the matter."

"Do the legions know the Claw is in Ascalon City?" said Dougal.

"They suspect," said the general. "But those who have attempted to find it have never come back out. You did."

"I was lucky," said Dougal, more to himself than anyone else.

"We could use that luck again," said Almorra.

There was a long silence in the room. At last Dougal said, "You *are* completely mad."

"The world is mad," General Soulkeeper observed. "We merely have to deal with it."

"All of Ascalon is haunted. Ascalon City is the heart of the Foefire and is overrun with ghosts. There is a reason the legions have never conquered it," said Dougal.

"Yet, you went there. And came out alive," said the general.

"I was young," said Dougal, "and stupid." He looked at Riona, but the other human's face was as unexpressive as a stone.

"And yet, you are alive," said Almorra.

"No," said Dougal, "I am sorry, but I am not interested in returning to Ascalon City."

The charr general, leader of the Vigil, blinked, and her ears flattened. "You agreed to come here."

"I agreed to listen to your proposal," said Dougal. "I did that. Now I am saying no, because you are chasing a madman's dream, and I will not be part of it. I'd like to go now." Dougal stood up, hefting his small pack over his shoulder. Killeen and Riona also stood up, but more slowly.

Another silence, and Dougal could almost feel the tension gathering in the room. Finally, General Soulkeeper stood up and said, "Of course. I'd like you to think about it, but I will respect your decision. If you could wait outside for a moment, I'd like to speak with Crusader Riona."

Dougal looked at Riona and raised an eyebrow, but the other human kept her eyes fixed on the general. Dougal and Killeen left the room, the hylek Naugatl opening the door to escort them back to the waiting area. As he closed the door to the meeting room behind him, Dougal caught Almorra's rising voice: "You mean you never *told* him what we wanted . . ." Then the door closed and muffled the angry voice of the charr general.

In the waiting area, Dougal sat down and looked at his hands. Killeen remained standing.

"I'm not afraid," started Dougal. "I want you to know that—"

"I'm going," said Killeen.

Dougal looked up and saw the sincerity in the sylvari's face. "Killeen, you don't know—"

"No, I don't," she said, "but I want to find out. I think what they're doing is for the best. For humans. For charr. For everyone."

Dougal shook his head, but Killeen pressed on. "Your races are fortunate. You've been here forever. My people have been here twenty-five years and have never known a world where the Elder Dragons were not present, gnawing at the corners of our lands, bringing us zombies and abominations and all forms of twisted creatures in their wake. My people are here for a reason—I think the dragons are that reason—and if I can do anything to help the other races put aside their squabbles and turn to the greater danger, I will do it."

"Killeen," said Dougal, "even the charr legions give Ascalon City a wide berth. It is a city filled with ghosts."

"Necromancer," reminded the sylvari, smiling, "that argument is not going to have a lot of traction."

"You don't stand a chance without me," said Dougal, standing up and looking down on her smiling green face.

"You should lead us, then," said Killeen. She shook her head at some private joke, then reached up and touched his forehead. "You humans. You think too much up here." She moved her hand down, resting on his chest, her fingers grazing the locket that hung around his neck. "You should be thinking from here as well."

Dougal's face darkened. Blushing, he turned away from her. He took a deep breath and said, "Killeen . . ."

The door opened and Riona entered. Her face was flushed as well, though in her case from barely contained anger. Dougal could imagine how unpleasant it must be to be chewed out by a charr, especially a superior who is a charr.

"She'd like to talk to you again," she said. "Come with me."

"I think I'll stay here," said Killeen. "You two may need a moment." Riona left the room without even seeming to have heard her.

In the hallway, Riona turned to him, angry. "Dougal Keane. What happened to you?"

"Riona, I really don't want to . . ." Dougal started, still shaken from Killeen's words.

But Riona would not be denied. "You used to take chances. You used to always talk about that big strike, that ultimate prize, that great treasure. The chance to prove to the world that you could beat it."

"I took that big chance. And in taking that chance we betrayed you," said Dougal.

"But you lost it," said Riona, ignoring him. "Whatever happened in Ascalon City. You lost more than the rest of our platoon. You lost your will. You lost your bravery. You started running and haven't stopped."

"Are you done?" said Dougal, fixing her with a glare as sharp and angry as her own.

Riona's mouth became a thin line. "Yes. I think we are."

"Fine," Dougal said. "Now bring me to your general."

A minute later, once Riona had left the chamber and closed the door behind her, Dougal said calmly, "Now, are *you* going to yell at me?"

"No," said General Soulkeeper, standing in front of the fire, staring into its depths as if looking for an answer. "Instead I want to tell you a story. I understand you left Ebonhawke five years ago, and you have not been back."

"I thought there was nothing for me there," said Dougal.

"I was part of the siege of Ebonhawke as well," said Almorra. "We may have hunted each other, or stared at each other across the battlements. My warband and your patrol."

Dougal said nothing but nodded. Almorra looked up from the fire to Dougal, and her gaze drilled into the human.

Her next words were heavy with emotion and memory. "I was there. Four years ago, when Kralkatorrik, the Crystal Dragon, awoke. I was in the Dragonbrand."

Dougal felt slightly ill. "I—I didn't know anyone survived that."

Soulkeeper grunted. "I served as a legionnaire in the Blood Legion at the time. Our centurion was in charge of interdicting enemy supplies and was overseeing the scores of our finest warbands stationed there. I was on patrol with my own warband in eastern Ascalon when the Crystal Dragon stirred.

"I felt it first rather than heard it. The creature's coming warped everything around it, and the vibrations reached me through the air, not as a low thunder but a strange feeling that reached into my bones and made every bit of my fur stand on end.

"Harthog Soulslasher, my second-in-command, saw it before the rest of us, coming over the edge of the mountains behind us, flying in from the north like an angry sun come to Tyria to scorch us all. Harthog was one of the bravest charr I'd ever known, but I saw his eyes bulge with terror as he raised his arm to point at the dragon.

"The others turned to see what could terrify such a charr as Soulslasher, but I reached out and grabbed my friend by the shoulders to shake the fear from him. As I did, I saw the changes start to take him.

"His eyes began to glow an unearthly purple, and his muzzle shrank back into his face, becoming like the soft but toothy maw of a giant leech. His fur became transparent as his armor sloughed off his thinning shoulders and his arms transformed into flailing, shard-like claws. The skin peeled back from his face, and his lips and nose and eyelids shriveled up and fell away.

"And then he turned into living glass, crystallizing in an instant before my eyes into his twisted form. And at my back, I could feel a pressure, like a great hand was pressing down on the entire world as the dragon passed overhead.

"Despite the fact the dragon soared hundreds of feet above us, its passage turned the land beneath the path of its flight black and transformed the plants into crystalline monstrosities. At the same time, the screams from the rest of my warband tore at my ears.

"I drew my blade just before the creature that had

been Soulslasher attacked, his splintered claws reaching for me as he screeched in horror at what he had become and the hunger that now drove him to drool at the thought of devouring me alive. I don't know what spared me from sharing his fate. Every other member of our warband succumbed to it. I was standing no more than a foot from Harthog, and he and the others were warped beyond recognition, yet I was spared.

"I slew the thing that had been Soulslasher then, but after I tore out his throat, his body kept coming at me. I had to shatter him into pieces to finally put him down. Then I turned, in the deafening silence after the dragon's passage, and saw the rest of my warband trying to kill each other, each twisted in a unique and horrible way.

"I waited for my warsiblings to tear each other apart, then stepped in and dispatched the survivors as best I could. When it was done, I looked before and behind me and saw that every part of the land that had passed beneath the dragon had been twisted in this same way. The grass shattered under my feet as I walked on it, grinding it into sand."

"The Dragonbrand." Dougal breathed the word with horrified respect.

Soulkeeper nodded. "The curse the dragon laid upon the land stretched for untold miles in the direction of the flight, coming from the north and reaching for the south. Everything in its path had been turned to crystal: the trees, the animals, even the land itself nearby.

"The worst part of it all is that the dragon didn't care about the destruction it caused. It was going elsewhere, on a mission known only to itself. To it, the Dragonbrand was worth nothing more than your boot prints are to you. We might as well have been ants. Everything I lost that day mattered to it not one bit.

"I fell into my own personal darkness, my friends slain by a force greater than I could hope to confront." General Almorra Soulkeeper seemed to forget that Dougal was there, her lips drawn back over bared teeth. "I became a gladium, a charr without a warband, and refused any aid in my darkness. At last, with the help of a few unlikely allies, I came to myself and knew what had to be done.

"I knew then that this was no foe that a single people could confront," Soulkeeper said. "To have any hope of defeating an Elder Dragon, the peoples of Tyria would have to band together to fight it."

"That's why you formed the Vigil," Dougal said.

"Yes," said Almorra. "And although I work to save Tyria, I also know I act to save myself." Almorra returned to the present time and the firelit chamber. Turning to face Dougal, she said, "Crusader Riona told me your companions died when you went into Ascalon City. They were your fellow warriors and your friends. I can understand your reticence to return there."

"I have a dozen reasons to stay away, and not one good one to return," said Dougal, "Yet, I accept your plan. I will lead a group into Ascalon City. I will find your Claw of the Khan-Ur. Provided, of course, you are willing to pay for my services."

"Pay?" said Almorra, suddenly brought up short, as if the idea that payment might be required had only now crossed her mind. "Of course. You can keep everything else you find, I suppose, and split it as you see fit with your companions. And our resources are not slender by any means. What do you need?"

"Well, first off," said Dougal, managing a tired, knowing smile, "I'll need a new sword."

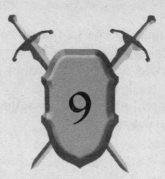

9

When we went to Ascalon City before"—Dougal jabbed a finger at the map of Tyria—"we crossed the Shiverpeaks up through the Snowden route. The Lionguard have established a string of havens up there to protect the trade."

He looked up at the two women. Killeen was soaking everything up with a focused, stern expression. Riona still had the self-satisfied smile that she wore ever since Dougal told them he had agreed to go with them to Ascalon City. As they discussed the journey, servants brought in a light lunch. Ewers of springwater were emptied, the plates of cheese, dried meats, and bread reduced to crumbs. There would be time for a real meal later, perhaps.

General Almorra, seated across from the three, said nothing but nodded.

"Then we hung north of the ruins of the Great Northern Wall and came down to the east of Ascalon City itself, looping back westward to its main gate. There were too many charr encampments otherwise," Dougal finished.

"I always thought that the northern flank was the weakest," said the general.

"Problem," said Riona. "Most of your previous route is underneath the Dragonbrand now. We'll probably see an increase in patrols along the edges of the brand now. We'll have to move carefully."

"No," said the general, "we don't have the time for a long journey. The legions' truce faction will not wait forever. Neither will the human queen."

"I am open to suggestions," said Dougal.

"Asura gate," said Almorra.

Dougal winced at the idea, but said, "There's no asura gate to Ascalon City."

Riona said, "There's one in Ebonhawke, but we would have to go back to Divinity's Reach to get use. There is no direct link between Lion's Arch and the fortress city."

"You'll be going through Ebonhawke," Almorra pointed out. "It is the closest available gate."

Dougal scowled at the map. "Possible," he said. "When we first left Ebonhawke"—he shot a glance at Riona— "we cut along to the south, so I know the area around Ebonhawke. But once we get closer to Ascalon, I'd be less sure.

"And while we can get to Ebonhawke," he continued, "once there, we're stuck. Even if we could sneak past the Iron Legion's siege of the city, we'd still have to hike scores of miles across charr-infested lands—and through the Dragonbrand, to boot—before we even reach Ascalon City."

"I thought of that," replied the general. "We have a contact in Ebonhawke as well who will get you out of the city. And as for a guide across the lands of the legions, I have already addressed that particular challenge as well."

Something heavy knocked on the door, and Dougal—who felt it reverberate through his body—jumped at the sound of it. Soulkeeper smiled.

"The answer to those concerns has arrived," the charr general said. Then she called out through the door: "Enter!"

The door swung inward on well-oiled hinges and revealed a powerful and lithe female charr standing at the threshold, younger than the general but no less impressive. She towered over Dougal, and the tips of her short horns brushed against the door's lintel as she entered. Her black lips were drawn back over her full set of vicious, gleaming white teeth and fangs, as if in a perpetual snarl. Her heavy yellow eyes scanned the room, assessing everything and everyone in it as a threat and then dismissing them as beneath her notice.

Where exposed, her amber fur bore black stripes on it, like those of a tiger, although a tuft of the snowiest white poked out from beneath the collar of her armor, right above the hollow of her throat. The armor that covered most of her fur moved as silently as she did, oiled for stealth as well as combat. She bore no weapon in her hands, but she didn't need one. She had her talons extended, each of which looked as sharp and long as a dagger.

Dougal realized how he had quickly come to accept General Almorra Soulkeeper's presence. The leader of the Vigil being a charr no longer concerned him. This new charr, however, brought back all of Dougal's previous worries; despite himself, he felt his muscles tense as if expecting some sudden attack.

"Riona Grady, this is one of your opposite numbers, working out of the Black Citadel," Soulkeeper said. "Killeen? Dougal Keane? Meet one of the finest warriors of this dragon-haunted generation: Crusader Ember Doomforge. She is to accompany you on your mission through the charr territories as both guard and guide."

Doomforge pointedly ignored the others and spoke instead to the leader of the Vigil. "With respect, General Soulkeeper, I do not need these weaklings by my side, not for such an important mission. They would only slow me down."

"Fine with me," Dougal said, edging away from the new charr. She stank of death and menace. "Send her, and the rest of us can go home."

"That is not possible," said Almorra, speaking to Dougal but intending her words for the new arrival. "Your knowledge will be key once you arrive at Ascalon City. Crusader Doomforge will help get you there."

"With respect . . ." Doomforge began once more, her eyes boring into her superior.

"Crusader Doomforge *will* help you get there," repeated General Almorra Soulkeeper, wheeling on the other charr and pulling herself to her full height, her own claws unsheathing. Dougal didn't think he would see a brawl break out in the general's chamber but that the two would establish a pecking order in the charr manner, through verbal threats and displays of power.

Doomforge, for her part, shrank a little under Soulkeeper's glare and took a step back. Dougal noted that the newcomer had retracted her claws into her paws as well.

"With respect," said Riona, softer than the charr but no less indignant, "if we are going to use an asura gate to get to Ebonhawke, we will have to backtrack to Divinity's Reach. We cannot bring a charr into Kryta, much less into the fortress city itself. Crusader Doomforge would be a liability."

"Say what you like"—Doomforge's nostrils twitched as she sniffed at the air—"they are craven, scared of the power of the charr. I can smell the fear on them from here."

Dougal smirked at the lie. "I'm surprised you can smell anything at all," he said. "What did you roll in on your way up here?"

Before Dougal could blink, Doomforge swung out a paw and grasped him by the shirtfront, slamming him against the stone wall. He tried to speak, but the pressure on his chest kept him from drawing a breath.

"Release him!" Soulkeeper barked out, and the pressure disappeared in an instant. Doomforge stood there with rage in her eyes.

Dougal peeled himself off the wall and gasped for breath.

"Crusader Doomforge!" Soulkeeper said sharply. "We spoke of this. For the Vigil's sake and for our ultimate goal, one must put aside old enmities."

Doomforge took one step back, glaring at Dougal the entire time. Dougal realized he had a tuft of orange fur from her forearms in each of his fists. He let the fur fall to the floor, then brushed his hands together.

"In the Vigil, you leave your old wars at the door," the general said to both Riona and the charr. "You *will* go into Ebonhawke together." She drew back her lips as she said it, showing her feral teeth.

It was hard to tell under all the fur, but Dougal thought he saw Doomforge go pale. "I don't see how sending me into the heart of a human stronghold will further the cause of peace," the charr warrior said.

An idea struck Dougal, and he spoke before he thought it through. "The only charr I've ever seen inside Ebonhawke were in chains," he said to Soulkeeper. He looked pointedly at Doomforge's wrists. "It's the only way she could make it through there alive."

Doomforge's slitted eyes widened into full circles as she realized what Dougal meant. "Absolutely not!" she growled. "No human will ever put me in chains!"

Soulkeeper was not nearly so upset. She ran her claws through the fur on her chin as she stared Doomforge up and down. Then she snorted. "She *might* make a convincing prisoner. I believe we have a set of shackles that would fit her."

"General!" Doomforge's orange fur bristled with the indignity. "You cannot be serious!"

"I am always serious," Soulkeeper said, and Dougal believed her. "Like a claw through a knot, this is the simplest solution to this problem."

Doomforge sputtered, "I will resign! I refuse to submit myself to such—"

Soulkeeper slammed both of her paws on her desktop. Everyone in the room fell silent, and when Soulkeeper spoke, her words lacked malice but not menace.

"I am your commander and you will obey my orders," she said to Doomforge. "I will not tolerate insubordination—least of all from you."

Doomforge forced a breath through her nose, then spoke with deliberate and measured words. "General. The humans of Ebonhawke will attack me on sight, and I will find it difficult to defend myself against them if I am in chains."

"We will be your guards," Killeen spoke up. "Everyone in Ebonhawke would stare at you, maybe even curse at you, but they would not dare touch you."

"We can't be dressed up as Vigil," said Dougal, "and we can't just pretend to be part of the Ebon Vanguard. They all know each other."

Riona nodded, understanding. "Independents, then. Thief-takers. Bounty hunters. Even so, we would have problems walking her into town in broad daylight."

"That would work," said General Soulkeeper. "I have to send word to our man in Ebonhawke to make arrangements. As for the problem with broad daylight, there is a solution for that as well."

Doomforge's eye twitched as she glared at Riona. "I think you're just walking me into an interrogator's cell in Ebonhawke."

"Stay here, then," Dougal said. "Kitty."

Doomforge opened her monstrous maw and roared at him for the insult. Her breath came at him like a hot wind, ruffling his hair and burning his eyes.

"Enough!" Soulkeeper's voice blared right over Doomforge's roar and cut it short.

The general glared at the soldier, her wide nostrils

flaring with frustration and shame at how undisciplined the younger charr's behavior made them both appear. "Your imperator remitted you to my command," Soulkeeper said. "You will control your temper and you will obey my orders. You. Do. Understand."

Doomforge's ears folded back at the general's barely restrained fury. She licked her lips as if to say something, then bit back those words. She bowed her head and nodded. "Yes. I do."

"Good." Soulkeeper turned to the others. "This is our plan. It's our best chance, whether any of you like it or not."

Using her wide yellow eyes, the general measured each of them up in turn. Dougal wasn't sure she liked what she saw, but she seemed resigned to work with what she had. She turned her back on them then and gazed deep into the fire.

"Stay for a moment, Doomforge," Soulkeeper said. "The rest of you are dismissed. I suggest you get some rest before dinner. You'll be shown to your rooms."

The two humans and the sylvari left the general's chamber. Dougal noticed that Riona had a grim, thoughtful grin on her face and probably could guess the nature of the conversation between the two charr on the far side of the door.

The hylek crusader took them to their rooms. Riona nodded at her door, then said, "I need to run a few errands here in Lion's Arch. I will join you at dinner."

"And I would like to explore the Vigil House further," said Killeen. "I think I saw some other sylvari in the halls."

"You two have fun," said Dougal. "I for one am going to follow General Soulkeeper's orders and take a nap. It has been too eventful a day already, and it is still early afternoon."

The three split up, Killeen leaving with the hylek, asking questions as they walked away. Dougal watched them leave and lingered for a long moment in the hall. Now that he was committed, he wondered if he had the right to drag Riona and Killeen back into the deathtrap that was Ascalon City. Perhaps the charr was right: traveling light and fast would be the best approach.

"Never adventure with people you would hate to see die," he said to himself. Lost in thought, he didn't realize that his door was already ajar as he strode into his quarters.

Dougal closed the door behind him without looking, staggered toward his bed, and set his pack down. The long day had finally caught up with him, and he wanted nothing more than to sleep. Almorra Soulkeeper had kept talking about how time was of the essence. If this was the last night he'd see a bed for a long while, they'd have to drag him out of it, even for dinner.

That's when he heard the heavy footfalls behind him.

Dougal spun about just in time to see a mountainous form emerge from the shadows behind the door and come straight for him. The norn stood over nine feet tall and had as much mass as a full-grown bear. He wore his bright blond hair tied back tightly behind him in a warrior's braid, and the light from the lanterns on either side of the bed glinted in his ice-blue eyes. His naked chest was crisscrossed with a maze of swirling tattoos, and he wore only a fur-trimmed kilt and a pair of soft leather boots, both of which bore black splotches of old blood.

The norn let out a bloodcurdling war cry that reverberated off the room's stone walls. Dougal ignored the scream to concentrate on the razor-sharp edge of the double-bladed axe the norn swung toward his head in a fatal arc.

Dougal let his feet spin out from beneath him as he hurled himself toward the bed. The axe sliced close enough to him for the rounded side of its steel head to glance off his temple as it passed over him. He bounced off the bed, which would have put him in the path of the axe's backswing but for the fact that the first strike had bit deep into one of the bedposts with a sickening crunch and stuck there.

Dougal scrambled away from the bed as the norn took hold of the axe's handle with two hands and pulled. Dougal cursed the fact that he still didn't have a sword and made a mental note to have Almorra make good on her promise, should he live that long. Away from the bed, he drew his knife, but when he looked up at the norn—who glanced back as he continued to struggle with and curse at his axe—the modest blade seemed next to useless.

Dougal hunted around the room for something else to use as a weapon. He spotted a toppled chair lying before an overturned desk near the large unshuttered window, and he dashed over to snatch it up over his head.

The norn snarled in frustration. "By the Bear!" he said in a booming, slightly slurred voice. "If you refuse to release my axe, you damned bedpost, then you will pay!"

The norn reached out and grabbed the top of the bedpost, then snapped it from the bed with a mighty twist of his wrist, which was thicker than the length of wood he now held. He querulously examined his handiwork and saw that although the post had been torn free from the base of the bed, the axe still hung embedded in it.

Dougal rushed forward and brought the chair down on the norn's head as hard as he could. As tall as the norn was, Dougal managed only to bash him in the neck, smashing the chair to pieces.

The norn turned around, still hefting the bedpost in one hand as if it were no heavier than a stick, and grinned. "Good job, boy!" he slurred. "That almost hurt."

Oh gods, thought Dougal, *he's drunk.* The only thing worse than a norn was a drunk norn.

While Dougal gaped at the norn's insane smile, the monstrous warrior brought the bedpost around like a club and knocked Dougal across the room. As Dougal smashed into the desk, the only thing he could think was how lucky he'd been that the double-bladed axe had been on the other side of the pole when it struck him. He lay there sprawled atop the desk, dazed and hurting, and struggled to collect any more thoughts than that.

The norn looked down at Dougal for a moment, nodding in satisfaction. "Ah, just like a human, though," he said. "Folds like a sheet." Then he put the bedpost on the ground and stood on it while he tried to pull his weapon from it with both hands. The force of his initial blow had jammed it tight. "Damnation," he said with an amused grunt. "I need to learn what kind of wood this is and make me a suit of armor from it." Then he laughed at the concept.

Riona appeared in the doorway, a look of irritation on her face. Dougal shouted to warn her off. She ignored him and, drawing her sword, moved in to attack the norn.

"Just hold on there, girl," the norn said, struggling past his hiccups as he cast a wary eye on her sword and edged toward Dougal. "I take no issue with you. Just let me do my duty and dispatch this boy."

Riona hesitated, her gaze flickering between Dougal and the norn. The norn saw the momentary distraction and launched himself forward, striking the human woman in the side with a roundhouse kick. Riona let out a shout as she was flung against the far wall. She was slow in getting up.

A huge shadow with tiger stripes appeared in the doorway. Ember Doomforge unleashed a battle cry that rumbled off the room's walls. Dougal would have covered his ears if he hadn't needed his hands to steady himself on the floor as he scrambled away from the norn.

The norn turned to face the charr and let loose a hearty laugh filled with bloodlusty glee. "Good! A foe worthy of my axe—if I could get the bloody thing free!"

Doomforge leaped at the norn, her claws popped from her fingers like a dragon's talons. The norn brought his axe and its attached bedpost up before him like a shield, and the charr slammed into it, knocking them both to the floor.

Flat on his back, the norn shoved hard with both

hands against his axe, trying to keep the charr at arm's length. Snarling like an angry wolf, Doomforge struggled to force her way past the bedpost, raking at the wood and the norn's arms with her claws.

Dougal shouted, "He's drunk and crazy!" hoping the information would help Doomforge. He knew it would only be a matter of seconds before one of them found some advantage over the other and the battle would be over. If the charr managed to bash the bedpost aside, she would tear the norn to pieces; but if the norn could hold her off until he could find some leverage, he might pin Doomforge under the bedpost and choke her to death.

Dougal scooped up a leg from the smashed chair. It wasn't a sword, but it would have to do. He charged right at the norn, howling all the way, hoping to at least distract him and give Doomforge a chance to dispatch him.

Seeing Dougal coming, the norn kicked his feet up hard and flipped Doomforge over him. The charr bowled straight into Dougal, rolling them both into a tangle of arms and legs that careened into the wall behind him.

Doomforge yowled in frustration and shoved Dougal away. He scrambled away from her, afraid that she might gore him in her fury, but he pulled up short when he saw the norn stand up before him.

The norn bashed his axe against a wall, smashing the bedpost from it. His weapon finally free, he hefted it in a meaty fist, ready to make quick work of Dougal and anyone who stood between them.

"Hold it!" Killeen shouted as she appeared in the doorway. "What are you doing?"

At first, Dougal thought the sylvari was talking to him, but she rushed into the room and grabbed the norn by the arm. "Gullik!" she said. "Stop! You'll get yourself killed!"

Dougal wondered just whose side the sylvari was on. Doomforge didn't bother to ask. She shoved Dougal aside and sprang at the norn, her claws flung wide to deny any escape. Behind him, Riona had gotten to her feet and regained her sword.

Killeen sprang between charr and norn, throwing one hand out toward each. "No! Don't! He's a friend!"

Doomforge hauled up short, her claws inches from Killeen's face. She glared at the norn clear over the head of the sylvari, who looked like a child stuck between two giants. "Explain," the charr said through her gritted fangs, her eyes daring the norn to attack.

The norn lowered his axe to the floor and leaned on its handle as if it were a cane. Dougal realized he had seen a norn do that before, in the crypts beneath Divinity's Reach. With the scuffle suspended, at least for the moment, the adrenaline drained from the norn's blood, and he wavered there, unsteady on his feet. He spoke slowly, with the precision of a drunk man trying to convince others that he was not drunk.

"Thunder and blood! This should have been so simple. Find the man who was with my beloved cousin at her death. Take my revenge on his triple-damned soul." He pointed at Dougal with a shaky hand. "Exit with my honor, and hers, preserved."

"So much for that," Riona muttered, her blade still out and at the ready.

The norn ignored her and squinted at Dougal with glassy eyes. "Bear's bile, though, damn me if I can see how a scrawny thing like you could have cut down such a prime specimen of female norn." He blinked, then added, "Norness. Nornitude."

Killeen tried to say something, but the norn cut her off. He let out a deep sigh, and Dougal swore he could see tears in the corner of the norn's great eyes.

"She was such a gentle creature," the norn said, "always tagging along in my footsteps. Who could blame her for being dazzled by my heroism? But mine are massive boots to fill, and now poor little Gyda is dead."

"Gyda?" Dougal's jaw dropped. "She was your—? But I didn't kill her."

The norn gave Dougal a long, lazy wink. "Of course not, little one. But what else would a human say when the finest warrior in all the Shiverpeaks came calling for his head?"

The norn reached out and put a massive hand on Dougal's shoulder. Doomforge and Riona stepped closer, ready with claw and blade. But the norn only stood there, staring at Dougal, weaving as he stood. Dougal wondered if the norn would collapse and he would have to catch his huge form.

"By Raven's black heart, who would blame you if you had killed yourself by now in terror?" He gazed into Dougal's confused face. "You are a brave one, aren't you? I can see it in your soul."

Dougal opened his mouth to protest, but the norn

shushed him. "Of course you didn't kill her," the norn said. "Just look at you. How could anyone imagine you could manage that?"

The norn paused for a moment to swallow hard, and Dougal feared that the drunken warrior might become sick. "But that's not the point," the norn said, recovering. "Not at all. It's not that sweet Gyda is dead. It's that you've failed to say a word about it to anyone. I heard she died, but nothing else. There's an epic tale to be spun there, I'm sure, and Gyda deserves for her part in the grand saga to be told. No true norn fears death—only being forgotten."

The norn's hand grew heavier then, and Dougal put up his arms to help steady the tottering giant, whose spirit-laden breath smelled strong enough to make Dougal's eyes water. As he did, he knew that he was too late. The norn's eyes rolled back up into his head as he crumpled forward.

Dougal tried to slip out of the way, but the norn was too big to avoid. The massive warrior's chest came down hard on Dougal's legs, pinning him to the ground. Dougal howled more in frustration than pain.

"Dougal!" Riona rushed to his side. "Are you all right?"

"I'm fine." Dougal struggled to extract his feet from beneath the norn's bulk. "Just get him off of me!"

Scowling in disgust, Doomforge reached down with both hands and heaved the slumbering norn onto his back.

"Who is he?" Dougal asked as he pulled himself to his feet.

"Gullik Oddsson," Killeen said.

Doomforge whistled at this, a strange, low note that emerged not from her lips but her teeth. "*The* Oddsson? I heard he single-handedly defeated a score of destroyers in the old dwarf mines beneath the Dredgehaunt Cliffs."

Riona blew out a long breath. "He's supposed to have stormed aboard the schooner *Watery Gravestone*, slaughtered Captain Deadbeard, and then taken command of the ship to terrorize the Sea of Sirens."

"Gyda told me he slew a mad grawl with his bare hands when he was only a child, no taller than me," said Killeen.

"He's a drunken ass who tried to kill me and nearly broke my legs," said Dougal. He kicked Gullik in the shoulder. The norn didn't even stop snoring long enough to acknowledge it. "And he's not sleeping in here."

Doomforge grunted. "How do you suggest we move him?"

Crusader Naugatl and a squad of guards showed up then, drawn by the sounds of the battle. They gaped at the norn and then at Doomforge, but they put their swords away at a sign from her.

"Leave him here," she said. "Secure the door and window. Post a squad of guards, and come find me as soon as he shows signs of rousing." She pointed at one of the guards. "Have another room prepared for Keane. Right now."

A guard ran off to fulfill his orders, and Doomforge sauntered after him, motioning for the others to follow. "Come," she said. "I can't speak for you, but after that, I need a drink." Killeen produced a blanket and laid it over the snoring norn's chest, then turned to the door as well.

"Are you coming?" she said.

"I was serious about that nap," said Dougal.

"I still need to get something from the bazaar," said Riona. To Dougal she said, "Can we leave you alone for more than five minutes?"

"Maybe," said Dougal, "if the rest of the world will stop beating me up long enough so I can get some sleep."

It isn't mind-reading," said Killeen, "and we aren't all connected into one big mass mind. However, before we come into the world, the sylvari are united in the Dream of Dreams."

The three of them sat at the end of a table large enough for a platoon. Dougal had slept at least six hours in the most comfortable bed in all of Lion's Arch, and had been roused only unwillingly by Killeen saying that Riona was back and dinner was in a half hour. It was already dark, and a heavy moon shown through the tall windows.

Dinner was excellent, a rare treat for Dougal. He had spent many of his years on the road, able to eat only what he was willing to carry with him. As a result, he had survived on mostly water and hardtack and the occasional bit of small game he brought down.

Tonight, though, Soulkeeper had made sure that he, Riona, and Killeen had the finest food and drink available in Lion's Arch. They dined on succulent roast mutton, braised moa, fresh breads, and a selection of the finest fruits available from the city's busy harbor market. They also split a pair of bottles of wine that was older than anyone at the table and finer than any Dougal had ever tasted.

It was not the first "last meal" Dougal had enjoyed before heading off on a job from which he had no assurance he would ever return. He hoped it would not be the final one despite his misgivings, and he was determined to make the most of it either way.

Riona had set Killeen off by asking the question "You're five years old. How do you know so much?" Indeed, it was a question that plagued Dougal as well. Unlike Riona, he had known a number of sylvari, and they always surprised him with the depth and breadth of their knowledge.

By the same token, there were matters that were completely beyond them. Emotions seemed to be a hard concept for them to understand fully, as was tact. The sylvari he had dealt with over the years would often unknowingly offend others by pointing out obvious and uncomfortable truths.

"We are the bounty of the Pale Tree, which grows at the center of the Grove," said Killeen. "Long ago there was a human warrior named Ronan who found the seed of the Pale Tree in a cavern. Ronan tired of war and, along with a former foe, a centaur named Ventari, traveled to the south and planted the tree in what would become the Grove.

"Ronan passed on, and so, too, in time did Ventari, who spent his life tending to the young sapling. Before he died, Ventari carved his tablet and set it down at the base of the tree. When we awakened, that tablet became our law, and we were infused with the spirit of both brave Ronan and gentle Ventari.

"We were not there when all this happened, but we know it because of the Dream of Dreams. While we were quickening within the golden fruit of the Pale Tree, the tree spoke to us of the world outside. She taught us, if you will, of the nature of the waking world.

"We are not all-knowing," she continued. "The Dream of Dreams is not like a tome of all knowledge. But it does give us a life before our life, in which we learn much of the world we are coming into. Fire is hot. Wild animals can be dangerous, but many can be tamed. Here is the proper way to use a sword. This is how you cast a spell, if you are so disposed. We come into the world with knowledge of the world, but not necessarily the experience."

Riona shook her head. "Is there a difference? Experience gives you knowledge."

"For humans, most likely," said Killeen, "but not for us." She picked up an oversized drumstick. "This is the leg of a young moa. I know that it was a moa from the Dream, and further that it is well cooked but not overcooked. I know what it tastes like but have never tasted it myself." She took a bite of the leg, and chewed for a moment or two. "Chicken," she said at last, the word muffled by the food in her cheek.

"I don't know what is weirder," said Riona, looking a little uneasy, "your telepathic dreams or the fact I am watching a plant eat an animal."

"Many plants eat animals," countered Killeen. "Flytraps, ibogas, jacarandas, pitcher plants. The oakhearts chase down and mash animals they encounter and use the remains to fertilize their young."

"Of course they do," said Riona. She turned to Dougal and whispered, loudly, "Creepy!"

If Killeen heard the comment, she did not respond to it. "But we don't have telepathic dreams. In the Dream of Dreams, one grows one's identity. When one is Awakened into the world, we leave the Dream behind, for the most part. But what we learn in the world goes back into the Dream to help new sylvari understand. The Firstborn entered into a world without sylvari, but what they learned helped all that followed them. So, too, what I learn will help future generations."

"Must make it hard for sylvari to keep secrets," said Riona, and Dougal realized what she was thinking: Killeen knew everything they knew about the mission. Who else has emerged, newly fallen from the Pale Tree who knew about this?

"We try not to keep secrets," said Killeen, almost smugly. "But knowledge is rarely specific. A face, an item, perhaps a name, may stay with us once we Awaken. We may feel drawn to a particular place or person, or feel that some task needs to be done. Occasionally, something in the Dream echoes back to an awakened sylvari, but it is more of a feeling than a vision filled with details and specifics. That is one reason so many sylvari wish to fight the Elder Dragons: we dream of a great shadow in the Dream, and awaken to a world where the dragons cast an equally deep shadow on the land.

"As an example"—she motioned at Dougal with her moa bird—"I know about the long war between the charr and the humans, but not as much about the reasons why, or what happened in Ascalon City." She looked at Dougal and took another big bite of moa flesh to indicate she was done talking for a while.

Riona took another slug from her wineglass, then reached for the bottle again. "Give her the abridged version, please."

Dougal wiped his mouth on his napkin, sat back in his chair, and began.

"As General Soulkeeper said, the charr were here on Tyria first and ran wild over the entire continent. When humans arrived, they were the first serious challenge to charr supremacy in centuries. But if it hadn't been for the death of the Khan-Ur, humanity might not have survived those ancient days. The Khan-Ur's children, who were also his four imperators—leaders of their own personal legions—fell to squabbling over his mantle, each accusing the others of treachery. They set their legions against each other. Blood, Iron, Flame, and Ash. None of them were strong enough to defeat the other three, though, and in the course of the civil war, the Claw of the Khan-Ur was lost. Yet, their internal dissension gave humanity some breathing room to develop, and with that time we conquered Ascalon.

"Several generations later, when the charr got their act together, we fought to keep them out of what we now considered our land. To that end, the kings of Ascalon began building a massive wall that ran west from the Shiverpeaks all the way to the Blazeridge Mountains on the Eastern Frontier. It took nine hundred years to complete, but it kept the charr to the north of it, where they belonged. Indeed, backed by the strength of the wall, we pushed them even further north, so that for most Ascalonians the charr were a distant but always present threat.

"The Northern Wall stood unbreached for nearly two hundred years, but way back in 1070, the charr discovered a great magic, based on mighty cauldrons filled with mystic energy. The charr shamans, in particular those that commanded the Flame Legion, unlocked the secrets of the cauldrons and brought about the Searing. Great burning crystals fell from the sky and scourged the lands around them, breaking the Great Northern Wall.

"The charr flowed through the wall in an unstoppable wave that washed all the way through Ascalon until it crashed on the shores of Orr. In Orr, its most powerful vizier cast a forbidden spell of his own that stopped the charr cold, but only at the sacrifice of his entire nation, sinking Orr beneath the sea. But that, as they say, is another story.

"The Searing forced King Adelbern to move his throne from Rin to Ascalon City, the only major city in his nation that still stood. There, he felt, he would make his last stand against the charr invasion.

"The king's sole heir, Prince Rurik, disagreed with him and led a large portion of his people over the Shiverpeaks to safety in Kryta rather than wait for their doom with their king. Prince Rurik, by the way, never made it to Kryta with his followers: he gave his own life so that they might find their freedom. It is said that Prince Rurik's death hurt King Adelbern worse than the fall of Rin itself.

"Back in Ascalon City, the Flame Legion prepared for a final assault on the place's walls. The imperator of the Flame Legion somehow got his hands on the Claw."

"So this Flame Legion imperator was really the last Khan-Ur?" asked Killeen.

Dougal clicked his tongue at that. "Not quite. The Claw is a powerful weapon, legends say, a force that would allow one to unite the legions under a single banner. But you still have to convince the other legions and earn the title of Khan-Ur to seal the deal, as it were. The Flame imperator decided that conquering Ascalon City and beheading King Adelbern with the Claw would cement his claim, so that's what he set out to do."

"The legions, led by the shamans of the Flame Legion, assaulted the walls of Ascalon City with their forces, their tamed siege devourers, and their magical cauldrons. The charr armies overran the defenders and surmounted the walls. Adelbern fought until the last, armed with his great magical sword, Magdaer. Magdaer was an artifact from ancient Arah, the City of the Gods, and infused with power. It is said that Magdaer's twin, Sohothin, was in the hands of his son, Rurik, when he died. In any event, Adelbern single-handedly brought down wave upon wave of charr warbands, making his last great stand on the battlements of his own tower.

"At last King Adelbern faced the Flame Legion imperator, the leader of the charr forces, who himself bore the Claw of the Khan-Ur. When the two weapons met, the energies within both exploded in a great jet of power that was seen from the Shiverpeaks themselves."

"The Foefire," said Killeen.

Dougal fell silent then, picturing that terrible event in his mind, making it match up with the horrible images he'd witnessed on his own venture into the harrowed city.

"Tell me more about the Foefire," Killeen said. "As a necromancer, that fascinates me."

A gruff voice—Dougal recognized it as Doomforge's—spoke from the darkness of the hallway. Dougal wondered how long the charr had been there and what she had heard.

"The Foefire destroyed every charr within Ascalon City, and for leagues around as well. The buildings, the farms, and the land were unharmed, but every charr within its reach was destroyed. The humans, however, suffered a different fate. Their souls were peeled loose from their shredded bodies, and they survive eternally as guardian ghosts to jealously protect the land. Adelbern, whom we call the Sorcerer-King, damned his people to destroy the charr. Adelbern did with cursed magic what his army had not been able to manage in years, and he cheated the charr of our triumph."

Doomforge stood in the room's arched entrance and waited for someone to gainsay her. Dougal resisted the temptation, and neither Riona nor Killeen seemed inclined to take the bait.

Doomforge grunted at the lack of any challenge. "General Soulkeeper sends me with her regrets. She cannot join us tonight."

" 'Us'?" Dougal said.

Doomforge moved into the room and cast her eye over the ruins of the meal. She had taken off her armor and now wore just a set of simple rope and leather clothes that Dougal could only describe as a harness. Dougal supposed that with all her fur she didn't need clothes for warmth, only charr standards of modesty. It covered just enough of her to manage that, although on a human it would have been considered scandalous. Despite her casual attire, she seemed far less relaxed than she had been in her armor.

"Soulkeeper asked me to dine with you so that we might become better acquainted." She looked down at the table. "But I see you are nearly finished."

Dougal waited for the charr to turn around and leave. He enjoyed watching her try to decide how long she would have to endure their company to fulfill her orders. Despite her actions against the norn, he wasn't about to make her feel at home.

Killeen, on the other hand, had no trouble with that at all. She leaped to her feet and scurried over to take the charr by the paw and escort her to a seat at the table. "The general is as wise as she is generous," she said. "I'm thrilled to have someone like you as a part of our guild."

Dougal winced at that word and saw Doomforge do the same as she accepted the seat the much smaller sylvari shoved in behind her. "I have a warband already," the charr said. "I do not need a guild."

Dougal nodded at that, finally finding something he and Doomforge could agree upon. "We are in no way a guild," he said. "Guilds are permanent organizations. They are created and maintained by their own membership, and are usually set up with long-term goals. We are four individuals gathered together for a single mission. We are a team, a company, maybe even what the asura call a krewe. And I don't even like teams that much." Riona failed to suppress a rude snort at that, but he ignored her. "It is often better to work alone."

Killeen smiled at them both as if they were slow-headed children. "But you're not working alone, are you? And you"—she turned back to Doomforge—"don't have your warband with you. I suppose, in a way, we're your warband."

Dougal almost choked on his wine at this, but Doom-forge's reaction drowned out his own. "I am charr," she said, pronouncing each word carefully. "My warband is to me what humans would consider a family. We were raised together as cubs in the crèche, in the fahrar. We were trained to fight together as a unit. We may not share blood, for we honor our elders and forebears, but the bonds of battle hold stronger than any family tie."

"A family?" Killeen said, tilting her head at a curi-ous angle. "All sylvari are a single family. We all sprang from the same source, the Pale Tree, but the Dream—our communal history and subconscious—binds us together even more than that. Perhaps that is why we treasure our individualism. When you have so much in common, the new experiences you have—those that separate you from the others—are what make you unique."

A servant swept in with a roast suckling pig on a platter and placed it before the charr. Doomforge eyed it for a long moment, then set to picking at it with a sin-gle talon, slicing the flesh from the bones like a master butcher. "By that," the charr said, "I mean that I already have a 'family' or 'guild' or 'warband' or whatever you wish to call it. I have no need for another."

"You can always use another family," said Killeen.

Having dismembered the pig, Doomforge stuffed it into her mouth. Piece by piece, its pink flesh disappeared into her maw. The way Doomforge's jaws and teeth worked in concert to annihilate the pig fascinated Dougal. He could not look away, no matter how much Doomforge glared at him over the bones she picked clean.

"All right," said Killeen. "Not a family. We can at least be a team."

Doomforge scowled as she reached for a goblet of ale a servant had brought her while she consumed her meal. "You forget that I am to enter Ebonhawke not as a friend but as a prisoner."

The charr looked as though she wished she could hack up that last word, spit it on the floor, and grind it under her boot. "This is not a wandering adventure. It is not a battle in some arena, for the sake of glory and recognition. It is a mission. I neither want nor need friends nor a family nor a team. I need only to follow my orders, and this I will do."

"I see," said Dougal. "And have you spent enough time with us to have fulfilled your orders?"

"No," said the charr, and for a moment Dougal swore Doomforge's features softened for a moment. "There is another matter. I came to apologize as well. To you, Dougal Keane."

Dougal's eyebrows rose but the charr just took a deep breath and pressed on.

Doomforge stared at the table as she spoke. "I acted rashly in the general's presence, and I am to convey to you my apologies for doing so. As long as you do not provoke me, it will not happen again.

"Further"—Doomforge's brows furrowed—"to allow a norn—even one as notorious as Gullik Oddsson—to slip past our guards is inexcusable. He apparently scaled the building and broke in through a window in broad daylight. Were he more competent, or less inebriated, he would have succeeded, and our mission would have become doubly impossible. I have spoken with the guards and it will not happen again. Oddsson has been sobered up, and I understand that he is facing General Soulkeeper's wrath as we speak."

Dougal waved off her apology. They were not going to be here long enough for any security changes to matter. "All I care about, Doomforge, is getting on our way before something like this happens again."

Doomforge reached for her glass but did not pick it up. "Ember."

"Excuse me?"

"Call me Ember."

"Seriously?" said Dougal, trying not to smile at the uncomfortable charr. He tried to remember when he had ever been on a first-name basis with a charr, and came up empty.

"The general suggested I request it."

"Are we supposed to be friends, then?"

"Not at all," she said, and Dougal was certain that the charr smiled as she said it.

Dougal nodded. "Then call me Dougal."

"I only have my one name," Killeen put in with a helpful smile.

Riona scowled. "Call me Crusader, charr, and I will call you the same, out of respect for our order. But it is good to see you kids playing nice."

"Just as long as we make it through Ebonhawke," said Dougal. To Ember Doomforge he said, "I have been trying to come up with a better plan but, short of a potion of invisibility, I am at a loss."

Killeen put a hand on Ember's free paw. "Are you going to be all right about wearing the chains?"

Ember bared her teeth for a moment before she spoke. "I hate it. I hate the very idea of it. But the general is correct that there is no other way, so I will do it."

"It's just a ruse," said Killeen. "It doesn't mean anything."

"If you believe that," Ember snarled, "then you know nothing of the charr."

Dougal tossed back another gulp of the liquor. "It's about Scorchrazor, isn't it?"

Ember started at the mention of the name. She cast Dougal an angry look, then nodded.

"Scorchrazor?" asked Killeen.

"Kalla Scorchrazor," said Dougal. "Even the humans in Ebonhawke know about her. One of the most famous charr since the time of the Searing. Back in the day, when the shamans of the Flame Legion commanded the charr armies, female charr didn't have much status among their people. They never went to war and were relegated to subordinate positions. Many of them served in chains. Scorchrazor changed all that. She destroyed the charr shamans and nearly took down an entire legion of them."

"How typically human," Ember said, "blathering on about things you know very little about. Your race has just enough knowledge to be dangerous."

"All right," Dougal said, his own curiosity rising. "Enlighten us."

Ember pulled a tuft of fur from her arm and held it over a candle flickering in the center of the table. The hair ignited, and Ember dropped it into her glass. The liquor in it burst into a bluish flame.

Lit by the flame in her glass, Ember spoke, her voice no longer carrying its usual menace. "In the days when humans still presented a challenge for the charr, we did something terribly foolish that we have long since sworn never to do again: we worshipped gods.

"Before humans came to Tyria, we had no gods. We knew about creatures with power we could barely comprehend, but we thought of them as foes to be defeated, not gods to be placated. When we suffered our first defeats at the hairless hands of humans, though, many charr blamed this on the fact that they could plead to their gods for help while we fought alone, relying only on ourselves.

"A warband from the Flame Legion came to the rest of the charr one day and announced that they had found gods for us to worship. These were creatures later called titans, but they were powerful enough that such labels mattered little. The shamans who led their worship used braziers of fire as icons of their newfound gods. The other legions hesitated to follow their lead, but the Flame Legion had so much success at converting others—often by force—that many assumed that they must have gods on their side. It was the titans that gave us the cauldrons that allowed us to breach the Great Northern Wall.

"One famous charr stood against them: Bathea Havocbringer of the Blood Legion. She sniffed out the foul plans of the Flame Legion and their new shamans, who directed the worship of their gods in ways that brought themselves power and profit. She said, 'I will bow before no one and nothing, be it mortal or god,' and she persuaded many other charr to follow her lead.

"Because of this, the shamans gathered in the night to plot against her. They captured her and made a blood sacrifice of her to their new gods. They declared her a traitor and accused her of using her sexuality to tempt the males from the true path of the gods. To prevent any more such treachery, they marked all females with the same brand of deceit and banned them from serving in the legions, where they would mix with the males.

"Many females objected to this, as did some males. Several shared Havocbringer's fate, and eventually the others saw no choice but to submit themselves to their new gods' will. We lived like this for centuries, long enough that most of us could not remember there ever having been another way."

Ember put her paw over her glass of lit liquor. The flames had burned low, and her paw sealing off the glass from the surrounding air soon snuffed them out entirely. If the heat from the fire hurt her, she did not show it.

"After the Searing, some charr realized that the shamans of the Flame Legion—who had long abused their powers—had tricked us. A warrior named Pyre Fierceshot helped spur the rest of us to stand up to the Flame Legion, but we did not triumph until his granddaughter, Kalla Scorchrazor, led a rebellion that restored female charr to their rightful place."

"How did she manage that?" asked Killeen.

Ember chuckled at this. "Males who think females are beneath them are poor at keeping secrets from them. The females watched the shamans and learned that they were cheating the charr of their right to chart their own destiny. Armed with that knowledge, they spread it far and wide throughout the charr lands, until most charr females—and many of their chosen males—sided with Scorchrazor.

"Before Scorchrazor entered the rebellion, plenty of other charr had already lined up to be counted against the shamans of the Flame Legion, following in the tracks of Pyre Fierceshot. As their numbers grew, so did the ferocity with which the shamans tried to keep them down. With Scorchrazor's help, though, the rebels finally had a chance at winning.

"Scorchrazor pointed out that the shamans of the Flame Legion lacked one thing the rebels had: open minds. If the rebels could see their way fit to allowing the females to fight beside them, they could effectively double their numbers overnight. This would give them the soldiers they needed to be able to overwhelm the shamans and their magic. And, eventually, the human kingdoms as well.

"Having grown up with their females in servitude to them for centuries, though, many of the male charr were reluctant to go against this 'tradition.' They argued that the females had stayed at home for too long and were no longer suited for the battlefield—if they had ever been.

"To counter this argument, Scorchrazor threw down a challenge before her detractors. The most important of these was Forge Ironstrike, imperator of the Iron Legion, and he agreed to meet her in single combat. If she could defeat him, he would acknowledge that female charr were just as qualified to become soldiers as the males. Otherwise, he would kill her as an example to the other females who were confused about their places.

"The battle took place in the ruins of Rin, the old human capital of Ascalon, which we have now restored as the Black Citadel. The imperators of the Blood and Ash Legions stood as seconds. Blood backed its daughter Scorchrazor, while Ash sided with Iron. Scores of others watched, from the highest tribune all the way down to the lowliest gladium."

Ember knocked back a bit more of her drink, thought for a moment, and then spoke. She was warming to both the spirits and to her tale. "Scores of charr came to watch the battle in the ruined arena in Rin. The two warriors were well matched. As a male of our race, Ironstrike was the larger and stronger of the two, but Scorchrazor was by far the faster and more skilled.

"Time after time Ironstrike charged, his claws stretching for Scorchrazor's throat, but each time she dodged him and sliced him with her own claws as he passed her by. Eventually, the frustration and the loss of blood took its toll, and Ironstrike grew tired. Then Scorchrazor switched to the attack.

"She drove the battered Ironstrike back until he ran out of room to retreat. He summoned the last of his strength for one last charge, but she dodged that, too, and knocked him flat. She pounced on him as he sprawled on the arena's dusty floor and forced his surrender from him.

"Released, Ironstrike honored the terms of their deal. He acknowledged her right to battle alongside him, and he welcomed the rest of the female charr to join their rebellion. Even the shamans from the Iron, Blood, and Ash Legions rallied to their cause.

"The forces of the Flame Legion and its shamans met those arrayed against them in final battle on the Plains of Golghein. Because the Flame Legion had told their females to 'stay home where they belonged,' they were so outnumbered that they surrendered rather than be slaughtered.

"To her credit, Scorchrazor accepted the surrender, but only so that the charr would not be stripped of the power of the Flame Legion, which had more shamans than all of the other legions combined. Even without gods behind it—perhaps especially—magic has its uses.

"The imperator of the Flame Legion was so shamed by his surrender that when he finally met Scorchrazor, he stabbed her with a poisoned dagger. Charr may do anything to win a battle, but only the worst cowards would violate a surrender so. His treachery cost Scorchrazor her life, but her last words were 'At least I die knowing my sisters are free.'"

"Which is why you had such a strong reaction against wearing chains," said Riona.

Ember pressed her lips together so hard, they paled. Then she polished off the rest of the liquor in her glass in a single swallow.

"What happened to the assassin?" asked Killeen, her hand still covering her mouth in disbelief. "Did he get away with it?"

Ember shook her head. "Imperator Ironstrike himself throated the coward on the spot. The Flame Legion imperator went to his reward before Scorchrazor did."

"And tomorrow," said Dougal, "we're off to find the weapon that an early Flame Legion imperator dropped during the Foefire, years before that."

Ember nodded. "We seek the Claw to bring peace between your people and mine. For the sake of my people, I will wear your chains—but I will think of Kalla Scorchrazor every moment they restrain me."

She rallied for a moment, and her face grew sharp and feral once more. "My orders are to complete this mission by any means necessary, and I will do just that. Know, however, that if any of you get in my way—if you become more of a hindrance than a help—I will not hesitate to strike you down on the spot and leave you to die."

With that, she spun on her heel and left.

Riona rolled her eyes, then slumped in her chair with a hand on her forehead. Dougal reached again for the wine. Killeen smiled with delight as the servants brought in a chilled custard for their dessert.

The sylvari raised her glass of wine. "An inspirational beginning. We may not be a guild, or a warband, or a krewe, or even a family. But we are a company, adventurers gathered together to a single purpose. For the moment, that is enough. I drink to our success!"

11

Dougal felt warm and full as he returned to his room. He checked behind the door as he entered and made sure that the night shutters on the window were secure, on the off chance that Gyda had any more irate relatives lurking about. Determining that all was clear, he sat down on the bed and thought about his new companions.

All of them were more determined than he was. Riona seemed dedicated to the Vigil cause. The charr crusader was going to follow her orders to the letter. And Killeen would not be dissuaded from visiting a city filled with ghosts.

The problem, thought Dougal, was that none of them had any idea of what lay waiting for them in Ascalon City. He had been there, at horrendous cost. They didn't seem too interested in listening to his warnings here in the safety of Lion's Arch; would they listen to him when they were surrounded by the howling masses of spirits?

Dougal leaned back and looked at the ceiling, and the next thing he knew there was a loud thumping on the door. He blinked himself awake and noticed that the room's single oil lamp was still lit and no light peeked through the night shutters. He could not have been asleep more than two hours.

Staggering to the door, he found the hylek, Naugatl, standing there, his wide amphibian orbs equally bleary. "Gather your things," the hylek said. "You are leaving."

Dougal stared at the creature, who repeated his message, then waddled down the hall. The creature thumped on the next door and was greeted by a feminine curse.

Realizing that Riona was just as irritated as he was, Dougal almost smiled as he put together his meager belongings. He splashed some ice-cold water from a pitcher on his face to brace himself awake, briefly considered changing out of the clothes he had slept in, decided it was not worth the time, and shambled down to the meeting room.

He got there before Riona, which pleased him in some perverse manner. Killeen had arrived early, but even she seemed bleary-eyed and worn-out. Only Ember seemed unaffected by the early hour, picking at the remains of the moa platter from dinner.

They sat there for a few long minutes. Servants brought in a platter of cheese and a new ewer of wine. Dougal helped himself to the cheese but abjured the wine.

"Riona's late. Perhaps we will have to leave without her," Killeen said, yawning.

Dougal smiled at the thought of Riona chasing after them as they left the safe house. "Perhaps we should."

Killeen stared at Dougal with her wide green eyes.

After a moment he decided he'd become uncomfortable with it.

"What?" he asked.

"Just wondering what your bones will look like."

Dougal frowned at her. Ember stopped picking the moa and glared at the sylvari.

"What are your wishes in the event of your demise?" she added, smiling at Dougal.

"What?" he responded.

Killeen shrugged. "There's a possibility that some of us will not survive this mission. It's only wise that we make each other aware of our last wishes. Would you prefer a burial, a burning, or something else entirely?"

Dougal shrugged. "Do whatever you like. At that point, I'll be beyond caring."

"Really?" Killeen's eyes lit up like the rising sun glaring off the sea. "That's refreshing. Most humans prefer to be buried, but with all the undead streaming out of Orr these days, a growing number are choosing to be burned instead. Just to make sure that they don't end up as some sort of zombie or skeleton in the service of the dragon Zhaitan, of course. Not that it's really them: their spirit should have fled by that point, after all. Most people either can't or don't bother to make the distinction."

She looked him up and down as if she were sizing up a side of beef. "You would make an excellent undead servant." She circled around him, checking him out from every angle. "Are you sure you wouldn't mind?"

Despite himself, Dougal shuddered. "Riona's right," he said, "you *are* creepy sometimes."

Killeen showed all her bright teeth as she smiled at him. "I am who I am."

A deep voice booming from the hallway interrupted the conversation. "Hail, my new friends! This shall be a saga our grandchildren will sing with pride!"

At first Dougal had felt relieved to be spared any more of Killeen's curiosity, but then he turned to see the norn walking toward them with a wide grin on his tremendous face. Dougal's muscles bunched in case Gullik was prepared to finish the job he had started the day before.

But Gullik seemed sober today, and not immediately bent on Dougal's murder, so there were those points in his favor. The norn walked up to Ember's place, nodded at the charr, examined the remains of the sadly depleted moa, let out a sigh, and contented himself with a handful of cheese.

Riona trotted up behind the norn, and Soulkeeper strode after them, unhurried.

"Wait!" Riona said to Gullik. "The general only asked if you might be interested in joining us. We haven't agreed on anything."

Gullik shrugged as he pulled his long, loose hair back behind him and wrapped a leather strip through it, binding it in place. "It's an adventure for the ages," he said. "It's exactly the challenge I've been needing. Life in these lowlands has bored me to tears of late, and I can think of nothing I'd rather do than make another mark upon history."

He stopped in front of Dougal, leaned forward, and gave him a conspiratorial wink. "After all, even *I* can't keep at this forever, and I have an image to burnish. The bards shall sing our names in the same chorus alongside those of Destiny's Edge and the other great heroes of our age!"

"And how are you feeling this morning?" Dougal asked, smiling wanly.

"Like a hedgehog got loose in my skull and fouled itself between my ears," the norn said with a knowing smile. "Never better!"

Gullik leaned down and spoke to Dougal in a confidential tone. "My regrets for yesterday," he said. "Bear's tongue, I haven't drunk that much since I had to barricade myself inside the Busted Flagon tavern in Divinity's Reach. They threatened to banish me forever."

"And when was that?"

The norn rubbed his stubble-dotted chin as he thought about this. "A month ago. No, maybe last year. It's been a while. In any case, I hope I didn't do anything earlier that I might regret."

"You passed out right after you failed to kill me," Dougal said.

"Excellent!" Gullik placed a massive hand on Dougal's shoulder, and for a moment Dougal wondered if he were about to be strangled to death. "I remember every bit of that. Well, most of it. Enough to know I was being hasty and happy to give you a chance to make amends on our way to Ascalon City."

Riona breathed in and out through her nose to compose herself, then explained. "When Gullik finally woke up, he was brought to General Soulkeeper. She asked him personally to not interfere further with you, as you are on a vital mission for the Vigil. When he learned that, he insisted on joining us." From Riona's expression, she did not approve of this new addition at all, and was seriously looking to Dougal for support in rejecting his offer.

Soulkeeper said calmly, "You could use some more muscle." She looked up at the norn, who gave her a little laugh. "Even with Doomforge along as your guide, you're sure to have plenty of fighting ahead of you."

"I do not need his help," Ember said, but did not press the point. It was clear that the charr had been fully cowed and would not challenge the general further. Riona didn't say anything, but glared at Dougal again.

Dougal, for his part, held his tongue. Even on best behavior, a charr in the party would be problematic, and the presence of a norn, even a norn like Gullik, would work to their advantage. Riona saw he was not going to enter into the discussion and let out a deep, frustrated sigh.

"You need more help than even a single norn can provide," Soulkeeper said, "but you will make do with his. At the very least, Gullik Oddsson here should be able to provide you with an excellent distraction for your foes."

"Hey-ho!" the norn shouted in response, raising his fist into the ceiling. "I am nothing if not distracting."

Soulkeeper caught Dougal's eye and gave a very human-looking shrug. "I was going to offer him his freedom in return for joining your mission, but he volunteered before I could get that far."

"Speaking of offers," Dougal said, "we were talking about a sword earlier. Among other things."

"Indeed." Soulkeeper scratched the side of her muzzle and glanced at the empty scabbard still hanging from Dougal's belt. "You're like a declawed charr. We can't send a human out into the world without a proper blade, can we?"

Dougal shook his head. Riona said, "A proper blade that he won't break, I hope."

Soulkeeper gestured for Naugatl, who was lurking in the shadows of the hallway. The frog-man hopped forward on long, rubbery legs, bearing a long bundle in his thin arms.

"You made a good choice, dryskin!" the hylek boomed in a gravelly voice. "This blade, she is too good for you!"

"But the mission isn't?" said Dougal, scowling at the hylek.

"No." The hylek winked a transparent eyelid at Dougal as he unwrapped the sword and handed it over. "That is too bad for you."

Dougal took the blade and unsheathed it in a single movement. It leaped silently from its scabbard as if on springs. The blade glistened in the firelight, black and oily. The ebony color seemed to have not been applied to the metal but to run straight through it.

"What does it do?" Dougal asked as he hefted it and gave it a few swings to test its balance. It felt natural, like an extension of his arm.

"What? You mean, does it shoot lightning or burst into flame or something like that?" General Soulkeeper bared her teeth in a smile.

"Something like that."

"I am afraid not," said the general.

"So what's so special about the blade?" Even as he said the words, Dougal realized he didn't care. This sword felt perfect, as if he'd been looking for it his entire life and not even realized he was missing it until now.

"It kills," said Soulkeeper. The hylek let loose a throaty laugh that, had he been human, would have sounded as though he were about to vomit. "It kills very, very well. Isn't that what a sword's for?"

Dougal could not argue with that. He glanced over at Ember, who was losing the battle to consume the roast moa with the norn. The charr casually pitched a moa leg bone toward Dougal, and Dougal swung the sword at it effortlessly as if merely pointing at it. The remnants of the bone fell into two neat halves at his feet.

Dougal looked at it and nodded his approval at Soulkeeper. "It's a good start," he said as he sheathed the blade. He looked at the general long and hard. "Why are we up at this gods-forsaken hour?"

"You need to get to Ebonhawke," said Soulkeeper.

"If we are traveling by asura gate, we have to go through Divinity's Reach," said Dougal. "No one will be up at this hour."

"You're right about the last part," said the general, "but you're not going back to Divinity's Reach. You're going straight through to Ebonhawke."

Now Riona finally spoke up: "That's impossible. The only solid gate to Ebonhawke is from Divinity's Reach."

"Did I say you were using an established asura gate?" said Soulkeeper, her jaw open with amusement. "We can tune the Lion's Arch gate to Ebonhawke's aetheric frequency. We have a very talented man on the other side to do the same. From what I understand, we can bring the two gates into alignment briefly and send you through. But we have to be quick about it: we have a very slender window in time."

Riona's voice rose now. "You mean there is a flaw in the asura gate system? Could the charr use this to break into Ebonhawke?"

"You would need an agent on the Ebonhawke side," said Soulkeeper. "And even if they had one, the charr leadership would be reticent to try it. They are distrustful of asuran magic."

"They aren't the only ones," said Dougal softly.

"So if anyone asks, we didn't do this," Soulkeeper said sternly, looking at Ember and then at Gullik. The big norn shrugged, comfortable in the fact that he didn't understand what was going on in the first place. "Further, you won't want to mention the Vigil at all. Good fortune to you all. Now, dismissed!"

Soulkeeper placed her fist over her heart and Naugatl, Riona, and Ember returned the salute. Dougal just hoisted his bag and followed the hylek out of the room. They wound through passages and emerged at the same nondescript entrance by which they had entered the safe house.

They stumbled out into the empty streets of Lion's Arch. A lamplighter moved slowly down the street from them, but it was otherwise empty. The breeze was at their backs, pouring back into the sea, but Dougal still tasted salt.

"This is never going to work," said Dougal to Riona.

"We've got too many people to be stealthy, and too few to be effective."

"I know," Riona said quietly. "But we will do as best as we can. My goal is to get you to Ascalon City. We may have to pay a heavy price for that."

"You talked our way past the Seraph," said Killeen. "I'm sure you and your purple-stamped orders can do the same here."

"The Ebon Vanguard is a different order entirely from the Seraph," said Dougal. "They are not so easily swayed."

"Don't they answer to your Queen Jennah?" asked Killeen.

"The Ebon Vanguard? Yes and no. Back before the Searing, they started out as the Ascalon Vanguard, an elite unit that fought alongside Prince Rurik and later ventured into the charr lands to take the battle to them. Many of the human slaves they rescued from the charr joined them and swelled their ranks. Since they weren't part of the Ascalonian army anymore, they changed their name to the Ebon Vanguard. Later, Adelbern recalled those soldiers and asked them to fortify Ebonhawke in an attempt to solidify the capital's supply lines and establish a last-ditch holdout position."

"So Prince Rurik founded Ebonhawke?" Killeen showed real interest.

Dougal shook his head. "Rurik died while crossing the Shiverpeaks. By the time the Vanguard came to Ebonhawke, a hero named Gwen Thackeray was in charge. She forged the city into what it is today, and she led its defense during its darkest times, right after the

Foefire, which—as you might imagine—sent every surviving charr in Tyria into a rage. Under her guidance,
the walls of Ebonhawke stood strong—so strong that
they remain unbroken to this day."

"Nothing lasts forever," Ember growled.

"She still sounds like an amazing woman," said
Killeen.

"The greatest ever," Riona said. "She was the finest
hero of her age. She was just a child at the time of the
Searing, and she spent years as a charr slave before she
escaped. She joined the Ebon Vanguard and climbed its
ranks to become its leader. She turned Ebonhawke from
an outpost into a fortress, which still remains as the last
hope in the War of Ascalon Independence."

Ember snarled at this. "You mean the Ascalon Insurrection."

Dougal tried to bring the conversation back on track.
"Gwen fought the charr. She hated them for what they'd
done to her and her family, but she changed her mind
about them after she worked with Pyre Fierceshot to
help bring down the destroyers."

"Some woman," Ember growled.

"Did you know that Logan Thackeray is related to
Gwen?" Dougal said to Killeen.

"That would make sense," said the sylvari. "He struck
me as being very dedicated to his queen and country."

"I've read Gwen's journals," said Dougal. "They're
kept in the Durmand Priory. She married a ranger in
the Ebon Vanguard. His name was Kieran Thackeray.
Logan is their direct descendant."

"Heroism must run in his blood."

"Oh, spare me," Ember said, her voice barely a low sneer.

"Pardon me?" said Riona.

"I said spare me your human lies." The charr's voice was taut and tense. "Gwen the Goremonger killed scores of my people. She was no hero."

"To us, she was," Riona said. "Without her, the charr would have overrun Ascalon long ago. Where would we be then?"

"The distant memories you should be." Ember's fur bristled as she spoke. "Tyria belonged to the charr before you mice burrowed your way into our lands, and we will have it long after you're all gone."

Riona snorted. "You should think before your speak. Remember, we're going to be your captors, kitty."

Ember moved effortlessly and suddenly, bringing her elbow around hard. Her first swat knocked Riona off her feet. Ember followed her, weaponless, but with her claws extended from her paw. She raised her paw again, this time for a blow that would rip Riona's armor off.

Before the charr could bring down her arm, though, Gullik's hand snaked out and plucked the fur on the back of Ember's neck. With a sharp yank, he hauled her back so hard that Dougal wondered if Ember's head might separate from her shoulders.

Snarling, Ember spun and launched herself at Gullik instead. He brought his free arm around and smacked her across her snout hard enough to knock her from her feet. Ember yowled at the norn. Dougal stepped between the two, his black blade in his hand, ready to put it to use if the charr came up swinging.

"Wait!" Riona said. "Don't do it! We need her!"

Dougal glared down at the charr. Riona had provoked the attack but now was trying to undo the damage. Perhaps she didn't want to go back to General Soulkeeper and explain what had happened. To Ember he said, "Are you done?"

Ember's mouth twisted, and Dougal thought she might be preparing to bite off his face. Then the fight went out of her, and she nodded at him without speaking.

"It seems," said the charr, measuring her words, "that I must make a habit of apologizing to you, Dougal Keane." She touched the corner of her mouth, and her fur came away spattered with blood. To Riona she said, "But you had best remember that you have your stories, and we have ours, and the two differ greatly."

Dougal sheathed his sword and stepped away from the charr. Gullik, his earlier violence forgotten, hauled Ember up and set her on her feet. "You are a ferocious warrior," he told the charr. "I would enjoy fighting alongside you in battle someday. But put your claws away today."

Dougal looked around: the alleyway was as empty as before. In Divinity's Reach a half-dozen Seraph would have been on top of them, and shutters would be slamming shut and secured up and down the street. Here it was just another morning brawl.

They moved through the back alleys to the covered merchant district. The banked braziers and forges of the bazaar lit the blue sailcloth from below, giving the area an otherworldly feeling. The few merchant guards watched them carefully until they left their particular areas, then returned to their bottles and warm blankets.

Within sight of the asura gates, Riona called a halt. At this point she produced the manacles from Gullik's pack, which also held Ember's armor and weapon. Ember flinched at the sight of them but then held up her hands, wrists together.

"Wolf's teeth!" said Gullik, softly. "A charr allowing a human to put her in chains? I must still be dreaming."

"I have my orders." Ember growled out her words. "I follow them."

"You are braver than I," said Gullik.

"It's the only way we can get her through Ebonhawke." Riona fixed Gullik with a glare that insisted he say nothing more, but he showed no signs of understanding it.

The norn sighed. "Ah, Ebonhawke. I know it well! I haven't been there since they threw me out of the city for destroying one of their pubs."

Ignoring Riona's protests, Ember turned and stood up right in the norn's face. Gullik's smile vanished. "That's something you failed to mention before. That's not going to present a problem for us, is it?" the charr asked.

Gullik put up his hands to reassure her. "Of course not. That was years ago, and I'm sure they've rebuilt it by now."

Ember turned back to Riona and let her finish attaching the chains. "If this fails to work, the Ebon Vanguard will hang me as a spy," she said,. "But before I go, I'll kill anyone responsible for causing that failure. This I promise."

"She's touchy," Gullik said to Dougal. "But still as regal as a lioness. I think I like her!"

They emerged from the market near the half circle of asura gates, their stone and metal ovals flickering with stray, erratic flickers of eldritch power. At the Divinity's Reach gate stood a trio of asura that Dougal had noticed coming in. They were practically vibrating with excitement, running from crystal to crystal and rune to rune, adjusting, modifying, and trying to tune the gate to the proper aetheric frequency.

"I'm not getting anything," snapped one.

"Try the sympathetic diathuergic connection!" suggested the next.

"Hang on, I'm seeing the handshake invocation come through. Tuning in the test chord."

"Got it!" said the first. "We are a go! Planar boring up and operating. Full chord registry. Amazing! We are live by five!"

"Kranxx, you are simply magnificent," said the second to herself with admiration, staring at the gate.

"You lot," snapped the third at Dougal's group, "get up there! We can't hold this for more than ten heartbeats! After that, the hard-linked resonant dampers reset and who knows where you'd end up."

Ember held up her chains and shook them, then nodded at Riona, who was holding the other end. Riona adjusted her helmet and nodded back. They ran up the ramp and stepped through the gate. Dougal followed them.

He felt his skin dry as he stepped through the gate. He had not felt damp in seaside Lion's Arch, but now all the moisture evaporated from his flesh, and the dry night air, still warm, forced its way into his lungs. Ebonhawke was perched on the edge of the Crystal Desert, and even in the dead of night the residual heat pulled the sweat from exposed flesh.

The far side of the gate was similar to that of Divinity's Reach: set atop a low mound, surrounded by a thick wall with a parapet pointed in toward the gate. In the event that something unpleasant pushed its way through from the other side, there would be a welcoming committee on this side.

Except that the guard posts were empty at this time of night. And at the base of the stone mound a single nervous, frustrated asura stood rubbing his short fingers through a tangled thatch of long hair.

Of course, thought Dougal, *Soulkeeper's "man" in Ebonhawke would have to be an asura.*

The asura looked at the adventurers. "You all made it? Good. Let me reset the dampers." He toggled a few runes on the plinth, resetting the crystals to their original positions. The shimmering meniscus of the gate surface faded behind them. "We need to move quickly. And just so you know, this was Soulkeeper's worst idea ever."

"Hold!" came a voice from the gateway. A trio of Ebonhawke soldiers strode through the gates. Others, armed with rifles, appeared on the parapets surrounding the gate grounds.

"Put your hands up!" snarled the officer. "Reach for your weapons and you will be slain where you stand!"

They were trapped.

12

"Have you lost your minds?" said the lead guardsman. "Where do you think you're going with that charr?"

Dougal looked around him. Riona stood stock-still, her hands gripping the chain linked to Ember's manacles. The charr was equally quiet, but Dougal saw that her leg muscles were bunched for sudden flight. Killeen, always accommodating, smiled and raised both arms. Gullik crossed his, scowled, but said nothing.

"Officers," said Dougal, raising both hands in front of him as if to ward off an expected blow, "we have a good explanation for this."

"Explanations later," said the officer. "Hand over that prisoner—now! Hand it over!"

Dougal looked at Riona. She bit her lower lip, then offered him the charr's chain. "Very well, then."

Ember's eyes went wide and white, and Dougal was sure the charr was going to try to bolt. She would not make it ten feet before the riflemen on the walls cut all of them down.

The asura running the gate stepped between Ember and the officer. "Just a moment, Lieutenant. What are you doing with *my* property?"

"Your property, Master Kranxx?" said the officer, towering over the small asura but no longer reaching out for the chain. "Why are *you* smuggling a charr into Ebonhawke?"

"My studies, of course," said Kranxx. "Your superiors keep pressing me for new and better ways to kill charr. I hired these"—he waved a small hand at Dougal's group, searching for a word—"*individuals* to bring me a living, breathing representative of the race."

"We could have brought you charr," said the lieutenant. "We have more than enough of them outside our walls."

"You didn't hear me," said Kranxx. "I need one alive and breathing. The ones you bring in are usually in poor condition."

Dougal shot a look at Ember. She was no longer as panicked. She was, however, angry.

"Why would you bring a charr here in the middle of the night?" asked the lieutenant.

"Idiot of a human," said Kranxx. "Can you imagine the riot that would ensue if I brought a live charr in with the regular supplies from Divinity's Reach? I suggested it, of course, but your Commander Samuelsson would not hear of it."

"Samuelsson knows about this?" said the guard.

"Of course," lied the asura, without missing a beat. "You think I would do something like this without checking it up the line? You humans care too much about chain of command for your own good, you know. Let's go wake up your Commander Samuelsson in the wee hours of the morning, and I'm sure he'll be glad to send me on my way, and then have a nice long discussion with you about the perils of personal initiative."

The guard's face hardened. "What are your intentions with this charr?"

"Vivisection," said Kranxx, and Ember jumped in surprise, almost pulling the chain out of Riona's hands. Gullik put a heavy hand on the charr's shoulder and let out a deep, throaty warning.

The lieutenant nodded and said, "And you're going to keep it in your workshop?"

"I have a cage prepared for it," said the asura. "If you want, I can make a rug out of its skin for you when I'm done."

"Very well," said the officer. "Olsen! Gregory! Escort Master Kranxx to his workshop and stand guard outside. I will send relief in the morning."

"Excellent!" said the asura, and motioned to Dougal and Riona. "You lot: Bring the prisoner and follow along! I have much to do before sunrise!"

As they walked away under the watchful eyes of the heavily armed Ebon Vanguard on the walls, Dougal started to say, "That was very—"

"Silence!" snapped the asura, raising a hand to hush Dougal but not missing a step with the two guards. "Don't talk: Watch the prisoner! I don't want it to bolt now, before I get a chance to peel back its ribs!"

Dougal fell back alongside Riona, wondering if he was dealing with one of Clagg's relatives.

They trod through the cobblestone streets of Ebonhawke, and even in the darkness Dougal felt a pang of homesickness. The streets were empty and the night shutters of the upper stories bolted tight: curfew was still in force, as it had been in his youth. There was no one visible on the streets, but Dougal knew that the alleyways were alive with sneak thieves looking for targets and teenagers daring the wrath of the authorities. He had done both in his time.

The buildings and walls were mostly of gray stone, carved in the quarries behind the city and shaped to fit together like pieces of a puzzle. The upper floors were whitewashed but in daylight were a dingy gray from the regular dust storms that blew up from the south. In the wan moonlight, they were as pale as phantoms.

Still, here was an old storefront he used to visit, and there was the fountain he remembered, and last was the tavern where he and Dak and Jervis and Vala and Marga would gather after patrol. He thought of them all, in that pale, dead city, and his heart sank again.

He looked at the others. Killeen had her hood up, and Gullik looked particularly bored. Ember looked about, possibly scouting for escape routes. His eyes locked with Riona's for a moment, and he saw in them the same sadness that he felt.

At last they reached a particularly thick reinforced door attached to a particularly dingy and windowless building. The guards took up positions on either side of the door as Kranxx fumbled with a set of oversized keys. He made a great production of opening no less than three sets of locks and swinging the door inward, then stepped aside. To the guards he said, "See you in the morning." To Dougal he said, "You lot! Inside! Quit wasting my time!"

The group dutifully entered, Ember giving token resistance on her chains and being pushed forward by Gullik. The asura stood by the door, slammed it after they entered, and resecured the locks, adding a pair of dead bolts as well.

Dougal looked around. The room was small, low-ceilinged—Gullik had to duck to miss the crossbeams—and littered with all manner of anvils, forges, odd-shaped rocks, skulls, glassware, and a variety of tools. What the room missed was the obvious cage that Kranxx had mentioned to the Vanguard lieutenant.

The asura finished barring the door and picked up something that looked like an elongated tuning fork. He tapped it against a metal plate and a bolt of lightning arced between the tines.

"I'm going to need you to scream," he said to Ember quietly.

Ember looked down at the asura, her shoulders hunched, "Why should I . . ."

"We have two guards outside who overheard me talking about skinning you," said the asura. "I do not doubt that one if not both have their ears pressed against the door, waiting to hear your screams. We should oblige them."

Ember looked angrily at the asura, then let out a loud snarl.

Kranxx shook his head. "Pitiful. I said a *scream,*" said Kranxx. He smacked the tuning fork against the metal plate again and it cracked like a lightning bolt, casting harsh shadows of the group behind them.

The manacled charr, standing ten feet away from him, unharmed, scowled. Then she bellowed, "No! I will never submit! *Argggghhh!*"

"Into the cage, beast!" shouted the asura.

"A charr will never—*Arggh!* The pain! My fur! *I'm burning!*" cried Ember.

"You do not know pain yet! Into the cage!" Kranxx tapped the fork a third time and it exploded in a shower of sparks, matched by Ember's own ear-piercing scream.

"Throw it in the cage and we can begin!" said the asura.

"Yes, Master Kranxx!" shouted Gullik enthusiastically. Riona and Ember both looked at the norn, their mouths open in disbelief. Gullik raised his eyebrows and said, "Just trying to help."

"Good!" cried Kranxx in triumph. "Now administer the sedative and we can begin. I want to flay that creature alive!" And he calmly set down his lightning fork and said in a low voice, "That was very good, charr. Have you done that professionally?"

"I have had my opportunities," said Ember, no longer as panicked as she had once appeared.

"Very well," said the asura, listening for a moment to his door, then nodding to the others. "Come, we should be out of here. Lieutenant Stafford will not dare wake his commander, but you can bet he'll be there in his office with the first dawn's light. And don't touch that." The last was directed at Gullik, who had reached out for the lightning fork.

Kranxx pulled a bag from one side of his worktable and put the fork into it, along with a couple flasks of bluish liquid and a couple other tools. He adjusted a few things on his workbench. He looked around the workshop and let out a sigh, then turned toward a back wall stacked with barrels. He opened one of the barrels, reached in, and pulled a switch, and the entire wall, complete with false barrel fronts, swung outward, revealing a narrow set of stairs descending into the earth.

"Follow me," said the asura, pulling a small gem from his pocket and blowing on it. It glowed with an amber radiance. As he walked down the stairs, other gems set into walls glimmered to life, with wan flames that provided a minimum of guidance.

Riona, still holding on to Ember's chain, followed Kranxx; Killeen and Gullik went next; and Dougal brought up the rear. He looked around the empty, windowless workshop and thought he heard the sound of cooling metal ticking away as it contracted. He wondered how long the guards outside would be content with listening to a sedated charr behind closed doors.

As Dougal worked his way through the passage, he noted that the smaller gemstones were already fading. They walked for what he estimated were two city blocks, then turned right and walked another one. Dougal tried to visualize where that put him in the city, but failed.

They emerged in the large basement of another building, probably a warehouse, at the top of a ramp. The ramp switched back twice before opening up into a space large enough to be a throne room but stacked with storage shelves. Little sat on the shelves but a few basic supplies plus several slabs of stone and ingots of metal stacked in a haphazard way, all wreathed in shadow. Several half-built golems lay in a pile in one corner, and along one wall was the half-constructed form of an asura gate. The shelves had been cleared away from the front of the room, the centerpiece of which was a long, circular lab table set at the perfect height for an asura to work at.

Kranxx slapped a small panel as he came into the room, and a flame leaped to life under a pot sitting on a metal surface. "Pardon the mess," he said. "I don't often have guests."

Ember crinkled her snout as she sniffed at the air. "I can see why," she said. "It smells like something died down here."

"No one can prove that," said Kranxx, smiling. "And if they can, I wasn't anywhere near here when it happened."

He turned to Riona. "Are you in charge here, or were you just the only one willing to hold the charr's chain?"

Riona nodded indignantly. "While we appreciate your aid, our business here is our own. We must leave this place as soon as possible, by orders of the queen of Kryta."

"Right," Kranxx said. "And I'm really Master Snaff of Destiny's Edge."

"I assume you are the general's 'man' in Ebonhawke," said Dougal.

Kranxx sneered at that. "She didn't mention me by

name? That sounds like Soulkeeper coming and going. She is too clever by half, sometimes. Thinks she's running the Order of Whispers or something."

"The what?" asked Killeen.

"Tactician Kranxx, of the Vigil," said the asura, quickly introducing himself with a small bow. Returning to Riona: "You're a crusader. Almorra recruits people like you."

"We are both crusaders of the Vigil," said Ember. "I am Ember Doomforge. The human female is Riona Grady. And she speaks the truth: our mission is on behalf of the queen of Kryta."

Kranxx nodded. "Soulkeeper warned me you people might not be too sharp, but when I joined the Vigil, I had no idea that it might ever sink this low. Smuggling a charr into Ebonhawke! Has she lost her mind?"

Killeen opened her mouth to point out it had been Dougal's idea, but Dougal raised a hand and silently pleaded with her to keep her helpful truths to herself.

"What did General Soulkeeper say in her message?" said Riona.

"Very little," said Kranxx. "Very need-to-know, she is. 'Expect visitors that will need to leave Ebonhawke quietly. Some may be problematic.' Problematic! She is a master of understatement. And she provided the date and time to reconfigure the gate. *That* was some mighty arcane kludging, by the way. They're going to have to recalibrate an entire bank of crystals after that one. Don't touch that, either." Gullik had found a pack hanging on a nearby peg intriguing, and looked at the asura sheepishly as he edged away from it.

"Very well," said Riona, "you have gotten us here and past the Ebon Vanguard. Where do we go from here?"

"I have to go out and make a few final arrangements," said Kranxx. "Plant a few false leads and wrap up some personal business. Then we will go out by way of the sewers."

"Sewers?" said Riona.

"We?" said Dougal.

"We," said Kranxx. "After this, I'm burned as an asset. And there will likely be an investigation and some changes regarding using and protecting the asura gate as well. Once Commander Samuelsson gets up and the lieutenant talks to him, I am going to become a person of interest. So, like it or not, I am coming with you. Where are we going?"

"Ascalon City," said Dougal.

Kranxx let out a low whistle. "Almorra," he said, "you never do anything in halves. Very well, then, get a bit of rest—you're going to need it. I will be back. And in the name of the Eternal Alchemy"—he looked at Gullik—"don't touch anything."

Gullik looked disappointed and collapsed onto a pile of sacks in the corner. The sides of one of the sacks split and potatoes rolled out. Killeen lowered herself down next to him and tried to make herself comfortable using the norn's pack as a pillow.

Ember held out her manacled hands and let out a low growl.

"Not yet," said Riona. "We aren't out of Ebonhawke."

"You must be kidding," snarled the charr. "We're in a

basement. If the Vanguard finds us, we're better off if I can pull my own weight."

"I don't think—" said Riona.

"Do it," said Dougal sharply. "Ember's right."

"We're taking all sorts of risks—" Riona started again.

"Unlock her," said Dougal, "or I'll fish out my tools and break the locks myself."

Riona shot Dougal a hot flash of anger but pulled the keys from her pouch and tripped the tumblers in Ember's wrist and neck manacles. The charr immediately stretched herself out to her full height, raised her arms, and let out a powerful growl. "You have no idea how good that feels," she said.

"You'd be surprised," said Riona, but Ember ignored her and joined the other two on the pile of potato sacks.

Riona turned to Dougal. Her face was bunched with anger and, Dougal thought, a little confusion. Instead she said, "You going to get some rest? I'll stand watch until Tactician Kranxx gets back."

"You froze," said Dougal. "At the asura gate. You were willing to hand over Ember."

"You would have thought of something," said Riona, but Dougal shook his head.

"You could have handed over your magic purple-stamped letter," Dougal said pointedly. "Orders from the queen of Kryta and Logan Thackeray."

"Thackeray's name doesn't hold the weight around here it once did," she said. "And as for Queen Jennah, you know that most of us here think that she is distant authority at best."

Dougal ignored her and continued, still keeping his

voice down. "But instead you would have handed one of your fellow crusaders over."

"A charr crusader," said Riona, her voice low but her face flushed. "And she knew the risks."

"Beside the point," said Dougal.

Riona was angry now. "You remember the other night, when Crusader Doomforge said she would do anything to make sure the mission succeeded—even if it meant the death of one of us?" Dougal nodded, and she continued hotly, "I feel the same way. If we were going to fight and die there at the gate, the mission would have failed. You know that. Ember knew that. She would have sacrificed herself if she had to: that's how the Vigil operates."

"We were lucky," said Dougal.

"*You* are lucky," said Riona, calming herself. "That's why you've survived long enough to come along. And are you *really* one to lecture me about sacrificing allies?"

Dougal opened his mouth but nothing came out. Riona nodded in triumph. "Now, if you don't mind, I could use some time away from all of you." And with that, she retreated to the far side of the room and wrapped herself up in her cloak, watching Ember and the others. Gullik was already snoring loudly.

Dougal let out a long breath and looked at the brooding Riona at one side of the room and the three non-humans on the other side. He walked up to the low asura-height table and tested it. It seemed strong enough to support a full-grown norn. Dougal lay down on the tabletop, wrapped himself in his cloak, and was asleep in moments.

His sleep must have been dreamless, because the next thing he realized, he was being shaken by the shoulders by a small child.

"Wake up, you bookah!" snapped Kranxx, rolling off him as Dougal sat up, blinking back his slumber and wondering if he was ever again going to sleep through an entire night.

As Kranxx's angry face came into focus, he managed a mumbled "What now?"

"Where is she?" said Kranxx, and looked over at the others. Killeen was pulling herself to her feet, and Ember was shaking the norn from his deep slumbers.

"She?" was all Dougal could manage.

"The girl, Riona!" said Kranxx. "While you've been sleeping, she's wandered off!"

13

We should leave her behind," said Ember. In his heart, Dougal knew the charr was right. However, what he said was: "How long do we have to find her?"

"An hour, at the outside," Kranxx answered, irritated. "One thing I did while I was out was to prepare a small incendiary in my old workshop. The smoke should alert the guards, but by the time they put the fire out, I was planning to be long gone."

"One thing?" said Ember.

"I also thumped on the ostler's door and demanded he have a large wagon with supplies ready to go for me by noon," Kranxx replied sharply. "I have no intention to pick up that wagon, but it will delay them further. And I *also* left a note for my assistant that stated I was leaving for Elona and putting the Ebonhawke gate and all attendant responsibilities for dealing with the authorities in his care." He paused a moment, then added, "I don't like my assistant that much."

"Okay," said Dougal. "Let's figure a half hour at best."

He looked at the others. "Killeen, any idea where she went?"

"I was asleep," said the sylvari. "And if you're asking about the Dream, it doesn't work that way."

"Fine. You come with me anyway," said Dougal. "Ember, brief Kranxx on the whys and wherefores of what we're doing. Gullik should understand what we're facing as well. We should be back within a half hour."

"And if you are not?" asked Ember.

"We go with your plan," said Dougal. "You leave without us. We'll catch up if we can. Killeen, with me."

Dougal stepped out of the building above the warehouse and cursed inwardly. The sky was already starting to lighten in the east, and the city was coming awake. Already the heavy shutters against the night air were swinging open, and a honey wagon drawn by a heavy dolyak was rattling along the street. No Vanguard in sight, but that was only a matter of minutes. Far in the distance he could hear bugles sounding reveille.

"Right. We split up," he said. "You go into the city, I'll head toward the Hawkgates. Ten minutes, then turn back. Don't get lost."

"She is up on the battlements," said Killeen.

"I thought you said the Dream wouldn't tell you where she was," said Dougal.

"I still have eyes," said Killeen. "She's up there." And Dougal followed her pointing hand to show Riona, in her traveling cloak, up on one of the city's interior walls, looking out past the gates.

Dougal set off at once, Killeen following him. He

knew the mazework of stairs and streets that was Ebonhawke. The nearest stair up was close at hand

The city itself had been a small fortress, nestled in the southern juncture of the Shiverpeaks and the Blazeridge mountain range. The steep mountains on several sides provided an ideal location just north of the Crystal Desert. With the Searing, its location grew in importance, and King Adelbern of Ascalon saw it as an ultimate bastion against the charr incursions. In the end, before the Foefire, he dispatched the Ebon Vanguard here to reinforce it.

And reinforce it they did. They spread the initial fortress walls outward, continuing to build as they took more territory against the regular charr raids. They erected the mighty Hawkgates at the northern entrance to the city. They mined the hills behind the walls for stone and made more living space for the refugees from the abandoned human cities to the north. And they trained their growing populace in the dangers that stood right outside their gates, from the siege engines of the charr.

Dougal knew where Riona stood, and why she was there. From that internal wall she could see over the lower walls, past the Hawkgates and all the way to the Fields of Ruin beyond. He climbed the stairs three at a time, leaving the sylvari far behind him.

"Riona," he said, and she jumped at the sound of his voice. She had not heard him approach.

"Dougal!" she said, her voice confused for a moment, almost weak. "I didn't hear you."

"We should go," he said. "Kranxx is back, and we don't have much time."

"I know," she agreed. "But look."

He followed her stare and could see it as well, and the sight stopped him in his tracks, as it always did.

Far to the north and west of the city were the front lines of the charr siege of Ebonhawke. They were positioned at the exact range of the human defensive ballistas—not one foot closer or farther away.

The front line of the charr entrenchments was a line of war wagons, parked in their positions for so long that trees had grown up next to them, providing shade for their crews. The war wagons were mobile walls of metal, each crowned with a spearlike palisade. Joined together in the field, they were an instant fortification for the charr military camps.

Behind them were the camps themselves, and with them a variety of siege engines and military units. Here were siege devourers, living engines of destruction, also equipped with ballista and cannon. In years past, when the charr improved their range, they pelted the walls and closer human districts with heavy stones and burning pitch. When the human machines could reach them, they pulled back farther and established new lines. The Iron Legion, the legion that had the most interest in engines of destruction, had been in charge of the siege for over a century, and used the city as a testing ground for its latest developments.

There were flames along the line: bonfires and forges and cooking fires for the awakening military units. There was the sound of distant horns—loud, blaring trumpets—and drums. The charr were waking to war as well.

Dougal looked out and saw what he had seen in his youth: the front lines of the war with the charr. In his days and nights here, in the cauldron of war, every day there had been sallies from the fortress and assaults on the walls. It was a hard, brutal life, and one became hard in return.

Or one left, as he and the others did. Leaving Riona behind.

Killeen had caught up with them. "We were worried," she said to Riona. "The others are waiting."

Riona shook her head and said, "I don't know."

"We should go," Dougal repeated, tearing himself away from the sight of what had for so many years been the enemy. And still was.

"I think I have to stay," said Riona. "I have doubts about what we're doing. I thought I didn't, but now that I'm back here, I feel myself falling back into what I once was—that we should be here, not at the Vigil or trying to find lost treasures. We should be here to protect Ebon-hawke."

"Riona, that's wrong," said Dougal.

"We have guards coming up," said Killeen, suddenly and clearly. Dougal looked to his left and saw a pair of Vanguard moving along the battlement toward them. They were moving with the slow, relaxed pace of two soldiers near the end of their duty shift. They were not actively seeking charr who had broken into the Fortress City, or the humans that had aided it.

For that, Dougal was thankful, but when he turned back to Riona, he saw that her face had fallen and she seemed on the verge of falling apart.

"I will delay them," said Killeen. "You talk to her." Before Dougal could stop her, she moved toward the guards, letting her hood drop to reveal her long, vegetative braids.

Dougal turned back to Riona. "This was all your idea," he said firmly.

"I know," she said, and sighed deeply, her forehead furrowing. "And when it was just finding you, and then sneaking into an ancient human city, it seemed doable. Now we have picked up a menagerie of castoffs and volunteers. And the more our numbers grow, the less likely we are going to succeed."

Dougal shrugged in agreement. "The less likely we will succeed without losing people."

Riona lowered her chin to her chest. "We could go off on our own."

Dougal started, but Riona continued hurriedly, "Two humans could sneak out of here easier than our clown carnival. Norn, charr, sylvari, and now an asura. Hardly the easiest party to conceal in open fields. We could reach Ascalon City, retrieve the Claw, and return it here, to Ebonhawke. Then we could keep it here. It would be a coup, a rallying point for our people."

"And for the charr as well," said Dougal. "If the charr thought that the Claw was here, they would stop at nothing to regain it. It would be worse than the worst of the assaults of seventy years ago, when the charr reached the base of the outer walls and undermined the outer district."

"You think so?" said Riona, and slid closer to him, her eyes never leaving the quiet battlefield.

"Look at it this way," said Dougal. "The charr want the Claw so badly that they are willing to talk about peace with the humans. What do *you* think?"

Riona nodded. "If this peace faction—"

"Truce faction," said Dougal.

"Truce faction," repeated Riona. "If they get the Claw, they will be able to force the rest of the charr to at least lift the siege and start talking. That's the theory."

"And then maybe we'll finally get a better view from here." Dougal kept his voice light, but Riona just scowled and stared at the charr front lines. Then she said, "You were right."

Dougal looked at her and she continued. "I froze back there, at the gate. I thought I could come up with a way to get us all past the guards if there was trouble, but when the time came, I found myself empty. I'm just rattled. Second-guessing myself."

Dougal's lips became a thin line, and he chose his words carefully. "This is about Ember."

"Do you trust her?" asked Riona. "Really?"

Dougal said, "She is part of your order. She is a crusader for the Vigil."

"I know," said Riona. "And I don't feel that way about General Soulkeeper. She's a charr, too, one that fought our people for many years. But the way Ember acts, she reminds me so much of . . . them." She pointed a chin at the distant war wagons.

"If it helps, I feel the same way," said Dougal. "After five minutes with Soulkeeper, I could forget she was charr. She commands naturally, and everything else just flows from that. Ember is part of her people, just like we're part of ours. You can see her struggle when she talks to us."

"Like I'm struggling," said Riona. "Still, I want you to know that I'm glad I found you. I'm glad you're here. *You* I trust." She slid close to him, and despite himself, he raised his arm to hold her. The weight of the locket felt heavy around his neck.

"I trust you too," said Dougal. "And this will pass. No matter what that Kranxx says, Soulkeeper's plan is a good one. We will get the Claw. Together. Promise."

They stood there for a long moment, and Dougal realized he had forgotten about Killeen talking to the guards. When he turned, Riona was still in his arms and the sylvari was heading toward them, raising her hood again. The guards were wandering back the way they had come from.

"Are we ready?" asked Killeen.

"I think so," said Dougal. Riona separated from him and nodded. They started down the steps.

"I had a curious chat with the guards," said Killeen. "It is interesting what people will tell you when you look at them with wide eyes and act like you just fell out of the tree. Apparently the siege has been quiet for the past few months: no new assaults from the charr lines. And, more interestingly, a moratorium on this side from sallies and patrols. They say some bigwigs made the decision."

"The truce faction," said Dougal, "and the queen."

"Yes," said Killeen, "but it is making everyone here very, very nervous. They are expecting some huge charr assault, and a lot of the human soldiers want to attack now, before it comes."

"You took a huge risk," said Riona. "They could have been looking for us."

"Everyone saw the charr; most would remember the norn," said Killeen. "Very few would pay attention to the sylvari in a cloak."

"How did you explain us?" asked Dougal. They were already at the door of the warehouse.

"I told them you were young lovers making a rendez-vous," said Killeen, "and acted like I did not know what that meant. They thought that was amusing as well."

By the time they had gotten back to the secret warehouse, the others were ready. Kranxx was packing a backpack with numerous small parcels carefully wrapped in waterproof waxed paper. Ember was fitting herself into the armor Gullik had been carrying on his back: sleek, black lacquered plates that glided silently over each other. For his part, Gullik was stroking his scruffy chin and, for the first time, seemed to be deep in thought. Riona picked up her helmet and quickly strapped on her scabbard.

"We're late," said Kranxx, hoisting the satchel onto his back and grabbing a loose piece of cloth that, only when he put it on his wide head, was recognizable as a hat. He pulled out a small lantern and lit it.

"You're in your armor," Riona said to Ember firmly.

"Kranxx pointed out that if we are spotted, whether I am wearing armor or not is a moot point," replied the charr, adjusting her scabbard and resting a hand on a heavy charr-made pistol on her opposite hip.

"At least have Gullik carry your weapons," said Riona. "And wear the shackles."

Anger flashed in Ember's eyes, and Dougal added, "At least until we're clear of the city."

Ember looked at Dougal. Dougal nodded toward Riona. Letting the air out in a long, hissing breath, Ember unfastened her belt and handed it, scabbard, sword, and holstered pistol to the norn. Then she held up her wrists once more. Gullik fished out the chains and Riona fitted them, loosely but locked, once more on her wrists and neck.

"Until we're clear of the city," said Ember, looking harshly at Dougal.

Kranxx poked his head through the door, then motioned for the others to follow. It was almost light now, the eastern sky reddening and drawing back the widow's veil that had hung protectively on Ebonhawke.

Then something exploded off to the north, just beyond the first wall. Screams and shouts sounded right after, and a call to arms went up among the Vanguard. Kranxx's letter of resignation.

Quickly but not panicked, the asura ducked into the mouth of an alley, then hustled everyone in after him. They huddled there in the darkness as a column of soldiers in black-and-gold uniforms tromped past, racing from their barracks to the (hopefully) now-burning shop.

Dougal watched the faces of the soldiers as they passed their hiding place: grim, weary, and determined. These were people who hated their jobs but were proud to do them and refused to falter for an instant. Dougal had been one of their number, as had Riona. To see them in action again, marching off to protect the city, made him flush with shame for not being among them. He felt grateful that the alley stood shrouded in darkness so that no one would see.

He expected Kranxx to lead them in the direction the soldiers came from, but instead he plunged them deeper into the alleyway, into a maze of small back passages that snaked between granaries and shuttered workshops. Once they crossed a major thoroughfare, then ducked back into alleyways that even Dougal was unfamiliar with. He figured they were heading west through the city, until at last they reached a dead end with a hatch nearly flush with the ground at its base.

Kranxx pulled out a key and fitted it into a lock on the hatch. He motioned to Gullik, who began struggling to open the heavy iron lid.

"Do we really have to go in there?" Dougal asked, peering down into the blackness. He pinched his nose so tight that it hurt, and the stench that escaped from the hatch still made his eyes water.

"It's the only way to get out of Ebonhawke without having to deal with the Vanguard," Kranxx said. "You *could* approach the commander and ask him permission to depart, but—given the nature of your mission and the fact that he's probably looking for you by now—he'd probably toss you into one of our lovely prison cells."

At the mention of Ebonhawke's prison, Dougal glanced at Riona. In the growing light of the morning, he could see the muscles in her face tighten, but she showed no other reaction.

"It's too bad the walls are so high," Gullik grunted, straining as he fitted his fingers under an edge and lifted. "And that you're all so small. Were we all norn warriors, we could just scale the wall and be gone."

Despite herself, Riona snorted. "You'd be filled with arrows and rifle shot before we made it halfway to the top. And then the charr would get to shoot at you on the way down."

Kranxx's lantern's light cast deep shadows on the asura's face. "The Ebon Vanguard built this place to stand against the charr forever," he said. "They drew on the experience Ascalon accumulated during the construction of the Northern Wall, and they've had over two hundred years of keeping the charr out of the city to help them figure out where the weak parts are and what they need to do to keep them plugged."

"Then how have you noticed something they haven't?" asked Dougal.

Kranxx allowed himself a chuckle. "Because I'm asura, and they're human. They think in terms of reiterations. They build something that they hope will stand, then they shore it up the best they can in the places they get wrong. People with brains think not in terms of single bits, like *walls*, but in terms of systems—especially interlocking systems and how they work together. The thing that lets Ebonhawke survive isn't the wall or the Vanguard. It's the asura gate. Without that, the charr would have been able to starve the humans out of here long ago. With it, the humans have managed a record-breaking stand against a truly determined foe."

"Granted," said Ember, whose hair bristled at the mention of her people's failure to wipe this settlement from Ascalon. "Many charr believe that Ebonhawke is impregnable, and taking it a waste of effort better spent elsewhere. The strongest dissenters are among the Iron Legion. This is why they have taken over the siege."

"And with their machines, they might someday manage to do it," said Riona, louder than she needed to. "One more reason we must work for this truce."

"Breaking down a wall isn't all that challenging, children," said Kranxx. "It just requires the right machines, and the charr have developed many crude but effective machines that could manage it. The trick is getting those machines into the right places. The Vanguard has gotten extremely good at keeping the charr from reaching those places."

Gullik hefted the iron hatch again and it rose another couple inches. The darkness beyond it gaped like an open, infected wound.

"So, why do we have to go down there, again?" asked Dougal.

"Because there's one spot in the wall that the Vanguard rarely watches and the charr don't attack: the sewage exit. Ebonhawke mostly gets its water from streams that flow down into it from the mountains, and they tap an underground river with a few deep wells. But they also need to get rid of all the waste they generate. Otherwise, the city would eventually be overwhelmed with it."

Even under her fur, Ember seemed to be turning a little green.

"The honey wagons dump the waste into a few well-positioned central depositories, each of which sits downstream from the wells and the point at which they divert some of the mountain streams into the sewer's main tunnel. The diverted water then carries the refuse under the city until it spills out of the far side of the mountain a couple hundred yards away from the wall."

Dougal's stomach turned. "You're kidding," he said, although he knew the asura wasn't.

The asura smiled. "The charr can't stand the smell. Every now and then, the Vanguard sends someone up to check out the sewage tunnel's exit, but he finds it locked up tight, and that's a good enough excuse for them to forget about it. The Vanguard isn't made up of complete idiots. They know about the sewage exit, of course, and they've secured it fairly well against attacks—from the outside."

"But not from the inside!" said Gullik, who had finally lifted the iron hatch and stood there, splay-legged, holding it up. "By the Snow Leopard's lazy tail, this just might work!"

"Might work? Of course it will work. It's foolproof!" He scanned the faces of the others. "It has to be when you're working with fools."

Ember growled at the asura, who let out a nervous laugh. "Present company partially excepted, of course."

"Then we have to go," said Riona. "And now, before the guards are done with Kranxx's foolishness and organize a proper search."

The set of her jaw told him everything Dougal needed to know. She hadn't lost an iota of her determination. She would do anything to see her mission through.

Dougal pointed into the darkness beyond the iron door that Kranxx had opened. A wrought-iron ladder disappeared into the abyss below.

"Let's get it over with."

14

The descent was interminable, and Dougal wondered how deep the original sewers ran in Ebonhawke. Gullik went last, securing the now-unlocked iron hatch behind them with what the norn probably thought was stealth but, to the others in the narrow vertical passage, sounded like the toll of a dead man's bell.

At the bottom of the ladder Kranxx handed his lantern to Gullik, then reached into his pack and pulled out and unlimbered a long pole made up of several hinged sections with a hook on one end. He shoved the other end into a pole-width pocket sewn into the back of his pack, then dug out and hung a glowing blue rock from the end of the hook. He shouldered the pack again so that the rock hung above him, about five feet off the ground, lighting his way, and he led them into the sewer.

Killeen followed right after Kranxx, peering at everything she saw in repulsed fascination. Dougal and Riona followed behind Killeen, with Ember after them and Gullik hunkering along in the rear, his head and shoulders held down tight to keep from scraping against the tunnel's ceiling.

The tunnel had been cut straight out of the side of the mountain, then covered over with fitted stones. Wooden trusses held up most of the roof, although in spots it had caved in or begun to sag. Far less care had been taken with these tunnels than with the elaborate underground structures in Divinity's Reach. Dougal supposed that had been determined by what each had been designed for. Here in Ebonhawke, they didn't have enough space for a graveyard: they burned their dead and watched the smoke from the fire carry their spirits off to the Mists.

At first, the floor of the tunnel was flat and dry, just like the passages that Dougal and Riona had been caught in as kids; but Dougal could hear the sound of running water up ahead. They soon came to a T with another tunnel. A wide stream ran through a deep notch cut into the left of this, leaving just enough space on the right for a human to walk.

The stench did not improve. It was awful.

"Wolf's nose!" Gullik said. "This smells worse than the latrines I had to muck out as a young warrior in the Battle of the Burning Pass."

Dougal peered into the filthy waters and tried to ignore the things he saw floating downstream. Mountain streams ran as clear as the rain, but the surface of this muck was so opaque, he could not discern its depths.

Kranxx led the way along the right-hand side of the stream, where a narrow walkway was perched over the flow. He could walk normally. Killeen, Riona, and Dougal had to follow more slowly, edging along. For Ember and Gullik, there would be no other choice than to wade through the edges of the muck.

And suddenly Ember stopped.

"Not a chance," the charr said, her voice filled with revulsion. "There has to be another way."

"We've already been over this," Kranxx said, calling back down the tunnel. His voice echoed off the slick masonry that lined the walls.

"I cannot—" Ember bit her tongue and swallowed back the bile rising in her throat.

"You are a brave and powerful warrior from a proud and magnificent people," Gullik said. "You have the strength to do this, and I will be there with you."

After a moment of trying to steel herself, Ember held out her hands instead. "Take off these chains," she said.

Riona shook her head. "Not until we are away from Ebonhawke. What if the Vanguard found us with you unchained?"

"I am not going to forge my way through that filth while bound in chains." Ember's tone made it clear that this point was not negotiable.

"She has a point," said Killeen. "What if there's a drop-off and she needs to swim?"

The thought of Ember falling all the way under the sewage made Dougal want to gag.

"No," Riona said. "She agreed to the plan, and we're going to stick to it." Her earlier softness, during the discussion up on the wall, was completely absent now. The Riona who led the party was back in charge.

"Then I go no further," said Ember. "I will make my way back to the surface and lead off any pursuit. I do not fear death, but this is no way for a charr to die."

"Leave a charr in the heart of Ebonhawke?" said Riona sharply. "That is not an option."

Dougal couldn't think of anything else to say. Instead, he walked back to where Ember stood at the intersection of the two tunnels and stood before her. She watched him patiently as he reached into a pocket and produced the moleskin package that held his lock picks. He held them up before the charr's face. Ember lifted her wrists to him with a smile, and he got to work.

"What do you think you're doing, Dougal?" Riona stormed toward him, her hand on the hilt of her sword. Before she could reach him, though, Gullik stepped between them, blocking her way. She tried to push her way past him, but he widened his stance to make it clear that he would not give way.

"Do you need a light?" said the norn helpfully, ignoring Riona's struggles and curses behind him.

Dougal ignored Riona as well, and a moment later Ember's hands were free. He reached up to undo the attached collar next.

Riona growled in frustration and craned her neck to see around the norn's bulk. "Dougal Keane!" she said. "I order you to stop!"

"Following your orders," Dougal said. The collar came open, and the set of shackles cascaded to the wet stones. "Oops, too late."

Ember scooped them up and hefted them in her hands, contemplating their steel links. Dougal thought she would throw them down the passage and into the sewer water. Instead she handed the chains to the norn, and Gullik for his part rooted around in his satchel for the charr's weapons. Dougal pocketed his picks once more, when Riona, now free of the norn's blocking frame, grabbed his wrist.

"How dare you?" she hissed, whirling him about.

Dougal braced himself, ready to knock aside her anticipated slap. Instead, when he opened his mouth to try to explain, she did something far worse.

She shoved him backward into the muck.

Dougal windmilled his arms to try to keep his balance, but failed. At the last moment he stopped fighting it and jumped in feetfirst instead, figuring that a controlled fall would be best. As he pierced the stream's surface, he had no idea how deep it might be, so he held his breath.

He blew it out right away once he realized that the sewage only came up to about his waist. When he realized it was so cold, he was surprised it hadn't frozen him instantly. He yowled in surprise, and his complaint rattled down the tunnels in every direction.

"You deserved that!" Riona said, still fuming.

Dougal pointed at Ember. "She needed out of those chains."

"And you *could* think of us as being outside the city, if you want," suggested Killeen.

Riona looked as if she were going to shout, then spun around and pushed Kranxx down the tunnel before her. Killeen followed along the thin ledge. Ember and Gullik stepped down into the stream. They groused at the stench and the cold, but the sewage didn't come up nearly as high on them as it did on Dougal.

Ember lifted Dougal out of the stream and set him down on the ledge. They nodded their gratitude to each other without a word. Dougal turned to scramble after Riona, and the charr and the norn waded right after him through the muck.

"In a group like this, such troubles are fated," Gullik said when they were all together again. "I've seen it happen before. Our differences are too great. Sooner or later we turn on each other."

"Riona and Ember are crusaders for the Vigil," Dougal said. "Despite their cultures, they should be able to work together." He sighed. "And remember, Riona and I are both come from Ebonhawke."

"I spoke not of cultures but of differences," said Gullik. "Between you two I sense a gulf the size of the sea."

Dougal glanced back at the grinning norn and couldn't help cracking a smile himself. "Gullik, my friend, you are wiser than you look."

"That's an exceedingly low threshold," Kranxx said from the head of the procession.

They walked in silence after that, following the tunnel through a series of switchbacks that brought them lower and lower through the side of the mountain. The muck got thicker and deeper, and the smell—if possible—got worse as they went.

Dougal tried not to think about how far they'd gone or how much farther they might have to go. He just focused his vision on the glowing rock hanging from the pole on Kranxx's back, and trudged on. Every now and then, he saw another tunnel head up and away from the sewer. Some of these were clean and dry, while others added their own small tributaries of filth to the mainstream.

When Kranxx reached a large intersection where a dry tunnel sloped down to where they were, he signaled to stop, and the others gathered closer behind him. Riona put her lantern down on the floor.

"We should rest," the old asura said. "This is the last place for a break before we reach the end of the line, and it's a bit of a haul from here to there."

As the words left Kranxx's lips, a line of torches burst into flame up the dry tunnel. Dougal put up an arm to shade his eyes against the light and gaped at the squad of Ebon Vanguard forming a solid phalanx in that tunnel. Two of the guards they'd run into at the asura gate stood at the head of the ranks.

The male officer, Lieutenant Stafford, raised his blade and shouted, "*This* is the end of the line for you! Cast down your weapons and surrender—now!"

"Hang on," Dougal said. "We can explain." Already he was trying to concoct a half-believable story that would buy enough time for the others to plan a break. He knew that there was little chance anyone would stop to listen to him, but he had to try.

'Lieutenant!" said one of the Vanguard. "The charr is free! And it has weapons!"

"Fire at will!" shouted the officer, wide-eyed and red-faced. "Then close to melee! Leave no survivors!"

The guardsmen in the front of the phalanx dropped

to one knee, revealing a second line behind them with muskets drawn. Dougal had time to curse and drop into a crouch as the breeches sparked and their tunnel was filled with noise and the smell of powder. Even as the bullets sang among them, the Vanguard dropped their muskets and pulled out their blades to join their fellows in a charge.

As the Ebon Vanguard raced toward them, Dougal found he had drawn his sword without noticing. Alongside him the others were recovering and preparing for the assault. Riona drew her slender blade. Killeen wove her hands in an intricate pattern. Kranxx, formerly in the lead, now faded back behind the others, dropped his pack, and started rummaging around in it. Ember had been the apparent target of the musket balls, and parts of her fur were smoking from several near misses. She extended her claws with a snarl and reared back to spring at their assailants.

Yet, before anyone else could react, Gullik let out a guttural roar, his flesh becoming thick and hairy, his face extending into a fuzzy, tooth-filled muzzle. Both attackers and defenders hesitated for a moment at the sight.

Of course, Dougal realized, Gullik would be able to take the form of a totem animal, and that form would be a bear's, just as his cousin's was a snow leopard.

The bear-Gullik dipped both of his massive paws into the sludge swirling around his thighs, then swung them forward like giant scoops, flinging their fetid contents over his companions' heads at the charging Vanguard. The guards howled in protest, blinded by the muck, their footing suddenly made treacherous by the sludge.

Ember leaped forward and gutted the lieutenant with a single slash of her claws. The man fell forward, gurgling blood. The charr moved past him and dove into the rear ranks of the guards rushing at them.

Riona stepped up and clashed blades with the female officer from the gate. "This is the queen's business!" Riona shouted, her voice almost pleading. "I demand you stand down!" Instead of answering, the Vanguard warded off Riona's initial blow and then followed it with a brutal riposte that clanged off the side of the crusader's helmet.

One of the Vanguard slipped past Ember and tried to run Dougal through, but Dougal parried him easily. The guard's sword seemed to slip along the oily surface of Dougal's blade until it smacked into the steel crossguard. Still, the way the man kept his balance and blocked Dougal's counterblow told Dougal he was in for a real fight.

Behind him, Dougal heard Killeen finish her spell. For a moment nothing happened, and he thought that perhaps she'd panicked and failed to make the incantation work or been interrupted by a stray blow. Then he heard squeaking in the distance, coming toward them from everywhere up and down the tunnels, and moving fast.

The guards heard it, too, and those who weren't directly engaged in the fight backed off, their swords at the ready, their eyes darting in all directions as they hunted for the source of the noise. The squeaking grew louder and higher, and the guards grew more and more anxious. One of them bellowed in frustration, his cry mixing with the rising squeaks.

The rats came scurrying from all around them, some wet and dripping with sludge, others dry as bone. Their eyes glittered red in the lights that Kranxx and the Vanguard still bore. They sounded hungry.

The guard who had screamed charged into the wave of rats, swinging his sword wildly. It clanged against the masonry rather than flesh, and then the rats swarmed over him. In an instant, they covered him from head to toe and began to tear him into tiny pieces.

While the first guard screamed in pain and terror, a pair of his fellows leaped to help him. The mass of rat flesh expanded to draw them in, and they began hollering for help too. In mere moments, the pleas stopped, and the guards collapsed under the weight of the murderous rats on top of them.

By this time Gullik had stormed into the dry tunnel. He had returned to his nornish form and now lashed out with his axe, left and right, and where it swung, men fell like saplings.

Dougal realized the guard he had battled would soon be the last of the Vanguard standing, but that didn't make the man any less determined to kill him. Dougal pressed the man hard, and when Gullik's axe sent a severed head sailing over his shoulder to bounce off the guard's helmet, Dougal took advantage of the distraction to backhand the guard off his feet.

The guard sprawled back against the side of the tunnel, and Dougal had the tip of his ebon sword under the man's unprotected chin before he could recover. The man froze, and Dougal looked into his terrified eyes and said, "Give up."

Knowing that he had no other option, the guard let go of his sword, and it clattered on the tunnel's floor. A moment later, Gullik's axe flew past Dougal's side to bury itself in the man's neck.

Dougal grabbed the guard to see if he could save him, but the man was already dead. Dougal spun to see the norn coming toward him to collect his axe.

"You stupid—" Dougal bit his tongue in an effort to control his fury. He was angrier at the norn than he'd been with the guard who'd been trying to kill him. "You didn't need to do that!"

Gullik smiled at him grimly. "And you, good fellow, are welcome! It's not every day I get to save a human's life."

Dougal gripped his sword so hard, he felt like his knuckles might pop out of his skin. "He surrendered!"

"He and his friends meant to kill us. They fired on us. They charged us, blades bared. This one chose his fate." The norn clapped Dougal on the back. "If it makes you feel better, I will speak well of him when I tell this part of my saga. And of the others as well."

Dougal surveyed the tunnel. The cooling corpses of the black-and-gold-uniformed guards who'd ambushed them littered the ground, their blood running down the tunnel that had brought them from the world above to spill into the river of sludge and be carried away. Most of the rats had run off as quickly as they'd come, but a few still nibbled on the bodies of the guards they'd killed.

Every one of his compatriots seemed fine. The hail of

bullets had ripped smoking channels through Ember's orange fur but not her flesh. She wiped the blood from her claws, while Gullik did the same with his axe. Killeen leaned over one of the rat-eaten guards, examining him closely. Riona knelt on one knee, staring down in abject horror at the woman she'd been battling. From the amount of the female officer's face that was missing, Dougal guessed that Ember had helped dispatch her.

Kranxx stood in front of his open pack, a bottle of bright blue fluid in his hand. "Anybody hurt?" he asked. "I've got a healing potion right here. I made it myself, and I'm eager to see how it turned out."

The asura's face fell when no one tried to claim his offered potion. "Anyone? Ember? No? All right, then." He rewrapped the potion and placed it back in his pack. "I'll just save it for later."

Dougal kicked the rats off the fallen guards, and they scampered away. Killeen noticed him shooing them away and blushed, turning a deeper shade of green.

"It's rare that I get to examine deaths this fresh," she said.

Dougal nodded, then sheathed his blade and put his head in his hands. He heard Killeen start to mutter something, but he ignored it. He needed to shut it all out for a minute.

"The Ebon Vanguard is the law in this city," Dougal said, to himself more than anyone else. "And we just killed them."

"Then it is good that we're leaving," said Ember. She arched her back and cracked her knuckles. "And better that we are not coming back."

Riona put a hand on Dougal's shoulder as he walked back toward the sewage tunnel. "I know," she said. Her voice was soft and low, but her eyes were wide and troubled: mirrors of Dougal's own. "They fired on us first. We had to defend ourselves." Unspoken was the question, *If you had listened to me—if Ember had been kept in her chains—could this have been avoided?*

Dougal grimaced as he looked down at the ruined corpse of the man he'd been fighting. He was younger than Dougal, but a stranger. If Dougal hadn't left Ebonhawke, they might have served together in the Vanguard. Now the man was dead, and although Dougal's hand hadn't been the one that had killed him, he still felt at fault.

"We need to keep moving," Ember said, heading for the dirty stream once more. "I doubt they came down here without telling anyone. There may be other patrols, and even if not, they will come looking for these people soon."

Dougal was less worried about getting away from the Vanguard now than he was about watching any more of them die. He glanced back up from the intersection and saw a guard—the woman who Riona had been fighting—back on her feet. She stood before the sylvari, who was now bathed in a greenish, necromantic glow.

"Killeen!" Dougal shouted.

The sylvari turned and flashed him a proud smile, then gestured at the guard to show Dougal her handiwork.

The creature had once been one of their foes but was now a bloodstained wreck, one arm shredded and the other obviously dislocated but still holding her sword in a literal death grip. The left side of her face had been torn from her skull, and the skin that remained was as pale as dried bone. Her eyes lolled about in her head as she moved, unseeing and unfocused, twitching with drained life.

Killeen had used her death magic. She had made the body walk again.

Killeen! Stop it!" Dougal said. "Let her go! Now!"
The ferocity of his revulsion stunned him, but he could not deny it. He'd seen the sylvari use her magics to animate corpses before, but not with someone so freshly dead, and not with a fallen member of the Ebon Vanguard.

Killeen's brow crinkled with concern. "What is it?" she said, examining the walking corpse. "Are her eyes falling out or something? I miss things like that sometimes."

Killeen's sincerity nearly deflated Dougal's anger. When he spoke again, he struggled to keep his words measured and his tone even. "Killeen," he said, "could you please let that woman rest in peace?"

"Why? Don't you think she'll make a good— Oh!" The sylvari clapped a hand to her forehead. When she pulled it away, regret twisted her face into a rueful frown. "I'm so sorry! I didn't even think about how that might offend you."

"It's all right," Dougal finally said. "Just let her go."

"No!" said Kranxx. He raced forward, peering up at the walking corpse from below. "Don't do that. She's perfect just the way she is."

"Dougal's right," said Riona, who looked just as distressed as Dougal felt. "This is beyond the pale. The guardswoman was just trying to do her job."

"And we're doing ours," said Kranxx. "There's a good chance that the sewage tunnel exit is trapped, and we could use a walking test case to send in first to check things out."

"That is exactly what I was thinking," said Killeen, obviously pleased that someone understood that she had only the best intentions.

"Trapped?" Dougal glared at Kranxx. "And why didn't you mention that before?"

Kranxx shrugged. "I didn't want to complicate the matter with other issues. I figured you—and I mean the collective 'you' here—would have a hard enough time making the right choice about how to get to Ascalon City from here without having to sift through extraneous points of data."

"Wolf's breath!" said Gullik. "We've been wading through this river of sludge to reach a tunnel of traps?"

"Some of us have," said Kranxx. "Others have remained nice and clean."

"Maybe too clean," said Ember. "You didn't dirty your hands in that fight, did you?"

Kranxx cringed at the accusation. "I was trying to get a surprise for our foes out of my pack, but the rest of you made such quick work of them that I never had the chance."

"Sure," said Ember. "Lucky you."

Kranxx bristled at her words. "The next time I pull something from my pack, just remember this: Close your eyes."

"By the time you pull something from your pack, we all will be dead," muttered the charr.

Dougal returned to Killeen. "Just let the woman go."

"Wynne," Riona said in a voice thick and raw. "I know her. I mean, I knew her. Her name was Wynne. Her father was friends with my father when we were young. He ran the armorer's shop."

Dougal couldn't look at the woman anymore. He had to turn away.

"She's dead," said Ember. "But she may still be of some use. That seems like a good way to honor her life."

"Charr or not," Dougal said, "that's the coldest rationalization I've ever heard."

"Bear's blood!" said Gullik. "I've never heard a pack of warriors natter on so like a gaggle of old women squabbling over their weaving."

The norn turned to Killeen. "Next time, show some more respect to those you kill. Every one of them was someone's child once."

"I wasn't," the sylvari said.

Gullik waved off her point. "You know what I mean."

To Dougal, the norn said, "The deed is done. Rather than fight over that, let's make some use of it. Or would you prefer one of us to wind up sharing that woman's fate?"

Dougal groaned and looked at Wynne once more. Blood covered her from her head to her knees, to which she'd fallen after Ember had delivered the killing blow. Her mangled face was recognizable, but only just.

"All right," he said, shaking his head as he spoke. "Put her . . . it . . . in the front. Then we don't have to look at her face."

"What about the rest of them?" Riona said. "Do we just leave them like this? To be eaten by the rats?"

Dougal gave her a pained shrug. He shared her anguish, but he didn't see what they could do to fix it. "We can't burn them down here, and we can't bury them in stone. Someone will come looking for them soon enough." He grimaced. "We need to be as far away from here as we can be by then, if only so we aren't forced to thin the Vanguard's numbers even more."

Killeen put the shambling, dead Wynne in the lead. The sylvari followed right after her, with Kranxx on her heels. Riona trailed after them, and Dougal remained in the back of the line of people who could fit onto the walkway. Trudging through the stream, Ember and then Gullik swept along behind the rest of them.

They made their way through the last section of the sewer, which seemed to wind on forever. Dougal kept peering into the darkness, hoping to see even the faintest glow of light.

The first clue he had that they were near the exit was the way the walls of the tunnel seemed to vibrate in a tone lower than his ears could hear. He could feel it in the air, though, and eventually through the soles of his boots.

The silent thrumming slowly grew in pitch and volume until it became a dull roar. This, Dougal knew, must be the sound of the stream spilling out of the tunnel and tumbling down onto the mountainside beyond.

"We should be coming up on it soon," Kranxx said. Dougal detected a hint of worry in the asura's voice.

"You don't know? Haven't you been here before?" asked Riona.

"Of course not," said Kranxx. "Don't you know how dangerous this is? I've studied the maps many times, though."

Dougal did not find that reassuring. He was about to say something about it when Wynne disappeared.

The walkway in front of them had tilted under their weight. Pitching forward, it had thrown Wynne into the fast-moving waters. She floundered about at the surface for a moment, flapping her dead arms in some horrible mockery of an attempt to swim, and then disappeared beneath the surface.

Killeen screamed as she nearly toppled in after her undead servant. When the walkway tipped downward, she lost her balance and spun her arms in a vain attempt to recover it. Moving faster than Dougal had thought he could, Kranxx leaned forward, bending at the waist, and tapped Killeen on the shoulder with the hook attached to his back.

Killeen managed to snag the hook with her hand, but instead of the hook hauling her back, her weight pulled Kranxx forward, dragging him along to share her fate. However, this gave Dougal enough time to react, and he pushed past Riona to snag the asura by the top of his pack. For a moment he thought he might tumble in after the others, and the trap would manage to kill all three of them at once. But he dug in his heels and leaned back hard, bringing their forward progress to a halt. With Riona's help, he yanked both Kranxx and Killeen back to a solid part of the walkway, where they all collapsed in a heap.

"The bottom of the stream must drop off just ahead too," said Ember. "I can feel the undertow from here."

"Thanks for saying something before it became a problem," Riona said as she struggled to catch her breath.

Dougal checked to make sure the others were all right, then knelt down to examine the floor and see what had happened. Kranxx stood next to him, giving him plenty of light to work with.

There was a hinge on the floor, almost impossible to see, especially by a lantern's light. Dougal recognized the type of trap they'd triggered, and he cursed.

"Bear's breath! What's wrong now?" Gullik asked. "This filth is too cold to just stand here in it!"

"Lots of traps only work once," Dougal said. "This one resets itself automatically. From this hinge here onward, the walkway is actually a ramp. A set of counterweights underneath it holds it up horizontally, right up until there's enough weight on the end of the ramp. Then the ramp tips forward and dumps you right into the worst part of the sludge."

"And then you die," said Ember.

Dougal shook his head. "And then you find yourself trapped against the grating that covers the end of the tunnel, held up against it by the force of thousands of pounds of filthy water pressing you into it until you drown."

"And then you die," said Killeen.

Dougal nodded. "And then you're held there until your body rots enough for the water pressure to tear you into pieces so small that you flow out through the grate with the rest of Ebonhawke's waste."

Dougal pointed at Kranxx's glowing light. "Can you put that out?"

Kranxx pulled a heavy sack from his pack and hooded the stone with it, blocking its glow. Dougal stared ahead into the darkness until his eyes adjusted to it.

"Yes," he said, "I can see some light up ahead. I think we're near the entrance."

"Good," said Riona. "Now we just need to figure out how to get there—without dying."

Dougal glanced around, and his eyes fell on Gullik. He pointed at the norn's axe and said, "Give me that."

"You're as mad as Raven," said Gullik. "No warrior gives up his weapon until the fight is finished."

"I'm going to use it to fight the trap." Dougal put out his hands. "Trust me."

Gullik screwed up his lips as he evaluated the man and the moment, then reversed his axe and handed it to Dougal by the handle. "I expect it back in one piece."

Holding the weapon, Dougal realized just how heavy the thing was. He wasn't sure he could swing it over his head. Fortunately, he didn't have to.

He set the axe down on the walkway, then lowered himself into the sludge. It was just as nasty as it had been before. No matter how much he braced himself for the stench and the cold, it was horrible.

He took the axe and put it headfirst into the sludge before Gullik could stop him. Then he bent down deeper into the sludge until it came up to the tops of his shoulders. With a bit of wiggling, he managed to wedge the ax up under the ramp. He tested it for a moment, then let go. It was jammed in there hard enough that it stuck.

"I want my axe back," Gullik said. "I haven't lost a weapon since an icebrood I was fighting took my spear from me and used it as a toothpick."

"I just need to release the grating," said Dougal. "Then you can have it back."

He climbed out of the muck again and then beckoned Kranxx to come with him. "I need your lamp," he said, "and you're light enough to not trigger the trap with me." He looked past the aura. "The rest of you stay here. We'll be right back."

Dougal worked his way forward along the ramp on his hands and knees, waiting for the axe's handle to snap or to feel the telltale tipping sensation that meant his life would soon end. As he drew closer to the end of the ramp, he saw the outside.

The sewer exited the mountainside beneath a rocky overhang, which was why they could not see any daylight sooner. Even so, the light seemed muted, and Dougal guessed that the valley beyond the grate was probably still deep in shadow. The end of the sewer was sealed with an iron grate that had been coated with rust and slime over the past two centuries. The water surged through the grate, forming a cascade of muck that disappeared in fog below. The grate swung outward, but there was a lock on the grate that functioned only from this side, and it looked serviceable enough.

With Kranxx's light over his shoulder, Dougal crept forward until he could reach the grate and put his weight on it instead. It held as steady as the rocks in which it was anchored. He slipped his pouch of lock picks out of its pocket in his jacket and went to work. Because of the rust and filth, it took him another half-minute longer than it should have to force the lock to give, but it did.

The grate, however, was stuck.

Dougal smacked it with his hand, but that didn't do a thing. Then he tried a shoulder, but that only bruised his arm. Standing up, he charged right at it.

It gave, suddenly and too well.

As the grate swung wide, Dougal lost his footing on the wobbly ramp and pitched forward. Kranxx reached for him with the hook but missed. Unable to recover his balance, Dougal did the only thing he could think of instead: he kicked off from the ramp and stretched out into the gaping maw of fog and shadow before him.

His fingers closed on the slimy, slippery bars of the grate as it swung away from him, and he clung to them for his life. He glanced down below his dangling feet and saw that he hung over a dizzying drop that deposited Ebonhawke's sewage onto a cluster of jagged rocks. Despite himself, he shouted in terror, sure that he would not be able to maintain his tenuous grip on the treacherous grate.

"Hold on!" Riona said.

He could not turn to see what she and the others were

doing, but he hoped it involved saving his life, and soon. A moment later he heard Kranxx's voice saying, "What? Wait! No!"

Then the asura came sailing past Dougal's head and straight over the grate. A rope attached to his waist drew taut, and someone on the other end of it held it fast so that Kranxx did not tumble to his death. Then that same someone yanked on the rope to bring Kranxx closer.

Once Kranxx had the grate in his grip, Dougal glanced back to see that both Ember and Gullik held the far end of the rope and were pulling hard. The grate swung shut with a satisfying clang, and the flowing sewage pushed the lower half of Dougal's body hard up against it. He used this opportunity to find a foothold and then haul himself up out of the flowage.

"Thanks!" Dougal shouted backward.

"Hey! What about me?" Kranxx shouted from the other side of the grate.

"What can you see, Kranxx?" Dougal asked.

"That I'm about to die!"

"No, I mean down below you. Is there any way to get down from here?"

"Sure, lots!"

"That doesn't involve dying."

"That narrows it down quite a bit. Hold on!" Kranxx swung himself around on the end of the rope and craned his neck at all angles. "Hard to see through all the mist. Looks like a fairly sheer drop down about fifty feet or more."

The asura rummaged around in his pack and

produced another coil of rope. He tied one end securely to the grate and let the other end play out below him. Dougal worked his way over to where the lock stood. "Let out the rope," he said to Gullik and Ember. "Slowly!"

They did, and the pressure from the flowing sewage pushed the grate open on its hinges again. Once the gap was wide enough, Dougal swung himself around to the other side of the grate and grabbed on to the rope.

"Why didn't you get started down?" he asked Kranxx.

"Slide down on a filth-slick rope into a monster-infested wilderness?" The asura shook his head. "You go first."

Dougal motioned for Ember and Gullik to let the rope play out until the grate swung back far enough that it no longer hung over the sewage-coated rocks below. Then he stuck out one leg and wrapped the rope around it. He checked Kranxx's knot and found it solid, then lowered himself down.

The going was easy at first, until he got to the section of the rope that had dangled in the flowage. It was slick and nasty. Dougal had already been covered with so much filth that he didn't care much about the stench, but he had to hold on with all his might to keep from sliding down too fast. This soon proved impossible. No matter how he tried to clamp his hands on the rope, it was too slippery, and down he went in a barely controlled slide.

Dougal hit the ground hard, his legs buckling underneath him, but he rolled with the impact. He lost his grip on the rope and feared for a moment that he would tumble back into the pool at the base of the falls, or into a deep crevasse hidden in the darkness. He came to a stop, though, against a wall of jagged boulders instead.

The charr warband that had been waiting there burst out from behind the rocks and surrounded him in an instant.

16

Dougal cried out in surprise and leaped to his feet. Before he could draw his sword, one of the charr knocked him back down again, sending him sprawling face-first into the dirt. Another leaped onto his back, pinning him there.

"Scream, human, and I rip out your throat," the charr hissed in his ear.

Dougal wasn't sure he could draw enough air to scream with anyhow, so he nodded in assent. He tried to get a count of how many charr there were but, lying facedown on the ground, it proved impossible. Most warbands had less than twenty members, to keep them mobile, but there were always exceptions.

Dougal tried to raise his head to get a better look, and a paw drove his face back into the hardscrabble dirt. He grunted in pain and felt the tip of a claw pressed into the softest part of his throat.

Kranxx came down the rope next, more slowly than Dougal had managed. He landed softly and peered into the dun-colored mists. "Dougal?" he called.

Following Dougal's path across the dirt, the asura strode closer to the pool of shadow that the stand of boulders provided. "Don't tell me that after all that you broke your leg coming down that rope."

A pair of charr reached out from the shadows and pulled Kranxx in. If he had a chance to struggle, Dougal didn't hear it. He could, however, hear the others still in the tunnel above, even over the splashing of the sewage into the rocky pool below.

"Bear's buttocks!" Gullik said. "Give me a hand with retrieving my axe."

"The rest of you go," said Ember. "We will meet you below."

A moment later, the rope began wriggling again, and Killeen descended to the ground. "Dougal?" she said, sounding not scared but concerned. "Kranxx? Where are you?"

Dougal tensed to ready himself for a yell, but the charr on top of him jabbed his neck with his claw. Dougal felt warm wetness slowly trickle out of a fresh cut on his throat and onto the ground.

Riona appeared next to the sylvari then. In an instant she had out her sword, and she stared warily into the surrounding darkness. "Dougal?" she said. "This is not in the slightest bit funny."

The charr not holding down Dougal and Kranxx emerged from the surrounding fog and foliage then, showing Riona and Killeen that they had them surrounded on all sides, save for that of the fetid pool at their backs. Both women kept their hands away from their weapons and craned their necks to catch sight of Dougal or the asura.

"Yes!" Gullik shouted from above. "My axe is free!"

"Don't kiss it," Ember said in disgust.

One of the charr stood back and bellowed up at the pair in the tunnel. "We hear you up there, and we have your friends! Come down here now—and leave that grate open—or they die."

At first, Dougal heard nothing but some urgent whispers between Ember and Gullik. Then she spoke: "I am Ember Doomforge, and I answer only to General Almorra Soulkeeper."

"Ah! A charr? I should have guessed. I am Scorkin Bladebreaker of the Blade Warband, Blood Legion," said the charr who'd spoken before. "Good work! We have your prisoners captive. Join us, and we will plan our assault on Ebonhawke together."

Dougal squirmed under the charr holding him down but could not get free. He hadn't considered the possibility that Ember might leave the sewer grate open behind them so that the charr could slip into Ebonhawke. His captor wrestled him into a sitting position.

Ember leaped from the tunnel and caught the rope where it dangled below the grate, then zipped down it to land in the center of the clearing. She stood tall and pointed at Bladebreaker as she spoke. "These people you've captured are part of my mission, and you will leave them to me."

"I know of your Soulkeeper and her Vigil," Bladebreaker said. "What fool's errand brings you here?"

"That I cannot reveal," said Ember.

Bladebreaker sneered, "Then you may go on your way. We will take care of your prisoners for you."

Ember stalked closer to Bladebreaker. "You misunderstand. They are coming with me."

"Wait," Bladebreaker said suspiciously. "Are they your prisoners, or are you theirs?"

Ember snarled at the implication. "Neither. We work together as part of the Vigil, and you must allow us to pass."

Bladebreaker snorted. "You are free to go where you like, Doomforge, but I cannot allow these 'friends' of yours to wander free through Ascalon."

"You will let us pass. All of us." There was menace in Ember Doomforge's voice.

"Do you challenge me?" Bladebreaker's stance made it clear he relished that thought.

Ember let out a laughing growl. "Do you not think I would enjoy tearing these weaklings to pieces and then helping you storm Ebonhawke from within? I ache to exact revenge on our ancient foes, but I am after bigger game."

Dougal could not tell if Ember was bluffing or not, but for the first time Bladebreaker took a step backward, surprised. "Bigger game than the thorn of Ebonhawke? The city our people have laid siege to for over two hundred years?"

Ember ignored Bladebreaker's disbelief and nodded.

Bladebreaker gaped at her, then drew his jaws together into a determined wall of pointed teeth. "These are my prisoners."

"These are my allies," said Ember. "I challenge you for their lives."

"Accepted," said Bladebreaker. "Challenge, then, and all is fair."

Ember drew her sword, its wet blade shining. With a gesture, she directed Riona and Killeen to retreat to the edge of the sewage pond. The other charr motioned with their own weapons and the two women reluctantly complied. Both were somber, and Dougal knew each was looking for an opportunity to turn the tables on their captors.

"I tell you that I must bring these people with me and that my orders come from General Soulkeeper herself," said Ember, hefting her blade as if it were a trifle. "You must accept what I say. Or you must die for your error."

Bladebreaker drew his sword too. It was filthy black but for its single sharpened edge. The pair approached each other with the care of priests observing an ancient ritual. When they were within three feet of each other, they reached out with their swords and slapped them together. The sharp sound rang out through the narrow valley. From there, the fight was on.

Dougal looked around to see the charr engrossed in watching the fight, paying far more attention to it than to their foes. Kranxx had been allowed to sit up, too, and he had his massive pack in his lap, his arms hugging it possessively. Over by the pond, Riona stood tensed, her hand drifting to the pommel of her blade, and whispered to Killeen.

Ember struck first, charging Bladebreaker with her sword held high. He raised his weapon to parry it, but she brought her blow down so hard that her blade still glanced off the spiked armor on his shoulder. He countered with an underhanded swipe of his off hand that sliced across Ember's belly. His claws slashed through her fur in three parallel lines.

Ember howled, less in pain than protest, and rolled backward out of Bladebreaker's range. She wiped a hand across her middle, and it came back streaked with red.

Ember charged at Bladebreaker again, hammering at him with her sword. She fought unlike any human Dougal had ever seen. She brought every bit of her strength and speed into play and moved like a furious blur. She gave no thought to fending off a counterblow or to raising any sort of defense. She simply attacked, attacked, attacked.

Bladebreaker didn't seem as if he had a chance. Ember knocked him back on his heels with her first strike, and he never recovered. All he could do was offer up the best defense he could muster, unable to counter her fury.

Then Bladebreaker lived up to his name.

Dougal hadn't realized it, but Ember's ferocious attack had played perfectly into Bladebreaker's hands. Every time she swung her sword at him, he swung back, seeking the weakest point of her blade and striking it there. Eventually, he knew, his strategy would work, as long as she didn't kill him first.

On Ember's last stroke, Bladebreaker brought the edge of his sword around to meet the flat of hers. The blade shattered into several pieces, leaving her holding little more than a shard jutting from her hilt. She stared at it in shock for an instant and then moved to defend herself against Bladebreaker's own vicious attack.

Dougal tried to get up and help, but the charr holding him sat him back down hard. Riona and Killeen moved to assist Ember as well, but the charr on either side of them moved to block them. Dougal glanced at Kranxx and saw the asura slowly and quietly rummaging in his pack, the charr guarding him too busy cheering on Bladebreaker to notice.

Bladebreaker pressed his advantage as hard as he could. He wasn't nearly the warrior that Ember was, but he had a weapon and she did not. Ember blocked his blows as best she could with the hilt of her shattered sword. She had her claws extended and ready, but she could not find a way around Bladebreaker's flashing sword to slice into his flesh.

Forced to retreat, Ember stumbled over an unseen rock behind her and fell flat on her back. She reached to her side and her paw came up with her pistol, heavy and deadly. She pulled the trigger and there was a dull, mud-stained click. Ember cursed.

Bladebreaker raised his weapon high above his head to deliver the killing blow, but before he could bring down his arms, a loud clang sounded high overhead.

Dougal looked up to see that Gullik had slammed the grate over the sewer's exit shut and had cut the rope free to fall in the pool below. The norn belted out a bellow filled with the joy of battle as he kicked off from the grating, angling toward a tiny ledge on the cliff face below. He snagged it with his hand as he passed and used the momentum to swing his feet high about in the air, catapulting himself away from the wall and toward the clearing below. As he landed near Ember and Bladebreaker, he hurled his axe forward, and it caught the leader of the charr warband right in the center of his chest.

Bladebreaker stood there for a moment, staring at the weapon that seemed to have magically appeared with its blade already embedded several inches in his armor. He opened his mouth to say something but discovered he could not, then toppled over dead.

There was silence by the pool, save for the splash of the cut rope finally reaching the water.

"You idiot!" Ember screamed at the norn as she threw herself to her feet. "I only win the argument if *I* kill him."

Gullik gave her a wide and toothy grin. "Then I suppose that means the winner is me." He pointed at the rest of the charr. "Off with the lot of you, now, or I'll win arguments with each of you, too!"

The other charr joined in a horrific roar so loud that it pained Dougal's ears. Ember was right: had she slain the leader, the rest of the band would have been cowed enough to let them go. But now, incensed at the norn's insult more than Bladebreaker's death, they closed in as one and growled for Gullik's flesh.

Gullik then realized that he was unarmed, his axe still stuck in Bladebreaker's chest. "Ho!" he said, holding his hands up and grinning wider than ever. "Now *this* shall be a true challenge!" As he spoke, he attained his bear form, hairier and more massive, his hands becoming wicked claws.

The charr who had been holding Dougal jumped up to join his warband in tearing the norn apart. Seizing his chance, Dougal leaped to his feet, his sword instantly in his hand. The blade made no sound as it left its sheath, but Dougal's former guard caught sight of him drawing his weapon and spun around, drawing his own blade.

Dougal's head swam from getting up too fast after having had a charr crushing him for so long. He put his sword before him and hoped that the charr would not see its black blade and impale himself on it in his fury.

Before that could happen, Kranxx stood up and threw something into the middle of the clearing. It fizzed and sparked as it rolled to land near Gullik's hind legs.

"An asura invention!" Gullik said. "Would you look at that?"

"Eyes!" Kranxx shouted at the top of his lungs.

Dougal remembered to close his eyes tight. The flash from the device's detonation was so bright that even through his eyelids it nearly blinded him.

Dougal blinked away the few dots before his eyes and saw the charr all around the clearing clutching their faces and snarling in pain and frustration. This would not be a fair fight, he knew, but it never had been.

Dougal's blade slid easily into the neck of the charr who had cut him and then came right back out again, along with the charr's last breath. Another charr came stumbling at Dougal, swinging his sword blindly while homing in on his dying friend's final cry. Dougal steeled himself to the task, waited for the right moment, then ran the charr through.

Riona slew three of the charr herself, with the quick efficiency of a warrior who had seen far too much of battle and wanted this one to end quickly. Killeen intoned a spell that caused three more of their assailants to rot to death before her eyes. Kranxx spilled no blood, instead rooting around in his pack for some other trick to use. Gullik regained his natural form, pulled his axe from Bladebreaker's chest, and used it to split the last of the enemy charr in half.

Ember stood amid the carnage, roaring in frustration. She snatched up Bladebreaker's sword and waved it at the dying charr, but she did not use it against them.

"This did not have to happen!" she shouted at the other charr, not caring if any of them could still hear her. "You did not have to die. If you had just listened to me, we could have been on our way, and you would all have lived to try your luck against Ebonhawke another day." Then she pierced Bladebreaker with his own blade.

Again silence in the valley, save for the falling mire behind them.

Dougal came over to stand near Ember, although he stayed out of reach of her blade. "I know how you feel. I felt the same about the Vanguard in the sewer," he said.

"That's nothing like this," Ember said.

"Except that it is exactly," Riona said from over near the pond. She wiped her blade clean before returning it to its scabbard.

"No, it's not," Ember snarled. "You regret killing your people. I regret that my people were so foolish. Let us leave them to the scavengers."

"Not all of them are foolish," said Dougal, and as if to punctuate his words, distant horns sounded: a charr unit on the march.

"That's another patrol of the Blood Legion," said Ember. "They expect a response." She moved among the bodies and pulled a slightly bent warhorn from among the corpses. She raised it to her lips.

Riona took a step forward, but Dougal stopped her from saying anything. Ember let out a long, low blast, repeating the notes from the first horn they heard. There was a pause, then the distant horns sounded again, apparently in a different direction. Farther off, there was a similar response.

"That bought us some time," said Ember. "They won't know anything is amiss until the day's end, when the warbands return to camp. When they find that this warband has been slaughtered, they'll set out to hunt us down and kill us all."

Dougal glanced up. The sun had finally topped their canyon valley and turned the spattering waterfall into a rainbow of gems. They would have to find a secure place quickly.

"In that case," he said, "we'd better get moving."

17

The fetid stream from the sewer pond seeped into a dank mire before they even left the valley. They hugged the mountain's foothills, trying not to attract any attention while putting as much distance as possible between themselves and the grated sewer pipe.

The day was warmer now, and the filth that permeated their clothes and hair stiffened and flaked off, losing none of its pungency in the process. Dougal was pleased that the charr sense of smell was not as vaunted as legend said, but was aware that even a group of asura with head colds could smell them from a league away.

"Bah," said Gullik, swatting at a small cloud of flies that had adopted his offal-stained braids. "You would think we were grawl, for all that these flies love us!"

"More importantly, we need to find cover for the rest of the day," said Ember. "This area is riddled with box canyons like the one the sewer let out of. On occasion one of our warbands would investigate them as an excuse to get out of the sun."

"This way," suggested Killeen, pointing to a particularly nondescript cleft in the stone.

"Your Dream?" said Riona.

"Something like that," said the sylvari, but she sounded distracted.

The haze of the morning had thickened as they moved, and now a thick layer of grim clouds covered the steel-gray sky. Ember led them up a gully cut by a shallow creek and discovered a pool at the far end. They waded into the water fully clothed and rinsed out the worst of the foulness, then changed and laid out the wet clothes to dry. They nestled there under the shelter of the gully's winding walls, checking and drying their weapons and armor, and gnawing on cold rations.

Ember bit off a short curse. "Bathing in that sewer destroyed half my powder. I don't know if I can trust the rest." She swept the damp cartridges off the rock she was using as a worktable and carefully repacked the remaining shot and powder.

"I use a paper soaked in beeswax," suggested Kranxx, snapping the wetness out of his muck-spattered hat. "Didn't lose a thing."

"I know that we're all exhausted, but we should only rest for a few hours before pressing on," said Riona.

Dougal shook his head. "The charr patrols are most active during the day, and that's when they can see the farthest. You saw those hills in the distance, when we came out? A charr lookout atop one of those can see for miles in any direction, and once they spot us, we're in trouble."

"Absolutely right," said Ember. "We should stay here

until dusk. We have a long path ahead of us, and the rest will do us good."

Dougal looked at Riona and said, "About the chains, you . . ."

Riona held up a hand. "Don't say it." She shook her head. "What is done is done. If we break down into might-have-beens and recriminations, we'll be worse off than we are now."

Dougal nodded. "Still, they might still be alive."

"They were doing their duty," said Ember, "and foolish enough to be in the wrong place at the wrong time. The same as the Blade warband. There was no camp back there at the sewer entrance. They were on patrol. Their bad luck, and their bad judgment. "

"It's not like they were part of your warband," said Riona, "or even your legion. Am I right?"

Ember hesitated. "No," she said at last. "They were not."

Dougal narrowed his eyes at Ember. "Charr seem to value their ranks and their legions highly. Bladebreaker identified his legion from the start. You didn't."

"So?" grunted Ember.

"So, which of the legions is yours?" asked Dougal.

"It—it does not matter," said Ember. "I work for the Vigil now."

Dougal pressed harder. "Is there a reason you won't say?"

Ember remained silent. She slid Bladebreaker's sword, now cleaned and oiled, back in her scabbard. It fit well enough.

"Are you sure you people weren't looking at my little surprise when it went off?" Kranxx said with a nasty chuckle. "Because you all seem blind. Look at her armor. Look at her mannerisms. She's from the Ash Legion, or I'm a skritt."

"Are you sure?" Riona asked. "I thought they were all assassins and spies."

Ember shot Riona a withering look, but Dougal stared at Ember. Now that he thought about it, she did look like an Ash legionnaire. Her dark clothing, her wiry build, her style of killing—it all added up.

"Not all of them are spies and assassins," Dougal said. "Just the more successful ones. Iron Legion tends to attract warbands with a flair for explosives and weapons. Blood Legion gathers the stronger, more violent types. Flame Legion still has the most spellcasters and shamans of any group."

Riona strode over to confront the charr. "Then tell us who you're really working for, Crusader Doomforge."

Dougal expected the charr to react typically, leaping to her feet and snarling threats. Instead she remained seated and just looked up at Riona. "My orders come from General Soulkeeper. Those orders are to find the Claw of the Khan-Ur and return it to her."

"But who is your real master?"

"I have no 'master,'" Ember growled. "Yes, the asura is correct: I am part of the Ash Legion. Doom Warband. My imperator is Malice Swordshadow. She personally sent me to serve with the Vigil. She knew that I would prove valuable there."

"To who?" asked Riona.

Ember shifted uncomfortably. "To Soulkeeper, of course, and—and to the Ash Legion as well."

"So you've been spying on the Vigil for the Ash Legion?" Dougal asked.

Ember paused for a moment, then nodded. "General Soulkeeper knew this from the moment I reported to her. She is no fool."

"And she let you go on with your charade despite this?" Riona's tone betrayed her disbelief.

Ember nodded. "She got what she wanted: an effective soldier ready to do her bidding. And she gave Imperator Swordshadow what she wanted: a direct report on the Vigil's activities from someone she could trust. Their interests do not conflict. No harm is done."

"But if it had been, would you have cared?" said Killeen.

"I don't much care to work with spies," observed Gullik. "Only a fool trusts someone who lies for a living."

Riona shook her head. "It is impossible to keep many masters. Eventually you must decide where your loyalty lies."

Ember responded: "Then we are fortunate we have not reached that stage yet."

There was a long moment of silence then. Dougal broke it. "Swordshadow is part of the truce faction. That's it, isn't it? That's why there is no conflict."

"I could not say," said Ember. "We did not discuss the matter."

"Because if it were known that Swordshadow supported it, there would be direct opposition from the other legions," continued Dougal.

Ember nodded and said, "There are many, among all the legions, who would accept a truce, if couched in the proper terms. But at the same time, there are many who would seek to reconcile with the Flame Legion." The rising bile in her voice indicated where she stood on the issue.

Dougal nodded. "There are those among the humans who would see us succeed, and those who prefer to see us fail as well."

Kranxx coughed and said, "Which brings up something I've been thinking about."

The gathered group looked at the asura. He was frowning and turning his hat in his hands as he spoke.

"When you lot came through the gate from Divinity's Reach, the Vanguard wasn't supposed to be there. It was supposed to be Seraph guards who were manning the post this morning, and I had an . . . arrangement, if you want to call it that, with their officer of the day. I didn't notice that the Vanguard were on the walls until after you came through and all fresh hell broke loose." He looked around at the group and his eyes eventually fell on Riona. "Somehow word of your arrival preceded you."

Riona's back stiffened. "Are you saying we have a spy among us?"

"I thought we determined that," said Killeen. "That would be Ember." Dougal shushed her.

"That would be a conclusion to which I would not immediately jump," said Kranxx, "but since you broached the matter, let us have at it. Who else knows about your recent activities?"

Riona sat down and thought about it. "Almorra, of course."

"A clam," said Kranxx. "A veritable stone. She barely

gives enough information to her subordinates, much less some outside forces."

"Others in the Vigil, then," said Riona, and Ember slowly nodded in agreement.

"A good possibility," said Kranxx, "but Almorra also tends to recruit driven, dedicated men and women." He looked at Ember, then at Riona, then said, "You snuck out this morning, Riona. Where did you go?"

"You don't think . . ." Riona started, her voice rising.

"Riona went scouting," said Dougal quickly. He didn't want the others to know about her doubts and second thoughts in this matter—not at this time, on top of everything else. "She thought there was some way down off the walls. That is where we found her, not five minutes from your door. She was . . . concerned . . . that you might not return."

"Or that I might buy my own safety for your own," said Kranxx sharply. "Don't be shy. I know asura that would sell their own birth parents for a safe bunk and a solid sinecure. I could have brought the Vanguard back with me, if that had been my intention, and spared us all a stroll through the sewers."

"I could have done the same, I suppose," said Riona. "And then there is this shared dream the sylvari has."

Killeen started, "It doesn't . . ."

"Work like that," finished Dougal, his brow furrowed. "Agreed. But we've been moving around so much, on little sleep, that I haven't thought much about what is bothering *me* about all this." He turned to Gullik, who was resting against a large boulder, watching the others talk. "How did you find me?"

The norn blanched visibly, as if Dougal had struck him. "What do you mean?"

"In Divinity's Reach," said Dougal. "I arrive there, and within the day you were in my room, drunk and loaded for bear."

Gullik smiled weakly. "I thought we had gotten beyond all that. Surely our experiences since have convinced you of my good intentions."

"How did you know?" Dougal asked, pressing hard now.

Gullik's lips disappeared as the norn obviously thought about how to phrase things. Then abandoned any hope for dissembling and said, "The asura."

"Me?" said Kranxx, surprised.

"The other one," said Gullik, "the one that was with you and Gyda when she died."

"Clagg," said Killeen, and she made the name sound like a curse.

"Clagg?" said Kranxx.

"Clagg," said Gullik, snapping his fingers as the memory settled in. "He came to me. I had been drinking. The Salty Dog was the tavern, I think. He bought me a few drinks. Told me what a wretch and a scoundrel you were and that you claimed all the credit in the battle that cost my dear cousin her life. That you denied her her story. And then he told me where to find you."

"He wound you up and let you loose," said Kranxx. "Sounds like an asura to me."

"I did say I was sorry about all that," said Gullik. "That is one reason I wanted to help you, after I sobered up."

"Did Clagg tell you how he knew where I was?" said Dougal.

"At that moment, I was not concerned with such details," said Gullik.

"And yet he knew," said Riona. "If Clagg knew where Dougal was, what else did he know about the Vigil safe house?"

"Yeah," Dougal said. "And did he get to Ebonhawke before us?"

"Asura come through the gate all the time," said Kranxx. "None of them were named Clagg, but that means nothing. He could have walked in right under my nose."

"All this is meaningless now," said Ember. "Assuming that this asura was hunting you, we probably lost him back in Ebonhawke. I would like to see him follow us through those sewers and down that cliff."

"The sewers," said Riona. "We met the gate guards there as well."

"I'm aware of that," said Kranxx. "It is not outside the realm of possibility, though it would require more initiative than I've seen from most Ebonhawkers. Present company and all that." He waved at Dougal and Riona. "But add that to the fact that a charr patrol was just waiting for us at the bottom of that waterfall. We just dropped into their laps."

"But none of them seemed to know exactly what our merry band is up to," said Dougal. "Neither the Vanguard nor the warband."

"It is possible," said Riona, "that someone knows something is going on but is not sure what it is. There are those who would be opposed to any cooperation between charr and human, regardless of purpose."

"Or who merely don't like not knowing," said Kranxx.

A silence descended on the group, broken only by Gullik's deep yawn. "Right," said Dougal. "Now that we've pounded this subject flat, let's get some rest. I'll stand watch for the first few hours."

"Not alone," said Ember.

"I'll stay up," said Killeen. "Kranxx has been up since we met him and probably needs a rest."

"That's the smartest thing I've heard since I last opened my mouth," said Kranxx, lying down and using his lumpy pack as a pillow. He dropped his hat over his face and was asleep in an instant.

"I could use a rest as well," said Riona. She leaned over Dougal and softly whispered, "Thanks." Then she found a comfortable spot, not too far from where Ember curled up on herself, and was soon breathing deeply herself.

Dougal looked at Riona and wondered how long this calm would last before their next storm. Probably until he did something she didn't like, he thought.

He looked near the entrance to their small oasis and Killeen was there, cross-legged in the sun and perfectly still. She could be asleep, or dead, for all her outward appearance showed. He walked over and saw that although her eyes were open, her eyelids did not move. She did not blink, and Dougal wondered if the sylvari did that just to reassure other races.

Dougal cleared his throat and Killeen closed her eyes, then opened them again. Suddenly they were luminous and full of life once more. "Is there a problem, Dougal Keane?" she said. "You think me a spy?"

"No," said Dougal, "but I do want to talk to you about what you did back there."

"With the guard. Wynne." She dropped her chin to her chest in a very human impersonation of a pout. "I meant no harm. It was the same thing that I did before, beneath Lion's Arch, with that skeleton. And it served the same purpose: to set off a trap so we would not suffer from it. But as a result, now Crusader Riona is irritated at me." She looked at him with her luminous eyes. "As, I suspect, you are."

"Not irritated," said Dougal, "disturbed. Necromancers among the humans have been considered rather unsettling for centuries, even though they work in magic like elementalists, mesmers, and other practitioners."

"Yet, among my people it is just a type of magic," said Killeen, "no different than divination or golemancy or any of the strange mathematical offshoots that the asura practice."

"I think that's part of it," said Dougal. "The asura look strange, so they aren't really judged the same way. You look a bit more like us, and therefore . . ." He let his voice trail off, unsure where to go next.

"When we act differently, it reminds you how separate we really are as a people," she said.

"Pretty much," said Dougal. "In the future, I want you to think about how others will react to what you do."

"So you're saying," said Killeen, "you *don't* want me to turn you into a zombie once you die."

"I think the others would be disturbed by that," said Dougal. "And you shouldn't turn any of them into the undead, either."

"Not even Ember?" said Killeen, her words belied by her smile.

"Not even Ember," said Dougal.

"If you wish," said Killeen, and turned back to watch the entrance niche to the valley.

"Good," said Dougal, and when Killeen did not add anything, he walked a couple paces away and added, "Good."

He found his own spot, in the shade, from which to watch both Killeen and the entrance as well as the others. It was as close to tranquility as he could hope to find, here beyond the walls of Ebonhawke, on the verge of enemy territory.

He shook his head. Gullik was right: the differences of this group could tear it apart. Ember was loyal to the Ash Legion, known for their secretive ways. Riona was both warm and cold to him by turn, and probably was going through all the same conflicted feelings he felt. Killeen was sometimes brilliant, sometimes out of step with everyone else. He knew nothing about Kranxx other than he had just gotten them out of a sealed city.

And Gullik himself seemed much deeper than his bumpkin norn exterior appeared. Was there more going on with him as well?

Dougal let out a deep sigh and wondered how they would even reach Ascalon City, much less find the Claw. Even if it was where he thought it was.

He did not mean to fall asleep in the warm afternoon

shade, but Killeen was suddenly there, touching him on the shoulder.

"I thought I should wake you first," she said. "I didn't want the others to know you drifted off."

Dougal stood up and yawned and checked the sun. The shadows of the valley wall were just touching the far side of the vale, but it would be several hours before it was dark enough to move. Stretching, he stumbled off to wake Riona and Ember and then get himself some guiltless sleep.

18

Keep moving!" Ember growled the words through her fangs as she forged through the darkness of the mountainside and into the vast valley of Ascalon below. "If one of those patrols catches sight of us, we're finished." The moon was filling out now, and even behind its shroud of pallid clouds, its light made travel easy.

The charr led the way through the shattered landscape, and Dougal chased right after her, with Riona nipping at his heels. Killeen came next, moving her shorter legs faster just so she could keep up. In the rear, Gullik had given up trying to hustle the even shorter Kranxx along and had scooped up the asura and set him to ride on the norn's broad shoulders.

"Wolf's teeth!" said Gullik, a little too loud. "We should turn this hunt around and kill them all instead!"

"Shush!" Riona said. "They can find us as easily by sound as sight."

"Bring them on!" Gullik said, louder than ever. "I will bathe in their blood!"

Kranxx rapped the norn in the ear. "This is simple math," Kranxx said. "There are six of us. Each warband has up to twenty members. Ember? How many warbands are there in southern Ascalon?"

The charr answered without looking back. "The Iron Legion has centered here since being charged with the siege of Ebonhawke. They and the Blood Legion both have responsibility for the patrols. Count in some Ash Legion detachments as scouts. Probably hundreds of warbands roam the region."

"Right. That makes for thousands of charr wandering these lands. What happens when one of them finds us?"

"And they say the asura are as smart as Raven!" Gullik laughed. "We kill them, of course!"

"I'm sure we will, but what will they do first?" asked Kranxx.

"Quiver before our might!"

"And?"

"Quake too?"

Frustrated, Kranxx spoke slowly, enunciating each word. "They'll make noise. They'll sound the alarm. They'll bring more of their kind."

"Raven's eye! I do believe you're right!" Gullik tried to keep a straight face.

"So," Kranxx said ignoring the norn's bemused expresion, "discretion is the better part of . . . ?"

"Battle!"

"Valor," corrected the asura.

"And why might that be?"

Kranxx grabbed his head with his hands and nearly fell off of Gullik's shoulders. "It means that it's better to understand what you are up against before you get into a fight. It involves gathering intelligence, thinking broadly, and figuring the odds."

"Fine, friend Kranxx!" Gullik twisted his neck to grin up in the asura's direction. "I shall permit you to do the figuring and to tell me when a battle is too odd!"

Kranxx clapped a hand over his mouth to keep from cursing.

Dougal chuckled as he strove to keep up with Ember. The charr was as fast and nimble as a mountain cat, and she had a longer gait, so keeping pace with her, even in the darkness, took some sweat.

The ground was fairly open, dotted by small copses of trees and the foundations of ancient habitations. Occasionally there would be a weathered crater, a remnant of a centuries-old battle between the humans and charr. Sometimes the center of the crater was empty, and sometimes the water that had gathered in the hollow winked like a crystal in the wan light. The grass reached up to Dougal's calves and in the daytime probably sported a host of wildflower blossoms.

They kept to moonlit sides of the hills, risking detection to keep from spilling into unseen pitfalls and gullies.

The six moved silently through the dusk and into the night, now not speaking unless necessary. The blue-white shades of the shrouded moon were only interrupted by the towers of flame erupting from the distant charr camps. These lit the undersides of the clouds, and the reflection of that light washed everything in a faint, fiery orange.

Sometime after midnight, Ember signaled for a halt. The others froze, then followed her to hunker down in the shadows of a skeletal charr war wagon, its frame long since scavenged for parts and left rusting in the moonlight. Silently she pointed toward a torch she had seen burning in the night. As they remained hidden, it wound closer.

Dougal glanced over to see Gullik fingering his axe, ready to leap into action at the slightest hint that they had been spotted. Killeen put her hand on the norn's wrist—which looked like a child reaching out to hold her father's hand—and he stopped.

As the torch drew closer, Dougal heard a number of charr voices growling and snarling at each other. The voices grew louder for a while and then tapered off as the torchlight faded in the distance. When it seemed safe, Dougal tapped Ember on the elbow, and she nodded and stood up. They spoke in whispers.

"That was a patrol from the Iron Legion," she said.

"Were they looking for us?" asked Dougal.

Ember shook her head. "No. Not yet."

Dougal had to agree. There was no tension among the Iron Legion charr. They moved like night watchmen making their regular rounds, neither expecting trouble nor encountering any.

They waited another ten minutes before Ember gave the signal to head out.

As a gray dawn threatened to break over the mountains far to the east, Ember steered them to higher ground and found a cave for them to hide in.

"Wolf's haunches, I do not care for burrowing into a dredge-hole!" Gullik said.

Riona nodded. "If a patrol finds us here, we'll have no place to run."

"This is Ascalon," said Ember. "We charr own every bit of it but the place we came from and the place we're going to. There are no places for us to run."

"At least it will be cool," said Kranxx. "My next research project must include methods for capturing the incredible heat that norn give off when exerting themselves."

"And the cave mouth faces south, so I can see the sun," Killeen said with a smile.

"And there's a great view," said Dougal. He gazed back over where they'd been. Far to the south, he could still see the peaks of the mountains in which Ebonhawke nestled. The mountains had given way to gentler foothills, like the one they were holed up in now. Once there had been forests here, but the war had ravaged the earth, and now verdant grasses had covered these rolling lands.

Dougal had not come this way out to Ascalon City the first time around—five years earlier, he and his friends had crossed through the Shiverpeaks instead—but he had studied maps of Ascalon for much of his life. On the other side of the hill, he knew, the land would become even easier until he and the others would find themselves racing across wide, open plains. Then they would be at the most vulnerable, with few places to hide; but if they stuck to moving at night, he thought they might be able to manage it.

"Get as much rest as you can," said Ember. "We will move out at noon."

"What? Why?" asked Dougal. Before he could say

more, Gullik cut him off with a tremendous snore that echoed through the cave.

Riona nodded and spoke up to be heard over the rumbling. "I thought you said that traveling during the day would be dangerous."

"Yes, but we are close to the Dragonbrand," Ember said. "We would be better off not attempting to cross it at night."

Riona caught Dougal's eye and signaled that she would take the first shift today, along with Ember. He was too tired to realize that there wouldn't be a second, and he leaned against the back of the cave and tried to ignore the norn's snoring.

The time passed so fast that when Dougal woke up, he felt as if he'd not slept at all. He felt a hand covering his mouth, and his eyes flew wide open to see Riona hunched before him, a finger pressed to her lips. After Dougal nodded that he understood, Riona removed her hand from his face, and he sat up. She stood up and beckoned him to follow her. They crept past Ember, who watched them silently with her large eyes, then rose to follow them.

Riona led Dougal to the mouth of the cave, where she knelt down and pointed at a pair of pale figures meandering up the hill in the light of the breaking dawn. Dougal rubbed the sleep from his eyes and squinted down at the figures: an old shepherd and his young apprentice. For a heartbeat he wondered how such people could have possibly brought their flock this deep into Ascalon, and he even gazed around, looking for the sheep. Then he realized what the shepherds really were.

Dougal signaled for Riona to follow him back into the cave. When they reached Ember, they spoke in whispers.

"They're ghosts," Dougal said. "They must have been working the fields around here when Adelbern brought down the Foefire."

Riona rasped. "And their spirits have been trapped out here for over two centuries. Horrible."

"They seem harmless," said Ember.

Dougal shook his head. "Anything but. I run into a lot of ghosts in my line of work. Most restless spirits have some sort of reason for hanging around a place: an unfinished task, a wrong that needs righting, and so on. They're often coherent, and you can hold a reasonable conversation with them. They can be obsessive, or angry, but they're sane—sane for ghosts, at least."

"And those two are not?" asked Riona.

"The spirits created by the Foefire are frozen in time. To them, it's still the day of the Foefire, Adelbern is still their king, and the charr are still threatening at the gates."

"Like in Ebonhawke today," said Riona softly, but both Dougal and Ember ignored her.

Dougal continued. "When they run into someone still alive, they see that person as charr, or at best an ally of the charr. It doesn't matter who or what the person really is. It could be Queen Jennah herself, or a sylvari. To them, every person who invades their space is charr."

"The Foefire killed every human in the entire country," Ember said. "The Sorcerer-King's atrocity extended far beyond his city's walls."

Dougal nodded. "It affected every bit of the nation except for Ebonhawke."

"What should we do about them?" Riona asked.

"Nothing, unless they come into the cave," Dougal said. "We don't need a fight with them."

"That's too bad," Ember said. She moved back into the cave and picked up Bladebreaker's sword. The two humans followed her.

"You can't tell me you're going to go hunt those ghosts down," Riona said, shocked.

"I don't need to," Ember said, pointing her snout over Dougal's shoulder. "They're already here."

As Dougal spun about, the two spirits entered the cave and froze there in its mouth. They looked much as Dougal supposed they had in their breathing days, but with every ounce of life drained out of them. They were pale reflections of their former selves, and they trailed wisps of pale bluish ectoplasm behind them as if blasted by a wind only they could feel. It made them look as if they were constantly burning, and the way their faces contorted with rage and pain only added to that impression.

"Charr!" the old shepherd's ghost said. He brought his crooked staff forward and unleashed an inhuman screech.

"Kill them!" The young shepherd drew the sword at his hip and charged forward, matching the other ghost's cry in a horrible harmony that Dougal feared might make his ears bleed.

The others in the cave awoke in an instant. None of them, including Dougal and Riona, could do a thing before Ember threw herself between the two ghosts and began slashing about, her blade and claws cutting clean through their spectral forms as if they were no more than mist.

The ghosts' twinned screeches rose higher and higher in pitch until Dougal felt his eyes start to roll back in their sockets. Ember's snarls and growls added to the cacophony.

Ember yelped as the ghosts' pale weapons passed through her, not breaking her skin but harming her just the same. The ghosts screamed as her claws and sword cut through them. Her strikes drew no blood, but with every swipe they dragged away more of the glowing ectoplasm that made up the ghostly figures, diminishing them more each time.

Riona grabbed her own sword, but Dougal held the others back with a raised hand. "If we try to help her, she'll wind up slashing us too," he said. To the others he shouted, "Gather your things and get ready to move!" When Kranxx, Killeen, and Gullik hesitated, he turned toward them and barked, "Now!"

Ember spun about like a wolf, flailing all around her and doing her best to ignore the pain when the ghosts struck her back. Soon the older ghost dissipated entirely.

The younger ghost howled in the grip of his insane fury and redoubled his attacks. With only a single foe now, Ember concentrated on taking the ghost apart. Dougal realized that if the shepherds had been living, Ember would have killed them each several times over by now. As it was, the others were ready to leave by the time she managed to dispatch the second apparition.

Dougal scooped up Ember's pack. "Are you all right?" he asked her as she staggered over to him.

"I'll be fine," she said as she took her pack from him. "It only hurts when I breathe."

"I think I have something in my pack to help," said Kranxx, unlimbering his satchel.

The charr just waved him away. "Ghosts hurt the soul more than the flesh, though they are no less deadly."

"Well done!" Gullik said. "You made quick work of those spirits. I only wish I'd been allowed to destroy them myself!"

"You'll get your chance if we don't get out of here fast," said Dougal. "It is difficult to really kill a ghost." He pointed to the swirling gray mists that still moved about the cave's entrance. "They'll re-form in a matter of minutes. Maybe less."

"Let's not be here when that happens," Kranxx said as he crawled up onto the norn's shoulders again.

"I'd love to be able to remain here and study them for a while," Killeen said. "They probably used this cave as a resting place when they were tending their sheep."

"We have our mission to think of first," Riona said as she headed for the cave's mouth.

Moving fast in the growing, muddy dawn, Ember led the group around from the cave's entrance to the crest of the hill. As they topped the hill, the sun cleared the horizon, and Dougal saw the Dragonbrand for the first time.

He felt as if he'd been stabbed. If the arrival of the ghosts had disturbed him, witnessing the damage done

trees, and
amethyst.
landscape
again and
hat coated
n.

been here

plied. "In

ving," she
he saw the

he bone. While the hilltop
hine, to the north a ribbon
side of the sky to the other.
ee a bit of daylight peeking
torm, but to the north and
hed out to the horizons. The
that flowed from the north
ads scudding over it ignored
rest of the region and raced
gs being pulled downstream

h the storm clouds, and thunder rolled along the ribbon and out across the surrounding lands. Now that he saw this, Dougal knew that he had heard the noise while he'd been trying to sleep but had simply chalked it off to Gullik's snoring. Rain fell in patches in some sections of the wide ribbon but not in others, and the lightning paid it no mind, zapping down from the sky wherever it liked.

The terrain below the clouds disturbed Dougal the most. The land had turned entirely to sharp-angled crystals that appeared to glow with power, although Dougal could not tell if that light was simply reflected from the sun or actually came from within. Bent and twisted amethyst trees stood by the side of a frozen cobalt stream that rolled through a landscape covered with scattered scrub brush and patches of grass all transformed into crystals both fragile and sharp. Where the ground was bare, it was twisted upon itself in gray lava-like swirls and dotted with half-shattered bubbles that looked like hatched ebony eggs clustered at the base of the glittering trees.

Lightning smashed down into one of thos
it exploded into uncountable fragments of
The crystal shards tinkled against the glassy
as they cascaded to the ground and shattered
again until they formed a gray-violet dust
everything near where the tree had once bee

Ember elbowed Dougal. "I thought you had
before."

"We came through the Shiverpeaks," he r
any case, that was before all this."

Killeen goggled at the scene. "How terrif
said softly, "and yet starkly beautiful." When s
others staring at her, she asked, "A dragon did this?"

"Yes," Kranxx said, once more perched atop Gullik's
shoulders, "and without any effort at all. Its name was
Kralkatorrik. The creature is such an aberration that
this is what happened to the land it simply flew over. It
didn't even have to touch it."

"Bear, Snow Leopard, Raven, and Wolf," said Gullik. He spoke quietly, as if his voice might invite more
destruction.

"It's horrific," said Riona, aghast. "A crime against
nature."

Dougal nodded. "This is why we're doing this, right?
If we don't find a way to work together, we don't stand a
chance against the creatures that did this."

"Statistically, we don't have much of a chance no
matter what we do," said Kranxx. When Riona scowled
at him he added, "But uniting the peoples against the
dragons would elevate us from 'No chance at all' to 'Very
little chance' instead."

to Ascalon shook him to the bone. While the hilltop they were on stood in sunshine, to the north a ribbon of storm stretched from one side of the sky to the other. Dougal thought he could see a bit of daylight peeking out on the far side of the storm, but to the north and the west the darkness stretched out to the horizons. The storm seemed like a river that flowed from the north to the west. The thunderheads scudding over it ignored the prevailing winds in the rest of the region and raced along the same path like logs being pulled downstream through a set of rapids.

Lightning arced through the storm clouds, and thunder rolled along the ribbon and out across the surrounding lands. Now that he saw this, Dougal knew that he had heard the noise while he'd been trying to sleep but had simply chalked it off to Gullik's snoring. Rain fell in patches in some sections of the wide ribbon but not in others, and the lightning paid it no mind, zapping down from the sky wherever it liked.

The terrain below the clouds disturbed Dougal the most. The land had turned entirely to sharp-angled crystals that appeared to glow with power, although Dougal could not tell if that light was simply reflected from the sun or actually came from within. Bent and twisted amethyst trees stood by the side of a frozen cobalt stream that rolled through a landscape covered with scattered scrub brush and patches of grass all transformed into crystals both fragile and sharp. Where the ground was bare, it was twisted upon itself in gray lava-like swirls and dotted with half-shattered bubbles that looked like hatched ebony eggs clustered at the base of the glittering trees.

Lightning smashed down into one of those trees, and it exploded into uncountable fragments of amethyst. The crystal shards tinkled against the glassy landscape as they cascaded to the ground and shattered again and again until they formed a gray-violet dust that coated everything near where the tree had once been.

Ember elbowed Dougal. "I thought you had been here before."

"We came through the Shiverpeaks," he replied. "In any case, that was before all this."

Killeen goggled at the scene. "How terrifying," she said softly, "and yet starkly beautiful." When she saw the others staring at her, she asked, "A dragon did this?"

"Yes," Kranxx said, once more perched atop Gullik's shoulders, "and without any effort at all. Its name was Kralkatorrik. The creature is such an aberration that this is what happened to the land it simply flew over. It didn't even have to touch it."

"Bear, Snow Leopard, Raven, and Wolf," said Gullik. He spoke quietly, as if his voice might invite more destruction.

"It's horrific," said Riona, aghast. "A crime against nature."

Dougal nodded. "This is why we're doing this, right? If we don't find a way to work together, we don't stand a chance against the creatures that did this."

"Statistically, we don't have much of a chance no matter what we do," said Kranxx. When Riona scowled at him he added, "But uniting the peoples against the dragons would elevate us from 'No chance at all' to 'Very little chance' instead."

Without a word, Ember did the one thing that every fiber of Dougal's body screamed at him not to do. She launched herself down the hill and toward that raw, crystal-packed wound in the world. A moment later he found himself loping after her, along with the rest of the group.

The path to the Dragonbrand was wide and easy, the smoothest going since the team had left Ebonhawke behind. The sun shone down on their heads, and the grasses around them swayed in the gentle wind like waves in the sea. It felt good to be out in the open air and sunshine again.

Dougal glanced at Killeen. She had seemed a bit off after having had to spend so much time in the darkness of the night and then in the shade of the cave. Now, though, she grinned from ear to ear, seemingly one with the nature through which she passed. Looking at her, Dougal couldn't help but smile himself.

It did not take long to reach the Dragonbrand. It seemed as if the corrupted landscape sensed they were coming and gathered itself closer to be able to entrap them faster. Or maybe it was just how Dougal tried to treasure his last few moments in the untouched land that made that time slip by so fast.

Ember came to a halt on the edge of the Dragonbrand, just before she reached the border of the purplish, crystalline obscenity. The others fell into rank alongside her, each of them staring out across the twisted atrocity to wonder what horrors it might hide from them.

Then, after drawing a deep breath, Ember stepped into the weird landscape, and the others followed.

The glassy grass crunched to dust under their feet, and soon the shards of it became deep enough to cover their ankles. The air crackled with electricity that made Dougal's hair lift up. Although he could see no threats, he sensed danger from every angle. He drew his sword and saw the others ready their weapons too.

"This is fascinating," said Killeen. "It's as if all these plants have been frozen in this state between life and death. Do you think they still grow?"

"Not after we step on them," said Kranxx.

"I wonder how this works," the sylvari said. "It's so curious." She picked a sapphire bloom from an amethyst bush and watched it slowly crumble in her hand.

"Let's keep moving," said Dougal. "The sooner we're through this place, the better."

"Bear's blood!" said Gullik. "This is all very strange, but it can't be worse than Ascalon City itself, can it?"

There was the distant, faint sound of an explosion, and something skipped off the ground in front of the norn's feet. Once it had been a standing pool of water, but now cracks spiderwebbed from where the bullet had shattered it.

Dougal spun about to see where the shot had been fired from, but Ember had already spotted the source. "There!" she said, pointing back the way they had come.

A charr warband stood on the edge of the Dragon-brand, ten soldiers all told, heavily armored and ready for battle. The warrior in front raised his rifle and roared, and the others echoed his call.

"Run!" Kranxx said, batting Gullik on the top of his head.

The norn laughed and pulled his axe. "If they've already seen us, my tiny friend, then the time for stealth is over!" He hefted his weapon in response to the challenge. "Wolf's teeth, the time for battle has begun!"

"Hold it!" Dougal said. He cast a wary eye on the warband. "They don't seem to be charging."

Battle lust danced in Gullik's eyes. "Then we shall take the battle to them!"

Ember grabbed the norn's elbow before he could stomp off to fight. "If they meant to fight us, they would have attacked already." The other charr of the warband were scrambling with their rifles as well.

"Oh-ho!" The norn beamed with pride. "They are wiser than they would seem if they fear to engage us in battle!"

"I don't think it's us they're afraid of," said Riona. "They just don't want to come in here."

"Maybe they know something we don't," Dougal said as he glanced around them.

"There's another warband coming from the northeast," said Ember.

"And that looks like one in the southwest," said Riona.

"We need to keep moving," Dougal said. Another distant pop and another shot puffed the earth next to him. "Right now." The three warbands, all on the closer side of the tortured strip of land, now sounded horns to each other. Their message was clear.

Without a word, Ember turned to the northwest and started off again. The others fell into step behind her, the norn and his asura passenger last.

"By the Wolf's whimper," Gullik growled, "only cowards run from such a fight!"

"Don't think of it as running away from that fight," Kranxx said. "Think of it as running toward a bigger one."

The norn let out a deep chuckle. "I *do* enjoy your wisdom!"

"I still don't like it," Dougal said, keeping pace with Riona and Ember. "What could be in here that would be so terrifying that it would keep three warbands of charr from coming after us?"

Riona smirked at this. "Let's hope we don't have to find out."

The gunfire behind them intensified, but at this range they were minimal targets, and the worst it did was shatter some of the glass foliage near them. None of the shots came close to hitting anyone, but it didn't seem as if the charr were trying very hard.

"Hold it!" Dougal said.

Ember skidded to a halt in the shattered purple grass, and the others following her all did the same. "What is it?" the charr said.

Dougal shaded his eyes and gazed to the southwest. "There," he said. "They're not shooting at us anymore. Look."

The two charr warbands on the southern edge of the Brand had joined together and were busy unloading their rifles into a crystalline hill hunkered to their east. It was a larger target, Dougal noted, but had no effect on them and their flight.

"I haven't seen anything this odd since I stumbled upon that hylek fertility ritual!" said Gullik.

Dougal knew then exactly what was happening. He'd heard tales of minions created by the Elder Dragons to execute their will—and anyone who might trespass upon their lands. Here in the Dragonbrand, they stood squarely in the Crystal Dragon's territory. Its passage had scarred this land and claimed it as its own. It stood to reason the creatures that lived here would belong to the Crystal Dragon too.

"We need to get out of here right now!" Dougal said, grabbing Ember's shoulder.

She shrugged him off with a growl. "We should get to the far side of that hill for cover."

"No," Dougal said. "We need to head in the other direction as fast as possible."

"We can't go back to the south," said Riona. "Those warbands will tear us to pieces."

Killeen put a hand on Dougal's arm. "What's wrong?" she said.

Dougal stabbed a finger in the direction of the hill, which had started to shudder. "That!"

As they watched, the hill continued to quiver as if shaken by an earthquake, although the land that they stood on seemed as solid as ever. A terrible noise sprang from the hill. It sounded like thousands of glasses shattering all at once.

Then the hill raised its head and opened its eyes.

19

"Run!" snapped Riona. "Run for the northern edge!"

Ember sped off to the north at a dead sprint, with Riona chasing straight after her. Dougal took Killeen's hand and pulled her along as he followed them.

Gullik stood and watched the hill rise. Kranxx pounded on his head. "Time to go!" the asura said.

"Raven's beak!" the norn said. "It's beautiful!" He hefted his axe before him. "This shall be my greatest triumph—or the tragic end of my tale!"

Dougal glanced back over his shoulder and saw the norn still standing there. "Gullik!" he shouted. "Come on!"

"Join me here or farewell!" the norn shouted. "From this foe, I shall not turn!"

Dougal hauled up short, and Killeen along with him. "Damned heroes," Dougal said. "He's going to get them both killed."

The hill shuddered one last time and then clambered to its feet. Although shaped like a man, the resemblance ended there. It stood three times as tall as the norn and appeared to have been formed from a stack of priceless diamonds the size of boulders. Twin spots sparkled in its face where eyes would be, but it bore no mouth, nose, or ears. What it had been before the passing of Kralkatorrik was unknown, but now it was that dragon's champion, its guardian of this land of twisted black rock and crystal forests.

The creature's limbs scraped against each other as it pulled itself to its full height, and the horrible noise set Dougal's teeth on edge. Gullik stood there before it, his rumbling laughter reverberating in the crystals all around as he thumbed his axe.

"We talked about discretion, remember?" Kranxx yelled at the norn. "We have bigger things to do!"

Gullik leaned backward as he craned his neck to look up at the unfolding creature, and laughed. "Bigger than that? I think not!"

Unbalanced, Kranxx smacked Gullik on the head one more time and then slipped from the norn's shoulders.

"He's insane!" the asura shouted as he raced after Dougal and Killeen.

"True," Dougal said with grudging admiration, "but I wouldn't bet against him."

Once Kranxx was clear, Gullik stalked toward the dragon's minion, hunting for the opening for his first blow. He moved left, then right, and watched how the minion tracked his movements. Anxious to get to the battle, Gullik chopped down a crystal sapling in his path. It collapsed in a shower of shards.

The minion locked on the norn with its glowing eyes, then leaned toward him and charged.

Each of the minion's steps thundered against the crystal terrain and brought cracks of lightning crashing down nearby. Although it seemed slow, its long legs covered ground fast, and it was upon Gullik before Dougal could blink.

The minion drew back a blunt-fisted arm and brought it down at Gullik with devastating speed. The norn leaped to one side to avoid the blow, and it smashed into the ground instead.

Before the minion could ready another attack, Gullik took his axe in a double-handed grip and swung it at the creature's leg. The limb cracked straight through at the knee, and when the minion tried to take a step forward, it left its lower leg behind.

Unbalanced by the surprising loss of its leg, the creature swayed for a moment and then toppled forward. Dougal saw what was about to happen and shouted for Gullik to get out of the way. The minion was too large, though, and the norn too slow, and the bulk of the creature came down right on top of him, crushing him under its phenomenal weight.

Dougal stared at the scene in shock. He had thought Gullik was crazy for trying to take on the creature, but somewhere in his heart he hadn't believed that the much-larger-than-life norn could lose the fight. Especially not so quickly.

Kranxx smacked Dougal on the leg as he passed, then sprinted away. "Run!" the asura called back over his shoulder. Dougal turned back toward the hulking beast, looking for some sign that Gullik had survived the creature collapsing upon him.

That was when he realized that Killeen was no longer beside him. The sylvari had raced forward, and was now standing before the minion, carving the air in an intricate pattern to fashion a spell.

Dougal stopped and cupped his hands around his mouth to shout at the sylvari. "Killeen! Forget it! He's gone!"

"No!" she said, still concentrating on her spell, her face creased in concentration. "He can't die. I won't let that happen!"

Glowing blackness stretched from Killeen's hands to encircle the minion, turning the shadows of its flesh to a brilliant white and its glittering hide to night. The creature froze for a moment, then threw its arms over its head as if letting loose a silent scream.

Hope soared in Dougal's heart, but it came crashing down an instant later when the blackness around the creature cracked, and the minion slammed its arms back down onto the twisted landscape, unfazed by the incantation.

Dougal glanced back to see Riona, Ember, and Kranxx in the distance. They had stopped running, probably locked in their own argument about returning. He turned to see the minion bearing down on Killeen, slowed only slightly by the fact that Gullik had removed one of its legs below the knee. The sylvari scrambled backward, but even on its knees the minion was gaining on her.

Dougal cursed. It was one thing to let Gullik take a stand against the minion by himself: he was a norn—and, more importantly, a norn who was a veteran of many battles and who hoped for a legendary death. Killeen, for all her strangeness, was guilty of nothing other than helping a friend.

"On my way!" he shouted, and charged forward to help the sylvari.

Dougal drew his black sword and wondered if it would have any effect on the creature at all, or if attacking it would be like slashing a stone wall. He dragged the blade against a glittering bush, and it fell apart in a satisfying shower of diamonds. The minion halted its progress toward Killen and focused its eyes on him instead. For a moment Dougal looked deep into the eyes of the beast, and could feel nothing but hatred in their depths. Then as quickly as it gazed into Dougal's heart, it dismissed him and turned back to the necromancer.

Before Dougal could stop it, the diamond-hided minion drove an earthshaking punch down at the sylvari. Killeen dodged to one side to avoid the blow, but even so, the impact of the near-miss was enough to stagger her.

Dougal was upon them now, just as the minion was about to level another blow at Killeen. He lunged at it with his sword. To his surprise, the blade went into the creature as easily as if he'd rammed it into a sack of grain. Indeed, shining sand poured from the wound, glittering in the Dragonbrand's unearthly light.

The minion shivered in protest at the blow and its attack went wide, smashing the ground far from Killeen. But the sudden movement wrenched the sword from Dougal's grip, leaving him unarmed.

The minion wheeled and punched down at Dougal this time. Dougal dodged under the strike, diving past the creature's one good leg. As he did, he spotted Gullik hauling himself up out of the crater of glassy dust formed when the minion had landed on him. Blood flowed over every inch of the norn's exposed skin, and he looked as if he'd been run through a mill. Despite that, he grabbed his axe and let out a mighty cry—and then collapsed, disappearing once more into the crater.

Killeen started another spell while the minion reeled back to launch another blow in Dougal's direction. "It's shrugging off your spells!" Dougal said. "Get out of here!"

"I might not be able to harm it directly," the sylvari said, her jaw set at a determined angle, "but there are other ways!"

Dougal dove away from the minion's attack again and slipped on the crystalline glass. His legs flew out from under him and he fell flat on his back. He was close enough to the creature now to see right into its glittering eyes, which had taken on a redder hue.

The minion slammed down another fist at Dougal, but he rolled out of the way and scrambled to his hands and knees. The crystals splashed up from the blow's impact lanced his sides and legs. A second punch rained down at him, but he was already scrambling out of its way, heading toward where he thought his sword had landed. It was cradled in a crystalline bush, the buds of gemstone flowers already winding around it.

Dougal grasped the hilt and pulled, and the bush screeched as its branches and flowers shattered from the force. Then he spun around to see that the crystalline creature had decided to ignore him for a moment. It had returned to hunting Killeen instead.

The sylvari was at the crater's rim now, desperately trying to finish another spell. This time the target of her incantation was Gullik. The battered norn had finally managed to crawl out of the purple-powdered crater. He bled from countless wounds as he staggered to his feet, and Dougal was sure he saw bone sticking through his skin in at least three different places, but the norn would not let that stop him.

Killeen's spell enveloped Gullik in a bright red nimbus, although it was hard to tell if the color came from the magic or the blood dripping from the norn's skin. As the final words of the spell left the sylvari's lips, she let her concentration lapse and glanced up to see the minion swinging its injured arm in a backhanded slap, level with the twisted earth. The arm was attached to the rest of its body by a fraction of its width, and the creature snapped it like a whip.

Gullik fell backward, but Killeen was not so fortunate. The back of the creature's fist smacked into Killeen with a sickening crunch, and she went sailing off to the north, with most of the minion's arm following the same trajectory. Dougal watched them both arc through the air as if they'd been loosed from a catapult. He gasped in horror as the boulder-sized arm fragment smashed into the sylvari as she landed on the ground.

Furious, Dougal turned back, raised his sword over his head, and charged at the dragon's minion. The creature moved more slowly, now that it was missing two limbs, but it was still a deadly threat. Dougal slashed at the thing's head, and his sword cut a long line across its face, just below the eyes.

The minion brought up its one good arm and smashed it down at Dougal. Watching the arm coming down at him, Dougal thought he'd finally made his last mistake, but the blow missed him by inches. As he wondered why, he saw that Gullik had gotten close enough to chop the back of the creature's good leg with his axe.

The glow that had surrounded Gullik now expanded to envelop the minion's leg at the point where the norn had damaged it. Dougal saw one of the bones poking out of Gullik's lower leg pull itself back into him and the skin heal over the wound.

Dougal understood then what Killeen had done. The spell she'd cast on Gullik allowed him to steal life force from the minion and take it for his own. Every time the warrior hit the creature, the spell drained its life force and gave it to the norn instead.

Gullik's blow had gotten the minion's attention, and it tried to reach back with its good arm to swat the norn, but missed. Seeing his chance, Dougal ran forward and cut at the creature again with his sword. The minion reared back in silent pain: the mouth that Dougal had cut into it sagged open now. Apparently confused, it turned back toward the human.

Then its left eye exploded.

Dougal cast a quick glance to the right and saw smoke curling from Ember's pistol even as she dropped the gun and drew her sword. Riona was already closing the distance between them and the beast, and Kranxx had his lightning rod out. The last was a mistake, as the lightning homed in on it and smashed the ground around their feet, staggering all three of them.

Help was coming, but it was still critical moments before it would reach them—moments when the creature could take out its frustrations on Dougal. Dougal backpedaled furiously across the broken ground, while Gullik leaped up on the creature's back and brought his axe down on it.

The blow made the creature shudder from one end of its body to the other, but Gullik found some way to hold on. With the minion's energy surging into him again, he pulled himself forward and brought his axe back for a powerful, two-handed strike. It landed directly on the creature's neck, cracking it.

The minion's head held on for a moment, hanging from its shoulders, but then its neck shattered. Dougal covered his head with his arms to protect himself from the flying shards, then dove to the side to avoid the boulder-sized crystal head as it fell.

Gullik rode the creature's now limp body down as it crashed into the ground, sending up a new cloud of finely ground dust that exploded from the spot where the thing struck. The last Dougal saw of the norn, he still had one hand on the handle of his axe, which had become embedded in the minion's back. He had the other raised in a triumphant fist, and he shook it at the sky as he let loose a norn war cry that seemed loud enough to reach the distant Shiverpeaks.

When the dust cleared, Dougal picked himself up off the ground and shook as much of the purple crystals from his face and arms as he could. Once he could finally see again, he spotted Gullik standing on top of the fallen creature, his axe slung over his shoulder. Although the reddish glow had left him, he looked exhausted but as hale and hearty as ever.

The norn smiled, but that smile froze and his face fell. And Dougal remembered the cost at which that victory had come.

"Killeen," he whispered.

Dougal charged over to where the minion's fist had crushed the sylvari. He found her trapped beneath the gigantic hand from her waist down. Her eyes were open and unblinking, and she had long since stopped breathing.

20

Dougal knelt beside Killeen's crumpled form. Ember, Riona, and Kranxx came up behind him, Gullik last of all, still coated in purplish dust. Riona tried to put a hand on Dougal's shoulder, but he pushed it away. For a long while, all he could do was stand and stare at the dead sylvari and struggle to control the anger building inside him. As he did, the thunder around them grew louder, and rain began to fall.

No one said a word as they watched the drops of water start to wash the dust from Killeen.

"Dougal," Riona started, "I'm sorry—"

Dougal cut her off. "Don't," he muttered, his eyes not leaving Killeen's corpse.

"We should have run," Kranxx said. "All of us. Any idiot could see that our best chance of surviving such an encounter was to flee."

Dougal glanced up and hurled daggers at him with his eyes. "Well, it looks like one of us idiots paid the price."

Kranxx stammered a moment. "I tried my lightning rod, but it had an odd effect in this environment. Its metaspell solenoids are fried out now."

"Aye," said Ember, "and my first two shots misfired before I could take out that thing's eye."

Dougal's face flushed with anger and regret. "I should have dragged her away in the first place."

"If you had," said Ember, "we would have left Gullik behind to fight that creature alone."

"You should have," Gullik said as he looked down at Killeen. He spoke so softly that Dougal had to strain to hear him. "I did not expect any of you to be so foolhardy as to join me. Least of all, her."

"Stop this," Riona said. "We don't have time for it. The battle is sure to have drawn attention. The warbands that awoke the creature are still south of the Dragonbrand and may choose to resume the chase."

"They would challenge a foe who slew this beast that terrified them so?" asked Gullik.

"Some charr are like carrion," said Ember, "only too happy to take on a foe when he is at his weakest."

"Regardless," Riona said, her face a mask, "we need to move. Now."

Gullik pointed at Killeen's body. "She deserves a hero's funeral." Despite the rain falling on her figure freely now, her skin was already starting to turn black around the edges, like the petals of a plucked flower. He became the bear, and in his ursine form shouldered the sharp-edged boulder-fist and rolled it off the sylvari. Then, as a norn once more, he knelt down and picked her crushed form up, cradling it in his arms. "If nothing else, we will not leave her body here in this damned place."

Gunshots rang overhead. Dougal glanced to the south to see three full warbands of charr starting to nose their way, cautiously but relentlessly, into the Dragonbrand. With Killeen gone, they had only five to face off against sixty-some charr warriors who were fresh and spoiling for a fight.

Gullik looked south, rage overtaking his face, and for a moment Dougal was afraid the norn was going to charge off to meet them in battle. Grimacing, Dougal patted the norn on the arm. "I think we'd honor her sacrifice more if we lived."

Gullik put his hand on Dougal's shoulder as they began following the others north through the rain. "There's no glory in fighting so few charr anyway," he muttered.

In the end they laid her to rest on the northern side of the Dragonbrand, beneath a cairn of rough stones covered with a thin coating of wet sod. All except Kranxx did the work, while the asura watched the Dragonbrand to the south through a set of lenses from his voluminous pack.

Dougal and Ember were laying the last of the uprooted sod over the stones when Kranxx came down from his perch.

"The charr patrols have turned back," the asura said. "I think they ran into something in the Dragonbrand that was related to the thing we fought."

"They are not as foolish as I feared," said Ember, standing back to look at their handiwork.

Dougal patted the sod into place and stood up. "Were Killeen human, I would offer a prayer to the Six Gods to guide her safely through the Mists."

"The charr have no gods," said Ember. "But we are not stone, and were she a charr, we would praise her prowess and her bravery, and seek to measure up to it in our own lives."

"The asura believe in an Eternal Alchemy," said Kranxx, "a great machine of which we are merely component parts. Parts wear out or break, but that doesn't make their passing any less painful."

Gullik let out a deep sigh and said, "I met her in the forest of Caledon. I was hunting the great cats there, seeking their pelts, and several of them got the better of me. I was resting beneath one of their strange-shaped trees by the roadside, when she walked along. She asked me if I would like to stop bleeding. I told her I would, very much. She worked her greenish death-magic over my wounds and I regained enough of my life to accompany her to the next haven.

"We did not travel together long," he continued. "Yet, in that time she impressed me both with her disposition and her ability. She told me about her people and how they grew on trees and how it was important that they find out what their purpose was in the Awakened World. I told her about Bear and Raven and Snow Leopard and Wolf, and others of our spirits who were no more, like Owl. And she asked many questions, and a few days later we parted on friendly terms.

"I didn't see her again until that day in your room, Dougal. And she kept me from making a horrible error.

The rest you know. She always was searching for her place in life, and always was curious about what happened at the end. For all our sakes, I think she found the former in this group, and hope she finds the latter in the Mists of the Afterworld."

There was silence, the soft rain still falling around them. At last Riona said, "The warbands are no longer pursuing, but without a doubt they will report our presence. We must move on."

No one said anything in response, but one after another they pulled on their packs and started the climb into the rolling hills overlooking the Dragonbrand from the north. By the time they reached the crest of the hill, the rain had diminished to a light drizzle and the sun was coming out. Looking back, Dougal saw a rainbow along the edge of the Dragonbrand.

They made good time once they were back in untainted lands. Compared to the earth ruined by the Dragonbrand, the springiness of the ground here seemed to propel them forward. With some difficulty, Dougal turned his thoughts to the task ahead of them.

"We should not have to worry much about patrols here," Ember said. "The creatures bent by the Dragonbrand rarely leave it, and the charr trust the devastated land to protect their southern flank. There may be a few sentinels here and there keeping an eye on the inhabitants of the Dragonbrand, but nothing in the way of the continual patrols outside Ebonhawke."

"A solid if flawed theory," Kranxx said. "One that I'm happy we can take advantage of." He'd resumed his place upon Gullik's shoulders. The norn bore him as easily as ever, immune to any abuse the asura could heap on him, whether physical or verbal. Still, Gullik was mostly silent, his thoughts kept to himself.

They hiked steadily north and westward into the hills, stopping well before the sun kissed the far horizon. At length they came to an old human farm building, partially collapsed along its southern wall but still warm and dry along its northern half. From the detritus scattered about and the ashes in the fireplace, other travelers had used this place as well.

"We should be moving at night again," said Ember, "two, maybe three nights before we reach the outskirts of Ascalon City itself. We are going to come around through the Loreclaw Expanses on the southern edge of the Ascalon Basin; there are fewer patrols on the south side of the lake. The western edge of the lake may have more patrols, since that is a major artery for the charr military. We will try to avoid them and approach the city from the west."

Dougal nodded, but no one seemed to be much in the mood to talk. Kranxx broke out some lumpy nutbread he had brought with him and passed it out to have with their cold rations. It was sweet on the tongue and, if anything, made Dougal sadder.

"I've lived in Ebonhawke for years," said the asura, "but that was my first experience with the Dragonbrand. I hope I never have another."

"The Elder Dragons have warped Tyria," said Ember, picking out a walnut shard lodged between her teeth with a claw. "If the ghosts of the past, the humans of

Ebonhawke, and the Flame Legion were not enough, now Kralkatorrik has drawn this scar through our lands."

"My people know of the power of dragons," said the asura. "The first dragon, Primordus, made his home in a great hub of magical power. We built our central transfer chamber, a cluster of powerful asura gates, atop that site. When the dragon's herald, which the dwarves called the Great Destroyer, woke years ago, it crippled our network and drove us to the surface. As mighty as we may seem now, it's just a pale shadow of our past."

Gullik grunted. "I know of what you speak, small one. The norn once ruled the north, until Jormag the Ice Dragon rose from his tomb. We fought him but were overmatched, and were driven from our lands. One of our greatest heroes, Aesgir, battled the Ice Dragon and, with the aid of the Spirits of the Wild, lived to tell the tale. More than that, he brought back the sole trophy we have of our battles against the creature: a single fang from its maw. That tooth is the heart of our settlement at Hoelbrak, and our great heroes test their might against it. For our people have agreed that when someone breaks Jormag's tooth, it will be a sign for our people to rise once more and defeat the Ice Dragon once and for all."

"Kralkatorrik, Primordus, Jormag," said Dougal, "and Zhaitan, who rose in another place of power, from beneath Orr itself, and flooded Lion's Arch and now makes its lair in the heart of the City of the Gods. And for all we know, there may be more of them. It puts the battles between the charr and humans into perspective."

"All the more reason that we should succeed," growled Ember softly, almost to herself. "We all seem to be resting on the edge, and unless we deal with our individual challenges, the dragons will consume us all."

Dougal nodded. Three hundred years ago humans ruled Tyria. Now, with the centaur raids, the bandits, the rise of the dragons, and the draining war with the charr, the humans have been driven back to a fraction of their lands. Dougal wondered if he was a member of a dying race, like the dwarves, fated to fade from the greater world.

"Do we want to approach the city during the night or the day?" Riona's question shattered Dougal's reverie.

"What?" He blinked. "Oh. I would rather try it during the day. The ghosts are less active then."

"But the charr patrols will be far more likely to spot us," Ember pointed out. "How did you manage it the last time?"

"Poorly," said Dougal. "We were more worried about the charr than the ghosts, and slipped past the patrols and into the city at midnight on a night with a full moon. It—it was a disaster."

"But you, my friend, lived to tell the tale, to sing the saga of your friends and their deaths," said Gullik, smiling wanly. "And their lives well spent."

Dougal shook his head. "Don't romanticize it. There wasn't anything good about their deaths. We were stupid and we paid a price."

"What happened?" Riona's voice was soft but insistent. "We should know."

Dougal pondered this for a moment and looked at the others. Ember nodded in agreement with Riona. Gullik was looking at him blankly, waiting. Even Kranxx had stopped chewing and sat there expectantly.

He'd put this off as long as he could. Dougal took a deep breath. "I have not spoken of this before. The 'legend' of my surviving Ascalon City grew up over time, and while I've done nothing to stop it and even have profited from it, I've never told anyone what happened there. So please bear with me, because this is one story that I cannot make myself the hero of."

Gullik opened his mouth to say something, but Ember silenced him with a jabbed elbow to the rib. Dougal continued.

"You know Riona and I were in the same unit at Ebonhawke. One of our friends, Dak, had found the old map in some library in Ebonhawke. It showed the old city itself, where the towers and reception chambers were and, most importantly, the royal treasury. We all memorized that map, in case it was lost."

"You think the Claw is in the royal treasury?" said Ember.

"I do," said Dougal, and stopped there, not elaborating. He was thinking of what had happened next, and at last decided to skip over the part where they chose to desert and left Riona behind to take the blame. Finally he said, "Dak and I and some others thought we would become treasure hunters, and left Ebonhawke for Lion's Arch." He looked at Riona and she nodded: she was not going to bring up the matter here, in front of everyone.

"We collected as much information as we could find on Ascalon City and then set off from Lion's Arch. Dak, Jervis, Marga, Vala, and myself. We were all close friends, and hired a group of locals for added support. The adventurers from Lion's Arch thought we were just going to see what we could pick up in Ascalon City. We didn't mention the royal treasury. We left Lion's Arch, crossed over the Shiverpeaks, and came down into Ascalon, where we spent most of our time trying to dodge charr patrols. They were very effective, and we lost most of our associates before we even reached Ascalon City . . ." He let his voice trail off, the images of the past rushing up to meet him.

"What happened then?" asked Riona.

Dougal tried to swallow, but his throat was dry. He pulled out a waterskin and took a quick swig from it. The water didn't seem to help.

"What happened, Dougal?"

He looked at Riona. If anyone deserved to hear about this, it was her. She had the right to know what had happened to their lost friends. He had to be honest with her. He forgot the others were there, and spoke solely to her.

"It was . . . awful. By the time we reached the city's walls, only one of the Lion's Arch group was left, a woman named Cautive, an elementalist. We should have turned back, but we decided that we hadn't come that far to go home, so we pressed on into Ascalon City. That's when it all went indescribably bad.

"We hadn't been inside the walls for more than fifteen minutes when Cautive lost her mind. She had been a fragile thing to start with, and after seeing so many of her friends die on the way to Ascalon City, knowing that we were in a place infested with ghosts pushed her over the edge. When she saw the remains of all the bodies littering the streets, she started wailing, and no one could get her to stop. We all stood there, in a square in a haunted city, yelling at her to stop and squabbling with each other.

"Dak finally hit her, just once. She toppled over and smacked her head on the cobblestones. We tried to get her to wake up, but she never did.

"Any of us might have done it. There we were, racing into a city filled with angry ghosts, and she was honestly loud enough to wake the dead."

"You didn't have any potions?" asked Kranxx. "No magic to heal her?"

Dougal shook his head. "Maybe if we'd had more time. But the trouble wasn't that Dak had killed Cautive: it was that he'd silenced her too late.

"As Vala knelt down to try to help Cautive, the first ghosts appeared. There were probably a dozen of them. They—they looked much like they must have in life. They wore the old Ascalonian uniforms, and they carried swords. But they were colorless, so much so that you could see right through them.

"When they saw us, they froze, stunned. They just couldn't believe we were there. Then they attacked.

"As they came at us, they wailed even worse than Cautive had. They were mad in every sense of the word. They had no words for their anger, but they expressed it in noise and steel.

"You remember the ghosts of the shepherd and his apprentice. When you see a ghost, how insubstantial it looks, you wonder how such a thing could hurt you. Can a mist harm you? It seems ridiculous.

"But when the first ghost struck, he ran Dak straight through, and that sword of his was solid enough to bring blood up into Dak's mouth. Jervis started casting spells, but there were just too many of them. They actually picked him up, and Marga as well, and carried them away.

"I'll never forget their screams. They went on forever."

Dougal felt his throat tighten. After a moment, he continued.

"Vala gave up on trying to help Cautive and turned her attention to Dak. I left her with him while I tried to rescue Jervis and Marga.

"I followed their screams. By the time I caught up with Jervis and Marga, the ghosts had taken them to the main square. The place was filled with scores of ghosts, an entire army of them. And there, up on the battlements of the palace, loomed the ghost of King Adelbern, shouting at his dead soldiers.

"I climbed up the side of a building so I could get a better look. Marga was already dead, her body pulled apart and being tossed about like a rag doll by the spirits. The ghosts were pulling pieces off of Jervis a joint at a time. I had a bow with me, and my first arrow caught him in the chest, which only hurt him more and alerted the ghosts that I was there. I fired the second while they turned to charge at me. The third finally caught Jervis in the throat and put an end to him."

"You killed Jervis?" Riona spoke so softly that Dougal could barely hear her. He thought about pretending that he hadn't but then nodded.

"It was the best thing—the only thing—I could do for him." He closed his eyes and tried to banish the look on Jervis's face when the final arrow hit home. It had been a look of gratitude.

"Bear's blood!" said Gullik, solemn but insistent. "Don't stop there, man! What happened to the others?"

"I raced back to where I'd left Dak and Vala, but when I got there, all I found was Dak, dead in a pool of blood."

"What about the woman?" asked Ember. Dougal hadn't even been sure the charr was listening.

"I—I never found her. I looked, but . . . I heard her screaming for me once, screaming for me to run. But it was cut off. I tried to keep looking, but the ghosts found me and the pursuit began."

Kranxx shook his head in disbelief. "So there you were, alone and caught between a legion of charr and an army of angry ghosts. What did you do?"

"I did what I had to. I left. I fled. Like a dog in the night, I ran from Ascalon City and made my way back to Lion's Arch. We had told some people where we were going, and when I turned up alone, the stories started and a lot of people wanted to hire me, since I had survived the City of Ghosts. But they never realized I had failed, and those I cared about had paid for that failure."

Dougal put his head in his hands and discovered that his face was wet with tears. He had no idea how long they had been there.

Riona put a hand on Dougal's arm, and he did not

have it in him to brush it away. "I know," she said. "I'm sorry they're gone as well. They were our companions, our patrol, our teammates."

"They were more than that," said Dougal. "There's something else I have to tell you." He stressed the last word as he looked at Riona and fished out the locket around his neck. "Something I should have said before."

Dougal opened the locket and sighed as if he hoped he might finally get rid of his last breath. "Vala," he said, looking at the cameo. "Sweet, beautiful, wonderful Vala."

"What about her?"

"We . . . were married, right before we left Lion's Arch," Dougal said, his words falling like hammer blows. "Vala was my wife."

He looked up to see Riona scowling at him. Her eyes burned with anger and grief in the dying light of the setting sun. For a moment Dougal was sure she was going to strike him, and he wished she would.

But she didn't; rather, she stood up and stalked off, grabbing her traveling cloak and wrapping it tightly around her. She settled in the doorway of the ruined house, her back to the rest of the group.

Dougal stood up now, unsteady and wet-faced, and took two steps toward her. Gullik looked at him, hard, and shook his head. Dougal froze, then nodded in agreement. There was no comfort he could offer her, not for this. Instead the norn picked himself up and walked over toward the shattered doorway, setting himself down against a crumbling wall, not so close as to crowd the human woman, but not so far away that if she wanted to talk, she would have to raise her voice.

Ember and Kranxx laid out their own bedrolls without comment and, with muttered good nights, stretched themselves out. Dougal sat by the cold fireplace for a long time. As the sun died, he knew he would not get any rest before they had to move on.

21

They moved through the night in silence now, Ember leading. Riona would not stay near Dougal: when he was near her, she would change her position in the group, sometimes leading, sometimes trailing the party. Gullik remained somber as well, and nothing that Kranxx said could coax him out.

The land grew more open and rolling, and the forests thicker and older, like spots of dark ebony in the night. In the distance Dougal could see fires from the camps and homesteads of the charr, but none of them were close enough to pose any threat. They also encountered fence lines, metal wire strung between wooden posts and interrupted by rusted gates, simultaneously a sign of ownership and a reminder that these paths were not often used. This was a land unvisited by the wars with the humans.

Dougal kept his silence as well, until Ember finally said, "I don't understand you humans."

Dougal looked over at Riona, her eyes forward, marching straight ahead. "Don't ask me. I hardly understand us, either." Her anger of the previous night had abated into a cold, dull fury, and she had said not more than three words so far in the evening's march, and all of them to Ember.

"If I understand you correctly, you and Riona were, for lack of a better word, close," said the charr.

"For lack of a better word," admitted Dougal.

"Yet, she remained in Ebonhawke and you . . . left." Ember skirted around the question of desertion. "And you and another friend became . . . close . . . as well."

"More than close," said Dougal. "We were married. We wanted to spend the rest of our lives together."

"And so you did, at least in her case," said Ember, thinking it through but shaking her head. "What bothers me is that Riona was unfazed by the description of her friends being slain. Even when you had to admit slaying one of your companions to end his suffering. But when you admitted that one of them was your wife, then she got angry."

Dougal looked at Ember's shadowed form in the darkness. The charr seemed honestly curious. "Human relationships are hard to explain to other races."

Ember snorted, "Oh, I understand. Charr relationships have all that stage drama as well. We on occasion mate for life, though our relationships are usually more casual, and we have more than our share of jealousies, rivalries, expectations, and disappointments. Lovers come together, break apart, and come together years later. We recognize families, though our children enter the fahrar of one of their parents' legion once they have been weaned. There we learn how to fight alongside others and form bonds stronger than family or affection. But you had been apart over six years. Surely she could not expect you to be some sort of celibate?"

"Our relationship was . . . complicated," said Dougal. And more than a little undefined, he reminded himself. They had sparred and argued and made up several times even before the memorable night when they had decided to leave Ebonhawke. And after they had left the city, Vala had been supportive and caring, more so than she had been earlier.

Was there, Dougal wondered, more going on with either woman than he had thought at the time? It would not be the first time he had misread another's thinking.

"I think the news was unexpected for her," said Dougal at last. "She knew that the rest of our platoon were dead. I told her as much, and she had a chance to deal with it. To find out that I had married Vala and she did not know about it, that was sudden. She will come around. I hope."

"I hope as well, and the sooner the better, for all our sakes," said Ember, and moved into the darkness once more.

They ran into another fence and followed it along under the moonlight to a latched gate, then passed through it into another field, this one with shorter grass and fewer weeds. They walked for about ten minutes, then Gullik froze.

"What is it?" hissed Riona, behind them.

"Something is moving out there," said Gullik.

The asura scowled and looked westward. "I see it, too: several somethings."

Dougal and Ember had doubled back by this time and the five stood clustered together. To the west, dark shapes, heavy and blocky and as long as the norn was tall, were framed against the lighter grass. As they watched, one of them shifted and let out a soft lowing noise.

Dougal let out a breath of relief. "Cows. Of course."

"Cows?" said Kranxx, as if it were suddenly a new factor in his calculations.

Dougal almost laughed. "It makes sense. We're in a pasture, after all, and we've been moving though gated fences."

The tenseness in the group went out of them in single breath.

Ember explained, "Charr are mostly carnivores. Most of our land is cleared for ranches, and slaughterhouses dot the landscape. We grow feed for the winter. Cattle, sheep, hogs, dolyaks, and devourers all keep the legions moving."

Gullik chuckled and scratched his chin. "I wonder if—"

"No," said Kranxx, "you will not tip the cows."

The norn snorted and said, "You never let me have *any* fun."

More seriously, Ember said, "We are cutting across more settled terrain, and the moon is going down. We should find a safe haven for the rest of the night."

In the end they found a feed barn, one used to shelter and supply the herds in the winter months, but for the moment open-sided and disused. They would not risk a fire, but the remains of the last season's straw felt as good as the best bed in Lion's Arch.

"Ember," Dougal said, "when we first met you, you mocked my story of the Foefire. Now's your chance. Tell us the truth about the Foefire."

The charr snorted. "You don't need truth. You have your own lies. You don't need mine."

"The more lies, the better," said Dougal.

Riona raised an eyebrow at Dougal, the friendliest gesture she had made in the last twenty-four hours. "Are you saying the legends of our heroes are nothing but lies, Dougal Keane?"

"The last time I went to Ascalon City, I only knew one version of what happened with the Foefire," Dougal explained. "I didn't talk to any charr about it. So," he said, speaking now to Ember, "I want to know what you know."

Ember snorted through her snout and ground her teeth as she thought about this. "All right," she said, "I will tell it as I know it, but I will refuse to mute any part of it for your ears." The rest of the group nodded.

"The invasion of Ascalon City was supposed to be the moment of our greatest triumph," said the charr. "Conquering it would have eliminated the last outpost of human resistance in the region and heralded the end of the Ascalon Insurrection."

"Other than Ebonhawke, you mean," said Riona.

Ember held up a hand. "Is this your story?" she asked the woman.

Riona stood her ground, refusing to let the charr intimidate her. "It's about my country."

"That you stole from my people," replied Ember.

"Please," said Dougal. "I asked for Ember's unvarnished account of the Foefire. She can't give me that if you interrupt her."

"Raven's claws!" Gullik said. "Among the norn, we say, 'The best tales are lies that show you truths.' Let the charr speak!"

Riona screwed up her face, trying to parse the norn's words, but held her tongue. The charr bowed her head to Gullik and Dougal, and continued.

"The charr side of the tale is handed down to us from the mighty jaws of Frye Fireburn, legionnaire of the Flame Legion and hero of my people. Frye was the leader of one the greatest warbands of his time, the legendary Fireshadows. They served as an elite espionage and assassination team for the Flame imperator.

"And before you interrupt again"—Ember looked at Riona—"yes, I hate the Flame Legion with a passion. They crippled the old charr ways and led us into the worship of false gods. They made us soft and foolish, and I will fight to keep them from regaining even a fraction of their power. Yet, I say to you that Frye Fireburn of the Flame Legion was a hero, and so you will understand why, if you let me continue.

"As the Flame Legion surrounded Ascalon for one final assault on the city's walls, the legion's imperator called the Fireshadows to him and ordered them to sneak into the city and assassinate King Adelbern. He believed that this would decapitate the Ascalonian forces, and in their despair they would be unable to mount a viable defense against the charr attack."

"What was the imperator's name?" asked Dougal.

Ember fixed him with a stony glare.

"I'm not objecting to you, I'm just dying to know," he clarified. "The human tales never mention his name, other than the imperator of the Flame Legion."

Ember nodded. "I do not know. After his disgrace, his name was stricken from our records."

"Bear's tears, that's cold!" muttered Gullik.

"It is our way." She waited for a moment. "May I continue?"

Silence and polite nods from the others. Ember resumed: "Frye and his warband of assassins scaled the city's wall that night and worked their way to the king's private chambers. They killed many guards along the way, silently dispatching them by sword and by spell.

"When they made it to the king's private chambers, they found it empty. They thought that they had missed the hated Sorcerer-King, that perhaps he had learned of their mission and even set a trap for them. They had arrived in the middle of the night, after all, and he was not there.

"The Fireshadows searched the royal quarters. That was when one charr stumbled upon the body of a human lying under a table in the king's private bedchamber.

"Frye turned the human over. As he did, the human let out a deep breath and his expression flickered back to life. This human had a knife driven into his chest, but he still had enough breath in him to speak."

"Who planted the blade in his chest?" asked Riona. "A charr?"

Ember glowered at the new interruption but, rather than rise to Riona's bait, simply replied, "It was a human knife, the story goes. Had a charr done it, I would have not hesitated to say so.

"The dying human's name was Savione. He claimed to be the king's servant. It was clear even to Frye that he was no warrior.

" 'You must stop him,' said Savione. 'The king is mad with grief, and he plans to use a great magic. He will kill us all.'

"At this point, the servant choked on his own blood and nearly died, but one of the Fireshadows tended to him so that he could finish what he had to say.

"The servant Savione opened his eyes again and spoke: 'When Adelbern saw the legions amassing outside of the city, he despaired. We dug in and tried to withstand the siege for as long as we could. When we saw the latest wave of charr arrive, we knew our final moment had come, that our time had finally run out. His Majesty told me, "This is no longer a siege, Savione. This will become an assault. But if force of arms fails us, force of will shall not. Where swords may fail, sorcery may succeed."

" 'His Majesty bears on his hip a mighty blade, a relic of now-lost Orr and its City of the Gods.' This was the sword Magdaer, twin to Sohothin, as your story said. 'He drew the sword and looked deep into its depths.

" 'The king said, "I have long known that Magdaer had other powers—remnants of the gods themselves. We Ascalonians may be doomed, but Ascalon will live on forever!" '

"The human looked at the charr, his life breath

leaving his body. 'He is in the throne room,' said the servant, 'surrounded by his Royal Guard and as many other soldiers as the walls can spare. He will unleash the power of his sacred sword, Magdaer. He means to kill all the charr—but the price, the sacrifice . . .'

"Savione closed his eyes, and the Fireshadow healers could not do anything more for him. Frye took the counsel of his warband and made his decision. If the dying human spoke the truth, the entire legion was marching into a trap. The Sorcerer-King would be too well protected for them to reach him. They decided to abandon their mission and alert their imperator to the danger instead.

"When Frye Fireburn and his warband returned to tell their imperator—who still bore the Claw of the Khan-Ur, mind you, and the loyalty of the legions—about the Sorcerer-King's plan, he refused to listen to them. 'We will breach the walls of the city tonight,' the imperator said.

" 'It's a trap,' argued Frye. 'Once our forces enter the city, this mad king will kill us all.'

"The imperator spat on Frye and said, 'You must truly fear my wrath to come up with such ridiculous tales to distract me from your failure. I sent you in to kill a king, and you come back with wild excuses. I do not accept such incompetence in the Flame Legion.'

"Frye and his warband protested the imperator's accusation. They insisted that every word they had told him was true, and they demanded that he halt the invasion until they could figure out how to deal with this new threat from the Sorcerer-King.

"The imperator refused to listen to Frye and his

fellows, and he had them arrested. 'Because you have been faithful servants until this day,' the imperator said, 'I will not tear out your throats.'

"Instead, he ordered that Frye and his fellows be bound hand and foot and tied to stakes placed on the Viewing Hill. I do not know what the humans called it, but it provided a clear line of sight into Ascalon City.

"The imperator believed that this punishment would be worse than death. 'You will witness the triumph of your legion, but you will not be part of it. You will have to bear that shame until the day our gods bless you with death.'"

"Raven's beak!" said Gullik, despite himself. "I thought the charr were godless!"

Kranxx elbowed the norn, irritated by the new interruption. "That didn't happen until later, after Kalla Scorchrazor destroyed the shaman caste," he said. "Has living in the frozen mountains for so long broken your sense of time?"

Ember ignored them. "After Frye and the others were staked out here according to the imperator's wishes, they howled at the stars as the walls of Ascalon City finally crumbled under the charr assault. They had long hoped to see this day, but they feared the imperator's hubris would ruin it all.

"Frye and his warband watched, unable to turn away. Soon after the gates fell, the imperator stormed into the city's main square. Adelbern, the Sorcerer-King, stood defiant on the parapet of his tallest tower with his magical sword in his hands. It burned with a fire that swirled about its blade as if it were alive. He shouted at the soldiers below as they fled before the Flame Legion's forces, some of them escaping through the holes the charr had made in the walls.

" 'Retreat?' the Sorcerer-King shouted. 'Retreat is not an option!'

"With the Flame Legion flooding through the city's defenses, Ascalon City had already been lost. The human soldiers ignored their king's complaint as their retreat transformed into a rout.

"The insane king raised his sword—a relic from the ancient land of Orr—over his head and bellowed down at his men, 'We will never surrender! Never!'

"Then he plunged his sword downward. As it struck the stones beneath his feet, a gout of white fire shaped like a blade shot from the tower's roof, enveloping Adelbern. The tower collapsed then, its very stones unable to withstand the power of the Foefire. Adelbern rode the battered rocks all the way down, disappearing in a cloud of shattered stones and dust.

"The mystic light from the Foefire burned without abatement. When the last stone of the tower stopped tumbling, the light intensified for an instant, then burst out and engulfed the entire city. The wave of destruction spread out from there, soon engulfing nearly all of Ascalon.

"The charr nearest the tower—the imperator and his victorious guard—were immolated in a heartbeat, their fur igniting like tinder, their flesh blasted by the unearthly flames. Yet, what happened to the humans in the blast was infinitely worse.

"The air in Ascalon City rang with a choir of their screams as the humans died in their tracks. Their bodies were blasted into burning fragments, but their spirits remained standing. Their mortal forms were reduced to broken skeletons but their souls remained, eternally bound to Ascalon. Only the charr close to the city were destroyed in the blast, but every human for leagues around was suddenly transformed into a ghost.

"This is why we call him the Sorcerer-King." Ember nodded at Dougal and Riona. "He worked a spell as great as the Searing itself, and in a single blow denied the Flame Legion their ultimate victory and damned the humans of his own land. Before the night ended, not a single body in Ascalon City still drew a breath. The Foefire that towered over this carnage remains to this day.

"Eventually, Frye managed to free himself and then the other charr in his warband. Unbound, they slunk away from the disaster, determined to bring news of the atrocity to the rest of the charr.

"The Fireshadows returned to the invasion's staging grounds—the site of the Black Citadel today. When they delivered the news of the Flame imperator's defeat at Ascalon City, few who heard the news could believe their ears. Everyone who met Fireburn and his warband, though, trusted every word because they could see how the horrors they had witnessed had transformed them.

"From head to toe, the fur of each of them had turned a snowy white."

There was silence in the empty barn. Even Riona seemed cowed by the strength of Ember's story. At last Dougal said, "What of the Claw?"

"It was on the imperator," said Ember. "He was in the city. There were a few attempts at salvage by the charr after the Foefire, but there were too many ghosts, and the city itself was declared off-limits. We had assumed that it had been destroyed."

"Someone thinks otherwise," said Kranxx. "Why else would the truce faction demand it, and Almorra think we could provide it?"

Gullik added, "It would be wherever this nameless imperator fell, then?"

Dougal scowled for a moment, then said, "It is in the royal treasury."

All eyes turned to him and he continued: "On the back of Dak's map there was a list. Gold, silver, tribute, and gifts from different lands. Suits of ornate armor. An inventory of the royal treasury. And at the bottom of it, the word 'claw.' That's why I think it is there."

"How would anyone know it was there, if it disappeared in the Foefire?" said Riona. Her earlier irritation had evaporated by this point.

"That I do not know," said Dougal. "I suspect it was on another piece of parchment and transferred to the map later, perhaps by a group of salvagers that knew more legends than we did. If someone had uncovered the royal regalia of the treasury over the past two hundred years, whether they were charr or human, we would have heard of it."

"As with the Claw," said Riona.

"As with the Claw," agreed Dougal. "It is a tenuous link, but the most likely one."

"Mysteries upon mysteries," yawned Gullik. "I know I have spent a hard night walking, and more in sight. Let us think more of this later, after a good sleep."

Kranxx volunteered for the first watch. Dougal

offered to join him. Riona didn't say anything to him, but she was less frosty and more relaxed as she laid out her bedroll. The shock of the previous night had washed over her, Dougal decided, and she had come to terms with it. That did not surprise him. If Riona was anything, she was resilient.

Putting his back against one of the feed barn's walls, Dougal pulled out the locket with Vala's cameo. It felt warm and reassuring in the darkness. Dougal removed the Golem's Eye as well and saw a warm red spark dancing at its heart. He wondered if he could use it to see the cameo.

"Is that what I think it is?" Kranxx was suddenly at his side. "How did you get your hands on a vintage ambient thaumaturgic construct like that? They don't enchant them like that anymore."

Dougal wanted to hide the gem, to keep it a secret. Yet, hadn't keeping secrets done nothing but hurt him and the others? Slowly he held it up and let it catch the moonlight shining through the slots of the barn wall.

"I . . . recovered it," Dougal said, "with Killeen's help. From the tomb of an asura named Blimm."

At the mention of Blimm's name, Kranxx choked. Dougal smacked him on the back to help him clear his throat.

"May I . . . see it?" said the asura, with the voice of a child asking for a third piece of candy.

Dougal's mouth was a thin line, but hesitantly he handed the gem over.

The asura examined the gem closely. "It's been deactivated," he said. "That's standby illumination in the heart. That is old magic, from just after my ancestors emerged on the surface." The asura blinked at it, turned it over in his hands, whistled softly, then handed it back. Dougal noticed that Kranxx seemed to have the same problem returning it that he had had giving it.

"It did that automatically after we left the crypts beneath Divinity's Reach," said Dougal.

Kranxx grinned as Dougal pocketed the gem. "It's an archaic spell matrix, but I think I know just how to recharge it. If you're interested, of course."

Dougal felt uncomfortable. The Golem's Eye was a victory, messy and bought at a high price, but a victory nonetheless. And should everything go south, it would bring a pretty gold piece in Lion's Arch, or even Rata Sum.

And the sudden avarice in Kranxx's eye reminded him of Clagg.

"I think we have other things to worry about," said Dougal, and, to his surprise, the asura did not argue or offer any retort. Instead he just nodded and crossed to the far side of the barn and sat by the other entrance.

Yet, through the rest of their watch, Dougal felt that the asura was watching him, not the outside world. And when, after a few uneventful hours, Ember and Gullik took their watch, Dougal shifted the gem to another pocket, buttoned it, and then slept on that side for the rest of the evening.

It was almost morning when Dougal awoke, refreshed. His hand went to his pocket, but the gem was still there, and he cursed his own distrust. He looked around: Riona, Ember, and Kranxx were all asleep in the soft hay. Gullik was alone and awake by one of the barn doors.

"Couldn't sleep?" Dougal asked.

Gullik shook his head. "Normally I sleep like Bear herself, but sleep was a prey I could not catch this evening."

Dougal sat down next to the norn. Because of their difference in size, he felt like a child sitting with a parent.

"Thinking about Killeen?"

Gullik nodded.

"It's not your fault."

"Of course it is! If I had not charged into battle against that minion, we might have escaped from the Dragon-brand clean!"

"Or it might have run us down and killed us all."

"I would like to believe you are right."

Dougal thought about this for a moment, then spoke. "Gullik, you charge into battle. That's who you are, and we all know it. Killeen, she stuck by her friends, and we all knew that too. What happened was inevitable."

"You mean she had to die?"

"Not at all. I mean you had to fight the creature, and she had to help you."

"And you had to join us too!"

Dougal smiled a bit at this, the first time he'd managed it since Killeen had been killed. "Apparently. Either way, you can't fault yourself for being yourself. The rest of us don't."

Gullik let out a deep sigh. "It is a painful thing when friends perish. It is a worse thing when they die because of your choices."

"I understand," said Dougal. "And I've often thought

that you should never adventure with people you like, because it is difficult to lose them. But having friends with you makes the journey so much better."

The norn reached out and slapped Dougal on the back with a surprisingly soft blow. "You would make a good norn. And I don't toss around such an honor without reason!"

Gullik's loud voice woke the others up, and they pulled themselves awake. Already the sun was cresting the far horizon, throwing prison-bar shadows through the barn. They breakfasted on cold rations, and even Riona seemed the better for a good sleep.

"We should burrow in for the day," said Riona. "It is too dangerous to be out in daylight."

"No," said Ember, and for once her voice was subdued, almost worried. "There will be herdsmen out for the cattle. I doubt there will be any patrols, but the charr are very good at reporting trespassers."

"What do you recommend?" asked Dougal.

The charr took a deep breath and let the air out in a slow growl. "Gullik," she said, "do you still have those manacles?"

Gullik smiled and said, "Of course! You gave them to me, and I have held them for you!"

Riona's eyes went wide. "No," she said. "No, that is not what's going to happen."

"I'm afraid so," said Ember, hiding whatever delight she might be feeling behind a concerned exterior. "The only way you two humans can enter the Ascalon Basin is as my prisoners."

22

You have to be kidding," said Riona, flushing.

"I wish I were," said Ember. "We have been fortunate so far, but we are moving into areas occupied by charr settlers, warbands, and small patrols. We can travel by day as a charr and her captured human renegades."

Dougal nodded at the idea, but Riona said, "You cannot expect us to be unarmed and defenseless in the midst of charr territory."

"Remind me," said Gullik, "have we had this discussion before? It seems oddly familiar."

"Give me a moment," said Dougal, and steered Riona away from the others. She resisted stiffly but finally went with him. "You realize you sound like Ember when we were in Ebonhawke."

"And look how well that turned out," said Riona hotly.

"But she's right. And you asked me a while back if I trust her. I do, and you should as well."

"It's not *her* I'm suddenly doubting." She looked accusingly into his eyes. Despite himself, Dougal turned away, shamed and silenced.

"Here is what I need to know," she said. "What you said back on the battlements of Ebonhawke. You promised. Did you mean it? Will you help me get the Claw?"

Dougal felt his face grow hot. "Of course. Yes. I meant it. We will get the Claw of the Khan-Ur."

"All right, then," she said, and walked over to Ember, now holding the chains. She held her wrists up to be shackled. "Let's do this and get on the road."

In the end, the chained manacles, originally fitted for the charr's wrists, were too large for the humans. Kranxx rearranged the metal cuffs and chains, fitting one wrist manacle around Riona's neck and one around Dougal's, and settled for loose ropes around their wrists. The third large cuff, which had been fitted for the charr's neck, Ember handed to the norn.

"You are their keeper," said Ember. "Norn mercenaries are common enough. No one will question why a charr is using a norn to keep an eye on prisoners."

"And how do you explain me, perched on his shoulder?" said Kranxx.

"You'll be walking, I'm afraid," said Ember. "And pull out that lightning rod of yours."

"It's nonfunctional," said the asura. "The metaspell solenoids are shot."

"Then don't tell anyone that," said Ember. "Just threaten our prisoners with it and look superior."

"That I can do," said Kranxx.

"Please don't try to enjoy this," said Riona through gritted teeth.

"I promise to try," said Ember as Gullik put the humans' weapons into his satchel. Dougal hated to lose the sword, but Ember left him his locket and the Golem's Eye. And, most importantly, his lock picks.

Ember took a deep breath and squared her shoulders, then led their contingent out into the day.

The early going was as it had been the previous night: rolling fields interrupted by fenced paddocks. Dougal now saw that the fences were topped with sawtooth shards of metal, and was glad they had not stumbled into one of them. There were more herds of cattle, and clusters of larger, furrier creatures. Dolyaks. When they intruded on their fields, the dolyaks retreated into tight circular formations, their horns turned outward.

After about a mile, they reached a more established path, heading generally east to west. Ember turned the group west and their time improved.

Then, cresting a rise, they encountered another group of charr. Despite himself, Dougal almost stumbled in his chains, and Gullik shot him a stern, withering look.

There were only about ten of them, merchants and guards clustered around a single heavily laden wagon drawn by a tired-looking dolyak. At the sight of the group with the human prisoners, the charr visibly reacted, some reaching for their weapons. Ember saluted them and marched past, a somber, superior Gullik in her wake with the humans and Kranxx bringing up the rear.

Dougal tried to keep his head down but hazarded a glance at the charr as they passed. Some looked at them with curiosity, some with surprise, and a very few with open hostility, their lips curled back in anger. Dougal put his head back down and concentrated on the ground in front of them whenever they came upon another group.

The path gathered trails from other sides and became more of a road now, with two well-worn wagon ruts and a high, grassy crest in the middle. They passed more merchants and farmers as well, in ones or twos. The farmers or ranchers or civilians stood aside as Ember brought her group through, and mutters and whispers followed them.

They themselves stood aside when a Blood Legion warband marched up the road. Ember saluted again and the front ranks returned her salute, but no one stopped to question them. In the back ranks, a couple charr, male and female alike, thumped their chests and roared as they passed the humans, and then laughed with their fellows.

About midday they reached a crossroad set up with a ring of fully manned war wagons. Ember halted them a hundred feet from the perimeter and said to Gullik in a loud voice, "You two watch the prisoners. I need to eat. I may bring you something back." Then she set off, the norn pulling Riona and Dougal to one side. Kranxx took up a position nearby with his inoperative lightning wand.

"I swear," said Riona softly, "that she is enjoying all this."

Dougal shook his head. "She is worried, just like you were, back in Ebonhawke. Everything rests on her. One false move and we are all done."

A few more charr passed them, most of them scowling. Gullik scowled back. No one gave them any trouble, and after about ten minutes Ember returned with a satchel. She fished out a prodigious slab of beef for the Norn, smaller slices and rolls for the humans and asura.

"What is it?" said Riona.

"It's warm," said Kranxx with a laugh, and Dougal realized that in their furtive travel they had not had a fire or a warm meal since Ebonhawke.

"Feeding your pets, kitling?" said a rough, base voice, and Dougal looked up to see a broad-shouldered charr lurching toward them. Dougal would have guessed he was an older charr, as his muzzle was fuzzed with gray and his horns were dull and worn. He was in battered, archaic armor, and Dougal noted that his left hand was mangled, missing a few fingers.

Despite his appearance, Ember pounded her chest in a salute. "Ember Doomforge, Ash Legion."

The older charr returned her salute, though stiffly. "Fellblow the Savage, Iron Legion, before I mustered out. I notched my sword on enough of these mice over the years. Why are these ones still alive?"

Ember shrugged. "I don't question my superiors. I merely carry out their orders. These vermin go to Black Citadel. Imperator business. I think they're spies."

"Huh," said Fellblow. "You need them both alive?" Dougal's heart dropped into his boots.

"For the moment," said Ember, and forced a laugh. The Iron Legion charr laughed as well, and moved on. Dougal suddenly realized that he had been holding his breath.

Ember pointed to the west. She said quietly, "This road will eventually take us to the Black Citadel. Instead we'll cut north when no one else is on the road. The Loreclaws are north of us, and beyond them the Ascalon Basin. Beyond that is the city."

Gullik and Kranxx nodded. Dougal looked at Riona, and her eyes were alive with a terrible fury.

A half-mile west of the crossroads, the land turned rockier, and now there were fewer ranches and almost no road traffic. Ember led them off the road and up into the hills.

The land was much as it must have been before the charr invaded, perhaps as it was before the humans arrived. Great boulders and faces of gray granite framed the valleys, worn by water and the insidious roots of slender young trees. The wind kicked up from the north, bearing with it a cool breeze.

"It should be easier for a while," said Ember, "at least until we reach the basin itself."

"Then you should let us out of these," said Riona, pulling at the neck shackle. It was leaving a red welt on her flesh.

"Not yet." Ember looked at the humans. "I only said 'easier.' These lands are not without peril. There are bandits in these hills, some human, some charr, some other races. And there are patrols here. There is less of a chance that some group will come upon us, but that chance exists."

"What she is saying," put in Kranxx, "is that the legions rule this land like the human queen does hers. They rule the cities and control the roads, but in the wild lands between the villages and the camps, a traveler is on his own."

Ember ignored the asura and looked at Dougal. "If there is a problem, free her first." She pointed at Riona. Dougal nodded.

They walked through most of the day without major incident. Once they came upon a small family of devourers, huge scorpions with two poisonous tails, feasting on the corpse of a deer. The devourers hissed and arched their double tails in warning, and Ember gave them a clear berth.

They finished off the last of the food that Ember had purchased, and pressed on, looking for a suitable place for the evening. That was when they heard shouts ahead, the clash of metal, gunfire, and explosions.

Ember and Gullik looked at each other, then carefully made their way up the rocky hillside, the norn dragging Riona and Dougal with him. Kranxx kept an eye on their rear flank.

The charr and the norn crawled the last few feet to the crest of the hill, and the humans followed. Topping the rise, Dougal was surprised by what he saw.

Charr fighting charr.

There was a bowl-shaped valley beneath them, dominated by a great campfire and lined with about a half-dozen tents. The valley had a prominent entrance, and through that cleft a patrol of Blood Legion warriors were pressing their way into a group of charr in red-golden armor. The Blood Legion warriors were led by a great black-furred charr, armed with a fiery sword, who shouted orders as the turmoil milled around them. The red-golden defenders were being pushed back, but some of them were armed with rifles that shot fire, playing them over the attackers like water from a hose. Near the campfire a charr in ornate robes was shouting what Dougal could only think of as an incantation.

"Flame Legion," snarled Ember, her eyes alight and her lips pulled back from her teeth. To Gullik she said, "You stay here. I'll be right back."

Riona barked, "No!" but Ember had already risen and was half leaping, half tumbling down the far side of the hill.

Dougal cursed as well. He could think of no advantage in going into battle with the charr. In her dark armor Ember might be identified as a friend of the Blood Legion, but any human in their midst was a target.

Ember was down among the tents now, bearing down on the shaman by the fire, her heavy blade drawn. Already the charr shaman's voice was reaching a crescendo, and something large was stirring from among the timbers of the flame. As Dougal watched, a wicker-shod arm wrapped in flame issued from the heart of the great campfire.

Gullik cursed, and Dougal saw that the norn was trying to physically restrain himself from charging into the battle. He looked at the emerging creature, then back at the humans, then to the camp again like a dog desperate for a treat.

"An effigy," he said at last. "The Flame Legion has summoned a flame effigy. I've heard of them, but I've never seen one. Never fought one."

"Go," snapped Kranxx. "I'll keep watch up here. Just don't get killed."

Without further encouragement, Gullik dropped his end of the chain, pulled his battle-axe, and, with a cry that resounded through the bowl of the valley, threw himself down the steep inner hillside. Dougal thought that, at the norn's shout, every charr's head in the battle turned toward them, before resuming their internecine struggle.

There was gunfire, and shots passed over their heads from Blood legionnaires unsure if they were possible allies or reinforcements for the Flame Legion. Dougal, Riona, and Kranxx flattened themselves on the hilltop.

"Spring the lock," said Riona, pointing to her neck.

Dougal looked down at the battlefield. Ember had reached the Flame Legion shaman and in a single blow cut him down. He crumpled like a set of empty ropes, but his enchantment had succeeded. Another heavy arm reached out of the flame, and now rising from the heart of the campfire was a giant's head wrapped in fire—a mockery of a charr warrior's head. Gullik was making for it, fearful someone would reach it first and deny him his fair slaughter of the creature.

"Ember said if something happens, free me," said Riona sharply. "This qualifies. Do it."

Dougal pulled the pouch with his lock picks from his pocket, and as he did he noticed there was someone behind him.

The Flame Legion soldier had appeared at the base of their hill, away from the battle. He wore a cumbersome backpack and held a strange rifle attached to the backpack by a flexible pipe. Whether the charr was a deserter or a picket or a patrol, he spotted them now.

"Hurry," said Kranxx, "I'll keep him busy." The asura raced down the hill, brandishing his useless lightning wand.

The Flame charr lifted his rifle and a jet of fire spat from its barrel, a stream of liquid flame that lanced toward the asura. The asura yelped and threw himself out of the way, dancing into a thicket of brush.

Dougal bent his head and concentrated on foiling the lock. It was a simple matter, the lock known to him and sprung before, and it pulled away from Riona easily.

The Flame charr had followed Kranxx and now played his flame rifle through the thicket, igniting the brush. As a result, he did not see Riona bearing down on him until the last moment.

She slammed into him hard, and the pair tumbled together down the hillside. She pulled away from him as the tube connecting the rifle and the backpack broke and fire in a thick trail streamed behind the legionnaire. The air took on a smoky tang from the burning brush, and Dougal's eyes watered. At the bottom of the hill, the charr struggled loose from his backpack, which apparently carried the rifle's fuel, his fur smoking. Before him, slightly uphill, Riona faced him. She was armed with a rock she had picked up.

For a moment the two locked eyes, then the charr did something Dougal did not expect. He bolted. Turned and ran from a stone-wielding human. Riona let out a cry and chased after him.

Dougal shouted as well and started down the hill, gathering up the lengths of chain to use as a weapon. Halfway down, he heard some urgent coughing, and Kranxx stumbled out of the scalded brush. His bare arms were blistered, and his wide eyes rheumy from the smoke.

"You're alive," said Dougal, and realized how happy he was.

"Only for the moment," said the asura. "Get me to my pack."

Dougal looked at where Riona had disappeared, then back up the hill to where the packs still lay. He half walked, half carried the asura back up the hill, where he dug through his pack filled with waxed-paper wrappings, finally producing a reddish philter. He drank it down without further comment, and then spent a long moment spewing up black powder. The flesh on his bare limbs crusted and fell away, revealing new flesh, a lighter shade of gray, beneath.

Dougal looked down into the valley. The Flame Legion troops were breaking, and the Blood legionnaires were upon them, cutting them down in ones and twos. More importantly, Ember and Gullik had engaged the effigy, the charr dancing forward and lancing the creature with the tip of her sword, enraging it, while the norn hacked at its burning legs with the zeal of a crazed lumberjack. As Dougal watched, the huge creature swayed, then fell backward in a flurry of burning wicker and sparks.

Dougal turned back toward where Riona had disappeared, but Kranxx grabbed the chain. "No," said the asura. "She'll be back. I hope."

Dougal had to nod. Already the battle had abated to the point that members of the Blood Legion were pointing up at them on the hillside, and about a half-dozen members of the victorious legion were hustling up to collect them. Dougal had time to stow his picks and stand there docilely while Kranxx, conspicuously holding the other end of the chain, tried to look both in charge and nonthreatening.

The charr patrol gathered up their gear and pushed Dougal down the slope to the rest of the troops ahead of them. Ember was already arguing with some officer when they arrived.

"These are my prisoners," said Ember. "I demand you release them to me at once."

"We appreciate your help, Doomforge," replied the officer, another female charr with tawny fur, "but I cannot allow you to pass without knowing your business."

"I am on the business of Malice Swordshadow, the Ash Legion imperator," said Ember, snarling. "I cannot and will not tell you the nature of my mission."

"Nor should you," came a deep, resonate voice from the perimeter of the discussion. "I will be dining with Swordshadow at the end of the week, and I shall take the opportunity to ask the imperator about it."

The soldiers parted to reveal the commanding charr, the one with coal-black fur and hard, angry eyes. His fiery blade was now sheathed. Dougal could tell by his ease and swagger that he was the top cat in this army.

What surprised Dougal most of all was the way

that Ember immediately stiffened with the arrival of the newcomer, coming fully to attention and executing a perfect salute. She was more intimidated by this charr commander than she was by even Almorra Soulkeeper.

"Ember Doomforge, Ash Legion, Detached, sir!" she barked.

"At ease, soldier," said the dark-furred charr. Ember did not relax a single hair. "These are yours?"

"Yes, sir!" said Ember. "I am taking these prisoners in for questioning. They were found near the Dragonbrand!"

The dark-furred charr grunted. "You said 'prisoners.' Plural. I think you're missing one or more of them."

Ember wheeled and for the first time realized that Riona wasn't there. A look of shock and fear spread across her face. "Where *is* she?" she hissed at Kranxx.

The asura stammered for a moment, then managed, "We were assaulted by a Flame rifleman. We drove him away, but in the confusion the female human escaped. I express my deepest apology and will offer a refund."

"Just wonderful," muttered the dark-furred commander. Louder, he shouted, "We have a mouse loose! I want it caught—now! Get trackers on it, starting up on the hill."

"Sir?" said Ember, and Dougal could almost sense the fear on her. "I need the . . . prisoner . . . alive and unharmed."

The commander grunted again and bellowed, "I want the mouse alive and unharmed! Any of you bring her back in pieces, and I will have your guts for garters! Am I clear?"

There was a sharp expression of agreement, and the milling charr broke into teams. Some gathered the deceased Blood Legion charr by the campfire for burning. Others laid out the dead Flame legionnaires for the crows and vultures. Meanwhile, a large contingent headed up the hill.

"You will accompany us," said the commander. "We will talk later."

"Sir, yes, sir!" said Ember, who saluted again as the commander turned and marched over to where other charr were emptying the contents of the Flame Legion tents.

Ember did not relax as much as fall in on herself. A picket of other Blood Legion formed up around them. Gullik took the chain from Kranxx, and Ember made a show of checking Dougal's neck manacle.

"What happened?" said the charr, fussing with the still-locked cuff.

"We were ambushed, like Kranxx said," whispered Dougal. "The rifleman would have fried him, but I freed Riona and she tackled him. The rifleman lit out and Riona chased after him."

"Idiot," said Ember, and Dougal was unsure if she was talking about Kranxx, Dougal, Riona, or herself. Then she added, "Keep your mouth shut and pray to your foolish gods."

"What's wrong?" Dougal managed.

"I may have taken you from the skillet into the flames," said Ember. "A regular charr commander I could bluster my way past, but this—"

"What?"

"The commanding officer," said Ember. "He is Tribune Rytlock Brimstone, hero of my people. If he chooses to take you off my hands, there is nothing I can do to stop him."

23

The Blood Legion charr returned with Riona within the hour. She was battered and bruised, but the charr followed the tribune's orders to the letter. She was whole and her eyes blazed with anger.

The charr brought her before Ember, and the two locked eyes for a moment, then Ember pulled back and lashed out with a wicked backhand slap. It caught Riona on her chin, and she collapsed to her knees from the force of the blow.

"Chain her up," snarled Ember, pointing at Kranxx and Gullik, "and do it right this time, or I'll stake you out for the ravens!"

The charr who had captured Riona nodded with approval and told Ember how they had found her, crouched in a shallow cave. She had no weapons and had surrendered.

Gullik and Kranxx reattached the chains.

"She had to do that, you know" said Gullik softly. "She cannot show weakness."

Riona glowered. "That's not what I'm mad about. I lost the charr I was chasing. He got away."

"Wait for later to tell Ember that," suggested Kranxx.

The company formed up, with Ember and her prisoners in the center. No one but Ember was allowed to take control of the prisoners, but there was no way they could escape. Burning their dead with the tents of the Flame Legion, the company moved north, Rytlock Brimstone at its head.

They moved at a double-march speed, such that Kranxx was scurrying to keep up. Behind them curled the smoke from the burning tents, and having advertised their presence, Rytlock had no intention of remaining in the area.

Dougal could feel the sweat of exertion and fear run down his back. They were surrounded by charr, and he felt like a mouse among cats. The urge to bolt, to flee, was strong, and he was afraid it would overmatch his better judgment.

He looked at Riona and saw that she was staring ahead, the welt from Ember's strike still vivid on her face. She noticed Dougal looking at her and nodded. At the next rest break in the march, she leaned toward him.

"This commander is a slave driver," she said.

"Ember said the commander is Rytlock Brimstone," replied Dougal. "She's afraid of him. I don't blame her."

"You know about this Rytlock?" said Riona.

"Big-time charr hero," said Dougal, and one or two charr soldiers glanced toward them. He shut up until they looked away. "He was one of Destiny's Edge. Legendary adventurers. Captain Logan Thackeray was one of that group, along with the asura Snaff, the sylvari Caithe, and the norn Eir."

"Eir Stegalkin," said Gullik sternly. "She was a great hero, once." He stressed the word "was."

"So the slave driver hung out with us mere humans? Pitiful," said Riona, loud enough for a few charr heads to twist in her direction.

"The prisoner will be silent!" snapped Kranxx, and slapped Riona's haunch with the lightning rod. Dougal admired that Riona didn't strike out against the asura.

They marched through the heat of the day, reaching the base camp by the late afternoon. The beachside camp was on the shores of the lake dominating the Ascalon Basin, and was laid out with military precision, lines of tents arranged in grids. The troops were dismissed and returned to their assigned quarters, leaving Ember and her prisoners alone. The charr stood there, waiting, and within a few moments the black-furred tribune stormed up.

"Doomforge!" snapped Rytlock Brimstone.

"Sir, yes, sir!" said Ember, snapping to attention. Riona stifled a laugh and Dougal scowled at her.

"You are a mystery. I don't like mysteries in my camp," Brimstone snarled. "You will take the furthest tent, down by the shore."

"Yes, sir!" Ember looked petrified.

Brimstone ignored her discomfort. "There is an empty supply skiff moored there. We are going to abandon it and report it scuttled. I want you out of here before tomorrow morning. We are heading east along the coast. Choose a different direction."

"Understood, sir!"

"Understand this," said Brimstone. "I don't want to see your face again. Dismissed!"

Ember executed a crisp salute and said, "Yes sir!" She motioned to Gullik to pull the humans down toward the far end of the tents.

"And, Doomforge . . ." said Rytlock Brimstone.

"Yes, sir!"

"You have your grandmother's eyes," said the tribune, and managed what Dougal could only imagine was a smile.

"Thank you, sir!" said Ember, suddenly relaxing a fraction of an inch, and waving for the others to follow.

The selected tent had been newly erected a fair distance from the crisp lines and close to the abandoned skiff. Ember indicated to the others to step inside. "Get your rest, we'll leave once night has settled."

"He knows," said Kranxx, pulling off his rumpled hat and running his fingers through his hair. "He knows what we're doing."

"No," replied Ember. "That is, he knows I am up to something, and that Imperator Swordshadow is somehow involved. And that we are a mystery, and he hates mysteries. The sooner we sneak out, the sooner he will be relieved of thinking about what we're up to."

"And what did he mean about your grandmother's eyes?" said Riona.

"I thought it was obvious," said Ember, pausing at the entrance to the tent. "He knows my grandmother. You rest. You will need your energy." And then she was gone, leaving the others to make themselves comfortable as they saw fit. Dougal did not remove his chains, and Riona did not request it. They rested until dark.

For an abandoned skiff scheduled for scuttling the boat proved to be well stocked. A pair of heavy oars were set in muffled locks near the stern, and a long steering pole was laid alongside a gunwale. Beneath the seats were a few tins of boiled meat.

The asura took the bow, the humans and Ember behind him. Gullik pushed off from shore and, nimbly for his size, settled in at the rowing bench. They rowed away from the camp on quiet oars. No one would admit to seeing them leave.

Once they were far enough from the shore that the charr campfires were hot red dots, Ember unlocked the manacles. Dougal wanted to throw them into the lake but instead handed them over to Gullik, who paused from his rowing long enough to stash them back in his satchel and return Riona's and Dougal's weapons to them.

The moon was already up when they left the camp, but the lake swallowed its light utterly. They rowed through the darkness, the horizon only obvious from where the stars ended and complete blackness began. Far to the north there was a faint glow, something throwing the moonlight back into the sky.

Riona and Dougal took turns at the bow of the boat with the pole, feeling in the darkness for the bottom and moving aside logs and lakeweed in their path. There was a splashing off the port side, but when Dougal turned, all he could see was a flash of silver scales diving.

There was another light up ahead, this one the color of flames. As they closed, it resolved into two, then four,

then a dozen different fires, all contained within great
iron foundries.

"Irondock," said Ember, identifying the place. "It is
one of our weapons foundries. It runs all day and night.
Hang to the far bank."

Gullik proved to be a subtle and deft rower, and
moved the shallow-drafted skiff to the left side of the lake
and through a narrow passage. Now they could hear the
clanging of anvils and the roar of forges across the water,
combined with the snarling shouts of the overseers.

The lake narrowed and they could see the docks,
metal-shod boats bobbing at the quay. Then Gullik
passed them as well, and they were around a rock outcropping and turned back toward the north.

"You are making weapons," said Riona quietly.

"Aye," said Ember. "Even if there is peace with the
humans and Ebonhawke, the legions have no end of
enemies. Ghosts, Flame Legion, ogres, grawl . . ."

"And dragons," added Dougal.

"And dragons," agreed Ember, although in the darkness Dougal could not see the look on the charr's face.

Now the glow to the north resolved itself more clearly.
It was not a reflection of the racing moon but a brilliant radiance with its own source. As they cleared the
channel and the terrain opened up to the north, Dougal
could see it more fully and recognized it.

It was a single ray of brilliant white light reaching to
the heavens, raised like a sword over the northern darkness. And like a blade it cut Dougal to the heart, for at its
base was the center of the Foefire.

In its distant light, Dougal could see the faces of the

others. Ember was familiar with the sight and was unimpressed, but Riona and Kranxx stared at the beacon on the horizon. Even Gullik, reliable rower that he had been, stopped his labors and stared at it, openmouthed, before recovering himself and resuming his regular strokes.

The lake was shallower now, and Dougal was touching bottom with his pole more often than not. Trees started to appear at the shores: long-limbed mangroves fluttering with bats and nightswallows. Finally the water became marsh, which became land solid enough to walk upon. Ember pointed to an outcropping on the northern shore, and Gullik pulled the boat up on the thick mud. Ember started up the bank, and the others followed, although Dougal now knew the land well.

The northern horizon had changed, limned by the power of the Foefire's heart. It was now an irregular shadow, angular and blocky. The remains of Ascalon City itself.

At the top of the bank was a broad road, and after waiting a few moments the group skittered across it, avoiding any charr patrols. Only when they were on the northern side of the road did Ember react and make for one of the low hills overlooking the city in shadows. They climbed to the top, where they came upon the petrified remains of several great poles that had stood, undisturbed, for two centuries.

"The Viewing Hill," said Dougal, knowing it from the tale. "This was where Fireburn watched the Foefire."

"Yes," said Ember, "and here I complete my task and my knowledge fails me. We're going to need your knowledge of the city, come morning."

"And until dawn?" asked Dougal.

"We wait," said the charr.

They were close enough to the city now that there was little danger of charr patrols, but still beyond the city walls, and there was little risk of ghosts. Dougal could see the spires of the broken towers of the city, dimly lit by the brilliance of the Foefire. It looked like a ghost city, the perfect home for the dead. About an hour after they arrived, a bank of clouds moved in from the west, capturing the moon and overtaking the skyblade of the Foefire. The light from the heart of the curse splashed against the bottom of the clouds.

Now that they stood on the edge of the city, the group was uneasy. Rest would be good, but this close, none were in the mood. Ember prowled the perimeter, watchful for charr patrols. Kranxx fiddled with things in his pack. Gullik sat on the southern end of the hill, facing away from the city itself, looking out over the roads and lake to the south. Only Riona seemed willing to rest, but she was seated, her helmet and sword laid to one side, as if she were waiting for something.

As for Dougal, he tried to relax, looking up at the pattern the Foefire's beacon made across the sky. But at last he had to give up, and sat up, looking at the city's crumbling edifices.

Kranxx cleared his throat. "You still have that ambient thaumaturgic construct?" the asura asked.

"The Golem's Eye?" Dougal nodded.

"Can I see it?" Kranxx said.

Dougal fished the stone from his pocket and gazed at it again. It was worth more than he might otherwise make in a year, but that did him little good at the moment. "Sure," he said, dropping it into the asura's hand. "Just make sure you take care of it."

"Oh," Kranxx said, "that I can promise you. I had to leave most of my tools back in Ebonhawke, but I brought a matrixulator. I could recalibrate it into a recharging device, given sufficient sympathetic energy."

Dougal blinked at the asura, realizing for the first time what Kranxx had given up to come along. For most of the trip, he had thought the asura was concerned with his own skin. Now it was clear he had left behind his lab and his projects, which for an asura were as important as his life.

"Why don't you hold on to it," said Dougal, "and see if you can figure it out."

The asura's eyes opened wide and his long ears perked up. "Hang on!" he said, and ran back to his pack, rooted around in it a bit, then came back with one of his bottles, a red syrup oozing down its sides. "Here. Use this if you're injured. It's a good batch. I think."

Dougal smiled and put the untested potion in his pocket. "And if we don't find enough treasure in Ascalon City, that gem is yours. Buy yourself a new workshop."

Kranxx made a choking, gurgling noise and pulled out a device that looked like the product of a union between a violin and a crossbow. "Yes. Yes! You see, it is fully primed, but just needs some basic arcanic updates to handle the annual progression of the stars over the past two centuries!"

Dougal shook his head, understanding about one

word in three. Which when dealing with the asura, was better than usual. He looked up and saw Gullik's broad back, his legs hanging over the southern-facing cliff.

"If you'll excuse me . . ." said Dougal, standing up.

The asura looked almost disappointed. "You don't want to hear me explain how it works?"

"Later, perhaps," Dougal said. "I owe Gullik a story."

Dougal walked over to where Gullik was sitting, crossing paths with the patrolling charr. Ember just nodded at him and continued on her rounds. The human sat down next to the norn, looked out over the quiet emptiness south of the city, and coughed softly.

"I first met Gyda . . ." said Dougal, and noticed that Gullik flinched at the name. He started again. "I first met Gyda Oddsdottir in a second-story room in a tavern in Divinity's Reach. We had both been hired by Clagg, who you've met. And let me say that Clagg was the type of asura who would only be brave if he was backed up by a large golem or a norn. Clagg had both, and the norn was your powerful cousin, so you can imagine he was insufferable."

Gullik let out a chuckle, and Dougal continued. He spoke of their adventures beneath Divinity's Reach, of finding Blimm's tomb, and of the final battle with the skeletal tomb guardian. He did not mention Gyda's bullying or threats, and once or twice, when he spoke of her kind nature, Gullik gave him a sidewise glance and a smile. For the most part, he told the truth, but it was the truth you would speak about the dead for the benefit of the living.

When he had finished, Gullik clapped Dougal on the

shoulder. By that time the sky was lightening to the east, although its rise would be obscured by the gathering clouds. It would be an overcast and gray day in the dead city.

The slow, colorless dawn revealed a city of tombstones. Its outer walls were broken apart like a jumble of loose teeth, and its spires and structures were canted, their windows and doors shattered and empty. Dougal could make out the sites from his map and his earlier visit. There was the Sunrise Tower of the palace, its spire rising above all others. The royal treasury was within the palace complex. There had been a central tower, but that had fallen, taking King Adelbern and his curse with it. There was the hall of records, now roofless, its contents rotted by time and weather.

And there was the central plaza, where he had to shoot Jervis. His heart sank at the sight. The others came up behind him, but for the longest moment, no one spoke.

"It's a wreck," Riona said. "A horrible, terrible ruin. I—I knew the stories, of course, but I never . . ."

"It's worse on the inside," said Dougal.

"So," Ember said, looking to Dougal, "what is our plan of attack?"

Dougal turned to look at the other four. All were armed and waiting for him. There was no question of turning back now, even if they wanted to. They had paid too high a price to get this far.

"This way," said Dougal, although as he spoke he felt he was condemning all of them to their deaths.

Dougal led the others down to the city's crumbling

outer wall and followed it around to the right, away
from the gaping maw of the main gates. "This is how we
entered the last time," he said.

"And we all know how well that went," said Kranxx.

"Why don't we march in through the front gates?"
said Gullik.

"Every ghost in the city would come to meet us,"
Dougal said. "They're mostly mindless monsters, but
they remember being charged with protecting that
gate—and then watching it fall. They have watchers
there. Nothing—and no one—ever gets through it." He
pointed to a hole in the collapsed wall wide enough for
even Gullik to fit through. "Besides," he said, "I've been
this way before, so I know what to expect."

Riona looked at the wreckage of stone and mortar
around her. "I never imaged it would be this bad."

"Steel yourself, then," Dougal said as he climbed over
several feet of rubble to reach the back of an alley on the
wall's other side. "There are worse things in here than
ghosts."

"Bear's bones!" Gullik said. "What could be worse
than an army of ghosts?"

Dougal led the team to the mouth of the alley, which
opened up on a wide street that had once been a center of commerce in the city. As he reached the street,
Dougal stepped back and waved his arms to present the
scene to the others. "What's worse?" he said. "All the bodies from which they came."

The bones, armor, and weapons of the soldiers that
had been fighting at the time of the Foefire littered the
streets. Most of the skeletons lay there still intact, having

had to endure only a couple of centuries of weather and sun. Unlike on other battlefields, birds and other animals refused to pick at the flesh here, the ghosts and the Foefire itself keeping them far away.

The first bodies lay at the mouth of the alley, and as Gullik brushed past one of them, it fell to pieces. The bones clattered and the armor clanged on the cobblestones, startling them all. Gullik cursed his clumsiness, then withdrew behind Dougal again.

"Nothing is holding those bodies together but memories," said Riona.

"Those memories are fading fast," said Dougal. He pointed at a small square that the street opened onto. "That's the way we're headed."

"And where are we going?" asked Ember.

"Ultimately, to the royal treasury, beneath the palace. Finding a way down once we reach it is another challenge. When Adelbern set off the Foefire, the buildings were shifted, and some of the lower stories were crushed by the upper. The king's chamber, atop the Sunrise Tower, was mostly unscathed. It should have some access."

"You say 'should' like you do not know," said Kranxx.

"We never got that far," said Dougal. "But then, we broke into the city at night."

Dougal crept up the street slowly, picking his way past the bodies and struggling to find a path that was wide enough that he could reasonably expect Gullik to be able to navigate it. Although Dougal was certain he'd given the norn plenty of room, Gullik still bumped over an occasional body, sending bones, weapons, and armor clattering along the cobblestones.

Dougal hoped that the ghosts would not be as active now, with the sun still on the rise, as they might be at night. Due to the city's high walls and surrounding buildings, though, shadows would hold on to the night long into the day.

And despite the fact that they had previously encountered the ghosts at night, it did not mean they were afraid of the day. Or any less lethal.

Soon they reached the street that led to the main square. As they drew closer, Dougal grew more and more tense. At one point he noticed he was unconsciously holding his breath. He had to force himself to breathe.

It was then that he realized where he was. Intentionally or not, he had brought the others to the very place where he had last seen Vala and Dak alive. He had struggled so hard to blot it from his memories that he didn't recognize it at first. But when he saw a familiar set of armor lying on the street in the center of a large bloodstain that the years had not done enough to fade, it all came flooding back to him.

He knelt down next to the skeleton that had once been his friend, and he reached out to touch the front of the helmet it still wore. "Dak Turnbull," he said. "How did it all go so wrong?"

Riona came up behind him and put a hand on his shoulder. "Is it really him?" The pain on her face made her look much older.

Dougal stood up and found himself in Riona's embrace. "It's all right," she said. "Finishing the job here will make it right." Then she stopped and Dougal felt

Riona's breath catch in her chest at something she saw over his shoulder.

"Oh, no," she whispered in his ear.

She might have said something else, but Dougal couldn't hear it. The sound of someone shouting from up the street drowned her out.

"Alarm! Alarm!" an ethereal, strident voice cried. "The walls have been breached! Invaders are in Ascalon City! Alarm! Alarm!"

24

Dougal spun around to see who was screaming at them. A ghostly figure stood across the street, pointing and yelling at Ember. She wore Ebonhawke armor and bore a greatsword in both hands. For a moment Dougal thought it was Vala herself, returned from the dead, and for that moment he was transfixed by the idea. But the mists around her face cleared to reveal a stranger, one of the watchers. That was when Dougal realized someone else was yelling at him.

"Dougal Keane!" Ember shouted. She grabbed his shoulder and pulled him around to look at her.

"What?" he asked, still stunned by everything roiling about in his head.

"That!" Ember stabbed a finger in the direction of another street that emptied out into the square. Dougal remembered from his research that this road led to the soldiers' barracks, although he was sure it had been centuries since anyone had slept there.

A column of ghostly soldiers stormed down that road,

rushing into the main square. Dougal recognized them at once as part of the same force that had killed his friends the last time he'd braved the streets of Ascalon City. These were the spirits of people slaughtered by the Foefire, like the simple shepherds they'd met near the Dragonbrand, only far more dangerous. He gazed into their faces and saw no love there, no compassion for the living, just madness and an all-consuming lust for death.

"Bear's blood!" Gullik said as he unlimbered his axe. "This will be a battle worthy of any saga!"

"You're a fool!" said Ember. "You can't beat them all!"

"I will not die without a fight!"

"Try not dying at all!" Kranxx said as he smacked the norn on the back of the head. "Run!"

"This way!" Ember sprinted away from the column of ghosts. She moved with the lumbering grace of a lion, weaving her way between and over the bodies scattered along the ground.

"Dougal!" Riona reached for Dougal's shoulders. "We need to go!" She snatched Dougal's hand and pulled him along, following the charr. Dougal stumbled along after her as best he could, although his feet felt as if they were bound with stones.

"We can't outrun them!" said Riona. "Head back for the gates."

"Too many between there and us!" said Dougal. To the others he shouted, "Follow me! We're going to the palace!"

Riona shot Dougal a hard look, and he said, "The ghosts think as they did in life. They try not to leave the city itself. So they should not violate the king's chamber without approval." He grabbed her arm and hauled her along with him for a few steps until she was back up to speed. She punched him in the back as she finally matched his pace.

"You idiot!" she said. "Why did you wait? What did you see?"

Dougal bit his tongue. This wasn't the time for the kind of discussion such words demanded. Instead, he just ran.

They wound their way through the streets of the city, racing toward the royal chambers. Because Dougal knew the way, Ember and Gullik, still carrying Kranxx, slowed down for Riona and him to catch up. Now in the lead, Dougal sprinted straight for their goal, and hoped that it was still standing.

Ahead of them rose a pillar of light, the energies of the Foefire itself coalesced into a single blade raised against the sky. When Adelbern summoned the Foefire on the battlements, he opened a sinkhole down through the catacombs that laced the foundations of the city. From that sinkhole rose a tower of radiance, the lasting memory to his great spell.

They turned right before they reached the luminous pillar, snaking through narrow alleys half-filled with rubble, leaving the ghosts behind. At last they reached the open court before the palace itself.

Dougal's heart quailed for a moment, for the lower reaches of the palace were blocked, their entrances crushed, the upper floors pancaked onto the lower ones. A single long staircase reached up along an inner wall.

Dougal checked his mental map and saw that it would lead to the royal chambers themselves.

Unfortunately, the staircase was guarded. A squad of ghostly soldiers stood there waiting for them. When they saw Ember, the guards at the gate drew their swords and charged at her. "Death to the invaders!!" they shouted. "Death! Death!"

"Is there any other way out of here?" Ember said as she drew her sword.

"No!" Dougal glanced back to see the soldiers they'd run from in the main square gaining on them fast. "We need to go through the guards! The royal chambers are at the top of the stairs." Dougal unsheathed his sword then, and the ebon blade seemed to hum in his hand.

"There are fewer of them ahead of us than behind," said Riona, her own blade drawn.

"Forward we go, then!" Dougal growled, turning back toward the steps and immediately running into Gullik's massive form. The norn grabbed Dougal to prevent him from tumbling backward.

"Hold him." Gullik pressed Kranxx into Dougal's arms. "Bear's nose! He's a good friend but a lousy passenger! I will hold back the ghosts for you."

"But what—"

Before Dougal could finish his thought, much less his sentence, the norn leaped past him, swinging his axe over his head. "All right!" he bellowed at the oncoming horde of ghosts. "Who wants me to send them to their eternal rest first?"

Riona grabbed Dougal and pulled him past Gullik as the norn pressed forward toward the bunched ranks of spirits. Above them, Ember had already begun a doomed battle with the ghosts guarding the gate. Her flashing blade and claws bit into their ephemeral forms, cutting through them like smoke. While this did not seem to cause the ghosts any obvious pain, after enough such blows they began to dissipate like fog, and hope leaped in Dougal's heart.

Kranxx shoved hard against Dougal's grip. "Put me down! Right now!"

"You don't stand a chance against the ghosts," said Dougal. "And quit squirming!"

"Of course I don't stand a chance, you idiot! But *you* do. Put me down!" Dougal set the asura down on the stair beside him. "Now get in there and use that sword of yours!"

Before Dougal could reply, one of the ghosts that Ember had dispatched re-formed from the swirling mists surrounding her. It spotted Dougal and charged straight at him, screaming, "Death to the invaders! Death! Death!"

Working on reflexes, Dougal brought up his sword and stabbed it straight through the ghost. The creature stopped cold, clutched at the blade for an instant, then started to scream in pain. It dropped to the stairs and lay there for an instant before it entirely faded away.

Despite himself, Dougal smiled.

"Step aside, Ember!" he shouted. "I'm coming through!"

The charr twisted out of his way, moving with the powerful grace of a hunting cat. Dougal stepped up and slashed his weapon through the forms of three ghosts at once. Every one of them howled in protest and cringed at the weapon's touch, but after it had passed through them, they stood straight back up and threw themselves into the fight again.

Dougal cursed. "I'm hurting them, all right, but only while the blade is actually in them!"

"That might be good enough," Ember said. She shivered, nearly frozen from all the ghostly swords that had swung through her.

"Riona!" Dougal said. One of the ghost's swords sliced right through his sword and then through him. It felt like it was trying to freeze his organs. He groaned in pain, then said, "Grab Ember and make for the top of the stairs!"

"No!" she said. "We can't lose you!"

"I'll be right behind you," he said, slashing at the ghosts again, forcing them to keep their distance. "Promise!"

Snarling in protest but doing what she'd been asked, Riona took Ember by her arm, and the two of them raced around the mass of ghosts to the left as Dougal forced them to the right. Once Ember and Riona were past him, Dougal kept pressing in that direction, circling around until the ghosts no longer stood between him and the stairs up to the royal chambers.

Dougal was just about to break off the fight and race after the others when he realized that Kranxx hadn't gone with Riona and Ember. He looked down the stairs and saw Kranxx standing where he'd left him, still rummaging through his pack, hunting for one sort of gadget or another.

"Get moving!" Dougal called to the asura. "I can't do this much longer!"

"I have to have something in here to help him!" said Kranxx.

"Who?" But Dougal knew the answer as soon as the question left his lips. Still defending himself with his sword against increasingly wary ghosts, he gazed down past the creatures he was barely keeping at bay and spotted Gullik again, still taking on scores of the ghosts himself.

"By the Bear's bloody claws!" the norn bellowed as he swung his axe all about. "I will battle you until my dying breath! Whether sagas are sung of this day or not, no matter how fast you might finally kill me, you shall know you've been in the fight of your deaths!"

"Gullik!" shouted Dougal. "Break off and follow us!"

"And let them chase you down?" shouted Gullik, grinning from ear to ear. "Never!"

"The aquatic thunderator won't work," Kranxx said to himself. "I do have a darkness grenade, but I don't know if it's functional." He shook his head.

"Just get moving and get up here!" said Dougal.

The norn turned to Dougal and pointed up the stairs with his axe. "Remember me!" he said, and turned back to slashing apart the spirits. They streamed out in strands of fog beneath his blows, only to re-form moments later. Pressed on all sides now, Gullik bristled and began to transform into his ursine form.

"I have one last healing draught, but that's not— Aha! Wait!" Kranxx reached into his pack and yanked something out of one of the endless number of pockets in it.

"Yes!" he shouted, and flung the small orb into the center of the fray. Gullik grinned and turned to shout something. It might have been thanks.

Then the ball exploded in a ball of flame, the force of the blow driving both man and asura back against the stairs. When the conflagration cleared, there was sign of neither norn or the ghosts but only a shallow, scorched crater. Already the pale blue strands were re-forming into ghosts.

Kranxx stared at the devastation. "By the Eternal Alchemy! I used too much arcanic energy! I killed him! I thought it would help and I killed Gullik!"

The pair of ghosts nearest them, at the borders of the blast, re-formed the quickest. Dougal stabbed each of the ghosts right through the chest. After they retreated out of the reach of his blade, Dougal reached down and grabbed the panicked asura by the back of his collar. Then he turned and sprinted straight up the steps, dragging Kranxx along with him.

The staircase ascended forever, and Dougal could see Riona and Ember ahead, climbing the steep steps as fast as they could. Beneath him he could hear the entire city howl; looking down, he could see ghosts spilling from every doorway and trying to force themselves up the stairs behind them.

Dougal, bringing the still-frantic Kranxx along with him, dove through the wide-open doors at the top of the stairs, bursting into what his ancient map said were the royal chambers. They landed in a tangled ball in the center of the main chamber, and before Dougal could pull himself free, Ember and Riona grabbed them both and dragged them behind a tattered dressing screen that cut off the back half of the room from the front.

Dougal started to ask what was going on, but Ember clamped a hand over his mouth while Riona muzzled Kranxx. Dougal's eyes darted around and spotted a ghost standing right over them.

He cursed himself for believing that the city's soldiers would not follow them in here. Yet, a ghost stood there staring at him with a kind and gentle face.

The unexpected face stopped Dougal cold. The look in the ghost's eyes was not maddened or vicious. This ghost looked . . . sad.

Rather than armor, this ghost wore the rich and elegant clothes of a royal courtier. He was balding and potbellied, and his eyes bore the weight of having seen far too many things for too damned long. He carried no weapon—other than the handle of a ghostly knife still jutting from the wound in his chest.

Riona raised her blade, but Dougal held up a hand to stop her. Mortals and ghost viewed each other, and Dougal found his voice.

"Savione," he said. "You're the king's servant, Savione."

The ghost in ornate dress frowned and sniffed. "Chief courtier, thank you," said the ghost. "But I *am* Savione. And it is about time you got here. Or someone like you."

From the doorway near the head of the stairs, there arose the racket of the approaching mob. The ghost of Savione turned and walked back through the dressing screen, disturbing it less than a gentle breeze. Dougal could no longer see him, but the courtier's voice carried throughout the room.

"How dare you burst into the king's private quarters unannounced?" Savione said, his voice commanding and firm.

The ghost soldiers chanted at him, "There are invaders! We must protect Ascalon! We must protect the king!"

Savione scoffed at them. "I have been in these chambers this entire day, and have seen no brigands, no raiders, and no bandits. Off with you!"

The ghosts' voices became more subdued and confused. "We saw invaders!" said one, but they were unsure of themselves now.

Savione did not raise his voice, but his words dripped with menace. "Leave now, or I shall summon His Majesty, our great King Adelbern, to deal with your intrusion personally. Do not tarry, but hunt your invaders elsewhere."

The ghosts were cowed by the invoking of the king's name, then encouraged by the idea that the invaders were still at large somewhere else in the city. The soldiers' chanting faded as they left the chambers and went off in search of prey someplace outside the king's private rooms.

The ghost poked his head through the screen. "I believe it's safe to speak now," he said as he emerged wholly before the others. "Their dedication to the king is nearly as mindless as their bloodlust, and I can confuse them easily."

Dougal got to his feet and stared at the ghost, stunned to see that something of the man had survived for so long.

"See," Ember said, elbowing Dougal in the shoulder. "Fireburn was right. Savione."

The courtier didn't smile—he frowned less—but it had the same effect. To Dougal he said, "Yes. I am Savione, in the . . . well, not flesh, exactly. But I'm afraid you have me at a disadvantage, sir . . . ?"

Dougal blinked. "Keane. Dougal Keane."

"Keane." The ghost's eyes lit up. "No relation to Lieutenant Dorion Keane?"

Dougal's breath caught in his chest. "Ancestor."

The ghost nodded thoughtfully. "Yes. I think I see some resemblance. A good man. We could have used him here, but other duties called."

"How is this possible?" asked Riona. "I thought all of the ghosts in Ascalon City had been driven mad by the Foefire?"

"Remember the story I told," said Ember. "This is the Savione I spoke of. He was dead before Adelbern had used Magdaer to ignite the Foefire. I assume that this man certainly had unfinished business to attend to."

"This reunion is all very touching," Kranxx said, his voice rising to a furious stage whisper, "but we have bigger problems right now!"

"As long as they do not hear or see you, the soldiers will not enter here," said Savione. "They fear the king's wrath more than anything."

"Is he here?" Dougal's head snapped around as he looked for any sign of Adelbern.

"Oh, dear, no," said Savione. "He patrols the battlements of the North Wall night and day, waiting for any sign of another charr assault." At this, the ghost gave Ember a sidelong glance.

The wailing of the ghosts outside grew louder as these thoughts spun through Dougal's head. "Those ghosts seem like they're still hungry for blood," he said.

Savione grimaced with regret. "I've rarely seen them this agitated. No outsiders have ever gotten this close to the royal chambers since the Foefire. It *is* possible that they will eventually choose to ignore my orders and charge the tower on their own initiative if they realize you are here."

Riona frowned. "I wonder if they would be so quick to follow your commands if they knew you betrayed your king. If the charr's story is true, you fought against him, with the charr at the very gates."

"Untrue and unkind." Savione looked down his nose at Riona, offended. "I was doing my best to save the soldiers His Majesty was determined to murder! Adelbern was desperate to keep the charr from taking Ascalon City, and he was prepared to do anything to stop it. He was furious at our soldiers for failing to stop the charr advance, and thought them cowards."

"But they weren't cowards," said Dougal.

"Hardly! They were the bravest men and women I ever knew. But we were arrayed against an implacable foe with seemingly endless resources and arms."

Savione scowled at Riona. "The Searing drove us from Rin, and the shame of that imbalanced His Majesty. He began to argue with Prince Rurik, his only child, who advocated making peace with Adelbern's old enemies in Kryta and taking shelter within its borders. Then Rurik broke with the king and perished while leading a faction of Ascalonians into Kryta."

The ghost sighed at the ancient loss. "His Majesty was devastated by his son's death, but he became more determined than ever to stand up against the charr and prove his son wrong—that he could save the kingdom, single-handedly if need be. When it became clear that Ascalon City would fall and that he could not stop it, he . . . I think he went mad."

"I don't know," said Kranxx, his voice ragged and worn. "Looks to me like he got exactly what he wanted."

The others, including the ghost, gaped at him.

Dougal looked at Kranxx and could have sworn the asura had been crying. Still, he was an asura, and his logic outran his feelings. "What? Haven't any of you ever studied game theory? If you can't win, you do the next best thing: you make sure your enemy can't win, either. It works more often than you'd think, because it changes the parameters of the game without your opponent's permission. Often even without their knowledge. You're not playing to win any longer. You just want to keep them from winning, and that's a lot harder to stop."

The ghostly courtier blinked. "What sort of creature are you?" he said.

"I am asura," said Kranxx. "I am after your time."

"Indeed, but you impute a great deal of rationalism to a man who had clearly gone mad." Savione's chilly glare froze Kranxx solid on the spot. "I was there with him. I heard his rants. I saw the insanity dancing in his eyes, by the way, as he drove this dagger *into my chest!*"

As he spoke, Savione advanced on the asura, the

ghostly dagger embedded in his vest. Kranxx shrank behind Dougal rather than face the ghost's naked wrath. "Point taken," he squeaked.

"Death has done nothing to improve His Majesty's condition." Savione crossed his arms over his middle, resting just under the blade in his chest. "In death, his madness grows. He speaks as if Ascalon City were not in ruins, as if the charr have been pushed back, and as if his son still lived."

Dougal knew they needed to get moving fast. If Adelbern found them, Savione wouldn't be able to protect them. To the ghostly courtier he said, "We came here for a great treasure mentioned on an ancient map. Do you know where such a treasure would be?"

"Ah," said Savione, and now the ghost allowed himself a grim smile, "you got my note."

" 'Your note'?" said Dougal.

"During the first few years of my . . . undeath, I thought I could gain my revenge on Adelbern. I created maps and notes describing the city and the treasures in the vault. I cast them loose on the winds and watched them carry beyond the battlements. My hopes were that someone would arrive and dispatch Adlebern's ghost. There were those who came, driven by avarice and promised gold, but the army of ghosts and the mad king repelled them. Eventually I ran out of ink and patience, and I abandoned the effort."

Riona said quietly, "Dak's map." Dougal nodded. One of Savione's missives had ended up in the old archives and from there fell into Dak's hands.

But Dougal noted that, although Savione claimed

disinterest in the matter, he still seemed to be very interested in some form of vengeance against the king.

"I doubt we can slay a dead king," he said, "but we do seek one of his treasures. The weapon borne by the charr leader—an ungue set with gems. It is called the Claw of the Khan-Ur."

Savione nodded. "I know of such a weapon. His Majesty stripped it from the corpse of the imperator who brought it here. For many years His Majesty prowled through the city, salvaging armor, weapons, and anything of value. He sealed it in the vault of the royal treasury."

"So your ancient maps were correct," said Riona.

"Mostly," said Savione. "Most of the entrances to the palace itself were shattered in the Foefire, and those that survived have collapsed as the ruined buildings have settled. If you want to get to the royal vault, you would have to descend down the pit where the Heart of the Foefire lies."

Dougal overlaid the image of the current ruins with what he had memorized from the map. Yes, if he lowered himself into that pit, he should be relatively close.

"Will you help us?" asked Dougal.

"I already have," said the ghost. "And I think removing one of Adelbern's prizes will vex him greatly. If you can discomfort him in the process, I would be much obliged. While I cannot send the king's ghost to the Mists, I can still take some comfort in petty vengeance. Perhaps I can get him mad enough—" He would have said more, but Riona interrupted.

"He's here," said Riona, who had moved back from

the tower's entrance. She had dropped her voice to a whisper.

"What do you mean, 'He's here'?" asked Ember, matching her tone.

"I mean he's here," said Riona. "Adelbern. On the parapet right above us." She pointed to the ceiling, and everyone looked up and listened. Dougal heard nothing.

"He usually remains on the North Wall or under the castle, in the catacombs," said Savione. "What would he be doing above us?"

"How often do you get living visitors?" Dougal asked.

"Almost never," Savione admitted.

"He must have heard his soldiers chasing us," said Dougal. "He's up there looking for us."

A great voice that chilled Dougal to his bones rang out throughout the city.

"Guards!" bellowed King Adelbern. "I have found our invaders! Come to me, and we shall mete out our justice for their crimes!"

25

Responding to their king's command, a roar went up among the soldiers outside.

"We don't have much time," Savione said. "You must flee."

"I have a plan," said Riona. "The Claw of the Khan-Ur is in the catacombs, right? And we can get to it from the Heart of the Foefire, correct?"

"And between us and it stand scores of angry ghosts," said Ember. "I think we covered that part already."

"So we can't just walk up and grab it," Riona said, "unless someone can draw the ghosts away while the rest of us find the Claw."

"That would be me," said Kranxx solemnly. The others looked at him.

"I'm serious," he said, his eyes red-rimmed. "Brute force won't solve this problem. I'm smarter than the three of you combined, and I have a pack filled with little distractions. And I have an idea of something I could do, something special." He nodded at Dougal, but the human didn't know what he meant.

Dougal protested, "Kranxx, we've lost one person already . . ."

Kranxx shook his oversized head. "I need to do this. For Gullik if for no one else. I cost him his life. I don't plan on dying without giving him vengeance. He'd never forgive me if I didn't."

"You need someone to come with you," Ember said. "Your will is strong but your legs are short."

"Good idea," said Riona, nodding. "Who could be a better distraction for this group of ghosts than a charr? Just the sight of you should send them into a frenzy."

"I was thinking of you, actually," Ember said. "You are the least important part of our team, the one we could best stand to lose."

"Very well. I'll go with Kranxx," said Riona. "If Ember Doomforge is too much of a coward to stand up to a bunch of Ascalonian ghosts, then I'll let her run off with her tail between her legs."

"I am no coward, mouse!" Ember snarled down at Riona, and Dougal wondered if the charr might end the argument by tearing out Riona's throat.

"Prove it! I've seen kittens less skittish than you."

Ember grumbled at her. "Fine. If Kranxx is determined to play the decoy, then I will join him. I wouldn't leave him with you, in any event.

"We'll keep them occupied for as long as we can," said Ember. "You just move like the wind. The longer we must keep them chasing us, the more likely they'll catch us."

Dougal held out his hand to Ember and then Kranxx, shaking with each one of them. "Thank you," he said.

"Don't worry about us," Kranxx said with a somber wink. "I'm not quite out of tricks yet."

"This isn't farewell." Ember's fur bristled as she spoke. "We shall toast our foes' failures tonight!"

Ember and Kranxx moved to the doorway and down the long staircase. On their appearance, the king let out a rumbling shout, and in response, the ghostly hordes poured from every doorway. They crowded and milled in the courtyard below, and then, as if propelled by a cannon, shot up the staircase toward them.

Ember picked up Kranxx and, with a bellow of her own, charged down the stairs.

Dougal could not bear to look, but halfway down the stairs the charr took a sharp left, off the stairs themselves. The pair, charr and asura, landed on a rotted roof not less than ten feet below them. Slate tiles shot out from beneath Ember's feet, but she kept her footing and jumped again, landing on a lower roof, and repeated the action once more.

Ember landed on the edge of the avalanche of masonry. She held her feet out before her, stiff and wide, and when she hit the stones she did not tumble and fall. Instead, she kept her feet and slid down the shattered tumble of stone, straight toward the street below.

Kranxx screeched the whole way down.

The ghosts followed them, those on the stairs streaming over the railings and into the city itself, those at the bottom changing directions and surging after the fleeing pair.

Dougal watched the ghostly pursuers disappear down the streets.

"You should go, now," said Savione. "They cannot keep them busy for long."

Riona led, and Dougal followed. Ahead of them the staircase was clear, and near the base of the stairs, visible in the overcast daylight was the pit that caged the Foefire's Heart. Yet, Dougal felt that someone was watching him and, despite himself, turned and looked up at the parapets above the royal chamber.

And there stood the last king of Ascalon.

Adelbern had been middle-aged when he'd died, but he seemed as fit and trim as any soldier half his age. He wore a suit of armor that Dougal suspected would have sparkled had it still been real and not some strange, ghostly abstraction. His head was bare, and his white hair fluttered in the wind that whipped through the crumbling battlements. His piercing eyes glared down at Dougal, and a snarl curled on his lips.

Adelbern raised his fist over his head and then swung it down to point a pale finger at Dougal. "How dare you trespass in my kingdom, thief!" the king said, his voice strong and full of fury. "For this, you shall pay the ultimate price!"

Dougal knew that if they fled, Adelbern would just send more ghosts after him, and their whole plan would be destroyed. He needed to play for time. He dropped to one knee and hoped that Savione's story was true.

"No, Your Majesty!" Dougal said. "I am Ascalonian by heritage, and I have come to seek your blessing!"

This strange request took Adelbern back an instant, but his fury resurged. "The only thing of which I shall approve is your death!"

"But, Your Majesty," he said, "I come here on behalf of your son, Prince Rurik!"

This blatant lie brought the ghost up short. He stammered for a moment, suddenly distracted. "Rurik? My son?" For a moment his face softened, but then it grew dark again. "Rurik is dead! To me, he died the moment he left Ascalon!"

"Your son is dead, as you are." This voice came from atop the battlements. The king turned to see its source, and his face grew livid.

"Savione!" he said. "You worthless wretch! How dare you enter my presence without my bidding?"

"No, sire! These people are here to repair the damage that you've done! I won't let you hurt them!"

"Stand aside and let me slay this foul beast now, Savione! In honor of your years of service, I will give you one last chance!"

"Years!" Savione threw up his hands. "Try centuries! You killed me, and you still consider me to be in your service! Well, no more!"

The courtier stared at his king and spoke in short, cold phrases. "I renounce my position in your court. There's nothing more you can take from me, Adelbern. You cannot hurt me."

"So you think!" Adelbern reached forward and pulled the ghostly dagger from the courtier's chest. Then the mad king stepped forward and swung his blade at Savione. The ghostly servant did not move to avoid the blow, and the blade sliced through him, cutting him cleanly in two.

Dougal waited for Savione to re-form like the ghosts

that Ember had battled in the cave near the Dragon-brand. Instead, the two halves of Savione separated from each other and slid apart. His legs fell one way while his chest fell another.

Before he faded away entirely, Savione said one last word, his voice brimming with grim relief: "Finally." Then he disappeared, flowing away into the breeze atop the battlements like a half-remembered dream.

Adelbern turned away from the vanished shards of his former servant but found the staircase empty. Riona and Dougal were already lost among the shadowed buildings below.

Behind them, the human pair heard Adelbern's cry of frustration over the rooftops.

"I think we got under his skin," said Riona, hugging a wall.

"You think Savione is really gone?" asked Dougal.

Riona shrugged her shoulders. "I don't think it matters what happens to Savione, Ember, or Kranxx. What matters is we find the Claw of the Khan-Ur."

Dougal grimaced at her, then craned his neck to get a better look at the top of the tower again. "All right," he said. "You're right. I know you're right, but I don't have to like it. Let's move."

Dougal sprinted through the town as fast as he could. Riona lagged behind just a bit, but he could hear her behind him every step of the way. Soon they reached the main square, and Dougal skidded to a halt.

The carnage sprawled out before him stole his breath. From one side of the square to the other, the remains sat piled up as if tossed into some careless giant's abattoir, bones and weapons and armor stacked upon each other like kindling for a monstrous fire.

Most of the bodies, especially the ones nearest to and even inside the shattered gates, had once been part of the charr invading force. At a curving line that met roughly near a well in the center of the square, though, the charr corpses mingled with those of the force of human warriors once arrayed against them. The two sides overlapped for several yards, a stark example of the uncertainty and chaos of battle.

Dougal and Riona picked their way across the square, trying not to disturb the dead. At first Dougal tried to avoid stepping on any remains so as to show respect for those who'd fallen here. That soon proved impossible, so he switched to treading gently on the bones that he could not avoid.

Then a horrible howl from Ember rang throughout Ascalon City, followed by an explosion, and Dougal gave up and just charged as fast as he could without slipping on the remains scattered across the square.

They were near the far side of the square when the charr appeared, still carrying the struggling asura. Ember's mouth was rimed with a lathering froth, and the asura was pulling things out of his rapidly diminishing pack and tossing them back at the howling, hungry ghosts.

There was a brilliant flash behind them, and the side of the old archive wall slowly collapsed into the street, burying the ghosts beneath it. A cloud of dust rose from the crash, and the ghosts slowly pulled themselves from the wreckage.

Ember noticed the two humans, and she stood tall and snapped a salute to Dougal. She panted from the exertion but seemed otherwise unharmed.

"Get out of here!" Riona said. "You're supposed to lure them *away*!"

"Hold it!" Kranxx said as Ember turned to sprint away. "That's it!"

The charr froze, and the asura leaped down from her back to pluck a bleached charr skull from the top of the mound of bones that filled even that distant part of the square.

"Yes," the asura said, grinning into the skull's empty eye sockets. "Proximity to the Heart of the Foefire. Good solidity. Should have enough necrotic residue to tune. This should do nicely." He pulled from his pocket the device that looked like a cross between a violin and a crossbow.

Not bothering to acknowledge the others again, Ember scooped Kranxx up and raced away from them with the asura in her arms. The re-forming ghosts, now clear of the collapsed building, howled after them.

Dougal and Riona crouched at the far end of the square. After the last of the ghosts spiraled out of view, chasing the charr and the asura, they let out a held breath.

"All right," said Riona, "now we need to get—"

That was the moment that three ghosts wafted out of the surrounding ruins and descended on her. These were dressed in ancient Ascalonian armor and keened and wailed as they attacked. For Dougal it was all too familiar.

"Vala!" shouted Dougal, slicing his sword through the nearest ghost. It let out a scream and dissipated, struck to the heart by the ebon blade. "I'll get them!" Another blow and he chopped a ghost through the eyes. It popped like a soap bubble.

The third ghost turned from its attack on Riona and leaped at Dougal, too fast for him to riposte. The spirit passed through him, and he could feel his heart freeze with its passage. He spun as it emerged from his far side and snapped loose with the sword. It caught the ghost immediately, and before it could even scream, it was gone.

Riona staggered to her feet, her face wan from the chilling touch of the ghosts.

"We need to go," said Dougal, "before any other ghosts find us."

"Too late," said Riona, and looked over Dougal's shoulder at the bone-strewn square they had just crossed.

The square was now filled with ghosts: soldiers and citizens, men and women and children. They watched the pair silently, their eyes wide with curiosity and madness.

"What are they waiting for?" asked Dougal, but he immediately had his answer. On the opposite side of the square, atop the shards of a collapsed tower, Adelbern appeared in full armor and bearing the ghostly remains of Magdaer, his double-bladed sword.

"You have invaded my kingdom and threatened my people," said Adelbern, his long hair blown back by unseen breezes. "You are traitors to Ascalon and to humanity. I have found you guilty, and the verdict is death! Subjects! Carry out the—"

Adelbern did not finish his sentence, for the ground beneath their feet began to hum and shake. Slowly, one of the bones pulled loose from the others and arced out, over the nearby buildings, to the east. Then another leg bone, this one belonging to a charr. Then a skull. All of them were suddenly magnetic, pulled by some unseen force toward the east. The air was soon filled with the shards of bones, daggers, and clubs of skeletal remains forming a broad gray-white river.

"What is this?" shouted Adelbern. "What sorcery is this?"

"Kranxx," said Dougal, kneeling down next to Riona in the shade of a toppled pillar, safe from the blows. "He said he had one more trick. He must have gotten the Golem's Eye to work again."

The ghosts themselves were confused as the bones sailed through them, leaving ripples in their spiritual form. Then one, then another, turned and started to chase the airborne rainbow of remains. These may have been their own bones in life, and perhaps they were incensed that they were being disturbed.

"Halt!" shouted the king at his deserting followers. "I said halt! Kill these interlopers, and then we will deal with the sorcerer."

The was a huge thumping noise, as of a building filled with kettledrums collapsing, and Adelbern, the ghostly king of Ascalon, the Sorcerer-King who had struck fear in the hearts of the charr, turned, his face contorted in shock and awe.

Above the line of buildings behind him arose a titanic figure, humanoid at the top and serpentine at the bottom, made entirely of bones and bone fragments. It was the same shape as the tomb guardian Dougal and the others had fled, the defender of Blimm's tomb. Except it was made of every bone in Ascalon City.

And at the back of its neck rode a small figure with a large head, gripping the bones like a rider holding on to his saddle. In his other hand he held his misshapened hat and beat the side of the creature with it.

"I got it to work!" Dougal could hear the asura's thin voice from the height. "Praise the alchemy, I built myself a city guardian!"

"Destroy it!" shouted Adelbern. "Destroy the abomination!"

Now another serpent appeared, this one a thin blue-white one that snaked around the torso of the city guardian. This one was made entirely of ghosts, each crawling on the backs of others as it spiraled upward, trying to reach the small asura.

"Kill the little monster!" shouted the ghost king. "Kill it and take its power!"

Kranxx apparently noticed the ghosts trying climb its creature's form and kicked his great mount hard. The serpent-bodied city guardian lurched to the left, collapsing buildings in its way and scraping off hordes of ghosts. More spirits rose in their place, and Dougal could hear the king laugh.

"You will join my kingdom!" exhorted Adelbern. "You and all the world of the living! I shall take you, and you will join my generals, and we will march on your cities and sweep them all from our path."

"It'll be a cold day in Rata Sum!" snapped Kranxx,

and the city guardian got taller now, reaching up to the overcast clouds.

"I will command your power!" bellowed Adelbern, ghostly spittle flying from his lips.

"I'll give you your wish!" answered Kranxx, his eyes as mad as the ghost's. "This is for Gullik! I will send you and your minions back beneath the earth!"

And with that, the city guardian, made of all the mortal remains of the ghosts of Ascalon, lunged forward like an arcing cobra, its huge head and massive arms before it as it descended right onto Adelbern and his spire.

"Command *this,* bookah!" shouted Kranxx. The late king barely had time to scream.

And then the centuries-old remains of Ascalon City cascaded down onto the king in a tidal wave of bone. The ossified skeletons turned to dust as they hit, but they were relentless and eternal, and the rest of the body followed, pouring ton upon ton of disintegrating legs, arms, and skulls onto the king's bastion.

It went on for what seemed to be several long minutes. And when it stopped, a huge fog bank of dust and death hung over the city. And there was no sign of ghosts, kings, or asura.

26

The pair stumbled through the cloud of pulverized bone, making for the hazy pillar of
light.

"He must have pulled in every loose bone in the city,"
said Dougal, shaking his head.

"And the ghosts with them," said Riona. "It will be a
while if they re-form."

"You think he got Adelbern?" asked Dougal.

Riona shrugged. "I'm sure he drove him back. It is
going to be a long time before he shows his undead face
aboveground, though I bet he won't be alone when he
does."

The air was so thick, they almost toppled over the
edge of the pit without seeing it. The dust cleared enough
to show a huge beacon lancing from the bottom of the
pit toward the sky, punching through the low-hanging
clouds. Somewhere at the base were the remains of the
tower where Adelbern, the Sorcerer-King, invoked the
Foefire.

Dougal reached into his pack and pulled out a length

of rope. He handed it to Riona. "Find something solid to anchor this," he said. "I'm going in."

"I'm going with you," she said.

He shook his head as he peered down into the blackness of the well. "I need someone back here guarding my way out. Otherwise, I'm never coming out of there alive."

Riona frowned but nodded in agreement as she went to fasten the rope around the base of a nearby statue. Dougal recognized it as a portrayal of Adelbern in his younger days, soon after he had returned from his battles with Kryta to claim the crown. It hurt to think how far the king had fallen from that hopeful age. He and the rest of the world.

Once Riona secured the rope, Dougal swung his legs over the ridge of broken stone around the pit. He mentally overlaid Dak's map. No, Savione's map. Was that the ghostly courtier's curse: that he could not leave for the Mists until the ghostly dagger was removed? Would he return as well?

Carefully, Dougal climbed down the side of the pit, Riona playing out the rope from above. He could feel the intensity of the light on his back, almost pushing him against the wall. If he was right, he would not have to crawl all the way to the bottom of the shaft.

The wall was slippery as well, and slicked with moss. Dougal had a hard time finding handholds. The rope meant he didn't have to, but he didn't like to trust himself entirely to his equipment. Ropes had been known to snap, and there was always the chance the ghosts would find it and cut it loose. Of course, if that happened, the lack of a rope would likely be the least of his troubles.

There. About halfway down the pit, a passageway delved farther into the depths. At some distant point in time it had been framed by a pair of heavy doors, but one was missing and the other canted at an angle, its wooden face reduced to splinters. Now it reminded him of the empty eye sockets of a sun-bleached skull.

Dougal swung over to the entrance. There was a thin perch before the door. Dougal reached into his pack and fished out a small lantern on a lanyard. He lit it and hung it around his neck. He would need the light once he moved away from the Foefire.

"I'm there!" he shouted up to Riona.

Her head appeared at the rim of the pit. "Good. What do you see?"

"This must have been a secret escape route for the royal family," Dougal said as he moved deeper into the foundations under the main square. "I'm surprised to see so little security."

As the words left his lips, Dougal felt something under his foot click. He recognized the sensation right away: a pressure plate. He braced himself for something horrible.

Dougal froze and nothing happened. All right. Then the trap would spring when the pressure was removed.

The trap was probably meant to go off when he walked past the pressure plate. That meant that if he leaped backward, he might survive. The trap would go off where it expected him to be, and he'd be just fine.

Or maybe whatever it was would affect the entire tunnel and kill him anyhow.

Dougal decided that that was unlikely, if this tunnel had been made for people who had to get out of the royal chambers in a hurry. The artisans who had crafted the trap would have known that. They wouldn't have put in a trap that might accidentally kill the people they were trying to protect. A smart trap maker would have it so that it would affect only people entering the catacombs this way, not leaving them.

And it must be older than the charr invasion itself, made for earlier rulers. He could not imagine Adelbern ever using a tunnel to escape.

Dougal threw himself backward, spinning about and throwing himself flat on his face and covering his head with his arms.

The trap sprang as Dougal's weight left the pressure plate. Fire did not engulf the passage. The floor did not drop away. Instead, he heard something come crashing down into the passage, right where he would have been if he'd walked blithely past the trap.

Dougal sat up and looked back up the passageway. In the light from the tiny lantern still hanging from his chest, he saw a series of spiked poles that had stabbed down from a set of concealed holes in the ceiling. These would have run him through and left him impaled on the poles until he either bled to death or died of thirst.

Despite that, there was just enough room around the spikes for Dougal to squeeze his way past. "I'm all right!" he shouted back toward the entrance, but Riona said nothing. Perhaps she could no longer hear him.

Dougal snaked his way through the catacomb. There were multiple passages now, some doorways crushed, others as open as spoiled tombs. The Foefire had twisted the catacombs when it struck. The darkened halls here had probably stood tall and unshaken once, but now the place was littered with bricks that had fallen from the ceiling and walls. In some sections the roof had caved in entirely, and in others it looked as if it might do so in an instant.

Finally he reached the site of the vault on his mental map. It was a slab of stone that seemed solid enough to serve as the foundation for a castle. It showed no hinges, knobs, or other features, only a dark hole in its exact center, just a little bigger than the size of his fist.

Five years. It had taken him five years to get to this point.

Dougal scanned the door with his eyes and his fingertips, hoping to find some flaw in it, some hint of what he needed to do to make it swing open. Finding nothing, he knelt down, brought his light up to the hole in the middle of the door, and peered into it.

He started cursing right away. "It's a Thief's Nightmare," he said to himself. To work this sort of lock, you have to put your entire hand into the hole, grab the handle, and then turn it in the proper sequence. If you screw it up, a blade springs out to remove your hand at the wrist. Worse, you can't see what you're doing. Your arm blocks the way. Barbaric. And effective.

Dougal steeled himself and stuck his hand into the black hole, hoping that it would still be attached to him the next time he saw it. The metallic handle felt cool in his hand as he grabbed it.

He turned the handle counterclockwise until it reached a point of resistance, and there was a click. There was no sudden pain, no blade dropping. He had unfastened the first tumbler. Sweating now, he began to turn the handle in the other direction, past the original point. There was a bit of resistance. Was that the second tumbler, or was it the trap about to spring?

"Stop," said a voice in Dougal's ear, and for a moment he thought Riona had followed him down. He craned his head around, but he was alone before the stone door. Still, he had heard something. Or perhaps it was his own imagination, translating some shifting of the stone into words.

Nevertheless, his gut said he had gone far enough. He brought the handle back to where it had been, then started turning it counterclockwise again. Soon he felt the handle click into place. Yes. It had been the second tumbler.

Dougal adjusted his grip on the handle and turned it clockwise now. When Dougal reached the point of resistance this time, he felt something sharp push up against his wrist. He stopped cold.

"Good," the phantom voice seemed to say in his ear.

Screwing up his courage, Dougal took a deep breath. If he got this wrong, he'd soon be missing his favorite hand. He could only hope that he'd be able to open the door with his other hand before he passed out from a lack of blood.

Dougal cranked the handle with a sharp twist. The blade that had been pressed against his wrist moved away. Within the stone slab there was a grumbling as iron bolts wcrc withdrawn.

Dougal turned and looked behind him, but there was no one there, only a blue-white mist that curled around a statue of a female warrior and then was gone.

Dougal pulled on the handle, and the door swung outward on well-oiled hinges.

The vault of King Adelbern lay open to him at last.

Dougal stepped through the door and into a large room lined with shelves. Magical lights illuminated the place from ceiling to floor, glowing with a bluish hue that cast everything in an otherworldly light. The walls and ceiling of the room were made of perfectly fitted cut stone bound together with crisscrossing strips of iron. These had no doubt been made to keep thieves from drilling into the vault, but by the way the iron bands sagged violently in the center of the ceiling, Dougal knew that they'd also kept the room from collapsing under the pressure from the fallen tower above.

He hoped they'd hold just a few minutes longer.

The shelves on both sides were filled with terra-cotta jars, each filled to overflowing with gold coins and jewelry. At the base of the shelves were piles of ornate swords and armor salvaged by King Adelbern from the wreckage above and tucked away, much like an elderly woman might hide silver pieces throughout the house in case of burglars. Rough sacks of gold and platinum were tucked into every nook and cranny.

A particularly large, ironbound chest sat on the far side of the polished marble floor, its lid unlocked and flipped back to rest against the wall behind it. A few gold coins lay scattered about the place where they had spilled out of a single sack that sprawled open on the floor next to the chest.

Dougal slipped into the vault, moving carefully and scanning for traps of any kind. The adrenaline coursing through his veins magnified his senses. While he didn't expect to find any more dangers located behind such a complicated and lethal lock, he'd known many people who'd died from making such assumptions.

He reached the chest and looked inside.

The Claw of the Khan-Ur sat inside the chest, atop a bed of gold coins and precious gems. Diamonds, emeralds, sapphires, and rubies sparkled back at him in the tiny lantern's light.

But the Claw held Dougal's attention. Two blades pointing forward, two pointed back, a handgrip in the middle. An ungue. It was set with four gems—red, black, gray, and golden—for the four children of the imperator, and the four founders of the modern legions.

There was something else, though, hanging from the forward, upward-turned blade. A simple golden chain, and hanging from that chain, a locket, twin to Dougal's own.

Dougal picked up the locket and held it up to the light, then opened it, although he knew what he would find. His own cameo, jet, set in ivory.

He thought of the soft voice in the hallway. "Thank you, Vala," he said, not sure if she could hear and not caring if she didn't. He pocketed the locket and turned to the Claw itself.

Dougal reached into the chest and carefully grasped the Claw by its jewel-encrusted handle. No trap was sprung. He didn't expect that Adelbern would have the desire or knowledge to construct a trap in the chest, but he couldn't be sure. Time was wasting, though, and he needed to move fast. Steadying himself, he yanked the weapon from the chest with a single sharp movement.

The Claw came out of the chest without incident, and Dougal examined it in the light. It seemed undamaged, despite having survived the Foefire and the intervening centuries. It looked exactly as he'd described it to the others, right down to the gold plating and the colors of the four jewels embedded in its handle.

The blades were clean and sharp enough that he could see his reflection in them, something he'd not done in a long time. He had to admit—without any surprise, given everything he'd been through—that he looked horrible. Dirty and ragged and covered with a thin coating of bone dust. Still, he could not hold back a smile.

He handled the blade gingerly, as its construction seemed to threaten to poke him at every moment. He looked around at the scattered treasure and wondered if he should risk taking more. Almorra, after all, had promised him and the others any additional treasure they found. But anything would have to be hauled back up the pit and out of the city. In the end, he quickly chose two small sacks of gems—emeralds and diamonds—and a good-sized satchel of platinum coins stamped with the seal of the Royal House of Kryta.

Dougal turned and sped back through the catacombs, lacing his way back through the bars of the trap, leaving the vault doors open. When he reached the pit, the rope still hung there.

"I have it! And gems and platinum as well!" he shouted upward. Riona appeared at the top of the pit and waved. The Claw would be too bulky and sharp to carry up on his back, so he tied it to the rope and gave the line a tug. Riona hauled hard on the rope, and the Claw went up in an instant and disappeared over the rim of the pit.

Dougal waited for a moment for Riona to throw the rope back down.

But the rope didn't return.

"Riona?" he called. "We need to get out of here. Just cut the rope off the Claw and toss me the free end!" Had something happened? Had the ghosts gotten her?

Riona leaned over the top of the well, brandishing the untied Claw in her hand. "I have it! Thank you, Dougal!"

"Wait!" Dougal strove to keep the panic from his voice. "Throw the rope down."

Riona's voice cut like a sword. "I'm afraid I can't do that."

Something ice-cold struck Dougal in the heart. "What do you mean?" he managed, but the horrible realization was already dawning on him.

Riona gave a mirthless laugh. "I have what I came for and have to leave now. Thank you for all your help. I could not have done it without you."

Dougal's blood ran cold. "This was your plan from the start, wasn't it? You're the one who alerted the Ebonhawke guards."

Riona chuckled. "And told Clagg where to find you.

Almorra isn't the only one to send messengers through the asura gates. Though I will admit that I wasn't sure about it all until we returned to Ebonhawke, and I saw the charr forces arrayed against us."

"Why?" asked Dougal, but he was already scanning the slick rock wall ahead of him. It would be difficult to climb without a belaying rope, but not impossible.

"Why Clagg and the Ebonhawke guards?" said Riona. "I wanted to get rid of our unwanted allies. This was supposed to be a private party. I thought you and I could pull this off without them, and if you were of a like mind, we could take the Claw for ourselves. From what I knew of you, I thought you could be . . . convinced, as long as the others weren't around. But instead of reducing our menagerie, I ended up increasing it. Telling Clagg resulted in the oaf Gullik joining us, and we had to take the rat asura with us after he got us out of Ebonhawke."

"And the guards in the sewers?" said Dougal, thinking of the horror they had both felt killing other guards.

"A sad accident," said Riona, her voice wavering. "I had planted myself on the parapet to wait for the guards, but you and that vegetable got there first. No, they were just doing their jobs, like the charr patrol."

"You can't take the Claw back to Ebonhawke," said Dougal, and moved slowly along the ledge, toward the wall and out of Riona's view.

"Stay where I can see you, or I am gone," said Riona, and Dougal moved back. "You're right. That was my original plan when I first received my orders from Almorra to enlist you to find the Claw. I thought it my chance to return to Ebonhawke as a hero as opposed to someone who aided deserters. But after we talked on the wall, I realized you were right. The charr would stop at nothing if they knew. No, I could not give the Claw to Ebonhawke, or to Almorra."

"Then what are you going to do with it?" said Dougal, looking around. Perhaps if he could grab a rock, he might be able to stun her at a distance. It seemed a pitiful chance.

"The Flame Legion," said Riona brightly now. "I'm going to give it to the Flame Legion."

"What?" Dougal almost shouted.

"Think of it, Dougal," said Riona. "If the Flame Legion gained the Claw, there would be a civil war. The charr women, like Ember, would rebel at once, but there would be enough of those charr in the other legions who would follow a new Khan-Ur to schism the legions. The charr would collapse in a civil war, and we could break the siege, pitting one side against the other. The humans would be able to retake Ascalon. We would be able to retake Ascalon!"

Dougal's mind raced, and he said, "So you caught that Flame Legion soldier after all."

"And made a deal," said Riona.

"The others trusted you," said Dougal. "Killeen, Kranxx, Gullik, even Ember."

"Why should we care? They're not even human," Riona scoffed at him. "I'm a true daughter of Ebonhawke. You should be a true son. You know what happens to Ebonhawke if the queen and this truce faction manage to forge some kind of agreement? We lose. It's only a matter of time before the charr betray us and Ebonhawke falls."

Dougal gawked at her. "I trusted you too. You helped me believe."

"I thought I trusted you," said Riona. "I really did. I thought you were smart enough to see how things were. Everything I knew about you, from when you and the others deserted me, told me I could convince you. But no, you are still haunted by your late wife. Wife! When you told me, I knew it would be near impossible to convince you: you're still in love with a dead woman. That's why you really came here, isn't it?"

"We can talk," said Dougal, mentally planning handholds on the slick wall. He set down the bag of platinum coins. It would just slow him down.

"We can't," said Riona. "When I was attacked by ghosts, you called out *her* name, not mine. You still love her, Dougal. You came here to find her. And now I'm leaving you with her. Both of you can remain together in death."

Riona laughed, but her laugh turned into a scream of pain and surprise. Her silhouette disappeared from the top of the pit. There was a feral growl and the clash of metal on metal.

Dougal ran to the base of the wall and started climbing. He did not know if he could make it in time or what he would do once he reached the top.

But he knew one thing. Ember Doomforge was still alive.

27

Dougal dug his fingers into the wall and climbed faster and faster. To keep from slipping, he stabbed his fingers into the crumbling masonry over and over again. He scraped his hands raw forcing handholds in his race to reach the top.

He could hear Ember clearly now: "Traitor!" she bellowed, and there was the clash of metal again. Dougal redoubled his effort.

Dougal clawed his way to the top of the pit in time to see Riona standing, facing the charr. Parts of her bright armor had been ripped away, and she had claw marks along her exposed arms. Ember was worse off: her heavy blade was knocked aside and she clutched her bleeding midsection, struggling to hold her insides together.

As Dougal watched, Ember managed a curse, spitting blood, and dropped to her knees, then fell forward. Dougal climbed over the edge and rose to his feet as a nasty grin split Riona's face. "It always makes me so happy to see a charr die."

Dougal's ebony blade sprang from its sheath, and

he held it before him, his raw fingers smearing its hilt. "Don't make me hurt you, Riona," he said. "Just give me the Claw."

Riona wheeled, surprised by Dougal's appearance. As he watched, her expression turned from rage to a softness. "Dougal," she said, "I misread you. You have much more determination than even I suspected. I'm sorry I left you down there." She did not lower the Claw, but moved to her right. Dougal stepped away from the edge of the pit and circled her.

"This is your chance, Dougal," said Riona. "We go our separate ways. You go back to Divinity's Reach or Lion's Arch or wherever. You survived Ascalon City—twice. You have gems and gold to prove it. And while the charr legions tear each other apart, you can just wait for the dust to settle and for the humans to come back. All you have to do is walk away."

"I'm afraid I can't do that," said Dougal. "You know that."

Riona came at him, whipping the ungue around as she charged. Dougal realized that some of the bloody scratches were not from Ember but from the Claw itself. Riona was an amateur with the blade, and could injure herself just as easily as she could wound him. Yet, she could not drop it to pull her own sword.

Dougal countered her attack with a flurry of blows, but try as he might, he could not find a way past the Claw's four blades. While Riona might not know how to handle an ungue, Dougal stood before her beaten and exhausted, the blood from his fingers making his blade hard to handle. She'd always been the better soldier, and that edge proved enough to keep him from hurting her.

Dougal backed up again, giving himself some more room from the Claw's blades and hoping that Riona might trip on the uneven paving stones when coming after him.

The blades of the Claw flashed at him again and again, and it was all he could do to mount a decent defense against them. Every time he thought he might see a space for a counterattack, Riona closed it in an instant. Sometimes this meant cutting her own flesh with one of the other blades, but she didn't seem to care. He kept backing up slowly, buying himself time with space, circling as he moved, putting her between the pit and himself.

"Just walk away, Dougal!" Riona looked straight into his eyes. "I'll let you go for old time's sake. I'm taking the Claw either way. You don't have to die." She launched herself at him. Dougal turned just in time to parry her attack. One of the Claw's blades got past his guard and ripped a shallow channel in his leg.

Furiously, Riona pressed the attack, slicing and stabbing at Dougal with abandon. He stumbled backward over the stones, deflecting the most lethal of her blows. She was forcing him to move now, spinning him so his back was to the pit and his form was framed in the light of the Foefire.

He was the perfect target, which is what he wanted to be.

Riona let out a guttural cry that might have been a curse or a threat or a prayer, and charged him, her blades lashing out and laying open his left shoulder.

That's when Dougal struck, despite the pain, at Riona's heart. She managed to half parry the blow, and it slashed through her side rather than into her chest.

But, more importantly, she had to twist to ward off the blow, and her own charge carried her forward, to the edge of the pit. She slashed again at Dougal, and he raised his blade again, piercing Riona's chest through its chain links halfway up the blade's length.

Riona's eyes went wide with the shock, and she began to pitch backward, Dougal's name on her bloody lips, his sword still lodged in her chest.

Dougal let go of his sword and reached beyond the length of the blade. He grabbed the Claw of the Khan-Ur from Riona's tightly locked fingers and pulled. The Claw came free, but Riona kept arching backward, back into the pit.

She fell without making a sound, disappearing into the light. Dougal did not hear her land.

Dougal sat on the edge of the pit, breathing deeply, clutching the ungue. His shoulder wept blood, and tears streamed down his face.

A deep chuffing noise behind him shocked him and told him Ember had not fully given up the fight. He staggered over and slapped his pockets, at last finding the potion that Kranxx had given him. He rolled Ember onto her back and poured the liquid between her lips, then took a swig himself. It tasted like concentrated cranberry syrup, but he could feel a warmth in his leg and shoulder, a tingling as the damaged flesh tried to knit itself together.

He poured the remaining potion down the charr's

throat, and Ember let out a long coughing jag, then rolled over and vomited bits of her own flesh. She touched the skin beneath her slashed belly armor to make sure her flesh was solid.

"The traitor . . ." spat Ember.

"Dead," said Dougal, and looked over at the pit. "I'm going to need a new sword. Again."

Ember growled and nodded, then said, "What about you, Dougal Keane?"

"What *about* me?" Despite the potion, Dougal ached, and knew that, if it came to it, he could not fight a charr one-on-one.

"Are you going to return with me to the Vigil, and give the Claw of the Khan-Ur to Almorra Soulkeeper?" The charr's words sounded hostile but she looked concerned.

Dougal could not guess what the charr was thinking but slowly nodded. "I'd like to do that."

A toothy smile spread over Ember's face. "Good. Even with your kindness of a healing draught, I am in no shape to fight you."

"So you *do* want to go back . . ." said Dougal.

"Of course," said Ember. "I do not think I could face my grandmother empty-handed."

"Grandmother?" Dougal was startled. "Almorra is . . ."

"I have her eyes," said Ember, smiling weakly. "Though my mother was Ash Legion. Don't tell me that that is not obvious even to a human?"

There was a great shout from the far side of the courtyard, and both man and charr looked up, surprised. Gullik staggered into view.

"I don't believe it," muttered Ember.

"I do," said Dougal.

The norn was pale, his massive form almost drained of life. Not an inch of his outfit was not shredded, and not an inch of his exposed flesh was not bleeding. His warrior's braid was burned off to a charcoaled stump, and he was—as they were—covered with a thin coating of pulverized bone. But he was alive.

"By the Bear!" shouted the norn. "Did you kill them all without me? The asura did a wonderful thing, for his device gave me wings. I awoke in the remains of one of the houses and tried to find you." He paused a moment, then admitted with a shrug, "I am afraid I got lost. I wasn't paying much attention on the way in."

Dougal wanted to hug the norn and lumbered forward, but Ember beat him to it, embracing the norn and slapping his back. Gullik winced but got his vengeance slapping the charr on the back as well.

"Where is he?" said Gullik. "Where is that powerful asura?"

Dougal's face fell, and Ember said, "He's dead. Kranxx died defeating Adelbern."

Gullik grew somber immediately. "I see. Did he die well?"

Dougal said, "It was a death worth a legendary tale."

"One I would like very much to hear," said Gullik softly. "And Riona?"

Dougal and Ember looked at each other, then Ember said, "She's gone as well."

Gullik lowered himself onto the ground. "I am afraid," he said, "that I have to find less fragile friends."

The three were silent for a moment in the heart of the dead city.

"Do you still have your satchel, norn?" asked Ember.

"Of course," said Gullik, and shuffled the pack off one shoulder.

"We need to put something away," said the charr, and Dougal hefted the Claw.

Gullik raised an eyebrow. "So this is what all the fuss was about? Was it worth the deaths of friends?"

"Nothing ever is," said Dougal, "but since you have space in your satchel, there is a bag filled with platinum coins halfway down that pit, and more in a treasure room beyond. But we'd best be quick, before Adelbern re-forms his ghostly body and marshals his troops."

Gullik rose to his feet. "Let him!" he snorted. "I will take out my rage against him in Kranxx's name! Still"— and a smile played over his face—"the only thing better than returning from a city of the dead is to return from a city of the dead bearing great treasures. Down here, you say?" He walked to the edge of the pit.

Dougal laid the Claw in Gullik's satchel. There was more than enough room for several more sacks. And he would have to scare up another sword as well. To Ember, he said, "He's right, you know. It hardly looks like something worth all the worry."

"How so?" asked Ember.

"I expected some legendary weapon, like Magdaer itself," said Dougal. "Something all-powerful and magical. It's just a gaudy toy."

Ember made a chuffing noise that Dougal now knew to be laughter. "It is more than a weapon. It is a key—the key by which we will unlock the chance for peace between our peoples—and with *that,* a chance to defeat the Elder Dragons. It does not get more important than that."

Dougal nodded and closed the bag over the Claw. "We still have to get back," he said.

"We will assault that bridge when we get to it, Dougal Keane," said the charr, and put a large paw on the human's shoulder.

Gullik let out a cry. "Are you two old women going to swap tender lies, or are you going to help? Someone mentioned treasure down there, and if Adelbern is still around, I want to take his best tableware!"

The charr and human laughed, and together they walked to the pit's edge. They had much yet to do.

About the Authors

MATT FORBECK has worked full-time on games and fiction since 1989 with many top companies, including Adams Media, AEG, Atari, Boom! Studios, Atlas Games, Del Rey, Games Workshop, Green Ronin, High Voltage Studios, Human Head Studios, IDW, Image Comics, Mattel, Pinnacle Entertainment Group, Playmates Toys, Simon & Schuster, Ubisoft, Wizards of the Coast, and WizKids. He has designed collectible card games, role-playing games, miniatures games, and board games, and has written short fiction, comic books, novels, nonfiction, magazine articles, and computer game scripts and stories. His work has been published in at least a dozen different languages. Projects Matt has worked on have been nominated for twenty-four Origins Awards and have won thirteen. He has also won five ENnies. He has written more than a dozen novels, including the *Locus*-bestselling *Blood Bowl* and the upcoming *Amortals* and *Vegas Knights* from Angry Robot. His novelization of the *Mutant Chronicles* film won a Scribe Award. He is a proud member of the Alliterates writers group, the International Association of Media Tie-In Writers, the International Thriller Writers, and the International

Game Developers Association. He lives in Beloit, Wisconsin, with his wife, Ann, and their children, Marty, Pat, Nick, Ken, and Helen.

JEFF GRUBB is an award-winning game designer and author. He is the co-creator of the *Forgotten Realms* and one of the co-founders of *Dragonlance*, and his novels include *Forgotten Realms: Azure Bonds*, *Dragonlance: Lord Toede*, *Magic: The Gathering: The Brothers' War*, *Starcraft: Liberty's Crusade*, and *World of Warcraft: The Last Guardian*. He builds worlds for a living, which is nice work if you can get it. He lives in Seattle with his wife and oft-times co-author, Kate Novak, and two supremely disinterested cats.